Praise for *New York Times* bestselling author Julia London

"Julia London writes vibrant, emotional stories and sexy, richly drawn characters."

—Madeline Hunter,
New York Times bestselling author

"[E]nticing from the very first page!"

—*Publishers Weekly* on *Seduced by a Scot*

"Warm, witty and decidedly wicked—great entertainment."

— Stephanie Laurens, #1 *New York Times* bestselling author, on *Hard-Hearted Highlander*

"An absorbing read from a novelist at the top of her game."

—*Kirkus Reviews*, starred review, on *Wild Wicked Scot*

"Expert storytelling and believable characters make the romance [one that] readers will be sad to leave behind."

—*Publishers Weekly*, starred review, on *Wild Wicked Scot*

"London is at the top of her game in this thrilling tale of political intrigue and second chances."

—*Booklist*, starred review, on *Wild Wicked Scot*

Also available from
Julia London
and HQN Books

The Cabot Sisters

The Trouble with Honor
The Devil Takes a Bride
The Scoundrel and the Debutante

The Highland Grooms

Wild Wicked Scot
Sinful Scottish Laird
Hard-Hearted Highlander
Devil in Tartan
Tempting the Laird
Seduced by a Scot

JULIA LONDON

Recycling programs for this product may not exist in your area.

ISBN-13: 978-1-335-04153-1

The Princess Plan

This edition published by arrangement with Harlequin Books S.A.

For questions and comments about the quality of this book, please contact us at CustomerService@Harlequin.com.

www.HQNBooks.com

Printed in U.S.A.

THE
Princess
PLAN

CHAPTER ONE

London 1845

All of London has been on tenterhooks, desperate for a glimpse of Crown Prince Sebastian of Alucia during his highly anticipated visit. Windsor Castle was the scene of Her Majesty's banquet to welcome him. Sixty-and-one-hundred guests were on hand, feted in St. George's Hall beneath the various crests of the Order of the Garter. Two thousand pieces of silver cutlery were used, one thousand crystal glasses and goblets. The first course and main dish of lamb and potatoes were served on silver-gilded plates, followed by delicate fruits on French porcelain.

Prince Sebastian presented a large urn fashioned of green Alucian malachite to our Queen Victoria as a gift from his father the King of Alucia. The urn was festooned with delicate ropes of gold around the mouth and the neck.

The Alucian women were attired in dresses of heavy silk worn close to the body, the trains quite long and brought up and fastened with buttons to facilitate walking. Their hair was fashioned into elaborate knots worn at the nape. The Alucian gentlemen wore formal frock coats of black superfine wool that came to midcalf, as well as heavily embroidered waistcoats worn to the hip. It was reported that Crown Prince Sebastian is "rather tall and broad, with a square face and neatly trimmed beard, a full head of hair the color of tea, and eyes the color of moss," which the discerning reader might think of as a softer shade of green. It is said he possesses a regal air owing chiefly to the many medallions and ribbons he wore befitting his rank.

—Honeycutt's Gazette of Fashion and Domesticity for Ladies

THE RIGHT HONORABLE Justice William Tricklebank, a widower and justice of the Queen's Bench in Her Majesty's service, was very nearly blind, his eyesight having steadily eroded into varying and fuzzy shades of gray with age. He could no longer see so much as his hand, which was why his eldest daughter, Miss Eliza Tricklebank, read his papers to him.

Eliza had enlisted the help of Poppy, their housemaid, who was more family than servant, having come to them as an orphaned girl more than twenty years ago. Together, the two of them had anchored strings and ribbons halfway up the walls of his London townhome, and all the judge had to do was follow them with his hand to move from room to room. Among the hazards he faced was a pair of dogs that were far too enthusiastic in their wish to be of some use to him, and a cat who apparently wished him dead, judging by the number of times he put himself in the judge's path, or leapt into his lap as he sat, or walked across the knitting the judge liked to do while his daughter read to him, or unravelled his ball of yarn without the judge's notice.

The only other potential impediments to his health were his daughters—Eliza, a spinster, and her younger sister, Hollis, otherwise known as the Widow Honeycutt. They were often together in his home, and when they were, it seemed to him there was quite a lot of laughing at this and shrieking at that. His daughters disputed that they shrieked, and accused him of being old and easily startled. But the judge's hearing, unlike his eyesight, was quite acute, and those two shrieked with laughter. *Often.*

At eight-and-twenty, Eliza was unmarried, a fact that had long baffled the judge. There had been an unfortunate and rather infamous misunderstanding with one Mr. Asher Daughton-Cress, who the judge believed was despicable, but that had been ten years ago. Eliza had once been demure and a politely deferential young lady, but she'd shed any pretense of deference when her heart was broken. In the last few years she had emerged vibrant and carefree. He would think such demeanour would recommend her to gentlemen far and wide, but apparently it did not. She'd had only one suitor since her very public scandal, a gentleman some fifteen years older than Eliza. Mr. Norris had faithfully called every day until one day he did not. When the judge had inquired, Eliza had said, "It was not love that compelled him, Pappa. I prefer my life here with you—the work is more agreeable, and I suspect not as many hours as marriage to him would require."

His youngest, Hollis, had been tragically widowed after only two years of a marriage without issue. While she maintained her own home, she and her delightful wit were a faithful caller to his house at least once a day without fail, and sometimes as much as two or three times per day. He should like to see her remarried, but Hollis insisted she was in no rush to do so. The judge thought she rather preferred her sister's company to that of a man.

His daughters were thick as thieves, as the saying went, and were coconspirators in something that the judge did not altogether approve of. But he was blind, and they were determined to do what they pleased no matter what he said, so he'd given up trying to talk any practical sense into them.

That questionable activity was the publication of a ladies' gazette. Tricklebank didn't think ladies needed a gazette, much less one having to do with frivolous subjects such as fashion, gossip and beauty. But say what he might, his daughters turned a deaf ear to him. They were unfettered in their enthusiasm for this endeavour, and if the two of them could be believed, so was all of London.

The gazette had been established by Hollis's husband, Sir Percival Honeycutt. Except that Sir Percival had published an entirely different sort of gazette, obviously—one devoted to the latest political and financial news. Now *that* was a useful publication to the judge's way of thinking.

Sir Percival's death was the most tragic of accidents, the result of his carriage sliding off the road into a swollen river during a rain, which also saw the loss of a fine pair of grays. It was a great shock to them all, and the judge had worried about Hollis and her ability to cope with such a loss. But Hollis proved herself an indomitable spirit, and she had turned her grief into efforts to preserve her husband's name. But as she was a young woman without a man's education, and could not possibly comprehend the intricacies of politics or financial matters, she had turned the gazette on its head and dedicated it solely to topics that interested women, which naturally would be limited to the latest fashions and the most tantalizing on dits swirling about London's high society. It was the judge's impression that women had very little interest in the important matters of the world.

And yet, interestingly, the judge could not deny that Hollis's version of the gazette was more actively sought than her husband's had ever been. So much so that Eliza had been pressed into the service of helping her sister prepare her gazette each week. It was curious to Tricklebank that so many members of the Quality were rather desperate to be mentioned among the gazette's pages.

Today, his daughters were in an unusually high state of excitement, for they had secured the highly sought-after invitations to the Duke of Marlborough's masquerade ball in honor of the crown prince of Alucia. One would think the world had stopped spinning on its axis and that the heavens had parted and the seas had receded and this veritable God of All Royal Princes had shined his countenance upon London and blessed them all with his presence.

Hogwash.

Everyone knew the prince was here to strike an important trade deal with the English government in the name of King Karl. Alucia was a small European nation with impressive wealth for her size. It was perhaps best known for an ongoing dispute with the neighboring country of Wesloria—the two had a history of war and distrust as fraught as that between England and France.

The judge had read that it was the crown prince who

was pushing for modernization in Alucia, and who was the impetus behind the proposed trade agreement. Prince Sebastian envisioned increasing the prosperity of Alucia by trading cotton and iron ore for manufactured goods. But according to the judge's daughters, that was not the most important part of the trade negotiations. The *important* part was that the prince was also in search of a marriage bargain.

"It's what everyone says," Hollis had insisted to her father over supper recently.

"And how is it, my dear, that *everyone* knows what the prince intends?" the judge asked as he stroked the cat, Pris, on his lap. The cat had been named Princess when the family believed it a female. When the houseman Ben discovered that Princess was, in fact, a male, Eliza said it was too late to change the name. So they'd shortened it to Pris. "Did the prince send a letter? Announce it in the *Times*?"

"*Caro* says," Hollis countered, as if that were quite obvious to anyone with half a brain where she got her information. "She knows everything about everyone, Pappa."

"Aha. If Caro says it, then by all means, it must be true."

"You must yourself admit she is rarely wrong," Hollis had said with an indignant sniff.

Caro, or Lady Caroline Hawke, had been a lifelong friend to his daughters, and had been so often underfoot in the Tricklebank house that for many years, it seemed to the judge that he had three daughters.

Caroline was the only sibling of Lord Beckett Hawke and was also his ward. Long ago, a cholera outbreak had swept through London, and both Caro's mother and his children's mother had succumbed. Amelia, his wife, and Lady Hawke had been dear friends. They'd sent their children to the Hawke summer estate when Amelia had taken ill. Lady Hawke had insisted on caring for her friend and, well, in the end, they were both lost.

Lord Hawke was an up-and-coming young lord and politician, known for his progressive ideas in the House of Lords. He was rather handsome, Hollis said, a popular figure, and socially in high demand. Which meant that, by association, so was his sister. She, too, was quite comely, which made her presence all the easier to her brother's many friends, the judge suspected.

But Caroline *did* seem to know everyone in London, and was constantly calling on the Tricklebank household to spout the gossip she'd gleaned in homes across Mayfair. Here was an industrious young lady—she called on three salons a day if she called on one. The judge supposed her brother scarcely need worry about putting food in their cupboards, for the two of them were dining with this four-and-twenty or that ten-and-six almost every night. It was a wonder Caroline wasn't a plump little peach.

Perhaps she was. In truth, she was merely another shadow to the judge these days.

"And *she* was at Windsor and dined with the queen," Hollis added with superiority.

"You mean Caro was in the same room but one hundred persons away from the queen," the judge suggested. He knew how these fancy suppers went.

"Well, she was there, Pappa, and she met the Alucians, and she knows a great deal about them now. I am quite determined to discover who the prince intends to offer for and announce it in the gazette before anyone else. Can you imagine? I shall be the talk of London!"

This was precisely what Mr. Tricklebank didn't like about the gazette. He did not want his daughters to be the talk of London.

But it was not the day for him to make this point, for his daughters were restless, moving about the house with an urgency he was not accustomed to. Today was the day of the Royal Masquerade Ball, and the sound of crisp petticoats and silk rustled around him, and the scent of perfume wafted into his nose when they passed. His daughters were waiting impatiently for Lord Hawke's brougham to come round and fetch them. Their masks, he was given to understand, had already arrived at the Hawke House, commissioned, Eliza had breathlessly reported, from "Mrs. Cubison herself."

He did not know who Mrs. Cubison was.

And frankly, he didn't know how Caro had managed to finagle the invitations to a ball at Kensington Palace for *his* two daughters—for the good Lord knew the Tricklebanks did not have the necessary connections to achieve such a feat.

He could feel their eagerness, their anxiety in the nervous pitch of their giggling when they spoke to each other. Even Poppy seemed nervous. He supposed this was to be the ball by which all other balls in the history of mankind would forever be judged, but he was quite thankful he was too blind to attend.

When the knock at the door came, he was startled by such squealing and furious activity rushing by him that he could only surmise that the brougham had arrived and the time had come to go to the ball.

CHAPTER TWO

Kensington Palace was the site of a masquerade ball held in honor of the Alucian Court, Thursday past, at seven o'clock in the evening. The Duke of Marlborough hosted in Her Majesty's stead. The Alucians wore black masks, indistinguishable from one to the next, so that the identity of the crown prince would not be readily apparent, a ploy that might very well have succeeded had it not been for the long line of young Englishwomen who desired an introduction to the prince.

A certain English Kitty, much admired for her Wednesday salons, was so enthralled with the punch cups that a notable fox was on hand to help in any way he might, and thereby took unfair advantage of her in the King's Cloakroom. When the kitten realized what the fox was about, she demanded satisfaction, and was awarded the assistance of three liveried footmen to escort her out to a waiting carriage, which required such maneuvering around her gown and her ample person as to have knocked the peruke from the unfortunate head of one of the lads.

—Honeycutt's Gazette of Fashion and Domesticity for Ladies

WHEN ONE LIVED as simply as Eliza Tricklebank, one did not expect to gain an invitation to a ball, much less meet a prince. And yet, she had somehow managed to put herself in the receiving line to be introduced to a prince, without the slightest bit of assistance other than a wee bit of rum punch.

She couldn't even say which prince she was waiting to meet, or how many of them there were in total. She'd heard there were at least two of them presently in England, but for all she knew, there could be scores of them roaming about.

It seemed amusing now to think that this evening, and this moment, and the idea that Eliza might make the acquaintance of an actual prince, had all begun only days ago when Caroline had called at Bedford Square where Eliza lived with her father.

Caroline had news about the ball, gleaned from the revered Mrs. Cubison, the modiste from whom she'd commissioned masks for the three of them. "Mrs. Cubison offered that she'd been retained a month ago to provide masks for the Alucians, and that she and her ladies had worked for *days* to fulfill their wishes." She'd spoken quickly, with much excitement, even as she lazed on Eliza's bed.

Hollis had gasped and reached for paper. "Not another word until I have my pencil—"

"You won't believe what I tell you," Caroline had said.

"I will."

"The truth will be known soon enough, I suppose—"

"Caro, by all that is holy, if you don't tell us, I will squeeze it from you with my bare hands," Hollis had warned.

Caroline had laughed gaily. She enjoyed provoking Hollis, which Eliza had pointed out to her sister more than once. Hollis stubbornly refused to accept it.

"All right, here it is. Every single mask is *black* and *identical*."

Hollis and Eliza had stared at their best friend, who very calmly pillowed her hands behind her head and crossed her feet at the ankles.

"Why?" Eliza had asked, only slightly curious about this mask detail.

"So you can't tell the crown prince from the others!" Caroline had cried triumphantly.

Looking around her now, Eliza thought that was very forward thinking by the Alucians because it had worked—she could hardly tell one Alucian from the other. There were scores of tall men dressed in black and identical plain black masks—just like the one she'd encountered in that narrow passageway a quarter of an hour ago.

What a strange encounter *that* had been. Gentlemen were such odd creatures to her, now that she was at a remove from them by a spinster's arm length. They could be so presumptuous. She realized now she wouldn't be able to pick out that man in this crowd of identically dressed men even if she wanted to encounter him again. Which she did not. And while the Alucian women were distinguishable by their beautiful gowns, even they wore the same black mask.

It appeared as if she would have time to inspect them all, sandwiched as she was between ladies adorned in silk and muslin embroidered with perfect stitching, and topped with elaborately constructed masks for this masquerade ball. Eliza knew her gown was not as beautiful as any of the other garments here. It was rather plain in comparison, really. She and Poppy had created it from two dresses. Poppy was quite talented with a needle, as it happened.

Eliza was talented, curiously enough, with the repair of clocks.

Her gown, made of white silk and blue tarlatan with sprays of blue flowers, floated over three tiers of skirt. Her waist and sleeves were adorned with ribbons bought for a dear sum from Mr. Key's shop. The décolletage was scandalously low, but Hollis said that was the current fashion. It dipped into a little bouquet of gold and blue silk rosettes that bloomed between her breasts. "The gold matches your hair," Poppy had observed as she'd curled and roped tresses of Eliza's hair this evening, twining it with strands of gold leaf.

"Doesn't it seem as if a clump of sod was dropped here and flowers sprang?" Eliza asked, trying to adjust the low bodice.

Poppy had cocked her dark head to one side and considered it. "Not…especially." Her tone lacked conviction, and Eliza gave her a pointed look as she took in their reflections in the mirror, to let her know she didn't believe her.

Hollis had proclaimed Eliza's mask the best of the three that Caroline had bought from Mrs. Cubison, who was, according to Hollis, *the* premier modiste in all of London. It covered Eliza's forehead and nose, and gold scrolls had been painted around the eyes. The mask rose from the right side of her face, sweeping up and arcing over her head. "It's the Venetian style," Hollis informed her.

Eliza didn't know what style it was and would have

no occasion to know, and neither did she care. She was grateful to Caroline for the invitation and for the very generous gift of the mask, but it seemed an extravagant waste of money to Eliza's practical nature. Of the three of them, she was the one who seldom made social calls, who rarely received invitations that were not to do with her father. Who *never* had occasion to set foot in a masquerade ball. That was what happened to spinster caretakers—they fell from the view of society. Were it not for her dearest sister and wildly popular dearest friend, she'd never go anywhere at all. And even then, on the occasions she was included, she generally had her father to consider.

But tonight, she'd been utterly transformed into someone very different. She wore perfume where she generally smelled like old books and court papers. Her hair was artfully arranged instead of being bound haphazardly at her nape. And her borrowed shoes were embroidered, not scuffed like the ones she wore about the house every day. Thanks to Caroline's magic, she was standing in Kensington Palace in an evening gown and wearing an exotic mask. To say this ball was a luxury for her was a terrible understatement. She intended to breathe in every moment and carry the memory of it around with her for the rest of her days. She didn't fancy herself a Cinderella.

At least not until she discovered the glittery magic of the queen's rum punch.

Eliza wanted to tell Hollis and Caroline about the rum punch, but she'd been separated from them almost the moment they'd entered the palace by the mob at the entry. Eliza had tried to keep pace with them, but she was hindered in her progress when three ladies dressed in Alucian costumes crowded in front of her, and Eliza had been so enthralled with their gowns, made in the redingote style and cut tightly to their bodies, and their trains! She'd never in her life seen such beautifully made trains, and she admired how they were tucked up in the back and sides with elaborate fasteners. "What do you imagine is the *cost* of a gown like that?" she'd asked, and looked up, only to discover Hollis and Caroline had disappeared into the dizzying array of ball gowns and jewels, elaborate masks and the square, black shoulders of all the gentlemen.

At first Eliza was a bit desperate to find them. She'd never been to a ball, and definitely not to one where it was rumored the queen and prince consort might appear. She didn't know what she was to do.

But the crowd was so thick, and before she knew it, she was being carried up the grand King's Staircase, past the painted friezes of people standing at a balustrade watching the guests go up, and then down the hall, past more paintings and elaborately carved ceiling medallions and priceless porcelain vases on French consoles. Past gold-gilded mirrors that made it seem as if even more people had been stuffed inside the palace, which was really quite a lot. It was impossible to fathom that London had so many people of Quality, so *many* people deemed worthy enough to be extended an invitation to this royal ball.

The wave of people she was riding had poured into the ballroom, and once again Eliza was dumbstruck. At least fifteen crystal chandeliers with three tiers of candles glittered above the heads of the dancers. The ceiling soared above them, held aloft by full-length windows. Portraits of Important People lined the room.

Risers, covered in red velvet, had been installed on either side of the room, and men and women lounged on them as if they were in a park watching a parade while others danced a quadrille. In a small alcove high above the floor, she could see the musicians, squeezed in practically shoulder to shoulder, their bows moving quickly over their strings as a dizzying swirl of skirts and masks twirled around.

It was magic. Glittery, sparkly magic, and Eliza had to pinch herself to make sure she wasn't dreaming it.

She'd been given a dance card when they entered the palace, and she'd thought perhaps she ought to step aside and affix it to her wrist. But she'd been distracted by all the people, and gone up on her toes and craned her neck, looking for Hollis or Caroline, but she saw no one she could possibly recognize behind a mask.

That was when a short, broad woman with a plain gray mask that matched her tower of gray hair had cried, "*You* there!" and pointed at Eliza.

Eliza had looked behind her and, seeing no one obvious, pointed at her chest questioningly.

The woman had impatiently gestured her forward, snatched up her dance card when Eliza was close enough, then clucked her tongue. "You've none of them filled! What have you been doing?"

Eliza realized with a jolt that the woman must be one of the ballroom hostesses Caroline had warned them about. Her function was to ensure that all dance sets were filled, and all unattached ladies had a partner. "If you don't want to find yourself dancing with old, leering bachelors, you best avoid them," Caroline had advised.

The woman snorted her displeasure at Eliza and commanded her to hold out her wrist, tied her dance card to it, then pointed to a group of young women. "Wait there," she said, and turned away, presumably to find her an old, leering bachelor.

Eliza looked at the small group of women huddled in a corner. Well, that was a motley lot of wallflowers. One of them was picking at her sleeve, unravelling a thread. Another's mask was so large that she had to tilt her chin up to keep it on. Eliza might be an old spinster, but she was not joining that group.

She glanced slyly at the ballroom hostess, who was occupied with berating another young woman unfortunate enough to have been caught without a dance partner. She'd thought it curious how a gown and a proper mask could transform a person so utterly in the space of a moment, but Eliza was indeed transformed. Once upon a time, she'd been terribly obedient and quick to please. She'd thought that was the way good young women who would make good young wives were supposed to behave. A review of her life might suggest she was *too* quick to please, for when Mr. Asher Daughton-Cress had asked her to be patient with him and the offer he would *definitely* make for her hand, she had not questioned him, because she was naive. She had trusted him because he told her to. And besides, he'd assured her he *loved* her desperately. But she'd discovered, far too late, long after the situation could be repaired, well after everyone else knew what she did not, that he'd been courting another woman.

A woman with twenty thousand pounds a year, thank you.

To whom he was now married and with whom he shared three lovely children.

That incident, which was the talk of London for what

seemed weeks, had taught Eliza valuable lessons. One, she would never ever suffer the pains of a broken heart again, because there was nothing quite like it—she had wanted to die, unable to grasp even the idea that one person could lie to another person so completely and without remorse. And two, never again would she please others for the sake of pleasing, and tonight, of all nights, she would not abide it. She would never again have an opportunity to attend a royal ball and she refused to be shackled to a group of undesirable wallflowers whom men were forced by etiquette to dance with, or worse, around whom leering old gents lingered.

So she quickly glanced around and spotted a footman slipping through a door that was disguised as part of the wall. She brashly followed him on a hop and a skip, escaping the eagle-eyed gaze of the hostess and sliding in through the door behind the footman before anyone could stop her.

She found herself in a passageway of maybe five feet in length and perhaps only three feet in width. At the other end was a similarly disguised door. The walls in the passageway were panelled, and a single wall sconce provided light.

In other words, within ten minutes of entering the rarefied halls of Kensington Palace, Eliza had put herself in a servants' passageway. No wonder Caroline had insisted she stay close so that she wouldn't do anything inappropriate.

She didn't mean to stay for more than a moment. She'd just wanted to avoid the hostess until she'd gone off to terrorize someone else. While Eliza pondered how long that would take, the door at the opposite end of the passageway suddenly swung open. A servant entered, carrying a tray of drinks on his shoulder. He looked at her as he moved toward the door she'd just entered through. "You're not to be here, madam."

"My apologies. But the room is so crowded, is it not? I need only a moment." She made a show of fanning her face. "I won't move from here, I swear it."

The servant shrugged and took one of the glasses from his tray. "Might as well have one of these, then."

"What is it?"

"Punch."

He swung open the door into the ballroom, and a great cacophony of voices and music blasted the small space before the door swung closed behind him, silencing it all to a din.

Eliza sniffed at the punch. Then sipped it. Then imprudently downed it, draining the glass, because the punch was *delicious*. How tingly it made her feel!

Moments later, the footman suddenly appeared again and extended his nearly empty tray for her glass. "Thank you," Eliza said sheepishly. "That was *very* good." She took one of the last glasses on his tray.

"Aye, madam. It's been amply mixed with rum." He proceeded on, through the other door, behind which Eliza could hear the deep hum of masculine voices. And then it was quiet again.

Who knew that rum could be so delicious? Certainly not her. She liked the soft, blurry warmth that spread through her. The sort of warmth she liked to feel at night when she was drifting off to sleep, or in a hot, sudsy bath. And yet, not like that at all.

When the footman returned a moment later with a full tray again, Eliza was happy to take another one.

She rolled her eyes when he arched a judgmental brow before going out again.

She sipped the drink and closed her eyes as the warmth spread through her arms and legs, and then announced to herself with delight, "This is *very* good."

She supposed that the fizzy warmth of the rum was what kept her nerves from defeating her completely when the door at the other end of the passageway came open a few inches, as if someone coming through had paused. She listened curiously to the male voices all speaking the Alucian language, and then the door suddenly opened all the way, to reveal an Alucian gentleman stepping into the passageway.

The door swung shut behind him.

Eliza and the masked man were alone.

He tilted his head just slightly to the left, as if he was uncertain what he'd just found. She returned his gaze with a curious one of her own. His presence was so large and the passageway so small that she felt a bit as if she was pressed up against the wall. But thanks to the rum, she was feeling rather sparkly and untroubled and, with the help of the wall, managed to curtsy with a slight lean to the right and said, "How do you do?"

The Alucian didn't answer.

She supposed it was possible he didn't speak English. Or perhaps he was shy. If he was painfully shy, he deserved her compassion. She'd had a friend who had suffered terrible stomach pains for days when she was forced to be in society. She was married now, with six children. Apparently, she wasn't shy away from society.

Eliza held up her glass, making it tick-tock like a clock pendulum. "Have you tried the punch?"

He glanced at her glass.

"It's delicious," she proclaimed, and drank more of it. Perhaps as much as half of it. And then chuckled at her indelicacy. She'd forgotten most of what she knew about polite society, but she was fairly certain guzzling was frowned upon. "I hadn't realized I was quite so parched."

He stood mutely.

"It must be the language," she murmured to herself. *"Do you,"* she said, enunciating very clearly and gesturing to her mouth, *"speak English?"*

"Of course."

"Oh." *Well.* She could not guess what would cause a gentleman not to speak at all if he understood what was being said to him, but frankly, Eliza was more concerned with the whereabouts of the footman than the Alucian stranger. "Are you going through?" she asked, gesturing to the ballroom door.

"Not as yet."

The clean-shaven, tall man with the thick tobacco-colored hair and the pristine neckcloth had a lovely accent. She thought it sounded like a cross between French and something else. Spanish, perhaps? No, something else. "How do you find London?" Not that she cared, but it seemed odd to be looking at a gentleman when there were only the two of you in the passageway and not at least attempt to make polite conversation.

"Very well, thank you."

The door behind him swung open and very nearly hit the gentleman on the backside. The footman squeezed inside. "Pardon," he said, bowing deferentially before the Alucian gentleman. Eliza thought it curious the footman didn't offer the Alucian the punch but walked past him to take Eliza's glass and offer her another. "Oh dear. I really shouldn't." But she did.

The footman carried on into the ballroom.

All the while the Alucian gentleman watched Eliza as if she were one of the talking birds that were brought to Covent Garden Market from time to time.

Perhaps he was curious about her drink. “Would you like to sample it?” she asked.

The man’s eyes fell to her glass. He moved closer. Close enough that the skirt of her gown brushed against his legs. He leaned forward slightly, as if trying to determine what her glass contained.

“Rum punch,” she said. “I’ve never had rum punch until tonight, but I mean to remedy that oversight straightaway. You’ll see.” She held up the glass, teasing him.

He glanced up at her, and she noticed he had the most remarkable green eyes—the faded green of the oak leaves in her garden at autumn. His dark lashes were long and thick. She held the glass a little higher, smiling with amusement because she didn’t believe for a moment he would be so ill-mannered as to take her glass.

But the gentleman surprised her. He took the glass, his fingers brushing against hers. She watched with fascination as he put the glass to his lips and sipped the punch. He removed a handkerchief from his coat pocket, wiped the glass where his lips had touched it and handed it back to her. “*Je*, it is very good.”

She liked the way his voice slipped over her like a shawl, light on her skin. “Would you like a glass of your own? The footman and I have an arrangement.” She smiled.

He did not smile. He gave her a slight shake of his head.

She considered this lovely creature further as she sipped the punch. “Why are you here and not out there?”

A dark brow appeared above his mask "One might ask the same of you."

"Well, sir, as it happens, *I* have a very good reason. The hostess was not satisfied with my dance card."

His green eyes moved casually to her décolletage, and Eliza's skin warmed beneath his perusal.

"I'm not particularly good at dance," she admitted. "We all have our talents, I suppose, but dance is not mine." She laughed because it struck her as amusing that she would admit this unpardonable social sin to a stranger. The rum punch did indeed have magic qualities.

The Alucian shifted even closer—her petticoats rustled with the press of his leg against her. His eyes moved over her mask, tracing the scroll that arched overhead. "I would hazard a guess that you would like to tell me your particular *talent*," he said, clearly enunciating the last word.

Either the rum or the masculine rumble of his question had Eliza feeling swirly and warm. She had to think a minute. What *was* her talent? Repairing clocks? Embroidery? Or was her talent something as mundane as taking care of her father? She was certain her sister and her friend would be appalled if she admitted any of that to any gentleman. She couldn't, anyway—his gaze was piercing, rendering her momentarily speechless and a wee bit slushy.

No, that wasn't right. It was the *punch* making her feel slushy.

His gaze raked over her, from the top of her mask's scroll and down to her mouth, her décolletage and the ridiculous spray of flowers, then to her waist. When he lifted his eyes again, his gaze had gone very dark, and the shine in them had turned her blood into a river of heat. It felt as if the air had been sucked out of that passageway, and she felt the need to hide behind her glass and sip tiny little gulps of air, because she honestly didn't trust herself not to do something very ill-advised. Like touch his face. She had an insane desire to press her fingertips to his high cheekbones.

His gaze was on her mouth as he said, "Did you not mean to share your talent with me?"

"No, I did not," she said, her voice somewhere outside of her.

His gaze moved lower, lingering on the burst of gold flowers between her breasts. "Are you certain? I'd love to hear it."

He was attempting to seduce her. It was exciting and amusing and so very silly. "Your efforts, while admirable, will not work," she announced proudly. "I am not so easily seduced." Except that wasn't entirely true. She certainly liked the feeling of being seduced. It had been a very long time since anyone had even thought to attempt it, and although she was crammed into this narrow passageway and it was hardly the place she would have chosen to be seduced, she rather liked the idea of starting the ball in this manner. It made her feel electric.

Fortunately, she supposed, she at least had the presence of mind to recognize she probably *shouldn't* allow herself to be seduced by a perfect stranger.

The gentleman shifted imperceptibly closer, and his masculinity, which felt undeniably potent, wrapped around her and held her there. He lifted his hand and shamelessly, and slowly, traced a finger lightly across her collarbone, sending all manner of chills and shivers racing through her. "Is that not what you intended? To be easily seduced in a dark passageway?"

She snorted a laugh. The ridiculous confidence of men who believed that if a woman came near, they wanted to be seduced! "I *intended* to drink some punch and avoid the ballroom hostess." She lifted her hand, wrapped her fingers firmly around his wrist and pushed his hand away. "You think highly of yourself, sir. But I should explain that merely because a woman is standing in a passageway, having drunk a bit of rum, does not mean she desires your advances."

He smiled smugly. "You might be surprised. What other reason could a woman have for lurking in this passageway?"

"I can think of a hundred other reasons." She could only think of one. "And I know myself very well, and I would never be seduced in a passageway. So if you would please step away."

His eyes casually took her in, head to toe, and then he stepped to the side.

Eliza sipped more punch as if she wasn't the least bit bothered, but in fact, her skin felt as if it was flaming. Her pulse was fluttering. And the thought that she was too practical was playing at the edges of her thoughts. The Alucian gentleman, tall and lovely eyed, was quite enticing. Who would have been the wiser? She wouldn't mind in the least being kissed at a royal ball…but neither did she want to risk discovery and be tossed out before she'd met a prince.

As luck would have it, the door swung open and another Alucian stepped in. But he drew up short and stared down at her in surprise. He looked past her to the gentleman stranger and spoke in their language.

The gentleman responded quietly and stepped around Eliza as if nothing had been said between the two of them and went into the ballroom without so much as a *good evening.*

The door swung closed behind him.

The door at the other end opened and the footman entered once more with yet another tray of drinks. "Madam, you can't be in here," he reminded her.

"All right, I'm going," she said, and with her glass, she followed the Alucians into the ballroom.

She instantly spotted the hostess searching the room like an eagle surveying a valley from a high perch. So Eliza turned and walked quickly away from the group of undesirable dance partners. She skirted around the dance floor and, when she finally stopped to have a look around, she discovered she'd put herself in a group of women. It was some sort of gathering. In fact, two older women were corralling the young women together like a pair of sheepdogs.

And that was how Eliza had found herself in a line to meet a prince.

She hadn't realized it at first—she was too taken by the youth and beauty of the ladies, all of them adorned in beautiful masks and gowns, and holding themselves with discernible confidence, quite unlike the wallflowers across the room. *This* was her group.

Eliza thought perhaps she ought to dispose of her fourth rum punch lest the fizzy feeling extend to her tongue—if it hadn't already—and when she leaned forward to see around the ladies, she saw a group of Alucian men. Curious, Eliza tapped the very creamy shoulder of the slender and tall young woman before her.

The woman turned. She had dark hair and wore an

elaborate mask that included peacock feathers arranged in a clever way around her eyes. The blue and green of the peacock feathers matched the blue of her gown. The woman blinked through her mask, her gaze taking Eliza in.

"I beg your pardon, but who are they?" Eliza asked, nodding in the direction of the gentlemen.

The woman blinked. "I think the better question is who are *you*?" she responded curtly.

"Eliza Tricklebank." She bounced into a tiny curtsy. "I am happy to make your—"

"You're not to be in this queue," the woman said, cutting her off. "*This* queue is for selected guests only. You must have been invited to it by Lady Marlborough. Did Lady Marlborough invite you?"

Eliza had the punchy audacity to laugh. It was necessary to have an invitation to stand in line? But the peacock was frowning, and Eliza said, "Of course!" And then she snorted, as if it was ridiculous to even question her.

"Really," the woman said coolly.

"Really," Eliza said. "She said to stand here, just behind you."

The peacock didn't seem to believe her, but she didn't press it. She turned her back on Eliza and whispered to her companion.

Was it really necessary to be *invited* to stand in line? And for what? Frankly, Eliza couldn't imagine why anyone would stand in line to meet anyone else unless that someone was terribly important. Or rich. Important and rich and handing out bags of money. *That* was a queue she'd willingly join.

Or if it was queue to meet the queen or some other bit of royalty—

Eliza's fate suddenly dawned on her like a beacon from above, illuminating the path before her. *Of course!* She leaned forward again. The Alucian gentlemen, all dressed in black superfine wool and white waistcoats and identical masks, were distinguishable only by the color of their hair. Which, on inspection, was quite similar, all of them shades of darkly golden brown, much like that of the gentleman in the passageway. They were similar in height, too. Only one of them was perhaps an inch taller than the others. Another a few inches shorter than the others. And curiously, they were all clean-shaven. Caroline had said the crown prince had a beard.

It must be the younger one! She was in line to meet one of the Alucian princes! Eliza was beside herself with glee. She felt giggly and restless and looked around once more, desperately seeking her sister, who would never forgive Eliza if *she* met a prince and Hollis did not.

But Hollis was nowhere to be seen, so Eliza sipped liberally, then touched the woman's shoulder again. The woman turned impatiently. "What is it?"

"Is it the *prince*?"

Well. A pretty mask could not cover a good roll of the eyes.

"Good Lord, Miss Tricklebank. You've shown quite indelibly that you were *not* invited to join this line. You best walk on before Lady Marlborough finds you." And she jerked around and put her back firmly to Eliza.

Eliza was not about to move away, not *now*, not with a prince only feet from her. And having found no place to dispose of her punch, she continued to sip it as the line slowly inched along, amusing herself with all the ways she could imagine being introduced. Miss Eliza Tricklebank. Miss *Eliza* Tricklebank. Miss Eliza *Tricklebank*, of the Bedford Square Tricklebanks. Not to be confused with the Cheapside Tricklebanks, as there had been a rift in the family after her grandfather's death.

She bent to see around the ladies again, examining the gentlemen. The one in the middle looked oddly familiar.

No. Her stomach fluttered uncomfortably. It wasn't possible! Was it possible? Good Lord, it was entirely possible. *That* was the same gentleman she'd met in the passageway. It was a *prince* who'd tried to *seduce* her? Hollis would faint with shock. Eliza might, too. He'd *sipped* her punch! The prince! The younger prince—

No. No, that couldn't be, she suddenly realized. It was the *crown* prince who wanted to make a match. It had to be him—why else would these women be queued up like cattle to make his acquaintance?

All at once, she couldn't seem to catch her breath. To think she'd come so close to the *crown prince*. She might have kissed him! She very nearly had done! He was the crown prince!

She took a breath, forcing herself to calm down.

He seemed a bit stiff to her now, actually. He wasn't shimmering with the heat she'd felt in the passageway, nor spilling over with seductive energy. He looked to be spilling over with tedium at present. Eliza would think he'd at least attempt to be a bit more cordial if he was indeed searching for a wife. Nevertheless, she would magnanimously give him the benefit of the doubt—perhaps the stiffness in him was the result of a bad back from riding around on horses. Or fighting wars.

Didn't her father say there had been skirmishes with the Weslorians?

Whatever the reason, he clearly was not enthusiastic about these introductions. Certainly not as enthusiastic as the slight man who kept bringing young ladies forward to meet him. Now *that* man had a ready smile for each lady. He moved strangely, and she realized that he held a gloved hand against his side. It appeared to be misshapen and he used his right hand exclusively.

One by one, the smaller gentleman brought the ladies forward, and one by one, they curtsied before the prince. He never seemed to utter a word but would give a polite bob of his head, then turn his back and resume his conversations with fellow Alucians. It seemed shockingly rude to Eliza.

She wondered what he would say when he saw her. Would he find it amusing? She might offer him the rest of her punch. Or perhaps he would remark on her thirst for it and offer *her* a punch. Perhaps they'd laugh. *"Oh dear, I had no idea it was* you *in the passageway!"*

The peacock wouldn't like that.

Eliza pictured herself before him, sinking into a deep curtsy. She would say, *"Enchanté,"* because he surely spoke French, the language of royal courts. He would hold out his hand to help her rise, and perhaps then he would smile, and he'd say, in perfect French, that the ball was quite pleasing, and how did she find it? And she would say, in perfect French, her fluency having improved dramatically for the moment, that she found it quite pleasing, too. He would ask if she'd yet put any names on her dance card, and when she admitted she had not, he would escort her past all the other ladies to the floor for a dance.

"Move up!" someone behind her hissed.

"Oh! Pardon," she said, and took a sort of hop-step forward as the line advanced, as if she were playing the game "Mother May I."

The introductions continued like an assembly line. It was the same every time—the enthusiastic Alucian introduced a lady, the lady would wax excitedly about something, and the prince would bob his head then turn away, and the poor man making the introductions had to work to gain his attention again. Some of the ladies, tired of waiting, drifted away, lured by the dancing. Others doggedly waited their place in line, Eliza among them. Why should she not? She felt so sparkly on the inside that she could not keep the smile from her face, particularly when she glanced around the ornate ballroom at all these beautiful people—well, beautiful masks. She was in *Kensington Palace* at a *royal ball.* The *crown prince* of Alucia had sipped her punch!

But just as Eliza was closing in on the prince with her introduction in mind, standing behind only the peacock, the prince said something to the gentleman making the introductions and began to move away. The peacock froze with indecision. Her companion looked back at her, her alarm evident behind her mask. Eliza could imagine what the two of them were thinking—that one friend would have the introduction and not the other was unthinkable.

Eliza nudged her. "Step forward! We might still make his acquaintance—"

The peacock suddenly whirled around to her. "Don't push me! Miss Tricklebank, has it not occurred to you that you are far too old to be in *this* line?"

"What?" There was an age limit? There was no time

to discuss it—the prince was moving away without so much as a glance in their direction, and Eliza saw her chance slipping through her fingers. She'd had enough rum punch to feel justifiably emboldened, and suddenly leapt around the paralyzed woman and blurted, "Welcome to England!" for lack of anything better to say.

In the days to come, Eliza would believe that Prince Sebastian would never have acknowledged her at all had she not sort of lurched into his path at the very moment he was striding forward, which unfortunately caused him to step firmly on her foot.

Eliza gasped with the surprise and pain of it.

"I beg your pardon, are you all right?" He quickly moved his very large and heavy foot from hers.

"Quite," she said breathlessly and stuck out her hand as if he were the butcher who had just given her a very good price on pork. "Miss Eliza Tricklebank."

He looked at her gloved hand as if he didn't have the slightest idea what he was to do with it. Eliza smiled hopefully. He reluctantly and delicately took her hand in his, which felt like a vast plane of palm and fingers, and bowed over it. "Madam."

The feel of that strong hand holding hers so carefully fired through Eliza's veins. It was the zest of accomplishment, the thrill of having met an actual prince, not once, but *twice*. "I am very pleased to make your acquaintance again, Your Highness. Your *Royal* Highness." She smiled brightly. "Formally. Obviously, we met earlier." She beamed at him.

"Sir," one of the Alucian men said, and the prince let go her hand and turned away from her. Before Eliza could so much as draw a breath, he'd been swallowed up by several Alucians and hurried along.

The man who'd been introducing the women to the prince suddenly appeared at Eliza's side. "Are you hurt, madam? Shall we have a look at your foot?"

"Pardon? Oh, no need, there was no harm." She laughed a little hysterically. "I met the prince," she said to him.

The man smiled. "Indeed you did." He leaned forward and said, "You and your foot might have left a most indelible impression on him."

Eliza laughed with delight. Her mission had been accomplished. A broad smile of pride spread across her face, and she turned her head and cast that smile at the peacock. That woman gaped at her, still paralyzed.

"I met the prince!" Eliza said again, and with a bright laugh, she nodded at the kind Alucian and walked away, aware that the peacock's gaze was boring through her back.

That was another thing that happened when one became a spinster caretaker. One ceased to care what others thought of her.

CHAPTER THREE

Guests at the Royal Masquerade Ball were treated to three sets of Alucian dancing, all of which involve very intricate steps and require an agility and eye for precision demonstrably not possessed by a certain minister many consider to be past his prime.

Ladies, if your lovely ball gown has suffered a mishap, remember to put a teaspoon of Madeira wine to every gallon of water to remove the stain.

—Honeycutt's Gazette of Fashion and Domesticity for Ladies

SEBASTIAN CHARLES IVER CHARTIER, the crown prince of the kingdom of Alucia and the Duke of Sansonleon, was hot behind his bloody mask and desired more of the excellent rum punch. But he would accept any liquid that might quench his thirst.

What he disliked about balls and assemblies and state suppers in general was that there were too many expectations, too many people to please. And apparently, to hear the captain of his guard tell it, too many dangers lurking beneath the gowns and the coattails around him. He was not allowed to take a drink from a servant. Protocol demanded any drink or food be handed to him by an Alucian. *After* it was sampled by an Alucian. And the

Alucians were so intent on their duty that a reasonable man could easily believe there were hordes of rebels attempting to poison him at every turn.

Sebastian also disliked the necessity of dancing. He wasn't a bad dancer, quite the contrary. His position in this world demanded that he be a competent dancer, and to make sure of it, his parents had hired the best dance tutors when he was younger. Still, he didn't particularly enjoy it. He was wretched at making empty conversation, curt when answering the same questions while trying to keep names in his head. He was not adept at being social, not like his brother, Leopold.

Sebastian would much prefer to be on the back of a horse. Or in a gaming room with his few close friends. Or writing. He was currently engaged in a meticulous recording of Alucian military history. The topic interested him, but his acquaintances found his interest in the past rather dry. If he had his way, Sebastian would be more than content to keep to his study and read his documents and books. He could do without company for long periods of time. Or, he fancied he could. He didn't really know it to be true, because as the heir to the Alucian throne, he was forced to endure a contradictory private life while constantly in the presence of others. Servants. Secretaries. Advisors. Guards.

And in full view of the public from which he was supposed to be sheltered. People had a way of seeing past the veil. His every step was recorded.

Which might explain his aversion to such events as this. He was surrounded by people he didn't know who clambered to be close to him. People who wanted to breathe in his air and push a little closer. It was vexing and at times could be terribly unnerving. Once, when he'd been dispatched to the initial launch of one of their newest warships, two men had come from nowhere, putting their hands on his shoulder, trying to capture him or toss him into the sea before the Alucian guard fell on them and stopped them.

In large groups, he felt like a caged animal, a species on constant display.

This particular ball had been planned well before he'd ever stepped foot on England's shores, a courtesy extended by the English crown to the Alucian crown. Negotiations for it had been handled by Sebastian's personal secretary, Matous Reyno. It was Matous's idea for the masquerade.

Matous had been by Sebastian's side for many years, serving him since the day of his fifteenth birthday and investiture as crown prince. Seventeen years in all.

Outside his immediate family, Sebastian trusted no one as he trusted Matous. That said a lot for the man, really, for the Chartiers believed that no one in the Alucian Court could be trusted. The forty-year-old rift between Sebastian's father, King Karl, and his older half-brother, Felix, the Duke of Kenbulrook, had created an atmosphere of distrust and betrayal that had followed him all the way to England.

Sebastian didn't really fear betrayal—he tended to believe the good in most, and more than once had suggested to his father that perhaps the rift between him and his half-brother could be repaired. Sometimes men did unwise things when they were young, he'd suggested.

His father had responded with a murderous look.

His father's fear that all men had been sent by Felix to harm them had settled into the marrow of everyone that surrounded the royal family. Especially while in England—everything and everyone was suspect.

It was that overriding suspicion that had led Matous to suggest that if everyone wore a mask, and an identical one at that, Sebastian might have some semblance of privacy. Very little, Matous admitted, but it seemed far better than wearing the sashes and the medals and rings of the knight guard Sebastian would typically wear if the ball were more formal. "It is the only way that you might attend without great attention, I think. You will not be so easy a target. And the English like the idea."

Sebastian had laughed. "A silk mask will not protect me from all the assassins that supposedly lurk around me."

"It will not protect you, no, Your Highness, but your elite guard will. And it may serve to confuse detractors and menaces."

Sebastian thought his detractors and menaces were wilier than that, but then again, it hardly mattered what he thought. There were men in the crown's service paid to think of these things, and their nerves had put Sebastian on edge since his arrival more than a week ago.

The trade agreement he'd come to negotiate was vitally important to his country but perhaps even more important to him. His father had not wanted to pursue it. The prime minister of Alucia resented Sebastian's interference in the delicate matters of state, and insisted they ought to be thinking of the military. "We should focus on preparing for war with Wesloria," he'd advised the king, "not pursuing trade agreements with a country so far from our shores."

Sebastian saw it differently. This friction between Alucia and Wesloria had taken a toll on the kingdom's economy. Border skirmishes did not come cheap, and had dented the coffers. In the meantime, Alucia had not progressed like other countries, had not begun to manufacture goods like England or America. What they needed was a stronger economy, he'd argued. Alucia might be a small European kingdom, but it was rich in resources. They needed the tools of industrialization, which England had developed above all others. The resources mined in Alucia—iron ore and copper, for example—could be traded for England's help in creating new, viable industries. Cotton and wheat could be bartered for tobacco and sugar.

Industrialization would give Alucia the upper hand if they found themselves at war with Wesloria, where Uncle Felix continued to sow seeds of discord.

The crux of the dispute between the two royal half-brothers was that Uncle Felix, banished forty years ago to his family's home in Wesloria when Karl took the throne, believed he had a more legitimate claim to the throne than Karl.

The question of succession had its roots in a sixteenth-century civil war, when a Chartier had first assumed the throne. Felix's family, the Oberons, who lost that struggle and had retreated to Wesloria, propping up Weslorian kings along the way. They'd long claimed that the Chartier claim to rule Alucia was not as legitimate as theirs.

Felix had promised to unite Wesloria and Alucia under one rule if he was successful in gaining the Alucian throne, and with the many loyalists dedicated to the Oberon cause, the Chartiers feared they could be drawn into war.

Sebastian wanted to unite Wesloria and Alucia, too. He wanted the Chartiers and Oberons and their fellow countrymen to unite in the strength of industrialization and shared prosperity. Not by the ravages of war.

"The prime minister believes this to be a fool's errand," his father had said to Sebastian one night in his study, when the two of them had been alone save for the two footmen who stood quietly aside, ready to serve.

"The prime minister can't see the forest for the trees," Sebastian had said. "We won't survive a war by falling behind the times."

His father had harrumphed but said, "I will agree to your plan, but over the objections of my prime minister. He has threatened that the parliament may not ratify any trade agreement struck by you if it is not completely advantageous to Alucia."

"I understand."

"You must maintain the upper hand in negotiations," his father had warned.

Sebastian was well aware of that. Wasn't that the goal of any negotiation?

"There is one way you might appease me and the prime minister and perhaps pave a path to ratification."

"Oh? How?" Sebastian had asked curiously.

"Bring home a wife."

"Pardon?" Sebastian had laughed.

His father did not. "We've waited long enough. We must secure the question of succession—Felix's son Arman has two children. While England believes in our legitimacy, Queen Victoria's consort, Prince Albert, agrees with the view of his duchy of Saxe-Coburg and Gotha, who favors Felix. They depend on Wesloria for iron ore, as you know. We can cement your trade agreement and England's commitment to us with an English bride."

This had not been part of Sebastian's thinking, but instead of debating the point, he'd said nothing. He needed to think about it.

His father had pinned him with a look. "You're not a young man any longer. You're two-and-thirty. We must secure the succession—it's as simple as that, son. If you can't arrange it, then perhaps you have no business inserting yourself in these affairs."

"I understand."

"I hope you do. You should know that if you don't settle on a match, when you return, I'll settle on one for you. A bride from Saxe-Coburg and Gotha, perhaps."

Sebastian had had no choice but to agree.

Now that he was in London, the rumors of rebellion felt dangerously real, whereas in Alucia, the threats always seemed at a remove. His security was the best of his country, and yet, Sebastian felt exposed in London. He didn't know how his younger brother, Leopold, seemed to live relatively at ease while he studied at Cambridge.

"They're merely rumors," Leopold had said with a shrug when Sebastian had questioned him.

Perhaps Leopold did not hear the reports that support for their father was eroding under a relentless propaganda campaign coming from Felix. That was another thing that drove Sebastian—he believed if he could modernize the country, he could shore up support for his father.

And then again, it was entirely possible that those rumors were unfounded but louder in Sebastian's presence, as he was the heir, the future king. Perhaps they seemed stronger here because of Prince Albert's support of Felix and Wesloria.

Sebastian had to find a wife in this veritable sea of

unmarried English women. Alliances had to be formed, and the ministers of Alucia had hypothesized that a proper English bride with strong connections to the Parliament of the United Kingdom would secure support for Alucia in a deeper rift between Wesloria and Alucia. Which potential bride, however, was an ongoing debate between the ministers that had accompanied him.

Sebastian understood his duty. He wasn't particularly bothered by the marriage part of this bargain with his father. He'd never entertained the idea that a marriage to a woman could be made solely on the basis of compatibility and affection. He had always known it would be a political alliance in his case, just as his parents' had been. They'd dispatched their duty to the kingdom and had produced the obligatory heir and a spare. Now they lived separate lives for the most part, his mother generally spending her time in the mountains at their ducal estate, and his father settled in at the palace in the capital of Helenamar. Sebastian assumed his marriage would follow the same path.

The Alucians had narrowed the field of eligible wives to a handful, but the hopes of English parents were evergreen. In addition to hearing the rumors of his demise at every turn, Sebastian was also being bombarded with introductions to unmarried English women.

He'd just endured a long line of them. It was ridiculous, what with all the masks. And what could anyone hope to do in a few superficial moments? Did they think he would look at one of those masked faces and Cupid would sling his arrow into Sebastian's heart? He'd resented the need to do it, and he'd been so fatigued by the many introductions that he'd actually stepped on the foot of a woman who had greeted him with a hearty

Welcome to England, as if she were standing at the port of entry, waving weary travelers through.

"Do you intend to dance?" Matous asked after Sebastian had told him that he would not accept another introduction and had proceeded to walk away.

"No." Sebastian looked around for a waiter. What were they serving? Was it the punch?

"I would highly recommend it, sir. If you don't, it will be remarked and your identity revealed."

"Have I not already been remarked?" Sebastian complained. "You introduced two dozen young women to me in the corner of the ballroom."

"Two dozen out of what could potentially have been two hundred," Matous said with a deferential incline of his head. It was a habit of his; he sought to appear deferential when he was disagreeing or correcting Sebastian.

Sebastian groaned and looked around for a footman.

"Is there a…type…that would please you, sir?"

Matous was not asking after Sebastian's favorite type of dance. The "type" that would please him was a naked one, preferably on a bed somewhere far from this madness. "Red hair," he said. "I made her acquaintance at Windsor, do you recall? Widowed or separated or something like it. And a drink, man. Wine, punch, I don't care. I must have something."

"As you desire, sir," Matous said crisply, and with a flick of his right wrist, sent one of the four guards, who were dressed identically to Sebastian, hurrying off to find something for him to drink.

The guard returned a moment later with a glass, which he sipped before wiping the rim clean with his handkerchief and handing the drink to Sebastian.

Sebastian downed the drink. It was the rum punch,

and it was as good as the first time he'd sampled it. A thought flitted through his mind briefly—was the woman whose foot he'd mangled the same woman in the passageway? He mentally shrugged and thrust the glass at the guard. "More," he said.

While he waited for the guard to return with more of the drink, Matous went off to find the woman with the red hair. At about the same time as the guard returned with a second round of punch, Matous returned with a woman on his arm. She was wearing a deep blue gown. Her auburn hair looked quite stunning, and her green catlike eyes glittered at Sebastian from behind a mask. She sank into a very deep curtsy.

"Your Highness, may I present Mrs. Regina Forsythe," Matous said.

"Mrs. Forsythe," Sebastian said. "A pleasure to make your acquaintance again."

"The pleasure is assuredly mine, Your Royal Highness." She accepted the hand he'd offered and rose up with a pert smile.

"You intrigued me so with your conversation at Windsor," he remarked. "I hope it is not an imposition to resume it?"

She smiled coyly. "Which conversation was that? About the soup? Or the fact that my husband is stationed in India at present?"

She was saucy, and Sebastian liked that about her. At Windsor, when he'd asked why she had not accompanied her husband to India to give him comfort, she had slyly explained that her husband saw to his comfort, and she to hers. "Both," he said to her question. "May I have the honor of this dance?"

"The honor would be mine."

He presented his arm. She laid her hand lightly on it and allowed him to lead her onto the dance floor. The musicians played a waltz, and Sebastian bowed, then took her hand in his, placed his other hand high on her back, and led her into the dance.

"How are you finding London?" she asked.

"It has been a privilege." Never give an answer that could be in any way misconstrued.

"How do you find your rooms at Buckingham?" she asked, her eyes glittering.

A clever little inquiry. "We are not housed at Buckingham. The queen has graciously accommodated our large party here."

"How fortuitous." Her coy little smile went a little deeper. "I am familiar with all the hallways and rooms at Kensington. It's quite a complicated little palace, is it not?"

Sebastian smiled. "Quite." He understood her as well as she understood him, as well as she and Matous and he all understood one another. Sebastian knew, without having to ask, that arrangements for private accommodations would be made.

At the end of the dance, he whispered an invitation in Mrs. Forsythe's ear and how she might go about it if she were so inclined. The lady did not so much as blink. She slid him a look from the corner of her eye, flicked open her fan and whispered her response.

He bowed, escorted her from the dance floor, thanked her, then walked back to his group of men. He looked around for the ever-present Matous and spotted him across the room in an animated discussion with one very round Englishman. But Sebastian was quickly distracted by a couple sailing toward him at what looked like thirty knots. One of his guards stepped in front of him before the couple could accost him.

"How do you do," the gentleman said, and bowed, exposing the bald spot on his head. "We should like to welcome His Royal Highness."

Sebastian's guard said nothing.

"We'd like to invite him to join us for cake," the woman trilled. But she didn't look at Sebastian when she said it, and he realized that they didn't know who he was. They were hoping he or his guard would point out the prince to them.

His guard clucked his tongue at the lady. "I beg your pardon, madam, but the prince does not care for cake."

Well, *that* wasn't true at all. Sebastian very much liked cake and he could do with some now. He was starving.

"Would you be astonished to learn that my father, Mr. Cumbersark-Haynes, was acquainted with your king when they were lads at Oxford?" the man said. "Jolly good times they had, and I'm certain His Highness would enjoy the tale if you'd be so kind to point him out."

Another guard moved discreetly to stand beside the first, blocking the couple's view of Sebastian.

"Ah, I see. Yes, my lord," the guard said, "the prince is just there," and pointed across the room.

Both English heads swiveled around in the opposite direction of where Sebastian stood.

"Splendid, thank you very much indeed," the man said. And then he leaned in close to Sebastian's guard. "Is it true what they say? Is there to be war between Wesloria and Alucia?"

"In Alucia, we do not listen to rumor," the guard said.

"Oh, of course *not*," the woman said quickly, nodding her head so adamantly that the feathers atop her mask looked as if they were bracing against a gale force wind. "And neither do *we* listen to rumor."

Except, perhaps, the rumor that war was brewing with Wesloria.

"If you will excuse us," the guard said, and the couple were both nodding like a pair of *dumbledees*, the Alucian word for idiot.

The woman put her head next to her companion and began to whisper in his ear as they hurried off in search of the crown prince.

The first guard turned around to Sebastian. "I would recommend, Your Highness, that we adjourn to another part of the ballroom."

"I recommend we adjourn to the dining room. I'm famished."

"A private dining room has been set," the second guard said, and indicated with his chin the direction they were to walk.

As they made their way toward the door of the ballroom, Sebastian looked around again for Matous but did not see him. The Englishman he'd seen talking to his secretary was now in the company of other Englishmen, all of them laughing together at something.

He did not see Matous again until much later, after he'd been served in a dining room and had drunk more of the delicious rum punch. He was in better spirits, looking forward to his clandestine meeting with Mrs. Forsythe. He'd even danced again, this time in complete anonymity with a young woman who focused on her feet. And when the Alucian dances were played, he joined the line with Lady Sarafina Anastasan, his foreign minister's comely wife.

At half past midnight, Matous appeared at his side. He looked harried, a bit disheveled, and his hair was mussed. All quite unlike Matous. He said low, "All is at the ready, sir."

Sebastian nodded. As they made their way from the ballroom, Matous said, "If I may, sir, is there some place we might have a word?"

But Sebastian had availed himself of punch and was feeling randy and desperate to be out of the mask. Visions of Mrs. Forsythe's fair green eyes and unbound auburn hair had begun to play in his head in anticipation of what was to come. "Will it not wait?"

Matous hesitated. He glanced at the guard and pressed his lips together. "As you wish, sir."

Sebastian took pity on his secretary and said in Alucian, "Come to my suite in two hours. We can speak freely there."

Again, Matous hesitated. It was not like him at all—he was generally eager to please. Sebastian studied his face a moment. "Will that suit?"

"Je," Matous said in Alucian. *Yes.* He bowed his head.

Sebastian carried on, his thoughts already on his tryst.

Mrs. Forsythe was waiting just inside the vestibule of the entrance marked by a clock. She smiled when Sebastian jogged up the steps.

"You must be freezing," he said.

"I will be warm soon enough. Come." She boldly reached for his hand. "I've the perfect room."

Oh, he was certain she had the perfect room, probably procured for her by spies in the English government or perhaps even by rebels. He was well versed in all the ways someone might try and catch him in a compromising situation because he'd spent his life learning to subvert such ploys. He pulled her into him, caught her chin with his hand and touched his lips to hers. She sighed longingly.

"I've a different room, madam. Would you care to see it?" He wrapped his arm around her waist to escort her down the steps.

She resisted. "But I had the servant light a fire."

"There will be fire in this room, too," he assured her.

She gave a quick, furtive look behind her.

"Are you expecting someone other than me, Mrs. Forsythe?"

"Pardon?" She blanched. "No, Your Highness, of course not."

She lied. But Sebastian smiled. He was well guarded and didn't care what little scheme she'd cooked up. "Shall we?"

Whatever agreement she'd made, whatever bargain she'd struck, she surrendered it—she preferred pleasure to subterfuge. How fortuitous for him.

He put his arm around her waist and led her down the steps to the drive. They walked briskly behind an Alucian guard who led them around the corner and into a private garden, through a side door, and up the stairs to where the Alucian servants and guards had been quartered. Another guard was waiting at the entrance to one of the rooms. He opened the door for them, then quickly and quietly closed it behind them.

The room was small, but the hearth was lit, and the linens looked freshly washed. Sebastian did not hesitate to remove Mrs. Forsythe's mask. She was as pleasing to look at as he recalled from the state dinner at Windsor.

She reached up and removed his mask, too, and smiled prettily. "What a handsome man you are, sir. *Quite* pleasing."

Sebastian kissed her. She kissed him back. And before he knew it, he had her against the wall, moving with abandon, and she was crying out in pleasure like a hyena.

He never did make it back to his suite of rooms that night.

CHAPTER FOUR

The Royal Masquerade Ball at Kensington Palace included banqueting in a room that boasted wall coverings in rich red and gold, contrasted by tables set in snowy white linens and silver. Guests availed themselves of the twenty-foot buffet serving meats, cheeses, sandwiches, biscuits, sweet meats, towering cakes in delightful shapes, and the evening's most favored delectable, the royal tipsy cake, served on plates of fine bone Limoges china, and finished in 22 carat gold, produced in France for Her Majesty the Queen.

—Honeycutt's Gazette of Fashion and Domesticity for Ladies

THE DISCOVERY OF food was another delight for Eliza. In addition to being a wee bit in her cups, she was famished. With the excitement of the day on her mind and an extraordinary amount of time required to prepare, she'd not eaten a thing since morning. She wandered up and down the tables laden with food prepared by the palace kitchens, filling a plate well past the amount of food that was considered polite for a delicate woman to take. Well, she was not a delicate woman and she was hungry and she was terribly blasé about her personal circumstances. It wasn't as if she was hoping a gentleman might notice her and consider her a worthy prospect for marriage—Eliza knew better than that. She was eight-and-twenty, on the shelf, unremarkable, plainly dressed, and undesirable to anyone in this crowd. She appealed mostly to the Mr. Norrises of the world, who assumed, given their widowed status and her spinster status, that she would be delighted to clean their chamber pots and darn their socks. No, thank you. Her life suited her well enough and allowed her to eat at royal balls without qualm.

She had settled with her plate of food near the door, at a table that had been set a little away from the others to clear space for those wishing to exit the room. It was there, behind her sandwich, that she noticed once again the enthusiastic, slender Alucian gentleman who had been the one to make introductions to the prince. He seemed far less enthusiastic now. He was standing in the hall, and she wondered what he was doing, when suddenly a veritable armada of Alucian gentlemen came striding down the hall, the prince at the center. The slender Alucian quickly stepped into their path, and Eliza realized he'd been standing there so that he could intercept the prince.

Once again, the prince seemed impatient with the slender man, and very subtly tried to move around him. But the slender man was determined to have his say. Eliza took a rather large bite of her sandwich, chewing enthusiastically, and watched as the man spoke and the prince responded, and then stepped around him. Nevertheless, the prince hesitated before he moved along, but move along he did, and the slender man appeared a bit dejected, judging by the way his shoulders sagged, and he stared down at the floor as guests streamed around him.

Eliza didn't think she cared much for the haughty

prince, in spite of his fine green eyes. She wondered where he was off to at such a clip.

The slim man suddenly looked up and through the banquet hall door. His gaze seemed to land directly on Eliza. She froze, a chipmunk with her cheeks full of sandwich. *Was* he looking at her? It was difficult to tell with the mask. Surely not.

Well, if he was, he was frightened off, because he suddenly turned and walked briskly in the opposite direction. He walked up to a round Englishman and whisked him off to the side of the hall for animated discussion.

That porcine Englishman seemed terribly familiar to Eliza. She called up many faces in her head as she tried to sort it out.

"There you are!"

The shout startled Eliza so badly she fumbled her sandwich.

"Dear *Lord*, what are you *doing*, Eliza?" Caroline exclaimed in horror. "You're eating as if you've not dined in *weeks*."

"I'm hungry," Eliza informed Caroline. "The food is delicious. I want to try everything."

"Well, it looks like you have everything on your plate." Caroline sat heavily beside Eliza with a sigh. "I've danced to the point I don't think I can take another step." Even though her mask was slightly askew, Eliza thought Caroline was particularly lovely tonight. But that was Caroline for you—always impeccably dressed. She had the good fortune of fine looks and a fine figure. Even in her bedclothes and her hair tangled around her, she was quite lovely. She was tall and lithe, and her pale blond hair was put in loops above her ears, anchored there by the velvet ties of her gold mask. Her gown was made of gold and white muslin, and gold velvet ribbons wrapped around her sleeves. She wore a single strand of pearls around her neck.

But it was her mask that stood out above all else. It was a work of art. It was shaped like the oversized eyes of a cat and was covered in the same material as her gown. Cascades of beads hung from the corners and bordered the full mask.

When they'd dressed for the ball, Caroline had taken an inordinate amount of time in front of the mirror, admiring herself from all angles, making slight adjustments to her gown and mask, depending on her perspective. "Madam Rosenstern made the gown *especially* for me, *especially for* tonight," she'd informed Eliza and Hollis.

Caroline suddenly reached for Eliza's dance card dangling from her wrist. "Eliza! You've only three of them filled!"

"I was forced to dance a polka," Eliza said, and took another bite of sandwich. "Have you any idea how dreadfully I dance a polka?"

"I know how dreadfully you *dance*, darling, but I rather thought you'd do well enough with a quadrille, and yet, you haven't a partner for that dance. We must find a hostess—"

"No!"

"And will you put down the sandwich? A gentleman will not be inclined to consider a lady for a dance partner, much less a potential wife, if he fears he must feed her as much as his livestock."

Eliza put down her sandwich. "If a gentleman considers me for a potential wife, he must also consider that I eat. This may come as quite a shock to you, Caro, but I did not come to this ball in search of a husband. I came to meet a prince, and *that*, I have done. *Twice* over," she added pertly.

Caroline gasped. "You have? *When?*"

"When I was avoiding the ballroom hostess. Look there, do you see that thin Alucian gentleman speaking to the fat Englishman?"

Caroline looked around. "Which one?"

"One of his hands is in a black glove and he holds it at his side."

"What of him?"

"He was the one making introductions to the prince. Who, by the bye, has shaved the beard you swooned about."

"Ah. To add to his disguise, I suspect."

"Who is the gentleman speaking to?"

Caroline sat up a little straighter to see. "If I am not mistaken, that is Mr. John Heath, the banker. You've met his daughter, Lucille, haven't you?"

Eliza shook her head.

"No?" Caroline leaned forward and whispered, "The poor dear has been out two seasons without a single offer. I have heard it said that her modest dowry is not enough to make up for her plain looks. She is not considered a *catch*."

"She and I could be fast friends, then, couldn't we?"

Caroline gave her a little glare. Both women turned their attention to the two men and their discussion across the way. A second Englishman had joined them.

"How on earth did you gain an introduction to the prince?" Caroline demanded. "One must be *invited* to be introduced."

"So I was instructed." Eliza forked a healthy bite of the tipsy cake. "I encountered him in a passageway between a study of some sort and the ballroom."

"A what?"

"A passageway."

"What were you doing in a passageway?"

"Hiding," Eliza admitted. "He sampled my punch. Said it was very good. And then he tried to seduce me."

Caroline's eyes rounded. And then she burst out laughing. "You can't be serious!" she cried gleefully.

"I am *quite* serious. He tried to seduce me, plain as day. I didn't know he was the prince then, obviously, or I might have allowed it, but moments later I found myself in a line to meet him, and Caro, I perjured myself." She laughed. "I claimed to have an invitation, and would you believe that not one person challenged me? Well, that's not entirely true. There was a woman dressed as a peacock who challenged me, but she didn't call the authorities."

Caroline's eyes widened. "Eliza Tricklebank! You were in the group of debutantes invited to make his acquaintance?"

"Did you see them?"

"I heard of them in the retiring room. *Everyone* did. Sarah Montrose was bragging and Emily Peters was *crushed* that she was not invited to join. Apparently, she's been struck off the list."

Eliza had another bite of cake. "I wanted to meet a prince and I saw no other way to do it. His eyes are an amazing shade of green, Caro. I've never seen such a color. Oh, and he stepped on my foot."

"What?"

"Right across the top of it, with all his weight. It's

a wonder he didn't break it—he's quite a large man up close."

Caroline gaped at her.

"But I didn't mind," Eliza insisted through another bite of cake. "It was an accident, and I own some of the fault, because I leapt in front of him before he got away. I will never have another opportunity to meet a royal prince and I wasn't going to let it pass because of some unwritten rule that one must be *invited*."

Caroline's mouth dropped more. "What has *happened* to you?"

Eliza laughed. "Where is the harm? If he'd been swept off his feet by the sight of me and had sent all the other unmarried ladies home, I would apologize profusely for my behavior. But he wasn't, and he didn't, and therefore there is no harm. This isn't Cinderella after all."

"Well, this is certainly *not* Cinderella. At least she danced," Caroline said, and helped herself to a piece of cheese from Eliza's plate. "You are not the only one to have encountered a prince tonight, you know. I was meant to dance with Prince Leopold, whose name is very clearly written on my dance card, do you see?" she asked, shaking her dance card at Eliza.

Eliza peered at it. She saw the name clearly written.

"We are acquainted, as you know," Caroline said.

Eliza resisted a roll of her eyes. She loved Caroline, but Caroline adored every opportunity to mention any of her many important friends. She had told Eliza and Hollis the story of meeting Prince Leopold of Alucia at a country house last summer. She had told them more than once—several times over, if one was counting. The meeting had been very brief, but according to Caroline, hugely memorable to her and the prince both.

"We are more than acquainted, really, given our conversation in Chichester. Well, you'll not believe it—he pretended not to know me at all."

"Pardon?"

"As if we'd never met!" She reached for another piece of cheese. "I was given the cut direct, Eliza, and for no reason whatsoever."

"But…did he not write his name on your card?"

"Oh, that," Caroline said, and had a third piece of cheese. "Miss Williams wrote his name there because I had said, with certainty I believe I am due, that once I greeted him, he would naturally extend the invitation. Any gentleman would have done so. But he has cut me to the bone."

"The *bastard*," Eliza said in full solidarity with her friend.

"He will regret it, you may trust me," Caroline said confidently. "All right then, come along, and stop eating! Let's go and fill the rest of your dance card. There are only three sets left, and one of them is an Alucian dance."

"But I want the tipsy cake!" Eliza complained. "I don't want to dance the Alucian set. I'll make a fool of myself."

"Come," Caroline commanded.

Eliza stifled a belch and allowed Caroline to remove the tipsy cake from her reach.

They walked arm in arm to the ballroom, but the hall was very crowded and their progress slow. As they made their way, the peacock, all smiles now, passed on the arm of an Alucian gentleman. "That's her," Eliza said, indicating the woman with a tip of her chin. "She's the one who informed me I had to be invited to meet the prince."

Caroline blinked. "Do you *know* her?"

"No. Should I?"

Caroline squeezed Eliza's arm. "That is *Katherine Maugham*."

Eliza glanced over her shoulder as the peacock was swallowed into the crowd. "Who is *Katherine Maugham*?" she asked, mimicking Caroline's dramatic intonation.

"Eliza!"

"What?"

"Do you speak to *no one* but the judge? Haven't you heard of Lady Katherine Maugham? Surely Hollis has mentioned her."

Eliza shook her head. "If she did, I wasn't listening." At Caroline's withering look, she said, "I have quite a lot to do every day and I can't listen to *every* word my sister utters, for you may trust there are loads of words. Where *is* Hollis, by the bye? And are you going to tell me who Lady Katherine Maugham is?"

"*She* is the one everyone believed would catch the eye of the crown prince. Her father is particularly well positioned in the Lords and heir to a vast fortune. His ironworks company is one of the largest in all of England and this trade agreement would be a boon for him. I'm truly surprised Lady Katherine didn't tell you herself, for everyone knows she is certain to whisper it to whomever is nearby at the first available opportunity."

"Well, she didn't catch his eye in the introduction line. He walked on before she ever opened her mouth."

Caroline gasped. And then grinned. "*Really.* Tell me *everything*, especially how offended she was."

Eliza giggled. When they reached the ballroom, Caroline made Eliza stand to one side. "Don't move as much as an inch, will you promise?"

"I promise," Eliza said, and saluted her friend.

Caroline hurried off. As Eliza waited patiently—she was too full to do more than that—she became aware of a group of gentlemen very nearby. Alucians and Englishmen, she confirmed with a quick peek, and once again, she noticed the thin, wiry companion of the prince. He seemed particularly agitated now. Eliza sidled closer under the pretense of stepping out of the way of foot traffic as a dancing set came to a close.

"How dare they utter the *word* rebellion," one of the Alucians muttered, his words heavily accented. "Do they not understand that every whisper feeds the potential?"

"I think they do not understand your country," said one of the Englishmen. "They believe what they've been told by those who would do you harm."

That voice sounded familiar. Or did they all sound familiar to her?

"Then perhaps *they* should not have been invited," the Alucian snapped. "Surely you must know that he is—" He very abruptly stopped talking and turned around.

Eliza blinked with surprise. She hadn't realized she'd gotten so close. "I beg your pardon," she said, and turned away, hurrying toward the ballroom door before any of them could speak.

"Eliza!"

In her horror at having been caught eavesdropping, she'd forgotten Caroline's instruction. She whipped about to see Caroline walking toward her on the arm of a gentleman.

"Where are you off to?" Caroline said, and through her mask, Eliza could see her glare.

"Um..." She looked toward the door.

"I should like to introduce you to my friend, if I may?" Caroline was staring daggers, so Eliza straightened, smiled and curtsied to the gentleman. Should she have curtsied? Oh well. Caroline would be sure and critique her performance later.

Caroline's friend was no taller than Eliza. His mask rode up his nose, but he had a pleasant smile and he bowed.

"May I introduce Mr. Howard of Brighton?" Caroline said with proper aplomb. "Mr. Howard, please meet my dear friend, Miss Eliza Tricklebank."

"How do you do, Miss Tricklebank." He bowed. "May I be so bold as to request the pleasure of this dance? Lady Caroline informs me that your dance card is not yet full."

Eliza shot a look at Caroline, whose countenance had gone from impatience to smiles. "You'd like that, wouldn't you, Eliza?"

"They will be starting a quadrille," Mr. Howard said, glancing toward the dance floor.

"Thank you, Mr. Howard. I would like that very much," Eliza said, offering her hand to be placed on his arm. Which might have been poorly done. She couldn't keep all the rules in her head.

"You must enter his name," Caroline said, pointing at her dance card.

Eliza thrust her arm forward. "Perhaps you might do the honor for me, Caroline. I would so very much hate to make a mistake." If Caroline noticed her sarcasm, she gave no hint of it. She quickly wrote Mr. Howard's name. "There you are, off you go!" She smiled brightly, as if sending a child off to the schoolroom.

So Eliza trotted off to dance with Mr. Howard. After him, she danced with another gentleman, a friend of Mr. Howard's. And then, the dreaded Alucian set with an Alucian whose English was so heavily accented that she could hardly understand him as she concentrated on the intricate steps. She danced a quadrille—Caroline was right, she performed passably at the quadrille. And finally, a waltz with a gentleman who reeked of tobacco and liquor.

At this point in the evening, the masks had begun to come off, as people were perspiring behind them. The cacophony of voices grew louder and the punch ran low. Eliza doffed her mask, too, tying the ribbons together and looping it over her arm while she danced. Once or twice, she had to remind herself that she was in Kensington Palace at a royal masquerade ball. That the gentlemen with whom she danced were important and wealthy men. And the women around her who weren't already in desirable marriages were bound for them.

She might have smiled and flirted, might have pretended for the evening that she was not a spinster who looked after her father. But strangely, she had no desire to pretend. She was quite at ease as a dancing spinster fallen gaily into her cups.

And really, the only eyes she could recall at all in that vast sea of masks were a pair of autumn green eyes.

CHAPTER FIVE

At half past two in the morning, the buffet in the banquet room was replenished to the great appreciation of many after the rigor of the Alucian sets. Masks began to come off and revealed several surprises, including how the curious tastes of a northern lord extends to his costumes. There was not a single sighting of a particular royal visitor after one o'clock. Nor was there any hint of the whereabouts of a lady whose hair marked her identity where her mask attempted to hide it. There was no witching hour for revellers, as many of them were heard in the streets as they departed Kensington well past four o'clock.

Ladies, if a late night of dancing has left you with swollen eyes, the French practice of sleeping in a mask of raw veal is the perfect remedy. You'll awake fresh and doe-eyed.

—Honeycutt's Gazette of Fashion and Domesticity for Ladies

SEBASTIAN WOKE TO an empty bed.

He bolted upright, momentarily disoriented by the small room and the absence of any servant quietly arranging the tea service. But it quickly came rushing back to him—the woman with the brilliant red hair riding him, her fingers curling into the flesh of his chest. He looked down. *Je*, she'd left a mark.

Sebastian rubbed his hands through his hair, then got out of bed and found his clothes, everything but his discarded mask. He quit the room in a half-dressed state. His shirttails were out, his coat draped over his arm, his neckcloth dangling from his fingers.

Two guards were stationed just outside the door, both of them leaning against the wall, having learned the art of sleeping while standing up, a skill Sebastian himself did not possess. They quickly roused and silently led Sebastian out of the building, taking care to make sure the doors closed soundlessly behind them.

The day was just beginning to dawn when they reached a familiar part of the palace. When Sebastian entered his chambers, his valet, Egius, very nearly fell out of the chair where he'd been sleeping. Sebastian handed his coat and neckcloth to him. "A bath, please."

"*Je*, Your Highness." Egius bowed and went out to arrange it.

Sebastian walked to the basin, plunged his hands into ice-cold water and splashed his face. His belly rumbled with hunger. It had been a vigorous night—Mrs. Forsythe had a voracious appetite for the male body.

His butler entered the room and bowed, *"Bon den, mae principae."*

"Good morning, Patro," Sebastian returned in Alucian. "I'll breakfast after my bath. Bring round the foreign minister. Where is Matous?"

"I'll send a man to rouse him, sir," Patro said.

It was early yet, Sebastian realized with a yawn. Too early to wake a man. "Leave him for now," he said, with a wave of his hand. "Let the man sleep until breakfast."

When Sebastian's bath was readied in the adjoining room, he sank into the steaming water and closed his eyes. This was the first time since arriving in England that he felt so relaxed. He was grateful to Mrs. Forsythe for scratching an itch that badly needed tending.

He dozed lightly in the fragrant water as his mind wandered aimlessly through a forest of thoughts, including the dozens of women he'd been introduced to since arriving in London. There were *always* women—eager, hopeful women. His lack of interest in any one in particular concerned his country's ministers. It wasn't that he didn't care for women—nothing could be further from the truth. But it seemed to him, more often than not, that a woman's interest in him was more about a position of privilege and notoriety than it was about *him.*

Nevertheless, he understood that he had to marry. He had to produce heirs. He was two-and-thirty, well past the time to do the one thing required for his life of undeniable privilege and produce an heir.

He'd met scores of women in Alucia. He'd met scores of women tonight at the ball, and before that, at supper parties across Mayfair in the homes of notable Englishmen. And two days after his arrival, at the formal supper at Windsor—but there, he'd been captivated by the saucy Mrs. Forsythe. No one else had stood out to him.

It was the same wherever he went, in any country, on any continent. He was introduced to people who were eager to marry a daughter, niece, sister, granddaughter to him. There were so many young women, in fact, that they'd all begun to look alike. Pale English faces and narrow noses. Mrs. Forsythe had stood out for all the wrong reasons. Compatibility, affection—none of that seemed to matter other than that the woman would one day be a queen and the mother of the heir to the throne in Alucia, and thereby bring the family privilege and standing. Sebastian could be a beast and it wouldn't matter.

He sank lower into the tub and thought about calling for more hot water. Unfortunately, he had meetings to attend. Today, he was meeting with the English trade minister, who was clearly skeptical of the proposed agreement. Sebastian had to be at his best and convince the man.

And yet, he didn't move from the warmth of the water.

The problem with all these women, he mused, was that he looked at the task of finding a potential mate as another in a long line of tasks: meet with the English officials about the trade arrangements; form alliances with rich, important men; select a woman from the many presented to marry. It seemed an easy enough task to accomplish if a man could divorce his feelings from it, but there was a part of him that yearned to find one who was compatible with him in some way. One whom he could trust. One who could be a friend and lover before she was ever a queen. Was that possible? Probably not. His grandmother had once said to him that there were trades in everything a person encountered in life. Great wealth and responsibility must come at the expense of something else. He assumed she'd meant love.

Once, he'd said to Leopold that he desired a woman who was compatible, and his brother had laughed. Not at Sebastian, really, but at the absurdity of their lives. They both knew that it was nearly impossible to find people they could completely trust, and they could only hope for it. Wealth and influence and titles had a way of turning otherwise honest people into liars and actors. Not that Sebastian believed that every woman he met was untrustworthy—but he didn't know how to separate the trustworthy ones from the opportunists.

He would probably never know if the woman he married held any particular esteem for him. She could be bored beyond hope by his quiet life, and he'd not know it. Honestly, Sebastian didn't know if there was really anything for a woman to admire about him other than the fact that he would one day be king.

The water had cooled, and he grudgingly climbed out of the tub. He accepted a towel and thick wool robe from Egius. He stood in front of the fire and ran his fingers carelessly through his damp hair. When he felt warm and dry, he went into the sitting room, waving off the undershirt Egius tried to hand him. "I'll have my breakfast first," Sebastian said.

He took a seat at the dining table. A young Alucian servant poured coffee. Patro had put a neat stack of his briefing papers on the table. He would be presenting language for the agreement later today. He picked up the first one and scanned the writing...*power and strength, and to take use of all due means, courses and prescriptions, and execute due acquittance and discharge...*

There was a soft rap at the door, followed by Patro's entrance. He bowed low. "Your Royal Highness, Field Marshal Rostafan and Foreign Minister Anastasan."

The two men entered behind Patro, both of them looking a little bleary-eyed. "Gentlemen," Sebastian greeted them in Alucian. "Did you enjoy the evening, then?"

"Excessively," Rostafan said, and sat heavily at the table beside Sebastian. By the look of it, Alucia's top military officer had not combed his hair. He was a barrel-chested man, quite tall, with a ruddy complexion and a beard that was in desperate need of trimming. He wore his military ribbons with great pride and had a habit of chewing his bottom lip to the point it looked always chapped. He took very little notice of the protocols and customs when it came to dealing with members of the royal family and tended to treat the king and his sons as if they were all equals.

His manner was the very opposite of Caius Anastasan, the foreign minister. Where Rostafan was big and gruff, Anastasan was trim and fastidious in his manner and attention to Sebastian. His olive brown skin was smooth and flawless, save for the dark circles under his eyes this morning, and he had not a hair out of place in spite of the early hour.

Sebastian knew Caius well—they'd attended Oxford at the same time, and Sebastian had considered him a friend. But his investiture as the crown prince of Alucia had changed some of his earlier relationships, including the one with Caius. His old friend had become deferential, and when he was named foreign minister, his deference had turned almost cloying. Sometimes Sebastian wondered if he'd imagined those years at Oxford.

Caius waited until Sebastian invited him to sit, which he did with a gesture of his hand.

"How did you find the ball, Your Highness?" Caius asked.

"Tolerable," Sebastian said, then smiled slyly. "Particularly toward the end." His visitors chuckled knowingly. Sebastian was used to every detail of his life being known to the people around the throne. It was impossible for him to have any secrets for any length of time.

Patro returned, this time with two servants carrying trays of breakfast—eggs and sausages, toast points and jam.

The three of them ate heartily while the men regaled Sebastian with tales about the ball. The sight of the English attaché dancing one of the Alucian sets was the stuff of excellent comedy when Rostafan told it. As they finished their meal, the talk gradually turned toward the meeting Sebastian was to have that afternoon. Caius was speaking about the need to reduce tariffs on Alucian goods. "We should insist on lowering the tariffs for—"

Sebastian stopped Caius from speaking by lifting his hand. "I would have Matous here for this." He looked around for Patro.

The butler nodded and went out to fetch the private secretary.

Rostafan drummed his fingers on the table, obviously annoyed by the wait. He turned his attention to the window and craned his neck to have a look at the gardens. "Looks to be another gray, wet day," Rostafan said. "One cannot comprehend how an entire people can abide such gray, wet conditions day in and day—"

The door suddenly burst open and Patro, wild-eyed and ashen, rushed in.

Sebastian twisted in his seat, confused. "What is it?"

"Sir—Mr. Reyno does not rouse."

Rostafan chuckled. "He can't hold his drink."

But Sebastian could see by Patro's face that he didn't mean Matous had drunk too much. "What do you mean, he does not rouse?" Sebastian demanded as he gained his feet.

"Sir, I regret to tell you there is a great deal of blood."

Rostafan lurched forward, brushing Patro aside as he rushed from the room. Sebastian moved to go after him, but Caius caught his arm with a surprisingly strong grip. When Sebastian tried to shrug him off, Caius put both hands on Sebastian's chest and roughly shoved him back.

"You dare put your hands on me?" Sebastian shouted.

"Sir! We don't know what's happened. We don't know if it's an ambush or some plot to draw you out. Patro! Send in the guard!"

Sebastian again tried to follow Rostafan and pushed Caius aside, but he was stopped by the appearance of guards who blocked his exit.

"Your Highness," Caius said, his voice gentler. "You *must* wait here until we know it is safe."

Several guards filed in behind the first. Sebastian glared at them all, enraged. He didn't care that they had a duty—he only cared that they allow him to pass, to see what had happened to Matous.

With a roar of frustration, he whipped around and swept the breakfast dishes from the table, sending them crashing to the floor.

It seemed hours before Rostafan returned. His expression was dark, and his hands were covered in blood.

"Well?" Sebastian demanded.

"Murdered," Rostafan said. "His throat slit."

The news was so astounding that Sebastian lost his balance. He tipped into the breakfast table, catching himself with his hand. "It's not possible," he said. *Matous! His one true friend.* He felt sick. There was a pressure on his chest that felt as if it would crush it. He was aware of everyone in the room, crowded with men now. They all stared at him, awaiting his order of what was to be done. "How is this possible?"

No one answered.

"How is this possible?" Sebastian roared, and brought his fist down on the table.

He suddenly recalled Matous intercepting him on his way to rendezvous with Mrs. Forsythe. He'd wanted to speak to Sebastian, had seemed unusually flustered when Sebastian put him off.

He'd told him he would meet him here, in his rooms, and then he'd never come. *What had Matous said? What were his exact words?*

"Your Highness, with your permission, I will alert the proper authorities," Caius said. His voice sounded hollow.

Sebastian nodded numbly—he wasn't even certain who spoke. "Leopold," he croaked. "Find him and bring him at once."

More people left the room. More people came in. A maid to clean up the mess he'd made. Egius to dress him. He couldn't undertake a murder investigation in a dressing gown.

"I want to see him," Sebastian said to no one in particular.

"I would advise against it," said Rostafan.

"I want to *see* him," Sebastian insisted. He signaled Egius to follow him into the dressing room. When he was dressed, he entered the crowded sitting room again and looked at his field marshal. Without a word, Rostafan went to the door and opened it.

Sebastian followed him, striding down the carpeted hall to a door at the end. He braced himself, then stepped inside the small bedchamber and looked toward the bed. The first thing he saw was Matous's gloved hand hanging off the side of the bed. He'd been born with the deformity, a misshapen stump of a hand with no fingers. And while one would scarcely notice his hand, as Matous had adapted quite well, there were some things that were difficult for him. Sebastian would imagine that fighting off an attacker would be one of those things.

His belly churned, but he stepped closer. There was a massive amount of blood, and a gaping wound across Matous's throat. But Sebastian was surprised that his friend looked so peaceful in death, his face free of the creases of worry. He looked as if he was sleeping, his dreams gentle, and below his gentle, dreaming face, an ugly, bloody gash.

Who would have done this?

Who?

The English guards had arrived, and the Alucian guards were insistent that Sebastian leave the room. He was escorted back to his sitting room, which had filled with more people. Alucians, mostly, including the foreign minister's wife, who was quietly weeping in a corner, consoled by Rostafan. There were two Englishmen in heated conversation with Anastasan. Sebastian was surrounded, and yet, he had never felt so alone in his life.

He'd never felt such guilt, either. Matous had wanted to speak to him, but Sebastian had been ruled by his cock, too intent on relieving it with Mrs. Forsythe. He needed a moment to himself. He wanted to mourn his secretary and friend privately.

He would not be allowed that opportunity. He would be watched by everyone. Even now, as he tried to absorb the shock, a frail Englishman had inched forward. His moustache was in need of a trim, and his skin was a peculiar shade of gray. "I beg your pardon, Your Royal Highness, but if I may inquire as to the last time you saw Mr. Reyno alive?"

Sebastian felt sick, as if his breakfast would depart his body at any moment. He swallowed down the nausea. He'd been taught from the time he was a lad to put on a face to the public. "Last night, at the ball," he said calmly and prepared himself to answer more questions.

He would do anything to find who had done this to Matous.

CHAPTER SIX

Commissioned for a dear sum from the most prestigious milliners and modistes of London, the masks worn at the Royal Masquerade Ball were a sight to behold. Some of them defied the laws of gravity in their precarious perch upon unknown faces. Some defied the laws of fine taste, and in particular a keen eye was cast upon the bird's nest that sat upon a lady's head as if she expected her chicks would come home to roost at any moment.

—Honeycutt's Gazette of Fashion and Domesticity for Ladies

ELIZA, CAROLINE AND HOLLIS had returned to Caroline's lovely Mayfair home at a quarter till five in the morning, and slept like angels until one o'clock in the afternoon. When at last they did rise, they carried themselves down to the dining room, still in their nightgowns and dressing robes and their hair unbound. They had breakfast, lazily picking over the food as they reviewed the masquerade ball in detail.

"Did you see Lady Elizabeth Keene?" Hollis asked with much excitement. She'd drawn her legs up under her nightgown and wrapped one arm around them as she nibbled toast.

"Who?" Eliza asked.

"Lady Elizabeth *Keene*, darling. If you'd come with me to the recital at the zoological gardens, you would have seen her."

"I leave the gathering of gossip to you, Hollis, you know it very well. I am better use to you in putting the gazette together."

"Well, she and Lady Katherine Maugham are fierce rivals and she's livid she's not yet been noticed by Prince Sebastian when everyone said she would be. She was quite attentive to a certain English gentleman for spite."

"The bodice of Lady Elizabeth's gown was cut so low, I should think she might have had all the attention she pleased," Caroline said, waggling her brows as she bit off a piece from the slice of ham that she held delicately between two fingers. She had taken two chairs—one for sitting, one as an ottoman for her legs.

"But I thought Lady Katherine was livid *she'd* not yet been noticed by Prince Sebastian," Eliza said, confused as to who was livid about what.

"I hardly noticed Elizabeth's bodice at all," Hollis said. She was studying a bit of paper she'd smoothed on the table. It contained her notes. "I could not tear my eyes away from her mask. It looked like an awful bird's nest perched on her head."

Eliza gasped. "I *did* see her! I didn't know who she was, but I feared the poor thing had lost her fortune and had been forced to fashion her own mask."

Caroline giggled.

"Lady Elizabeth has forty thousand pounds a year, you know," Hollis announced without looking up from her notes. "Lady Katherine has only thirty thousand pounds a year."

Eliza and Caroline looked at each other. Their silence prompted Hollis to look up, too. "What?" She was clearly surprised by their surprise. "Did you think you're my only source of information, Caro?"

"I assure you, I was under no such illusion," Caroline drawled.

"All right, darlings, we must decide what will be recorded in the gazette about the ball!" Hollis said brightly. "Firstly, we must make comment on the gowns. I've made a few notes."

"There was a peculiar mix of them," Caroline began. She leaned to one side to allow a footman to pour tea into her cup. "Some of them so beautiful and some of them rather plain. I especially liked the Alucian gowns."

"Oh, *they* were beautiful," Eliza agreed. "But if I had to choose which gown dazzled more, I would say Hollis's."

Hollis gasped with delight. "*Would* you?"

"I would!" Eliza reached for a blue ribbon in Hollis's hair, which was so darkly brown it almost looked black. The ribbon had been missed in their blurry-eyed disrobing this morning. Hollis's gown, currently draped over a chaise upstairs, was made of the most gorgeous sapphire blue silk, trimmed in black, with a dramatic skirt that cascaded to the floor in panels. Poppy had worked several nights to bead the bodice with tiny black crystals. Hollis had added a stunning collar necklace made of black onyx, a gift from her late husband.

"The mask suited her, too, didn't it?" Caroline agreed, smiling at Hollis. "Mrs. Cubison was right about the blue. She was quite right about everything, really. If only she'd told me who was behind which mask! Now I'm cross all over again."

"So tight-lipped," Hollis agreed, also appearing to be cross with a modiste whom she'd never met.

"I'd hoped she might give me a hint of how certain people would be disguised, but alas she was a soul of discretion. She said, 'Lady Caroline, what is the point of a masquerade if you know the identity behind every mask?'" Caroline mimicked Mrs. Cubison's apparently deep voice.

"A valid point," Eliza agreed.

"Nevertheless, I persisted," Caroline said. "I *always* persist. Frankly, I *begged* her and I should think she would have obliged me as she owes me a small debt of gratitude."

"Why?" Eliza asked.

"Why!" Caroline blustered. "Can you not imagine how many clients I've sent to her in the last year alone?"

"How many?" Hollis asked curiously.

"I don't have a *number*, obviously, but I recommend her to anyone who asks. It doesn't matter, for she'd not divulge a *thing* about who'd commissioned what."

"What in bloody blazes is this? It looks like a harem in here, Caro!" a male voice thundered.

Lord Hawke, Caroline's brother, he of the handsome visage and trim figure, the gentleman who kept all the young ladies of London and their mothers guessing as to whom he might eventually take to wife, strolled into the dining room. He'd been out, apparently, or was going out, as he was wearing his greatcoat. And he looked quite refreshed, as if he'd had a full night's rest. It hardly seemed fair.

"Are you only just out of bed?" he asked incredulously, looking at each of them in turn.

"Of course!" Caroline said. "It was dawn before we

finally stumbled home. Had you stayed on, you'd still be abed, too."

"I would not have stayed on. It was personal sacrifice enough that I was forced to escort the three of you against my will. I don't care a fig about balls, and certainly not for the purpose of amusing some foreign prince. Even so, I am generally in good health and do not need much sleep. You should take your walks, the three of you. It's good for stamina." He reached across Caroline and helped himself to a slice of ham. "You're all too pale, really."

Eliza and Hollis took no offense. Beck had known the Tricklebank sisters since they'd been children, and tended to view them as children to this day. He paid them no heed, and they paid him even less.

"You won't believe it, Beck—I met the crown prince!" Eliza crowed.

Beck looked at her as if she'd lost her mind. "And?"

"And he's unmarried." Eliza winked at him before fitting a cherry into her mouth.

"Dear Lord," Beck said with alarm. "Surely I needn't explain to you gooses that *none* of you, not even *you*, Caro, have the sort of dowry or connections or the *appeal* that such a match would require. You're whistling in the wind! Frankly, if you ask me—"

"No one has," Caroline pointed out.

"If you ask me," he said a bit louder, "you'd all do well to be more practical in your dealings about town."

"Meaning?" Caroline asked.

"Meaning, set your sights on gentlemen who are more suited to your situation. A baronet or knight for you, Caro." He looked studiously at Hollis and Eliza. "I don't know, perhaps a clerk of some sort?" he suggested, just in case Hollis and Eliza thought so highly of themselves that they might have set their sights on a lord or, heaven forfend, a prince. "Instead of wasting your time worrying over ball gowns, endeavour to do something useful, such as learning about the care and feeding of a husband and children. You should not be chasing princes and certainly *not* writing your *gazette*," he added with much disdain and a pointed look at Hollis.

"There is not a single gentleman in our acquaintance who appreciates the work or the appeal of *Honeycutt's Gazette*," Hollis said pertly. "Am I the only one to notice this?"

"Trust me, Mrs. Honeycutt, you are not the only one to notice," Beck said.

Hollis was very protective of her enterprise and looked as if she might launch herself at Beck. But Caroline was quick to step in before anything untoward was said or done. "Thank you for your advice, dearest brother," she said sweetly. "Surely now that you've imparted your vastly superior wisdom, you'll want to find someone else in need of your advice and leave us to finish our breakfast?"

"You're dismissing me, are you?" Beck asked casually as he helped himself to bread. "Then you must not care to hear my news."

"What news?" Hollis asked.

"No, no," he said, wagging a finger at her. "This is not for your gazette, Hollis. *This* is strictly confidential. Do I have your word?"

"Really?" Eliza asked, perking up. "What is it? Has Mr. Clarence's wandering eye wandered again?"

"Nothing as mundane as *that*," Beck said, clearly disappointed by her guess. "Do I have your word?"

"Yes!" the three of them cried in impatient unison.

"Very well," Beck said, and ate a berry before announcing, quite casually, "This morning, the crown prince's personal secretary was found murdered in his bed at Kensington."

There was a moment of stunned silence. And then a burst of questions.

Beck held up his hand and looked around at them. "His throat had been cut as he lay sleeping. I suppose he lay sleeping. All I know is that he was found in his bed, dressed in nightclothes, from which one could deduce he'd been sleeping."

Caroline, Hollis and Eliza looked at one another, their mouths agape.

"But which one is his secretary?" Hollis asked. "They all wore identical masks."

Beck shrugged. "They say his hand was deformed—"

Eliza gasped. *"No!"* she croaked.

"Yes."

"But he was the one who managed the introductions to the prince! You remember, Caro, I pointed him out to you."

"Well, he won't be making introductions now," Beck said carelessly.

Caroline slapped her brother's arm as he reached across her again. "How can you be so heartless?"

"Really, Beck!" Eliza said, appalled by this news. "The man spoke to me! He asked if I'd been harmed."

"That's right," Hollis chimed in. "A man has lost his life and you are making jests."

"It's not a jest, it's fact. I'm not heartless, but I have

no personal knowledge of this man. It is therefore difficult for me to spring tears of grief for his demise."

"But *why*?" Hollis asked.

"Because I don't *know* him—"

"No, no, I mean why would someone kill him?"

"Well, that is the question on everyone's mind, isn't it? I suspect it has something to do with the rumors of rebellion that circulate. Perhaps the murderer meant to slay the prince and mistook his secretary."

"No," Eliza said. "The secretary was a slight man. The prince is tall and robust."

"I suspect they will know soon enough. Someone is bound to have seen something. One simply cannot go wandering about Kensington cutting throats and not be noticed. All right then, stop eating and dress. It's near to teatime and I'm expecting callers. I won't have a harem lounging in my dining room." Beck took another berry and sauntered out of the room. "Please do as I ask, Caro," he called over his shoulder before disappearing into the hall.

Caroline rolled her eyes and pulled a hunk of bread from a loaf and began to butter it.

"I can't *believe* it," Eliza said. "I can't believe that poor man was *murdered*." She thought about how earnest he was in making his introductions to the prince. How intolerably disgruntled the prince appeared to be, scarcely looking at the ladies. How kind he had been to her when she'd boasted of meeting a prince. He'd said she'd made an indelible impression.

"Why would someone *murder* him in a royal palace? Where there are guards and people and so many opportunities for capture?" Hollis added. "Beck is right—someone is bound to have seen something."

"But if one managed to evade capture, suspicion would fall to English *and* Alucian. Think how difficult it will be to sort it all out," Caroline remarked.

"Yes, but—"

Hollis's argument was never heard, for they suddenly heard Beck bellow for Caroline in a voice that clearly conveyed displeasure. "*Caro!* I will have an explanation for how you came to spend so much for one *dress*!"

"Oh dear," Caroline said. "My brother has discovered how extraordinarily generous he is."

Caroline had long been famous for spending Beck's money. He generally huffed and he puffed, but really, he could never truly say no to her.

"CAROLINE!"

"Well, then," she said, quickly gaining her feet. "I think it best if we retire at once to my rooms." She began to walk so quickly that her dressing gown billowed out behind her as she fled the scene. Hollis and Eliza scurried after her.

As the three of them dressed, Hollis couldn't contain her curiosity about the murder. She ran through several scenarios that would have led to the poor secretary's death. As she babbled on, Eliza wondered how the prince with the green eyes had taken the news.

OVER THE NEXT few days, the whole of London was abuzz about the sensational news of a murder at Kensington Palace. Hollis was a frequent visitor to the house in Bedford Square, updating her family on the most recent theories as to who or what had befallen the gentleman, whose name, she'd discovered, was Mr. Matous Reyno. At first it was suspected the culprit was English, perhaps someone opposed to the trade agreement, for who would have access to that part of Kensington but an Englishman? And yet all the servants at the palace had been questioned and no clue had emerged.

The queen herself had offered a reward for anyone with information who came forward.

When no one came forward, suspicion shifted to the Alucians—there was turmoil in their part of the world, everyone said, and surely it had to do with that. But the whereabouts of the Alucians, including their serving staff, were accounted for on the evening of the ball.

"One could conclude that poor Mr. Reyno cut his own throat," Hollis said drily. She reported that the Alucian princes were made distraught by the crime, and understandably so. "But the crown prince has conducted himself admirably in the course of the meetings in spite of his tragic loss," she said confidently. "He continues to push for the trade agreement."

Eliza thought of the green eyes behind the mask and tried to imagine them distraught.

"And now I've nothing for the gazette." Hollis sighed. "It seems rather gauche to speak of fashion in light of the tragedy, does it not?"

"Of course," Eliza agreed.

"Oh, well," Hollis said. "Mrs. Pendergrast gave me a lovely pattern for sewing a baby's christening gown."

The lack of tantalizing content for Hollis's gazette did not remain a problem for long, however. It changed one morning when Mr. French, who normally delivered the post, did not appear at the house in Bedford Square. In his place came a stout little fellow who was scarcely taller than a child, wearing a greasy cap and dirty coat. Eliza had seen him around a time or two lurking near the Covent Garden Market.

He handed the post to Eliza.

"Where is Mr. French?" she asked curiously as she gingerly took the post from hands that were gray with dirt.

"Dunno, miss." He seemed anxious to be on his way, and indeed, once she had taken the mail, he hurried down the steps and across the square as quickly as he could.

In that stack of mail was a handwritten note that would change the course of Eliza's life.

CHAPTER SEVEN

THERE IT WAS, in black-and-white—a rumor implicating Rostafan, printed in a women's fashion gazette, of all things.

> *The pomp and gaiety of the Royal Masquerade Ball was marred by the tragic death of an Alucian principal. While it would be untoward to speculate, one cannot help but wonder why or where a certain high-ranking Alucian official, with a generally large presence, would absent himself before the last set of dances?*
>
> *And neither should one speculate on what a recently wed lady, lithe in appearance and light of heart, will do when she discovers her husband has taken a keen interest in her dearest friend. Therefore, we will not speculate.*
>
> *—Honeycutt's Gazette of Fashion and Domesticity for Ladies*

"A generally large presence," Caius repeated, his brow furrowing. "Generally? General? A high-ranking general? Is it meant to implicate Rostafan?"

Caius, Sebastian and Leopold were bent over the gazette that Leopold had brought to Sebastian. Leopold said a friend had pointed out this rumor, this accusation, very plainly printed. But who would say such a thing? Based on what information?

Sebastian flipped through the pages of the gazette, looking for anything else that might inform him. The pages were mostly advertisements for ladies' dresses or products such as teething syrup for babies or pomade guaranteed to produce a thicker, longer head of hair if rubbed into the scalp three times a day. There were ads for household products that would make a home sparkle and a husband smile. There was a brief article detailing the proper way to set a table and instructions for making a child's christening gown.

But here, on the last page, under the heading News About Town, this...rumor? Jest? False clue? "I want to speak to whoever has seen fit to publish this rubbish," Sebastian said, pushing the gazette away with disgust. "What sort of person profits from gossip?" He focused on his foreign minister. "Who would allow such rubbish to be printed without any evidence whatsoever?"

Caius looked at Leopold. Leopold shrugged.

"Find out," Sebastian said curtly. "Bring him to me. I would speak with the author."

"You?" Leopold shook his head. "*You* can't speak to him, Bas. Anyone but you."

There was nothing Sebastian hated worse than being told what he could or could not do. "Why in bloody hell not?"

"You know why. The English authorities are handling the investigation. You can't undertake one of your own. Think of how it would appear if the crown prince of Alucia was chasing around London in search of clues like a common constable."

Sebastian flicked his wrist at his brother. He didn't

care what anyone would say of him. He was devastated by Matous's murder. He had to do something.

"All right, you don't care," Leopold said curtly. "But think of what our father the king would say about it."

That gave Sebastian pause. His father very much cared about appearances. King Karl believed that the appearance of fair and impartial rule, and his projection to the world as a true and just monarch were what kept him on the throne when there were whispers that Felix's claim was legitimate.

Sebastian looked out the window. He couldn't erase the image of Matous lying on that bed with his throat cut. He couldn't stop feeling the ravage of guilt for not having come back to his rooms that night. Had he come when he'd said he would, Matous would have been with him. "Find who wrote this," he said quietly.

No one moved for a moment. Sebastian kept his gaze on the window. "Why are you still here?"

Someone moved and went out the door. Then Leopold stepped in Sebastian's line of vision. He was the one person who didn't care what Sebastian's title was. "If you have something to say, say it," Sebastian said.

"I will. Don't be a fool, Bas. Let the appropriate people investigate his death. You'll only make things worse."

"You may very well be right, brother. But Matous was my friend, and I am not content to sit idly by and allow some faceless Englishman to do it."

"You are here to negotiate a trade agreement, Bas. *Your* trade agreement. If you turn your attention from it, you could very well lose control of the negotiations. And then where will you be? You must think of Alucia."

"I think of Alucia all the time," Sebastian said darkly. "My whole *life* has been about Alucia. But Matous was my friend, Leo, perhaps my only true *friend.* Would you do any less for your friends? For me? What sort of prince am I if I sit idly by and allow others to seek justice?"

Leopold groaned. He rubbed his face with his hands. "I can't stop you. But you won't do it alone. I won't allow it."

Sebastian turned his gaze to the window without a response. It seemed better to let Leopold believe he could somehow affect what Sebastian would do about this than to argue.

LATER THAT AFTERNOON, as Leopold took tea and Sebastian paced restlessly, Caius returned with Mr. Botley-Finch, the English attaché assigned as the conduit between Sebastian and the English government while he was in London.

"Do you know who this is?" Sebastian asked, tossing the gazette onto the table before the attaché.

Mr. Botley-Finch was a reed of a man with dark lips, sand-coloured skin and hair that had been elaborately combed to disguise the fact that he was going bald. He bowed in deference. "It is merely a ladies' magazine, Your Highness. Nothing of import. I hazard to guess they are simply attempting to increase readership." He gave a half-hearted shrug. "Women and their gossip."

Sebastian didn't care if children had published it. Someone had given them the idea. "Who publishes it?"

"I can't say for certain who is the publisher, but Justice William Tricklebank is listed as one of the primary proprietors. It seems the business of the gazette was left to him after the death of his son-in-law, Sir Percival Honeycutt."

"Did this Tricklebank attend the ball?" Sebastian asked.

"I should think not, sir. He is a high court justice on the Queen's Bench. And he is blind."

"Then what the devil is he doing printing papers about ladies' fashions and teething potions for babies?" Leopold asked sharply.

"I don't know the particulars, Your Highness, only that his name is attached to the enterprise. My advice, if I may, is not to dwell on this…rumor." He spit the word out like a brass tack. "It was done for attention and nothing more. There is no truth to it."

Sebastian studied the attaché, debating what he ought to do.

"Your Highness, if I may," Mr. Botley-Finch said with the sort of smile that suggested he thought Sebastian was being obtuse. "Her Majesty the queen has instructed the prime minister to use all necessary means to find whoever has done this to such an esteemed guest. There is no call to worry that appropriate measures are not being followed."

"I never said I was worried," Sebastian said smoothly. "But perhaps you can enlighten me with what you've uncovered thus far?"

Mr. Botley-Finch shifted from one leg to the other. "We are still investigating."

So they'd found nothing. Sebastian stood up. "Thank you for your time, sir."

"Your Highness," he said, and with a sharp bow, he quit the room, Caius with him.

When the two men had departed, there was no one left but Sebastian and Leopold and Egius, who was busy in the dressing room.

Sebastian looked at his brother. "Take me there."

"Where?"

"To this blind Tricklebank fellow."

"Bas," Leopold said reprovingly. "*No.* We've been over this."

"Disguise me if you must. No one will know me without the Alucian clothing. You can make me look like an Englishman, can't you, Egius?" he called.

Egius stopped in the doorway to the dressing room, looking as if he'd been struck. "I beg your pardon, sir. You wish to look like an *Englishman*?"

Sebastian waited for his answer.

Egius blinked. "I suppose…that is, if you require—"

"I do," Sebastian said, and snapped his attention back to Leopold. "Find where this Tricklebank resides. I want a word and I think Botley-Finch and his people do not intend to pursue this…*rumor*," he said, mimicking the attaché.

Leopold sighed. "Bloody hell, you've the heart of a mule." He rose from his seat and walked to the door of Sebastian's suite of rooms and held out his hand for his greatcoat. "Egius, he must have a hat that will cover his hair. And a cloak. Scuffed boots if you can find them. And a walking stick. The English love nothing better than to promenade about with a walking stick."

"*Je*, Your Highness," Egius said.

Leopold looked back at his brother. "I'll see what I can do, but I should like my objections to be fully understood. This is foolhardy. You jeopardize everything you came to England to accomplish."

"Noted," Sebastian said, just as curtly. He suspected Leopold would have every opportunity soon enough to tell him he'd been right.

CHAPTER EIGHT

A supper party at the home of Lord Morpeth of Hill Street produced, at its conclusion, a single, unclaimed ladies' kid-leather glove with four pearl buttons. The glove bore an uncanny resemblance to another glove dropped at the Royal Masquerade Ball as a particular flame hurried out after a particular prince, according to several who were in attendance.

Ladies, if you suffer from sleeplessness, wash your hair with lye soap, rubbing well into the scalp. Do not rinse, but wrap your hair in a kerchief and rinse in the morning. Do this for a fortnight and your sleeplessness will be cured. This cure is courtesy of the Glasgow Herald.

—Honeycutt's Gazette of Fashion and Domesticity for Ladies

THE LITTLE DOGS, Jack and John, the Tricklebanks' fearless defenders of The Door, announced intruders at a quarter to two with frenzied barking. Eliza, busy at her desk with a mantel clock she was repairing, heard their house steward, Ben, yelling at the dogs to stop their yapping, then a lot of scuttling about as he corralled the dogs into the kitchen.

The knocking continued, and Ben shouted, "I'm coming, I'm coming!"

Ben was not the sort who suffered lightly the impatience of others. Eliza heard him shuffle by, imagining him swiping his hands on his leather apron before he opened the door. The last she'd seen him, he'd been cleaning windows.

She heard male voices, and something trickled into her fierce concentration. Something that made her realize it was not business as usual at the door. She couldn't make out what anyone was saying, but she could hear what sounded to her like an accent.

Eliza put down her tool, popped up from her desk and paused to look at her reflection in a pier mirror between the two windows of the drawing room. She smoothed her hair and then her apron, and went out into the hall to have a look at who had come.

At the end of the hallway, Ben's wide frame filled the open door and blocked her view of the callers.

"But is he within?" an accented male voice asked Ben.

"Ben?" Eliza said.

Ben looked back. "Callers, miss. Come to call on the judge without an appointment."

"Who?" she asked curiously, moving down the hall to the open door. Over Ben's shoulder, she could see a man standing on her stoop. Tall and broad-shouldered, he wore a cloak, and his hat was pulled down low over his brow. Eliza moved closer, peeking around Ben. There was another man at the bottom of the entry stairs, similarly dressed. He was holding a walking stick, but not in the usual manner one might hold a stick to walk. He wielded it like a billy club and paced the sidewalk impatiently, pausing every few steps to glance up at the door.

Ben shifted so that Eliza could stand beside him. That was when she noticed more men dressed in cloaks and hats standing halfway down the street, but clearly watching what was happening at her door. “Who is calling?” she asked again.

The gentleman on the stoop touched the brim of his hat. “How do you do.” His accent was clearly Alucian—she’d heard enough of it at the ball to recognize it now. And he looked vaguely familiar. Had she danced with him? “We are calling on Justice Tricklebank.”

Oh dear. Now why on earth would Alucian gentlemen be calling on her father? Her father had very recently reported that he’d shared ale with two fellow justices, a Member of Parliament and a pair of Alucian barristers. Could it have something to do with that? Surely he would have told her if anything remarkable had occurred in that public house. Her father had said nothing more than a pleasant evening had been spent comparing laws in Alucia and in England.

She hoped to high heaven this had nothing to do with the note that had arrived here a few days ago. Jesus and Joseph, she surely hoped not. “May I inquire who is calling?”

“Ah…” The man glanced behind him to the man on the street. That one looked up, and Eliza peered down at him. Her mouth suddenly gaped—she knew immediately who he was. A spit of fire raced through her, because she would never forget those eyes. And she suddenly realized why the man before her looked so familiar. He had almost the same eyes. Their color was blue, but they were the same shape and had the same intensity to them.

“I am at liberty to say only that the gentleman is

concerned about a matter of some delicacy that is probably best heard by the justice's ears only." He gave her a thin smile.

Oh dear, oh dear. This *was* about the note, she just knew it! What else could it be? For heaven's sake, he hadn't come racing after her like Prince Charming after the ball. No, her instinct told her this was most decidedly about the note, and her heart began to do a bit of pitter-pattering in her chest. Where was Hollis when she needed her? She'd *told* Hollis it was a bad idea, but as usual, Hollis wouldn't listen and had been very persuasive in bringing Eliza around to her viewpoint. Eliza shuddered to think how angry their father was going to be. He'd told them expressly to leave it alone, to hand it over to the London City Police and let them deal with it.

The note had been penned anonymously, the handwriting flourishing and written in thick black ink. It read only, *Your Honor, the person responsible for the tragedy at Kensington is one of their own. Look to the field marshal.*

When Eliza read the note aloud to her father, he'd said, "Well, that's an odd thing to receive, isn't it?"

"Why would someone send this to you, Pappa?" she'd asked.

"I couldn't say, darling. Perhaps because my docket has included criminal cases this month? I can think of no other reason. Hand it to Mr. Frink," he instructed her, referring to his clerk. "He'll see it to the proper authorities. We'll not mention it to anyone else, as it's nothing to do with us."

Of course Eliza had done as her father asked, and handed the note to Mr. Frink when she escorted her father to court. Which might have been a day or two later than her father probably imagined, because first, she'd had to show it to Hollis.

Hollis and Eliza had agreed they did not want to go against their father, but the note was too tantalizing to ignore. Hollis had actually seen the Alucian field marshal at the ball. "He has a very grand presence," she'd said of him.

They had reasoned there was no harm in disguising the news and printing it for the gazette's loyal readers. No one could possibly determine who they were writing about, and besides, who would think to question women who published a ladies' gazette?

At least that was what Hollis had asserted. "Do you think the men who are investigating this crime will read the gazette? It's a game, Eliza, and no one will be the wiser. Really, we'd be *helping* them find the killer."

"If you put it that way, someone might read it and bring information forward, mightn't they?"

"Precisely," Hollis had said confidently.

Eliza had locked gazes with her sister for a long moment. "Are we not justifying our reasons for going against Pappa's wishes?"

"Or course not! We'd never do that," Hollis said airily.

That was hardly true. They'd been going against Pappa's wishes since they were girls.

It hardly mattered now why they'd decided to do it. They'd done it, and someone had read it, and now the crown prince was standing at her door. *Two* princes, actually. She didn't know if she should be impressed that the princes had read the gazette, or alarmed by how foolish she and Hollis could be at times.

"Miss?" the prince on her stoop said.

Eliza blinked. She noticed he was not wearing Alucian attire. None of them were. Why were they dressed like ordinary Englishmen? If they weren't clustered together like a mob, if one of them hadn't gripped his cane like a weapon, they might have been any gentlemen walking down the street. And what about her? She was wearing a gray day gown with a white apron, and her hair, still damp from this morning's bath, was loosely tied at her nape. This was not at all how she wished to receive the princes of Alucia. If Caroline could see her now, she'd swoon with shame.

Furthermore, Eliza did *not* want to receive them in their modest home with the lace curtains and the yapping dogs and the clocks stuffed in this nook and that cranny. This was the height of embarrassment, and Eliza did not wish to be embarrassed in this manner. She wanted to be dressed properly, her hair coiffed, and with perhaps a bit of rouge on her cheeks. She determined there was only one thing to do, the thing that no one in their right mind would do, and that was to turn the princes away. "I beg your pardon, but we were not expecting callers," she said, and nervously ran her fingertips over her cheeks on the chance ash or oil from a clock or, heaven forbid, ink was residing there.

"Madam," the prince said a little more insistently. "Is the justice *in*?"

"Give me the word, and I'll toss him off the stoop," Ben suggested, cracking his knuckles to emphasize how easily he could do that.

"I beg your pardon?" The prince was incredulous.

"You heard me," Ben warned him.

Eliza noticed that down on the street corner, Mrs. Spragg had come out on her stoop with a broom. But the broom was not moving. She was watching the commotion at Eliza's house. This was a development that was completely unacceptable—Mrs. Spragg was worse than Hollis when it came to repeating things she'd heard. Eliza knew this because Mrs. Spragg was a frequent caller, desperate to see a bit of gossip she'd collected printed in the gazette.

Eliza suddenly stepped back into the foyer. "It's all right, Ben. Do come in, sirs," she said.

The younger prince glanced over his shoulder at the crown prince and nodded.

It was odd, watching *two* princes jog up the steps and come inside. They crowded in next to each other in the foyer, doffed their hats and held them out to Ben as if he was a butler.

But Ben was not the butler, and he did not care to be thought of as such, and looked disdainfully at the hats, then at Eliza. She winced and gave him a small nod. Ben grudgingly took the hats. "I suppose the cloaks, too," he said curtly.

"If you'd be so kind," Eliza said.

"Thank you, that is not necessary," the younger prince said.

Apparently, he was the only prince who would speak. The crown prince was looking around him as if he wasn't certain where he was. He'd probably never seen a home like hers. He'd probably never stood in an entry as narrow as this, with cloaks hanging from the walls and boots lying against each other like drunken lads, and baskets for the market scattered haphazardly around. With a broken cuckoo clock on the floor, its door open, because the cat liked to sleep in there. With strings and ribbons tacked to the walls and leading off down the hall and turning into rooms.

Their house was modest and not fit for princes, but Eliza was quite proud of it all the same. It wasn't a palace or a castle, and it was a bit cluttered with the colors of their lives, but it was lovely and the arrogant prince could look around all he liked.

"This way," she said, and marched off to the parlor, annoyed with the intrusion. The moment she stepped foot inside, Jack and John leapt up from their beds and rushed forward, barking again as if the house was now on fire. "How did they get in here?" Eliza asked as they raced past her to examine the intruders. "Jack, John, stop that!" she cried. "Ben, will you please?"

"Aye, I've got them." Ben bent down, scooping up one dog and then the other. Ben's wife, Margaret, had probably let them out of their kitchen prison. Margaret was the housekeeper and did most of the household cooking and laundering. When she wasn't feeding the little monsters table scraps, she was allowing them to do whatever they pleased. She was terribly lenient with dogs.

Well. They all were, really.

"Come on, then, you pair of mutts," Ben said. "We'll see if Meg has found a bone for you, then." He went out with a dog stuffed under each arm.

Eliza glanced nervously at the princes. They stared after Ben. It must be quite shocking to them to see how the rest of the world lived. People picking up dogs, stepping over knitting, reluctant to take hats when there was no place to put them.

What was she to do with these men? She was certain there was some sort of protocol, but she had no earthly idea what it was. *Curtsy!* She ought to curtsy. "I beg your pardon," she said, dipping quickly and crookedly. What else was she forgetting? She wished she'd listened more attentively to Caroline when she was droning on and on about her presentations here and there. Eliza could have used her instruction in court etiquette on the slim chance foreign princes found their way into her parlor.

Someone in the house upset one of the dogs, because the three of them were startled by the sound of one of them barking excitedly. Eliza smiled sheepishly. "Do you have dogs?"

The princes did not offer if they owned dogs. In fact, neither of them spoke. They seemed at a loss for words and simply stared at her.

Eliza did a quick survey of the room. What a pity she hadn't thought to pick up her father's knitting before going to the door. And why hadn't anyone aired the room to get rid of the smell of his tobacco? The hearth was lit, thankfully, but the sofa had been haphazardly pulled around in front of it, presumably when her father had complained of cold. The dog beds were off a little to the side of the hearth—Jack and John liked the warmth of the fire. Currently, Pris the cat was stretched out across two dog beds, his back to the princes. He was not impressed by royal visitors.

A pair of upholstered chairs, both of them with worn arms and cushions that appeared misshapen, were arranged near the windows with a small table between them. The chairs looked worn, but that was what the Tricklebanks liked about them—they'd been worn into the shapes of their bodies and were quite comfortable for sitting and reading on wintry afternoons. Eliza was reluctant to replace them.

A lap rug was draped over the back of one chair, and on the table between them stood a stack of books and papers. The chintz curtains behind the chairs drooped a little, and the carpet was worn in the familiar paths they all took across the room. The mantel was crowded with clocks that were in need of repair.

And there was Eliza's desk, from which she managed this household. She wasn't the tidiest of persons, and her desk was a mess. In addition to the daily post, some documents she was to read to her father and the menus she'd made for Margaret, it was strewn with parts of the dismantled clock she'd been repairing.

This room, where they so often gathered, was the heart of their home. But the heart of their home looked as if it had been beating a thousand years and had worn itself out. What the princes must think, she couldn't begin to guess. She wasn't ashamed of it in the least… but perhaps a bit mortified that it suddenly seemed so cluttered and untidy.

"Would you care to sit?" she asked, gesturing to the sofa.

"No, thank you," the younger prince said.

Poppy suddenly appeared in the room as if she thought she might miss something. She hesitated when she saw the two men, dipped a curtsy, then looked at Eliza, eyes wide with curiosity.

"Will you bring tea, Poppy?"

"Thank you, no," the younger prince said. "As I said, ours is a matter of some urgency."

"Oh, it's no bother," Poppy said, and went out again as quickly as she'd come in.

"Well, then!" Eliza clasped her hands before her. "You wish to…?"

"Speak with Justice Tricklebank." As the younger prince spoke, the crown prince wandered over to the table between the two chairs. Copies of the gazette were scattered across the top of it, as well as some books she'd been reading aloud to her father.

"Will you please inform the judge that Mr. Chartier has come to call?"

Mr. Chartier? Who was *that*? "I beg your pardon, but I'm afraid the judge is napping just now." Eliza smiled sadly.

The crown prince exchanged a dark look with his brother. Eliza could feel the impatience rolling off him in waves. She had a sudden vision of Hollis, gasping and shouting, *"No, you can't be serious!"* when Eliza told her this extraordinary tale.

"If you like, you may tell me what you would have him know and I will happily relay the message." Unless it was about the rumor she and Hollis had printed in the gazette. It was fair to assume she'd not relay *that* message.

The two men turned their attention to her as if they couldn't determine what she'd said.

"What shall I tell him?" she asked with what she hoped was cheerful accommodation.

The crown prince muttered something in Alucian. The younger prince responded in kind, then stepped forward. "Madam, I must impress on you once again that we've come on a matter of some delicacy and would prefer to speak directly with the justice. Are you his housekeeper?"

"His house—" The blood began to drain from her face. She straightened her shoulders. "I beg your pardon, Your Royal Highness, but I am Justice Tricklebank's daughter, Miss Eliza Tricklebank."

Both princes reacted with surprise, and went suddenly stiff and still, taking her in from head to toe. The crown prince, in particular, was glaring at her, as if he thought she was lying about her identity.

Eliza tried very hard not to be offended. She self-consciously touched a loose strand of hair at her collarbone. "I've had the pleasure of making your acquaintance. Perhaps you don't recall?" A thought suddenly occurred to her. "Oh! Of course you don't. I was wearing a mask!" She laughed with relief, happy to have thought of it, because she would not like to think he'd sipped from her glass of punch, then stepped on her foot and have *no* memory of her. "We met once in the passageway, and then again in the ballroom, when you stepped on my foot." She'd meant only to remind him, and had not meant to make it sound so accusatory. "Accidentally, of course," she quickly amended.

The crown prince's eyes narrowed. He finally deigned to speak with a crisp, disbelieving "I beg your pardon?"

"My foot," she said, sliding the injured party out from under her hem. "You stepped on it."

He looked appalled. He'd clearly taken offense. "I did no such thing."

"Don't you recall? I was in the receiving line with the other ladies. But before my introduction could be made, you began to walk away. I admit that I rather leapt into your path, but when I did, you stepped on my foot."

Something flickered in his eyes.

"How odd that you don't remember," she said curiously. But she was struck with the notion that they'd suffered a great loss recently, and he probably had put the entire ball from his mind. "Lord, how very careless of me," she said, tapping a fist to her forehead. "Please, allow me to offer my deepest condolences for your loss."

The two princes continued to stare at her. Was she really so clumsy? She wished Caroline were here to whisper in her ear what to do. "I, um…we've all heard the news, I'm afraid."

The younger prince—*Prince Something, Prince Ssomething...why couldn't she remember his name?*—nodded. "Thank you."

"What a shock it must have been. It was to all of London, really—"

"Miss Tricklebank, will you wake the judge?" The younger prince interrupted before she could review what she'd heard.

"Unfortunately, I can't do that," Eliza said apologetically.

"I beg your pardon, Miss Tricklebank," the crown prince said in a voice that was calm and soft in spite of the fact that his eyes were positively radiating fire. "If you know who I am, then you surely must know you cannot refuse me."

Eliza was taken aback. She'd never cared for the way men thought that by virtue of their sex they were superior to women and could simply order them around and tell them what to do. She couldn't count how many gentlemen had been in this very parlor to call on her father, and thought it quite all right to tell her what to do. *Some tea, Miss Tricklebank,* or *Fetch your father's lap rug, Miss Tricklebank,* or *I'll have a port, Miss Tricklebank*. But this was *her* house, and she could refuse whoever she liked. "I beg *your* pardon, sir, but my father is blind and does not sleep through the night as you and I would, as he cannot sense the time. He needs his rest."

The crown prince's brows dipped low over his eyes, sparkling with ire. He moved closer to her. Very close. As close as he'd been in the passageway. His considerable size made it necessary for Eliza to tilt up her chin to look him square in the eye. She realized there was a time in her life she might have been intimidated by a rude prince. When she would have quickly, demurely, with all due haste, done as he bade her because young ladies were to do what gentlemen asked of them. That was before she'd been humiliated by a gentleman and had realized a thing or two about them. That was before she'd become a spinster and had stopped caring what anyone at all thought of her. And *this gentleman* had made her angry.

His glare turned darker. "We have asked you respectfully more than once to fetch your father. We have impressed on you that this call is very important." His voice was as calm as a baby's breath, but his eyes shot daggers through her. "The judge has printed a clue or piece of gossip about the death of my personal secretary in his ladies' gazette, and I should like to question him about it. Do you quite understand me, Miss Tricklebank? Now be a good lass and hie yourself off and bloody well *fetch* him."

Eliza's mouth dropped open. She'd never wanted to punch a man in the mouth, but *oh*, she wanted to punch him. Take a good swing and watch him tumble onto his princely arse. She didn't care how important or handsome or royal he was, she was infuriated that he thought he could speak to her in this manner, as if she were some lowly chambermaid who had failed to dust his crown properly.

Her hands found her waist. "You have no call to be so rude."

His hands found his waist. "What did you say?"

"I'm sorry, did you not hear me? Then allow me to speak plainly—you are *rude*. And for your information, it is not the judge's gazette. In fact, he has nothing to do with it. Furthermore, I will *not* wake him merely because you command me. The absolute *nerve*." She folded her arms.

His autumn green eyes widened with surprise. "Do you have any idea who you are speaking to? I could see you punished dearly for your impertinence."

"Ha," she said. "This is a free country, Your Highness. And while you may be someone's prince somewhere, you are not mine. I am not a child, I am not impertinent, I am the master of this house and I said *no*, you cannot see my father now, and frankly, I will thank you both to go now." She threw out her hand and pointed to the door. That was when she noticed Poppy standing there with a tea service, her mouth agape. "Poppy, do step aside. I should not like to give the slightest impediment to the *immediate* departure of these gentlemen."

Poppy was still so stunned she didn't move.

"Poppy!"

Poppy lurched forward and deposited the tea service on the table.

The men stared in shock at Eliza. Well, the younger one stared in shock. The other one glowered. Oh, she could well imagine they were *quite* unaccustomed to being tossed out of houses. She pointed again. "The door is that way."

The younger prince tried to smooth things over. "Miss Tricklebank, surely you can understand how distressed my brother is."

"Livid is more like it," the crown prince snapped and turned his back to Eliza. She watched his broad shoulders rise as if he drew a deep breath, then sink again as he released it.

"I would well imagine he is any number of things,

but that gives him no call to come into *my* home and speak to me as if I were a slave in your country—"

"A *slave*?" the crown prince said loudly, rounding on her again.

"Bas," the younger prince snapped, then spoke in Alucian, quickly and in a low voice. The crown prince turned his back to her again.

"Please do go." She pointed again.

And still neither of them moved. Poppy stared at Eliza in astonishment. Eliza frantically wondered what she would do if they didn't leave as she'd asked. "What are you waiting for?" she demanded.

The younger prince was the first to move, striding out of the room without another glance at Eliza.

The crown prince slowly turned to follow. But he made certain to pause just where Eliza stood and glare down at her with ferocity. She pursed her lips and returned his scowl with a ferocious one of her own.

And then he was gone.

When she heard the front door shut, Eliza almost collapsed to her knees, astoundingly short of breath. She looked at a wide-eyed Poppy who moved first, rushing to the window. Eliza was quickly on her heels, stumbling into the windowsill and leaning over it to have a look down at the street.

The princes appeared to be arguing.

"Who was that?" Poppy whispered.

"You won't believe me, Poppy, but those two are the princes of Alucia."

"What?" Poppy exclaimed as the two men turned and began to walk away from Bedford Square. "Prince Sebastian and Prince Leopold?"

"Leopold!" Eliza shouted. "That's it. I don't know

why I couldn't recall it, particularly as Caro has gone on about him."

Poppy whirled about and caught Eliza by the shoulders.

"Eliza! You kicked them out?" She squealed, shaking Eliza. "You ordered the *Alucian princes* to leave your house? Oh my stars! Oh my goodness!"

Eliza suddenly felt rather faint. She collapsed into one of the worn armchairs. "I did, didn't I?" At the moment he'd insulted her, it had seemed imperative. Now she was scandalized by what she'd done. "I can't believe it! I can't believe that I ordered the crown prince of Alucia from my house."

With a laugh of delight, Poppy bounced onto the chair next to her. "Can you imagine what Hollis will have to say about it?"

Eliza gasped and sat up. "Poppy! Go round to her house and tell her to come at once. And not a word to Pappa, do you promise?"

Poppy was instantly on her feet. "I promise!" She was already out the door.

Eliza sank into her chair. She pressed her palms to her belly and tried to swallow down a swell of nervous nausea. She had thrown the crown prince of Alucia from her humble house.

What was the *matter* with her?

CHAPTER NINE

A famous modiste in Mayfair who has a reputation for creating beautiful masks and bonnets has reported an unusual interest in kid-leather gloves in the last week. The interest comes not from ladies wishing to expand their wardrobes but gentlemen in search of a mate for a lost glove.

For your attention: Franklin Clothiers reports a surplus of blue and green tarlatan cloth, ideal for summer wear, for a limited time.

—Honeycutt's Gazette of Fashion and Domesticity for Ladies

HOLLIS ARRIVED ALMOST STRAIGHTAWAY, in the same manner someone might come running to douse a fire. She swept into the parlor, fetched her pencil and paper from her reticule and tossed the reticule aside. She perched on the edge of the chair with her pencil poised over her paper. "Tell me everything."

Eliza hadn't even opened her mouth when there was an insistent pounding on the door. She shot up from her seat, expecting the princes of Alucia to be at her door.

"That will be Caro," Hollis said. "I sent Poppy to her and told her to come at once."

"The High Council of War has been assembled," Eliza said. She'd regained some of her composure and walked to the door of the parlor just as Caroline rushed inside ahead of Poppy.

"I've been to Mrs. Cubison!" Caroline announced excitedly. "You know, don't you, that she is the *premier* designer of masks and *everyone* went to her for the Kensington ball?"

"How could we possibly *not* know it?" Eliza asked. "You've mentioned it no less than a dozen times."

"It bears repeating." Caroline tossed her hat and cloak onto a chair. "She gave me news about the glove," she said as she patted her hair into place.

"If you please, Poppy, might we have some tea?" Hollis asked.

"Make it whisky, Poppy," Eliza amended. "It's been quite the day."

"Where is the judge?" Caroline asked.

"He's sleeping," Eliza said.

"Does he know about the princes?" Hollis asked.

"No!" Eliza whispered loudly, looking anxiously to the door. "He'll be quite cross with us if he hears of it, Hollis. I don't intend to tell him."

"All right, I must have the news," Caroline said, and sat beside Hollis.

Eliza told them everything. How the princes had come to her door, wishing to speak to her father, having somehow come to the conclusion that *he* had printed the on dit about the field marshal in the gazette. But the crown prince's worst offense, far worse than his appalling lack of manners, was that he appeared to have no memory of Eliza whatsoever.

Hollis and Caroline listened with rapt attention, their eyes wide, gasping softly at the appropriate moments and glaring when the tale warranted it. When Eliza had finished, the three of them were silent for a moment.

"I can't imagine it," Caroline said at last. "I can't believe two foreign princes under so much scrutiny would simply appear at Bedford Square. I should think the prime minister might have prevented it."

"How exactly would the prime minister prevent it?" Eliza asked.

"I can't believe they were so *rude*," Hollis said.

"Prince Leopold was not particularly so," Eliza said, picking at a loose thread in the arm of her chair. "The fault lies entirely with the crown prince. He was wretched. I suppose if one is a crown prince one is not required to practice civility, and he most certainly did not. Frankly, I wouldn't be at all surprised if it was discovered that he himself committed the crime."

Hollis gasped, but Caroline laughed at her. "He'd not dirty his hands, darling. Who do you suppose killed the Alucian, really?"

"Oh, an Alucian," Hollis said with confidence. "An Englishman would have no reason to murder him, would he?"

"But he was arguing with the Englishman," Eliza pointed out. "You remember, Caro."

"Who?" Caroline seemed confused. "Oh! Mr. John Heath! He's the new governor of the Bank of England."

"Perhaps he has something to tell," Hollis suggested.

"I can't imagine what," Caroline said. She slumped back in her chair as if she was suddenly exhausted.

Poppy entered with a crystal decanter of whisky and four glasses.

"Perfect timing, Poppy," Caroline said. "All these princes and gloves are taxing on a person."

"But why wouldn't Mr. Heath have some information?" Hollis asked as Caroline accepted a glass of whisky from Poppy. "At the very least, he could describe what they talked about."

"I don't know," Caroline said. "He doesn't seem the type to be engaged in a conspiracy, does he? And besides, he spends his weekends at a house on the other side of the town." Her brows rose and she looked at the sisters expectantly.

"What house?" Eliza asked as Poppy handed her a whisky.

"She means a brothel," Poppy said.

"Oh!" Hollis quickly jotted something down before taking the glass Poppy offered. Poppy took the last glass and sat on the sofa beside Eliza.

"No matter what he does on the weekends, he spoke at least once to the poor murdered man at the ball. You know his daughter, Caro. Perhaps she knows about his conversation with the Alucian?" Eliza suggested. "I should think it noteworthy that one had a conversation with a man who was found dead the next day, don't you? Would he not mention it over supper?"

"That's right!" Hollis said excitedly. "Caro, didn't you say that Miss Heath is often in the company of her father? You must introduce us."

"Don't be absurd," Caroline said. "The two of you really shouldn't take this any further, don't you suppose?"

"Why not?" Eliza demanded. "Because the prince doesn't like it? I am weary unto death of men who think I haven't a brain in my head, that I can't understand complex matters."

Hollis, Caroline and Poppy looked at her with surprise.

Eliza sniffed. "I suppose the utter lack of regard I receive from gentlemen of the court has stuck in my craw. I tell you, I've read as much of the law as they have—"

"You could invite her to tea!" Poppy suggested before Eliza could begin a familiar rant of the disrespect she was afforded in her father's court, merely because she was a woman.

"I hardly know her well enough to invite her to tea," Caroline protested.

"Please. Any unmarried debutante would be *delighted* to come round to the Hawke House and hopefully lay eyes on the fine Lord Hawke. Any woman but Eliza," Hollis said with a side look to her sister.

Eliza clucked her tongue. "I should rather marry the crown prince of Alucia."

Caroline sighed. "Fine. I'll invite her to tea, then, but only if you tell me all again, Eliza. Especially the part how you tossed the crown prince out on his ear."

Eliza stood up and cleared her throat. *"If you know who I am, then you surely must know you cannot refuse me,"* she said, mimicking his accent and his low voice. *"Now be a good lass and hie yourself off and bloody well fetch your father!"*

Poppy, Hollis, and Caroline howled with outrageous laughter.

"And you told him to leave?" Hollis asked.

"I'll perform this part," Poppy said, hopping up from her seat. *"I am not a child, I am not impertinent, I am the master of this house and I said no, you cannot see my father now, and frankly, I will thank you both to go now!"* she said in a voice pitched higher than her own. "And she pointed to the door, lest they not find it on their own."

Caroline broke into peals of laughter.

"We are the only house in all of London who would turn them out!" Hollis said.

"We may not be the last for that sanctimonious foozler," Eliza said with a flick of her wrist.

"But Eliza, what of his fine eyes?" Hollis asked, gasping for breath. She was laughing so hard she was practically in tears.

"Eyes of the devil, that's what."

"Ooh, a *devil* is he. Well, the devil makes a better lover than an angel," Hollis opined.

"Hollis!" Poppy and Caroline exclaimed at the very same moment.

The women fell into fits of laughter.

The sudden barking of dogs silenced them. They could hear someone moving around above.

"That will be the judge, up from his nap," Poppy said, and hurried from the room.

Moments later she returned with the judge. "Who is here, Poppy?" he asked congenially as she moved him across the room to his favorite chair.

"Me, Pappa," Hollis said. "With Eliza."

"And me!" Caroline said. She came to her feet. "How dashing you appear today, Your Honor," she said, leaning over him to kiss his cheek.

"Oh, you flatter me, Caro. Had a nip, have you?" he asked as she moved away.

"Not a thing gets past your nose, does it?" Caroline said cheerfully.

The judge settled in his chair and groped around for his knitting. He'd been working on a long piece of ivory. What it was, Eliza couldn't say. He liked to keep his hands busy, and knitting was something he could feel his way through. He draped the piece across his lap and the ends of it pooled on the floor. That seemed to Pris a perfect place to nap, and he sauntered out from behind the bookcase to settle in on the end. Jack and John, who had accompanied the judge into the parlor, each circled three times before dropping into little mounds of dog on their beds.

"What are you four about today?" the judge asked jovially of the ceiling.

"Oh! I almost forgot," Caroline said. "I've been around to see Mrs. Cubison. You know Mrs. Cubison, Your Honor, don't you? She is the modiste that *everyone* sees."

"I've not seen her," he said.

"Pappa, don't tease," Hollis said pleadingly.

"I'd rather die by my own hand than tease you, darling."

"Well, she had quite a lot of news," Caroline continued. "A string of gentlemen have come to inquire about the glove."

"Glove? What glove?" the judge asked.

"The infamous glove dropped at Kensington. It seems that after the crown prince of Alucia left the ball, a glove was dropped outside of the private residences at Kensington. Some think it was a signal of some sort. You know, telling the murderer it was time," Hollis explained.

"Oh, *that* sort of signal," the judge mused. "Might it have simply been a dropped glove?"

"It might have been," Hollis admitted.

The judge nodded sagely. "But I don't suppose the modiste suggested a field marshal was wearing the glove, did she?"

"No, but I'm sure she *thought* it," Caroline said.

Eliza exchanged a look with her sister.

"I can assume from the sudden silence of my daughters that we all believe the modiste has indeed seen the written rumor of the field marshal. Eliza, darling, you were very wrong to take that note to Hollis. And Hollis, dearest, you were more wrong to have printed it."

"But Pappa, we might have been of service," Hollis attempted.

"You've not been of any service other than to kick up dust. I don't want my daughters to have any part in it." He put down his knitting and turned his head toward the center of the room, where Eliza was standing. "I must insist on having your word, the both of you. You might as well give yours, too, Caro, and you, Poppy. I will not have you involved in any way in the investigation into that poor man's demise. Do I have your word?"

The four of them sheepishly muttered their assent.

"Quite a lot of bother this ball has turned out to be," the judge groused. "I can hear you rolling your eyes at me."

"Pappa," Eliza said, glancing at Hollis with the unspoken question of whether or not she ought to tell her father the rest.

"Yes?" He picked up his knitting. "What more?"

Eliza swallowed. "We've had visitors." She told her father about the visit from the princes. She expected a good tongue-lashing, but when she related how the prince had spoken to her and her immediate response of throwing him out, her father chuckled.

"Well then, that alleviates any fear I had that one of these princes might whisk you away from me, Eliza. Poppy and I would be quite lost without you."

"I will leave the bachelors to Caro," Eliza said. "I

read in the *Gazette* just last month that she is highly prized on the marriage mart."

Caroline laughed. "Never doubt the benefit of having friends with a gazette. Now, then, I really must bid you all a good day. Beck and I are dining with the Montpassens this evening." She paused to pet Pris, who had jumped onto the judge's lap.

When she'd gone, Eliza returned to her clock, and Hollis scribbled down some notes. Life as they knew it returned to its normal flow.

Normal it remained until the next afternoon, when Caroline sent word that the tea with Lucille, the banker's daughter, had been set for Saturday afternoon.

There was never any need to question that they wouldn't follow through with their plans, despite the judge's admonishment.

The three of them never listened to what any man told them to do.

CHAPTER TEN

A little bird perched in the trees of Hyde Park on a royally brisk Saturday afternoon might have spotted three gentlemen dressed as English lords but speaking with curious accents. One might also have noticed a pretty little peacock trailing along behind them, spreading her feathers and hoping to be noticed.

—Honeycutt's Gazette of Fashion and Domesticity for Ladies

LEOPOLD WAS FURIOUS with Sebastian, and grudgingly, Sebastian had to admit he was right. Regrettably, when Miss Tricklebank had refused to rouse her father, he'd lost his temper. But in his defense, it had been a fraught few days, and Sebastian had never met a more disrespectful woman in all his life.

And that house. What a hodgepodge of clocks and pets and yarn and books! The strings and ribbons strung along the walls and into rooms, the scattering of shoes and shawls and papers. It was cluttered and close, and while it clearly suited the strange cluster of people living there, he'd found it terribly distracting.

He'd wanted to look at everything he saw. To observe how the English lived. To understand why one would stack books on the floor.

"You could not have done anything worse than what you did," Leopold said in a huff.

"All right, it was badly done," Sebastian agreed. "But you must agree there has never been a more impudent woman!"

"*Je*, she was impudent. What does it matter? She is no one. A charwoman."

"That is *precisely* why it matters," Sebastian had complained. "I have never in all my life been spoken to like that by a commoner. Mark me, Leo, if one allows commoners to treat a prince so ill, it is only a matter of time before the lords are spitting at your feet. The audacity of that woman!"

"You shouldn't have been there at all, Bas, and now you've only brought more attention to yourself. Trust me, the tale of you in that charwoman's parlor will spread through London like fire." He shook his head. "I can't believe I'm the one saying this to *you*."

Neither could Sebastian. Leopold had been called to task more than once for bad behavior, generally the result of too many celebrations that involved too much whisky and too many women.

Sebastian, however, was always the model of decorum. Frankly, he was surprised by how quickly he'd lost his temper with the woman. He wanted to believe it had to do with the strain of Matous's death, but in hindsight, he realized it might have more to do with the fact that no one ever said *no* to him—especially not a woman.

No one ever said anything except *Yes, Your Highness*, and *As you wish, Your Highness*. But she had not the least compunction to say no, and said it as easily as she might have said it to a child. He'd been shocked by her refusal—women were too solicitous of him, too keen on seeking his favor, no matter how small, no matter how meaningless. And this woman would demand, in outrageous fashion, that he leave her house? If she'd been an Alucian, he could have tossed her into a jail or seen to it that she washed floors for the rest of her life.

But that would never happen because no Alucian woman would ever attempt such a thing. He would hazard a guess that no other Englishwoman would, either.

This woman—he'd never met anyone quite like her. She was quite attractive, with golden brown hair and unusually bright blue-gray eyes. And yet she was different from the many attractive women he'd met in his life. At first, he'd not understood why, but then, upon reflection, it had become clear to him—she didn't look at him with starry hope swimming in her eyes. She knew who he was, and yet, she didn't look at him with any particular reverence. *None.*

It was oddly disconcerting. He didn't know how to return the gaze of a woman who eyed him like he was an intruder in her house. He didn't know how to feel about not being sought after or desired. It felt out of step with his everyday life.

Everything in England made him feel out of step with his life.

Nevertheless, Leopold was right—no matter what else, Sebastian had displayed an amazing lack of control. Moreover, he'd not gotten the information he wanted. That was what galled him most. Miss Tricklebank knew something, that much was obvious to him, and he'd ruined his chance for discovering it.

He tossed and turned that night, debating with himself, wondering what to do. The next morning he announced to Leopold he was returning to Bedford Square.

"I think you're turning mad before my very eyes," Leopold said sharply.

"I feel a bit mad. Matous's body is on its way home to Helenamar and his wife and children," he said, referring to the capital of Alucia. "And we are no closer to knowing who did this to him than we were the morning we found him. How can I possibly return to his wife and tell her I know nothing? That I did nothing?"

Their conversation was interrupted by a knock at the door. Patro announced Field Marshal Rostafan and Foreign Minister Anastasan. Sebastian stole a look at his brother as the two men came in. They were both thinking the same thing—they didn't know if they could trust the field marshal or Caius, for that matter. Everyone and everything was suspect now.

As usual, Rostafan sat at the table without invitation. Caius remained standing. He seemed uneasy to Sebastian, which was to be expected, given what had occurred. The events of the last week had rattled everyone but Rostafan, who reached for a cluster of grapes from the center of the table without invitation.

Sebastian wondered if he really knew any of these men around him. He'd never felt quite so alone. "What news?" he asked.

"They are incompetent," Rostafan groused. "That is the news. We have only their empty assurances that all avenues are being thoroughly investigated. If I may, Your Highness, I would have your leave to investigate. We can't trust the English. For all we know, this was a plot to gain the upper hand in negotiations."

"What upper hand could murder possibly give them?"

Sebastian asked. "I'll speak to Botley-Finch and learn what progress they've made."

"Botley-Finch spends more time at the gentlemen's club than he does with the business at hand," Rostafan complained. He sighed loudly and pushed back against the table. "As every day passes, we are losing opportunity."

"I understand," Sebastian said. "As I said, I will speak with Botley-Finch."

But Rostafan clearly wanted more and held Sebastian's gaze, waiting. When he didn't get whatever it was he was looking for, he abruptly stood. "If I may have your leave, then, Your Highness."

Sebastian gestured to the door.

The field marshal stalked from the room. Caius watched him go, then glanced at Sebastian, clearly confused. So was Sebastian—he couldn't begin to guess what Rostafan was thinking. For all he knew, the field marshal was hiding his own guilt. But he couldn't reconcile that idea to reason. Why would Rostafan kill Matous? What possible reason would anyone have to murder Matous?

"If you please, Caius, I would like a private word with my brother."

"Is there anything I can do to help?" Caius asked.

Sebastian shook his head.

Caius's expression was one of resignation. He bowed his head and quit the room. Sebastian nodded at Patro, dismissing him, too.

When he was satisfied they were completely alone, he said, "I'm going back to the justice."

Leopold opened his mouth to speak. Then closed

it. He leaned back in his chair with a heavy sigh and rubbed his eyes with the palms of his hands.

Sebastian stood and stalked to the window. "Do you think I should leave the investigation to Rostafan?"

"No."

"Neither do I. The only thing I know with certainty is that no one saw anyone come or go that night, and Rostafan has been accused in a ladies' gazette. That's all the information we have. I won't leave it alone, Leo."

"But the English are—"

"I'll go alone this time. I won't involve you. I'll need no more than a pair of men. But I need to know who has pointed a finger at our field marshal. I can scarcely look at him without wondering if he has betrayed me."

"You assume you can gain entrance," Leopold pointed out. "Have you forgotten you were asked to leave? For God's sake, let the English authorities do the hunting."

His brother was more concerned for appearances, just like their father. "I agree with Rostafan in this—they *aren't* investigating, at least not with any urgency." He looked back at his brother. "They don't share our desire to find the murderer. They think this has to do with rebellion, that a Weslorian or a traitorous Alucian has killed him, and they are probably right. Can we really wait any longer for answers? How do you know the culprit doesn't lie in wait for me?"

"If they do lie in wait for you, you would be an easy target walking around London without guard, Bas."

"They will never know it is me. I'll dress as a tradesman or some such. Give me two men and a carriage."

Leopold shook his head. "I will say it again—this is

foolhardy and reckless." But he got up to do as Sebastian had asked all the same.

THE NEXT AFTERNOON, Egius helped Sebastian dress in what they both thought might pass for a common Englishman on the street. He wore shirtsleeves and waistcoat, a greatcoat that looked as if it had been patched and sewn many times, and a hat so worn that the brim sank over his eyes. "What am I supposed to be?" he demanded of Egius.

"An Englishman, Your Highness."

"Yes, but a tradesman? A baker? A solicitor?"

Egius seemed stumped by the question. "An Englishman," he said again, but with less confidence.

Sebastian was in a borrowed carriage, too, one Leopold had managed to obtain. He didn't like dragging his brother into this charade, but he had no one else to help him, no one he could truly trust. How astounding that a man could be the future king of a nation and have no one to trust.

He instructed the two guards to park at the north end of the square. "Remain here," he instructed.

"His Royal Highness Prince Leopold has insisted we not allow you to go alone," one of the guards said in Alucian.

"When we return, you may confirm to Prince Leopold that I did not allow you to obey his command," Sebastian answered in English. No one needed to hear them speaking their native tongue and wonder why Alucians were dressed as Englishmen and lurking around this square. "Speak English."

"Your Highness," said the other one. "It's not safe—"

Sebastian threw open the door of the carriage and

leapt out of it. "Stay here." He shut the door and walked briskly to the red door at 34 Bedford Square.

His knock was answered by the frenzied barking of the two dogs, then furious scratching on the other side of the door. That sound was quickly drowned by the shouts of a woman telling them to behave. The door cracked open perhaps two inches, and a woman, her face obscured by the door, peeked out at Sebastian through the narrow opening. He realized she was the maid who had looked so stunned when her mistress had tossed them out from the parlor.

She didn't seem to recognize him. She gave him a quick look up and down as she used her foot to push the dogs back from the open door. "Deliveries and trades come round the back. Not the front door."

"I'm not—I beg your pardon, if you could inform Miss Tricklebank that the cr—" He caught himself. He was wretched at deceit. Which, under normal circumstances, he'd proudly admit. Today he found his inability to play this game vexing. "Will you please inform her that Mr. Chartier has called?"

She opened the door a little wider and peered down at him. "Who?"

"Mr. Chartier."

Her eyes narrowed slightly, and she eyed him closely, her gaze flicking the length of him and up again. "Wait here," she said, and shut the door. He could hear her loudly commanding the dogs to follow her, and the sound of woman and beasts receded from the door.

So there he stood like a suitor on the doorstep for all of England to see. It felt like an interminably long wait, too. He was a sitting duck, just as Leopold had feared he would be—anyone could shoot him or tackle him or rope him. He was exposed to the world, which was something his country had endeavoured all his life to ensure never happened.

Sebastian glanced once or twice over his shoulder at the carriage. He could imagine it being commandeered and then he'd be forced to navigate a city he didn't know. A city everyone else navigated every day. But he'd be wandering through the streets like a beggar without a purse.

The longer he stood waiting, the more his concern for being noticed ratcheted. He kept expecting someone to shout out his name, or rush him from behind.

At last, the door suddenly swung open, startling him, and this time, Miss Tricklebank stood in the doorway. She frowned. She dipped a half-hearted curtsy, which was really a generous description of what she did. "*You* again."

"Miss Tricklebank, I owe you an apology."

"You certainly do." She folded her arms and stared down at him with her unusually gray eyes.

"My behavior yesterday was…unwarranted."

"Mmm."

How much apologizing was he required to do? He was rather rusty at it—his life hardly ever afforded him occasion to apologize for anything, much less to a commoner.

"Do you…do you understand what I've said?" he asked.

"I speak English very well, thank you. What I understand is that you don't know how to apologize."

He blinked. "Rather, I think you don't know how to accept one."

She moved to shut the door.

Sebastian grabbed the door to stop her. "All right,"

he conceded. "My behavior was…rude," he said, borrowing a word from her. He winced inwardly. He was not a discourteous man, generally speaking. Or hadn't been, until yesterday. *The supreme art of war is to subdue one's enemy without fighting*, went the old Chinese saying. He'd been taught that sentiment as a boy and was failing miserably. "I have no excuse to offer other than my distress at having lost a fellow Alucian and personal friend. I apologize, Miss Tricklebank."

She dropped her hand from the door. "He was your friend? I didn't know he was a *friend*. If I didn't say so, I will say it now, that I am truly and terribly sorry for your loss."

She seemed to soften toward him. She even seemed sincere. He dropped his hand from the door. "May I please come in?" he asked quietly. "I give you my word I'll be courteous."

"Is it the prince?" the maid asked, her head popping up over Miss Tricklebank's shoulder.

Her question surprised Sebastian—he was not accustomed to servants asking questions at all, especially prying ones. They were to serve and keep silent while doing it, then disappear into the shadows. He waited for Miss Tricklebank to admonish her. She didn't. She said, "It *is* the prince again. Isn't it odd, Poppy, that all I wanted was to make the acquaintance of a royal prince so that I could say that I had, and now I've made this one's acquaintance so many times one might call us friends." She smiled prettily at him.

Sebastian thought the better of telling her they most certainly could *not* be called friends as he admired her smile.

Miss Tricklebank leaned forward and looked up and

down the street. "Only you today, Your Highness? You best come in. You've gained enough attention as it is."

"What? Where?" he asked, and looked over his shoulder. He saw no one.

"You may not notice how the curtains around here flutter, but I certainly do." She pulled the door open wide. "Come in, please."

"Thank you." He stepped through the door and politely took off his hat. He held it out, but neither Miss Tricklebank nor the maid seemed inclined to take it. So he slowly reeled in the offer of his hat. "May I inquire if the justice is in?"

"Not at present. Poppy, I suppose we should have tea and attempt to make a proper showing," Miss Tricklebank said, and then she laughed, as if a proper showing was impossible.

She gestured to the parlor. "Mind your step, Your Highness. We're moving a few books around today."

Sebastian followed. When he stepped across the threshold, the two dogs leapt from their beds at the hearth and rushed forward to have an accounting of his shoes. He stood awkwardly, uncertain what to do about the dogs or with his hat, which he clutched in both hands.

"For heaven's sake, Jack and John, leave the poor man be! To your bed," Miss Tricklebank ordered, and pointed at the dog beds. One of the dogs trotted off right away. The other one was less inclined to obey, so she scooped him up and plopped him onto his bed.

"May I ask when you expect the judge to return?" Sebastian asked as he carefully stepped around a stack of books on the floor.

"Not till five o'clock. He's at court." Miss Tricklebank peered at the grandfather clock in the room, ticking out the time to them all.

Sebastian glanced at the clock, too. It was standing proudly in a line of clocks in various stages of dismantling. For what purpose, he could not guess. And perched in between the clocks on the mantel was a black-and-white cat, eyeing him smugly.

It was only half past three, said all the clocks that were working, and Sebastian thought quickly how best to make his case for waiting until the judge's return. "If I may, Miss Tricklebank, I should like to impress on you again why it is imperative that I see your father. He has printed something of vital importance to me. Something that could lead to a clue as to who has murdered my friend."

"Yes," she said slowly. "But he didn't print it, Your Highness."

How could she deny it? It was in black-and-white, printed in the gazette that the judge owned. "It was plainly printed in his gazette—"

"I am aware—"

"I don't expect you to understand—"

"What?" She made a sound that he wasn't certain was a laugh or a bark. "Why ever not?"

"Well, I..." Her question caught him off guard. A million things went through his mind, such as how he didn't understand it himself, and couldn't possibly explain the layers of political intrigue that had enveloped the court in Alucia these past few years. If he didn't understand it, how could he expect a woman who was essentially only a caregiver to understand it?

"I can assure you that my father was not responsible for the printing. That person was...someone else." She gave a flick of her wrist and tipped her chin up, as if she expected him to challenge her.

"Someone else? Who, then? I must speak to him. It is very—"

"Urgent, urgent! Yes, Your Highness, I *do* understand. For heaven's sake, is it not obvious that the person you desire is me?"

What in blazes was she saying? Desired her for what?

She blushed. "I don't mean *desire* in that sense of the word, and I don't know why you must you look so disbelieving, but it's true, the person you want to speak to is me, for I am the one who received the news and mentioned it to, ah…the person who publishes the gazette."

Sebastian stared at her. "You have given poisonous gossip of a potential crime to someone for the sake of printing it in a ladies' gazette?"

She frowned a little, as if that thought hadn't occurred to her. "It wasn't gossip. It was a note, addressed to my father."

Sebastian's heart did a bit of a flip. "A *note*? *What* note? Written by whom? Why was it sent to your father?"

"It wasn't signed. It said only that it was the field marshal and nothing more. My father suspected it was sent to him as he had the criminal docket in his court this month. Perhaps whoever penned it thought he would see to it that it was investigated."

Sebastian was stunned. Someone had written a note implicating Rostafan? He slowly turned and deposited the damn hat on a desk. He turned back and studied Miss Tricklebank. She studied him, too, her expression wary. Could he trust her? Was it possible she was part of the subterfuge around Matous's death? His instincts told him not to trust her, and yet, there was something about her that gave him pause. Perhaps it was her stunning honesty with him thus far. She wasn't trying to hide her actions or that she'd received a note. She looked at him without the slightest hint of deceit.

And still, it made no sense. She seemed like the sort of woman who lived a quiet life. So why had *she* received a note? Why did she have anything to do with this at all? Or her father, for that matter? What could a blind justice have to do with Matous's death? He shook his head, then rubbed the space between his eyes. "Madam, please, I beg of you, tell me what you know. From the beginning, if you don't mind."

She shifted on her feet, as if she didn't know whether she ought to stand or sit for this. "That's all there is, really. A few days after the ball, a man delivered our morning post and the note was in that stack of letters."

"Your postman."

"Actually, he wasn't our regular postman. He handed me all the post and off he went. I brought it inside and went through it, and there it was. A folded note, addressed to my father."

"Do you have any idea why your father?"

"Only that he's a justice on the Queen's Bench, as I said. I think my father is right—whoever wrote the note thought he could affect any investigation."

"Is your father involved in the investigation?"

She shook her head. "I'm sure he would have mentioned it. He thought it seemed misdirected."

"May I see this note?"

Before she could answer, the maid banged into the room with a silver tea service that looked quite heavy. "Here we are!" she sang out.

Sebastian stifled a groan—he was just beginning to make some headway and wanted to see the note.

"You can put it there on the table, please, Poppy," Miss Tricklebank said.

The maid—or Poppy, apparently—smiled at Sebastian as she moved across the room. "It's a bit like yesterday all over again, isn't it?" She deposited the tea service on the desk. She poured two cups and handed one to Miss Tricklebank. She tried to hand the other to Sebastian, but he shook his head. Remarkably, the maid didn't put the cup down but decided to drink it. She positioned herself next to Miss Tricklebank, lifted the cup to her lips and blew softly across the tea's surface before sipping it.

What in the name of heaven was happening in this house? Since when did servants take tea? Since when did women feel not the least bit intimidated by the future king of Alucia? This was all very, *very* new to him. But never mind that now. "The note, Miss Tricklebank. May I see it?"

Miss Tricklebank was distracted. Her brow had furrowed and she was studying him up and down. "Why are you dressed like that?"

"Pardon?" Sebastian looked down, having forgotten his costume of sorts. "Obviously, to avoid being noticed."

"Really?" She and Poppy the maid exchanged a look. "But surely you're allowed to go wherever you please."

"Of course, but I—" He shook his head. There was no point in explaining it. "We were speaking of the note? I need to see it. I don't believe all avenues of inquiry are being explored, and when the rumor appeared in this...*gazette*—"

"Honeycutt's Gazette of Fashion and Domesticity for Ladies," Miss Tricklebank clarified.

"When the rumor appeared in the ladies' gazette, the English officials did not think it was important, and I—"

"I beg your pardon?" Poppy said, as if he'd affronted her.

"Can you believe it?" Miss Tricklebank said, and rolled her eyes.

"I can't believe it at all," Poppy exclaimed. "They're envious, the lot of them, that's what."

Sebastian had no idea what the women were talking about, or who was envious of whom.

"Well, of course," Miss Tricklebank agreed. "For all of history they've believed publishing to be a man's exclusive domain. We've proved them very wrong, haven't we?"

"We certainly have!"

"I beg your pardon, I don't know what this is about," Sebastian said. "It was unimportant to the Englishmen because they consider my secretary's murder to be an Alucian matter. And well it may be, Miss Tricklebank, but *someone* has implicated my field marshal, someone who brought a note to *you*, of all the people in London, and I should like to know why."

"Oh, to give a clue, I should think," Poppy said confidently and sipped her tea.

"Or to divert suspicion from the true culprit by falsely naming someone else," Miss Tricklebank countered.

Poppy smiled. "How *clever* you are, Eliza. Of course! The Alucian prime minister could be responsible for all we know and said that the field marshal was responsible or some such, and supposed everyone would accuse the field marshal."

"The prime minister is not in England," Sebastian said, trying to follow their reasoning.

"Or someone like him," Miss Tricklebank said, ignoring Sebastian and addressing Poppy. "I've read enough of Pappa's papers that I've developed a bit of expertise in the twisted ways of the criminal mind." She tapped a finger to her head.

"Don't know what the judge would do without you," Poppy agreed.

It was as if Sebastian was not standing in the room. For the first time in thirty-two years of living, he was not noticed or needed. "Miss Tricklebank!" he said loudly.

The ladies stopped their chattering and looked at him.

He glanced at the maid. Then at Miss Tricklebank. "May I speak with you privately? Please."

The two women looked at him as if he'd just asked them to lift the hems of their dresses. Poppy colored. *"Well."* She gingerly set aside the teacup. "I suppose I know when *I'm* a bother."

"Oh, darling, you're not!" Miss Tricklebank trilled.

"It's quite all right." Poppy's voice was light and airy, but the look of offense she cast at Sebastian before walking out said otherwise.

Miss Tricklebank watched the maid sail out of the parlor, then turned a very stark frown to Sebastian, her pretty eyes narrowed with irritation. "Now you've gone and done it."

"*I've* gone and done it?"

"Well, *I* didn't hurt her feelings."

He honestly didn't know if he should laugh or roar his frustration to the ceiling.

"I don't know how things are done in Alucia, but Poppy is very much part of our family and we treat her as such."

"What *is* this place?" Sebastian muttered to himself. He looked around him again at the clocks and the smug cat, the stacks of books, the balls of yarn. "On my word I don't understand. Is there *no* reverence for the fact that I am a crown prince of a foreign nation? None?"

Miss Tricklebank looked to the door Poppy had gone through. "Apparently not."

The truth left him speechless. Not in his wildest imaginings could he have conjured a situation like the one he found himself in. She stubbornly was not going to give him the deference he was due, and he had to accept that in this case, it didn't matter. It was not germane to the crisis at hand. He needed to know who had given her the note, and if the only way to find out was to cease to be a prince in this parlor, then so be it.

He tried one more time. "Miss Tricklebank, I am imploring you to give me the note that was brought to you."

"Well, I'd like nothing more."

"*Thank* you."

"If I had it. But I don't. Pappa said to give it to the authorities, so I did." She put down her teacup and walked across the room to the mantel and the many clocks there.

"Are you telling me you don't have the note in your possession?"

"Regrettably, no. Don't look at me so crossly. I hardly expected a prince to come knocking on the door." She paused and chuckled at that. "I certainly did not." She pulled a small stool from the wall and stood on it to examine a moon dial on the face of one of the clocks. "I think this is wrong. We won't have a full moon tonight, will we?"

Sebastian's head was beginning to swim. "But the gazette—"

"Oh, I gave the note to Mr. Frink *after* sharing it with…the person who prints the gazette." She adjusted the moon dial and hopped down off the stool, smiling. "Are you sure you won't have some tea?"

"Who is Mr. Frink?"

"My father's clerk. He helps him on the Bench during the course of his everyday work. I'm not allowed, you know. God forbid a woman should advise a justice on the Queen's Bench." She folded her arms and looked off a moment, apparently miffed by this.

"Where might I find this Mr. Frink?"

"Find him? Why would—Oh dear. He doesn't have the note, either. He gave it to the London City Police."

Sebastian's head might very well explode. He dragged his fingers through his hair, a nervous habit his childhood nurse had broken him of decades ago. "Who in the London City Police?"

"I couldn't rightly say. I would have thought someone might have mentioned it to you."

Sebastian clenched his jaw. This was beginning to feel a bit like a circus. "No one has mentioned it."

"Really?" Miss Tricklebank frowned again as if she was working something out. "You must be quite disheartened. Well, sir, I don't *have* the note, but I can tell you precisely what it said. It was very short and read, *'Your Honor, the person responsible for the tragedy at Kensington is one of their own. Look to the field marshal.'* And, as I said, it was not signed."

"What of the handwriting?"

"The handwriting? Lovely. A talent at penmanship to be admired. Thick strokes of the pen, which I've never conquered. A strong hand, I should think. Perhaps a female. But then again, it might have been a male."

Sebastian squeezed the bridge of his nose in an effort to stave off a ferocious headache that was beginning to press in behind his eyes. He'd had the best education a man might seek in this world, and yet, he couldn't work his way out of this morass.

"I intend to investigate further."

Now what was she talking about?

"The murder," she clarified. But she said it calmly, as if she expected to investigate a murder and then do her laundering.

"You."

"Yes, *me*, why not me? I'm curious and my father says I can be very clever about these things. No one will give me the least bit of credit."

This was quickly becoming the most absurd day of his life. As if he'd stepped into some port and had been whisked away to another land entirely. Everything that was up was now down. Once again, he studied her for some sign of deception but saw nothing except confidence and curiosity in her expression. "Don't be ridiculous, Miss Tricklebank. You can't *possibly* undertake an investigation yourself."

She blinked her pretty gray eyes, then squared her shoulders as if she intended to take a swing at him. "Well then, Your Highness, you seem very certain about what I can and can't do. I certainly *can* investigate. I saw him at the ball, you know. More than once."

"Saw *who*?"

"The, ah..." She cleared her throat. She made a

whirling motion as if trying to wring the word from her body. "The departed."

"What do you mean, you *saw* him?"

"Just that. The first time I saw him was in the receiving line, where you stepped on my foot."

He opened his mouth, but she added quickly, "*Accidentally.* But I also saw him at least twice more speaking to a banker."

A *banker*? Why would Matous be speaking to a banker? Which banker? "Who? And how do you know he was a banker? How do you know who he was at all? Everyone wore masks."

"Yes, well, Mr. John Heath has a very distinguishing figure."

She was mad. That was what was happening here—the woman, pretty as she was, was mad, and this was all her imagining. "There were several distinguishing figures at the ball that night."

"I mean that Mr. Heath is corpulent."

This interview had gone well past the point of useful. Sebastian studied her. Yes, he was onto something—she was a bit of a loon. Perhaps the best thing to do now was to retreat, to discuss this with Leopold. At least he now had a name of someone who had spoken to Matous more than once the evening of the ball. It was a start. "Thank you, Miss Tricklebank, for your help. I will take what you've told me and use the information wisely."

She smiled patiently, as if he was a child who didn't understand. "I'm taking tea with Mr. Heath's daughter," she said. "My friend, Lady Caroline Hawke, has invited me. It will be my pleasure to tell you what I learn, if anything."

What good would that do? "Thank you, but I hardly think that is necessary. I will speak to Mr. Heath myself."

She made a sound, as if trying to swallow down laughter. On closer inspection he saw that she was indeed trying to keep from laughing. At *him*? Was there no end to this woman's cheek? "May I ask why you find that so amusing?" he asked tightly.

"You may!" she said cheerfully. "It is amusing that you think you can step into another English home in your disguise and learn anything. It won't work, you know. If Mr. Heath knows anything, he won't tell you. He'll surely think he's in some sort of trouble and will prefer to tell his own countrymen rather than you. That's if he receives you at all. We are very indulgent here at Bedford Square, but I assure you, other homes are not so. And if there is anything to know, his daughter will tell us."

"Then I will speak to her," he insisted, although Sebastian didn't know how he could possibly call on another young woman in disguise. He felt as if he'd pushed the bounds of pretending.

"But that's impossible!" she said with more gay laughter.

He folded his arms with exasperation. "Go on, then. You haven't yet been shy about telling me why I am so wrong in so many things. Why is it impossible?"

"You really can't guess?"

He pressed his lips together and stared at her.

"Your Highness! If you pay a call to Miss Heath, everyone in London will think you've decided she is the one."

"The one what?"

Miss Tricklebank burst into laughter that sounded so

bright and carefree that if he hadn't been so perturbed, he would have laughed with her. She had a lovely laugh, the sort that settled on a person like summer sun. "The one you intend to marry, of course!"

Bloody hell, he'd forgotten all about that. He felt himself flush with the embarrassment of having every bloody Englishman watch his every bloody move while trying to predict whom he would make an offer of marriage to. He turned partially away from Miss Tricklebank, who was once again trying to stifle her mirth. He truly had never known anyone like her. What must *she* think of him? Appearing at her house in the clothes of a wastrel, unable to fend for himself or avenge his friend's death. He was an impotent prince here in England.

"No one would allow you to have an audience alone with her," she continued, her giggling subdued for the moment. "They'd want to negotiate the marriage settlement before they'd allow it."

He clucked his tongue at her.

She grinned so charmingly that he was knocked a little off balance. "And if you called on Mr. Heath, everyone would think that it had to do with your trade agreement."

"You are beginning to sound like my brother," he complained.

"Oh! I shall take that as a compliment." She solemnly inclined her head.

Miss Tricklebank was clever on her feet. And so very pretty, if he allowed himself to think about it. He particularly liked her smile, in spite of how many times she had used that lovely smile to laugh at him.

She arched a brow, a silent question about his perusal of her.

"I'm very sorry, Miss Tricklebank, but I can't leave this to you."

"Oh dear. Did I mistakenly ask your permission? I assure you, that was not my intent." She smiled again, her eyes sparkling with delight.

"You must be the most irreverent, disobedient person I have ever met in all my years," he said with exasperation.

"Really! In *all* your years? Perhaps you ought to go abroad more often, sir. I am disobedient because I am not your subject."

"Yes, you've made that exceedingly clear, Miss Tricklebank. That was my point. You are *not* my subject. How can I trust you to tell me what the young lady says or doesn't say?"

She looked surprised by this. "Because I said I would."

"This may come as a great shock to you, but I've learned in my life that trust is not an easy thing to bestow." He hesitated. He could feel a rush of emotion, of great sadness. "Matous Reyno was perhaps the one friend in this life whom I *could* trust, and I am…" He was cracking, his guilt and grief mixing together to form a powerful weight on his heart. "I am lost without him," he said, mortified that his voice should break.

He *was* lost without Matous. He'd taken him for granted, had relied on him so completely, and not once, that he could recall, had he thanked Matous for his loyalty or his friendship.

"Oh." Her smile faded. "I'm so very sorry for you, sir. I know a bit what it's like to lose someone very dear. But you should know that I honor my word, no matter what. And I have nothing to gain or lose by looking into this matter. It's my own curiosity that compels me now.

I think it's terrible what happened to your friend. He was very kind to me. He seemed a good man."

"He was," Sebastian said quietly. He felt another stab of regret and grief in his belly and looked away from her. In the days since the shock of Matous's death, it had become easier to cope with his loss, to accept what was. But the hole in Sebastian's chest remained.

"On my word, you may trust me, Your Highness."

He was probably losing his mind, but he rather thought he could. He roused himself from his despair and looked at her. "How will you get word to me?"

She smiled. "I assumed you would come round and demand it. But I can send a note if you like."

"When will you see her?"

"Saturday afternoon at four," Miss Tricklebank said. "At the home of Beckett, Lord Hawke, in Grosvenor Square, in the Mayfair district. Have you made his acquaintance?"

Sebastian shook his head. He picked up his hat from the table. "Thank you, Miss Tricklebank, for your help."

"You are very welcome. Shall I show you out?"

"No need. I know the way." He started for the door but paused and glanced back at Miss Tricklebank. She was up on the stool again, squinting at one of the many clocks. What a strange little parlor this was. What a strange little world.

He thought that had this been a different time, a different life, he might very much have liked it here. It had been a trying day, but he felt it to be new and very different to be in the company of someone who saw him as a mere gentleman.

Not a prince. Just a man.

It was refreshingly different in every way.

CHAPTER ELEVEN

An unmarried lady, who has banked her patience, recently took tea with a friend. A Hawk descended and speculation abounds that the Hawk has at last decided to choose a mate.

Guests at the tea were treated by the latest fashion of wide bell sleeves, worn with perfection by the daughter of a famous jurist. We predict these sleeves will be everywhere come spring.

Ladies, the latest advice on introducing the world to your newborn suggests that bright colors and objects should be brought in gradually, so as not to overwhelm the developing brain.

—Honeycutt's Gazette of Fashion and Domesticity for Ladies

ELIZA AND HOLLIS went to Holbren Hill the morning of the tea so that Hollis could purchase a goose and Eliza could buy tobacco for her father's pipe.

Hollis had in mind to host a supper party. "I've not invited people to dine since Percival passed. But that's been more than two years! I am determined to put away my widow's weeds and enjoy society again."

"You put away your widow's weeds months ago," Eliza reminded her.

"I may have shed the clothes months ago, my dear

Eliza, but I've only just shed them from my heart. Should I invite the crown prince of Alucia now that you are so well acquainted?"

Eliza gave her a wry smile. "Do you mean the prince who gads about town dressed like a cart driver?"

The two of them turned their attention to the geese and fowl the butcher had strung in three rows across the outside of his building. Eliza had, of course, told Hollis and Caroline everything that had happened on the prince's second visit to Bedford Square, and they'd reviewed it in great detail.

"I can't believe he's allowed to do so," Hollis said. "Can you imagine if the queen was traipsing about dressed as one of us—Excuse me! Pardon!" she called to the shopkeeper. "I'd like that one," she said, pointing to a very fat goose hanging on the first string at the very top of the shop.

The shopkeeper, dressed in a leather apron and shirtsleeves, peered up to the goose she'd pointed out.

"That ought to do for twelve, won't it?" Hollis asked.

"Aye, fifteen if you've a cook who knows how to cut them."

"Then that is the one I'd like."

The shopkeeper glanced up again. "Would you not like one from this row?" he asked, pointing to the birds hanging lower. "Any of them would suit twelve."

"No. I'd like that one," Hollis said, pointing to the goose overhead.

"I'll have to get a lad."

"I'll wait!" Hollis said cheerfully.

The shopkeeper frowned at her.

"If you don't mean to sell it, then why hang it?"

The man muttered under his breath and then whistled. A boy appeared. The shopkeeper told him to fetch the ladder.

As they waited, Hollis turned to her sister and took her hands in hers. "Do you know what I can't stop thinking about? That *you*, of everyone in London, of all the proper ladies with titles and dowries, have received the prince *twice*. Do you think he fancies you?"

Eliza burst out laughing. She caught the eye of Hollis's manservant, Donovan, who winked at her before turning his attention back to the lad with the ladder.

"He can hardly abide me, Hollis. He thinks I pay his title no heed and that he knows better than me on every subject."

"True on both counts. Nevertheless, *you* know *him* better than anyone."

"I don't know him at all, other than his nature is to be cross."

"He's handsome," Hollis observed.

"So is Donovan."

Hollis blushed. Everyone was always pointing out to Hollis that Donovan was the most handsome of men. He was tall and solidy built, with lovely brown eyes and thick dark hair. For Eliza, the most appealing thing about him was his steadfast loyalty to Hollis. She couldn't imagine how Hollis might have survived those days and weeks after Percival's death without Donovan to manage things. Still, sometimes Eliza and Caroline giggled and imagined all sorts of intimate things that might have happened between Hollis and Donovan behind closed doors. She was, after all, a lively widow and no one would be the wiser.

But Eliza also knew her sister very well. No one would ever hold a candle to Percival. And if Hollis had ever thought of even kissing Donovan, she would have told Eliza everything. She had never mentioned any attraction at all.

"What does Poppy think of the prince?" Hollis asked, drawing Eliza back to the present.

"Poppy can scarcely abide him," Eliza said. "She stayed for tea when he called, and he asked her to leave. She was quite offended."

"Well," Hollis said with a shrug. "No one but the Tricklebanks expect a maid to take tea, Eliza."

"That is not true—you take tea with Donovan. And you know very well that Poppy is more than a maid."

"Well, *I* know that, but perhaps you ought not to ask her to bring tea when someone calls. That makes her appear a servant, and a future king would not expect to take tea in the parlor with a servant. It must have been quite unsettling for him."

"Poor dear, forced to take tea with a young woman who is not a maid. Never mind Poppy, anyway," Eliza said. "He was rude." But he'd also been rather vulnerable, which had surprised her. When he spoke about his secretary's death, he had been visibly distraught. It had made her want to put her arms around him and hold him tight.

The lad had reached the top of the ladder and was leaning far to his right to take down the goose Hollis wanted. The ladder started to slide. The crowd below sent up a cry of alarm.

"I, for one, can't fault him for his bad humor," Hollis said as she watched the lad. "Someone was murdered. For all he knows, they mean to murder *him*."

Another cry went up from the crowd—the lad's ladder was sliding farther to the right. The shopkeeper noticed it from below and righted it before the boy and the goose tumbled to the ground.

"What are you talking about?" Eliza asked.

"I've done some study of Alucia. They say the prince's uncle wants his throne. That the prince's father *took* it from him."

"Really?" Eliza asked. "I thought the prince's father was the true king and the uncle wanted to take the throne from him."

Hollis shrugged. "I didn't study it *that* closely, and I don't know all the details, obviously, but something is amiss in Alucia, and everyone knows it. Maybe *he* is the thing that is amiss."

"Here you are, madam, that will be one pound, one shilling," the shopkeeper said, holding out the goose to her. Donovan quietly stepped forward to take the bird.

"One pound, one shilling? That's outrageous!" Hollis exclaimed. "I'll give you one pound for it."

"Bird weighs one and a half stones," the shopkeeper said. "One pound, one shilling."

"If it weighs one and half stones, that young boy could not have carried it down. One pound, sir, or you can have the lad take it right back up."

The man grumbled, but he snatched the money from her hand all the same.

Hollis smiled sweetly. "*Thank* you."

The shopkeeper turned away, the money tucked into his apron. "Who's next, then?"

With that purchase completed, they made their way down the street to the tobacco shop, Donovan trailing a few feet behind them with the goose. "I can't come to the tea to meet Miss Heath," Hollis reminded her. She'd been invited by Caroline but had conflicting plans. "I'll want to know everything. I've heard she's quite shy and will scarcely utter a word."

"Oh dear, I hope that's not the case."

"Eliza." Hollis put her hand on her sister's arm and said somberly, "Don't let Caro do all the talking."

Eliza laughed. It was impossible to keep Caroline from doing all the talking.

"And be careful. It's bad business, murder. It may seem easy enough to ask a few questions here and there, but who knows where it will lead."

"Don't worry, Hollis. I know what I'm doing."

Hollis looped her arm through Eliza's. "Neither would I would want to see you unduly hurt in any other way."

Eliza almost rolled her eyes. "What's the matter, darling? Do you think the prince will sweep me off my feet and I will be the *only* one in London who doesn't know he's made an offer of marriage to someone else?"

"Of course I don't think that," Hollis scoffed. "But by all accounts he is very handsome." She nudged Eliza. "And rich. That is a powerful broom if one is inclined to be swept."

Eliza laughed. "Don't worry about me. I am a completely different person than I was then."

"You're still a woman," Hollis said.

Eliza was accustomed to her family's protective feelings for her. Her mistake with Asher had been quite spectacular. "It's nothing like that," Eliza assured her. "I'd just as soon be swept off my feet by Mr. Norris."

"No!" Hollis cried, and they broke into a fit of giggles, recalling the hapless, would-be suitor several years ago, whose wiry hair had stuck up in several directions at once.

"I'll come round Saturday evening to hear all the details," Hollis said. "Don't forget a single one. *Especially* Beck's reaction when he realizes what role he is to play." The two sisters looked at each other and laughed again.

They'd concocted a plan for the tea, of course. They would have Miss Heath warm to them by having Beck make an appearance and make some vague suggestions that perhaps Lord Hawke was at last ready to settle on a match. That, they reasoned, would loosen the woman's lips in the spirit of cooperation and a desire to know more. Eliza and Hollis were skeptical that Caroline could arrange this surprise appearance, because Beck enjoyed being uncooperative, but she'd assured them Beck would bend to her will. Once Miss Heath had made Beck's acquaintance, they would bring the conversation around to Miss Heath's father, and then Eliza would casually mention what she'd seen at the ball. It seemed very straightforward to Eliza.

When she'd purchased her tobacco, Eliza and Hollis hugged goodbye.

"You'll wear the blue dress," Hollis instructed her.

"Yes," Eliza agreed.

Hollis patted her sister's cheek. "Good luck. See you tonight!" She and Donovan started down the street, Donovan towering over Hollis, the goose slung carelessly over his shoulder. Hollis was going on about something, judging by the way her hand was waving about as they walked.

Eliza sighed and went in the opposite direction with her father's tobacco.

Late that afternoon, she emerged from her rooms in the dress Hollis had suggested she wear. It was the blue of a robin's egg, with sleeves so wide at the wrist that she could have tucked Pris away in one of them and no one would have been the wiser.

Her father was in the parlor, Jack and John on their beds and Pris nowhere to be seen. Her father was knitting, the steady *click click click* of his needles sounding like one of the clocks. Ben was tending the fire.

"I'm off to tea at Caro's, Pappa," she said, leaning over to kiss the top of his head.

"Oh? Who's coming?"

"Miss Lucille Heath. The daughter of Mr. John Heath."

"The banker?"

"The very one."

Poppy entered the study holding Eliza's cape. "Oooh, look at you, Eliza. How pretty your dress! Do you see her, Ben?"

"Aye. 'tis lovely, Miss Eliza."

"It's a lovely shade of blue, Your Honor, with very fashionable sleeves," Poppy explained.

"New, is it?" her father asked the space before him.

"Rejuvenated," Eliza said. "With the new sleeves. Hollis says the wide sleeves are a must."

"Well then, if Hollis says it, you must have wide sleeves," her father said. "Give my regards to our Caro and Miss Heath. Shall Ben hire a cab for you?"

"No, thank you. It's a lovely day. I intend to walk." Donning the cape, Eliza bade them all goodbye. She walked out into the cluttered foyer, took her bonnet from a peg on the wall and struck out for Caroline's, striding down the street with purpose as she tied the ribbons of her bonnet beneath her chin.

At the corner, she looked up at the windows of Mrs. Spragg's house, where the drapery had been pushed aside just enough to give Mrs. Spragg a view of the street. Eliza waved, then carried on, past the butcher shop and down the street to another corner. There, she paused in front of the confectioner's to admire the sweets in the shop window.

She was perusing a tray of freshly baked lemon tarts, debating if she should have one, when she became aware of someone behind her. That someone turned into the looming shadow of a man reflected in the shop's window, and gave Eliza such a start that she whirled around, her hand to her heart. When she saw who stood behind her, she groaned and dropped her hand. "What in blazes are you doing? You gave me quite a fright!"

"I beg your pardon, that was not my intent. I mean to accompany you to your tea," the prince said. "I have a carriage." He gestured to one just down the street.

Eliza looked at the carriage, then at him. "I don't need a carriage. You shouldn't go sneaking up on people like that, Your Highness."

"If you could refrain from addressing me formally, please?" he asked, and cast an anxious glance around them. "I don't want any undue attention."

"Then perhaps you shouldn't be wandering about like a lost traveler. Where are your men?"

"Nearby. Could you please manage to keep your voice below a shout?"

She tried to see around him to his men. He moved slightly so she couldn't. "You needn't worry," he said low. "I am well protected."

She blinked. He was impossible. Did he really think she feared for him? It was herself she had in mind to worry over. "*I'm* not worried, but *you* should be. Or perhaps I *should* be worried because I think, sir, that you are quite mad!"

He seemed surprised by her admonishment and then terribly amused, judging by the way he smiled. The effect was so dazzling that Eliza was momentarily stunned by it. "That's rich, Miss Tricklebank. You may think your kettle is a shiny copper one, but trust me, it is as black as my pot."

She folded her arms. It was possible that he had a point. Nevertheless.

She looked him up and down. "Why do you insist on dressing like a cart driver, Your Highness?"

"For God's sake," he said, glancing nervously around them. "Don't call me that."

"Well? Why would you accost me dressed like this?"

He took exception to her characterization of his dress, looking down. "I did not *accost* you. And I am dressed as a typical Englishman. You may address me as Mr. Chartier."

"A typical Englishman! You look like a scoundrel in that ragged coat and hat."

He gave her the sort of look a parent might give a recalcitrant child. "If you will put yourself in my carriage, you may cast all the aspersions you like on my clothing."

She laughed. "I am not getting in your carriage, *Mr. Chartier*."

He sighed. He glanced heavenward for a moment as if garnering patience or strength. "You have an *astounding* capacity to say no to me, Miss Tricklebank. A carriage is the safest form of travel for us both, which I should think is obvious, but if you desire to be stubborn about it, we will walk on. But let us please walk *on*—if we continue to stand here, people will begin to notice."

He was full of ideas for what she ought to do, and Eliza didn't care for it. "*We* will not walk on, and I don't rightly care what anyone thinks of who I speak to on the street."

He snorted. "Of course you do." He firmly took her elbow and turned her about.

"I *don't*," she insisted, falling into step beside him. "Anyone who knows me would find it more remarkable that I have an escort, as I rarely do. I don't require a gentleman to escort *me* about. I walk these streets quite on my own." There was a bit of pride in her voice, she realized. What an odd thing to be prideful about, but she was. Miss Williams, who lived across Bedford Square, was never allowed to go to market without a maid or someone to accompany her. Eliza went all the time, whenever she fancied.

"How happy I am for you," he said, and let go her elbow, clasping his hands behind his back. "I don't understand why you don't, however. You're pretty enough."

She immediately stopped walking and stared at him. "I'm pretty *enough*? Why, thank you so very much for that *generous* compliment, Mr. Chartier."

"I didn't intend any offense," he said, his eyes straight ahead. "I meant that you're very comely and I should think gentlemen would be eager to escort you."

The so-called Mr. Chartier put his hand to the small of her back. "Do keep walking, please."

She forgot to object to his command as a thrill had raced through her body and had stunned her tongue into paralysis for a moment, because he'd just proclaimed her very comely. Eliza was generally immune to compliments freely handed out by men to gain favor, but this one made her chest swell a little. *Very comely.* She couldn't wait to discuss this with Caroline and Hollis and Poppy.

"You don't need to sprint, Miss Tricklebank," he said. "People will think you're running from me."

She was startled back to the present. "Perhaps I should run from you. How is it that you can traipse around London without anyone knowing? Isn't someone somewhere wanting an audience with you? Don't you have important trade papers to sign or some such?"

"It is Saturday. The negotiations will resume on Monday. In the meantime, my butler will explain that I am indisposed."

That seemed so absurd that Eliza chuckled. "Do you mean to say that your butler tells people what, that you have a headache, so you can dress in a worn coat and hat and walk around London?"

He gave her an impatient, sidelong look. "You have no idea how difficult it is to live my life, particularly here in England. Someone wants my attention at all times. If I'm to have any modicum of privacy, it is sometimes necessary to lie, Miss Tricklebank."

She supposed that was probably true. "Please, call me Eliza if we're going to be friends, which I suppose we are since you've told me your secret."

He clucked his tongue at her. "We are not friends and I've not told you any secret."

"You've told me two, in fact. One, that you can't trust anyone, and two, that you have no privacy. I know these things because I've had more of your time than probably anyone in London. You even drank from my glass."

"Pardon?" He peered down at her with a confused expression.

"In the passageway, the night of the ball. You drank from my glass and tried to seduce me."

He stopped walking and stared at her in disbelief. "*That* was you?"

She stopped walking, too. "Should I be offended that you don't seem to have any recollection of me? You drank from my glass, you stepped on my foot—do you remember *anything* from the night of the ball?"

His gaze flicked over her and then locked on her face. She looked into those autumn green eyes and felt the flare of a thrill race through her again when he said, "Actually, I remember some parts of it rather keenly."

"That makes two of us, then."

One of his dark brows rose above the other, as if surprised or amused by this. Eliza remembered some parts more than keenly. Her memories of that night with a foreign prince were knitted into her fibre now. "And clearly, I remember far more than you. I met an entirely different man that evening."

"Did you? How so?"

"You weren't as…as *vexing* as you are now. And that night, you'd intended something entirely untoward."

His gaze moved over her again, a little slower now, casually taking her in. "I remember more than you think, Miss Tricklebank," he said in a low voice. "You are correct, however—I had intended something quite different that night." He slowly lifted his gaze and pierced hers with it. "But I would not call it untoward."

Well. Now it felt as if a flock of robins was beating its wings in her chest. She didn't know what to do with all those wings. She faced forward and started walking again. “Nevertheless, my point remains, Mr. Chartier. We are very much in each other’s company and we have a shared interest, which I think recommends us as friends. Therefore, you should call me Eliza and, if I may be so bold, I should call you Sebastian.”

He gave a bark of laughter. “My God, you *are* bold.”

“And brash,” she added pertly. “You must admit that one must be brash if one is forced to keep saying things like, *‘You’re wrong, Sebastian,’* or *‘What are you doing here, Sebastian,’* or *‘You’re mad, Sebastian.’*”

A smile turned up the corners of his mouth. “I don’t know if you realize just how fortunate you are that you’re not an Alucian.”

“On the contrary, I am quite clear on the advantages of being a British subject. Is Sebastian a family name?”

“It was the name of my great-great-grandfather, King Sebastian I. And yours?”

“It belonged to no one. My mother liked the name, that’s all.”

“Where is your mother now?”

“Long dead. Yours?”

“In Alucia.”

“You’re a lucky one, then. I would very much like to have my mother nearby.” Eliza glanced over her shoulder. She saw two men walking behind them, also dressed like cart drivers. “Are they your men?” she whispered.

“If you mean my guards, yes,” he playfully whispered back. “And you will draw less attention to them if you didn’t look at them at all.”

Eliza turned her gaze straight ahead. She suddenly laughed and grinned at him. “*They* must think you’ve lost your fool mind.”

"Oh, I've no doubt of it," he said agreeably, and smiled back. "But they would never have the gall to offer that opinion. For all I know, one of them is responsible for Matous's death."

Eliza gasped. "*No.* Wait, do you truly think so?"

He shrugged. "I honestly don't know what to think, Miss... Eliza."

Ooh, but her name sounded delicious when he said it in his deep dulcet tones, with his alarmingly arousing accent.

They had come to the corner and she turned left. A sudden gust of cold wind very nearly took her bonnet off. The wind was picking up, and low clouds were beginning to slide in over the tops of chimneys.

"How much farther?" he asked.

"A quarter of an hour at most." Another gust of wind caught her bonnet again, and she grabbed the brim at the same time she tried to pull her cloak around her. When she did, she almost stepped off the sidewalk, but the prince caught her with a steadying hand to the small of her back. "Careful."

This was the second time he'd touched her there, and the shock of his touch shot through her body. She'd never been so easily stimulated by a mere touch as she had been this day.

He removed his hand at once, of course, and when she turned to look at him, those lovely green eyes were on hers, the color deeper and darker somehow. She noticed his square jaw. His full lips the color of dark rose. She had the fleeting question of what it would be like to kiss those lips, followed by a general curiosity of what they would taste like, and then a more pressing curiosity of how passionately those lips might descend on her lips. Or against the skin of her neck. Her arm. Her throat. And everywhere else, points low and high.

She had to look away, lest her imagination take flight. Or she had to remove her cloak for a bit of air.

They walked along in companionable silence. When they reached Grosvenor Square and Upper Brook Street, she pointed to number 22. "Lady Caroline Hawke resides there."

The prince looked at the large house without comment. "How long will you be?"

"An hour or so, perhaps more. If you like, I'll send a note of the outcome through one of your men."

"I'll wait."

"Someone will see you," she pointed out. "And it's getting cold."

"I have a carriage. And no one has given me a second look as we've walked here." He took off his hat and dragged his fingers through his hair, then seated the hat again. "It's actually freeing to be standing in the middle of a city like London without a horse guard or trumpets blaring."

It was odd to think of it. She stood in the middle of London without fanfare all the time. How strange it was that someone would need to wish for that. "Suit yourself," she said. She gave him a fleeting smile and walked up the steps to Caroline's door.

She could feel his eyes on her as she waited for the door to be opened. Or, it was more accurate to say she could feel his eyes boring holes through her back—boring clean through her, looking out the other side of her. She risked a glance back.

The prince was standing precisely where she'd left

him, his gaze fixed on her. He smiled a little, as if he wasn't certain he should smile at all.

Another little shiver coursed through her. She turned back. She really needed to have some tea or something to stop those tiny quakes in her.

Garrett, the Hawke butler, opened the door. "Miss Tricklebank." He bowed.

"Eliza!" Caroline sailed in behind the butler, all smiles. She reached around Garrett and took Eliza's arm, yanking her inside. "Come in, come in," she whispered and gave a furtive, backward glance at Garrett. "She's in there, and she has scarcely said a word! Hardly a how-do-you-do! How will we *ever* make her talk?"

Eliza calmly removed her bonnet and cloak and handed them to Garrett. "Let's have a look, shall we?"

Arm in arm, she and Caroline walked into the green salon to chat up Miss Heath while a pair of green eyes worked along the edges of Eliza's thoughts.

CHAPTER TWELVE

A fiery wife without a husband near has received visitors from the queen's privy. It remains unknown if the lady was wearing one glove or two when she received them. Curiosity abounds, but word is that the woman is merely clumsy with her gloves and does not use the expensive kid leather to signal her partners in a vast conspiracy.

Ladies, a drop of lemon juice in the corner of your eye will widen the iris to achieve the doe-eyed look made popular by the lovely Duchess of Inverness.

—Honeycutt's Gazette of Fashion and Domesticity for Ladies

AN HOUR CAME and went.

Sebastian was pacing now, questioning everything he'd ever known about himself. Miss Tricklebank—Eliza—was right about him. He was mad, beyond mad, to be wandering about in this park until he was chased away by an old man who shouted that the park was not for vagrants but for residents only.

He would speak to Egius about more suitable clothing.

He restlessly walked around the perimeter of the gardens, waiting for news from a banker's daughter who surely knew nothing.

It was his fault for listening to Eliza. To a woman who lived in a cluttered house in a nondescript part of London. She would discover nothing—how could she possibly? What could the banker's daughter know? So why, then, was he clinging to anything she could tell him about Matous on the last night of his life?

And how was it that Eliza had noticed his private secretary more than he had that night? Was it his guilt that compelled him to act like a fool, chasing after ghosts of clues? Or was it perhaps the impotency of his position, his inability to do anything for himself? All he knew was that this was one thing he could do, one way he could at least pretend to avenge Matous's death. He could not return to Helenamar with nothing to tell his widow, Maribel. He couldn't imagine Maribel's devastation. Sebastian had long had the impression that the Reyno marriage was one made of true felicity and love. They seemed to truly enjoy each other's company. It was the sort of marriage that, had Sebastian been anyone else, he would have aspired to.

How Maribel would miss Matous. How he missed his friend.

Then again, it was entirely possible that the sensation in his chest was something else, something as yet unidentified or understood that drove him to pace this square like a madman.

He'd never felt anything quite like this, at this intensity. It was so unique and unexpected that he didn't know what to do with it, or how to make it go away. He didn't know if he even wanted to make it go away. Whatever it was, it felt like it had the capacity to consume all rational thought.

All right, he could say it, at least to himself—he esteemed Eliza Tricklebank. He'd gone from despising her, to being surprised by her, to appreciating her unusual place in this world. As they'd strolled along, he'd wanted to touch her, to look in her gray eyes and see the sparkle there. He hadn't even cared that she didn't seem to esteem him in quite the same manner, and in fact, held no regard for him at all. That just made her all the more intriguing.

But he realized, as he walked around that square, that he wanted her to feel some regard for him. He wanted her to esteem him, too. The terrifying thing was that he didn't know how to create that regard in her. He'd never had to do it, never had to impress anyone. He'd never had to do anything but breathe, and the people flocked to him.

This absurd notion was beginning to chip away at his thoughts. He wondered what was taking so long, because this idea of his regard for her, and all the reasons why he wanted it returned, were consuming him to the point that he could not walk away from the gardens at Grosvenor if he wanted. His conscience was pushing him to try to gain her favor.

The wait was tedious. He avoided his carriage and his guards. They waited, one of them with his back against the wall in an alley, the other leaning against one of the horses.

Twice, Sebastian settled and watched people come and go, hurrying home or out for the evening. The wind was steadily gusting now, and he could detect the scent of rain. He looked up to a clock tower on the corner—it was half past five. He felt anxious—they'd be looking for him at Kensington by now. He couldn't wait for her much longer.

A fat plop of rain hit him on the shoulder. Sebastian

glanced around, saw no one in the gardens, and slipped inside to stand under the broad spreading limbs of a tree. He had pulled the collar of his greatcoat up around his ears and his hat lower on his head. He folded his arms and waited. He must have dozed a little leaning against the tree, because he was startled when the door of number 22 swung open and a woman in a brown cloak and bonnet and wearing wire-rimmed glasses that slid down to the tip of her nose hurried out. On the entry landing, she whirled around, shook another woman's hand quite vigorously. She then darted down the steps and around the corner to where a cabriolet was parked at the curb. A gentleman got out and handed her up, drew the curtains across the opening, then climbed up onto the driver's seat and set the horses to a trot.

At the door of 22, Eliza Tricklebank stepped out, and damn it if Sebastian's heart didn't skip a single beat. She was speaking to another woman as she tied the ribbons of her bonnet.

Sebastian strode out from the gardens, prepared to intercept her and escort her home, but then the women were joined by a gentleman on the landing. He had his hands on his waist, and looking rather perturbed, seemed to be arguing with Eliza's friend. Sebastian couldn't comprehend what they were saying, but he understood the tenor of their voices too well. He watched as Eliza quickly kissed her friend's cheek, dipped a curtsy to the gentleman, then hopped down the steps, leaping from the last one onto the walk.

Sebastian took a few steps toward her but instantly realized his mistake—her friend had spotted him immediately. Whatever the gentleman was saying to her, she ignored. Her gaze was fixed on him. Even from across the street, Sebastian knew that she'd recognized him, and he felt a sick turn in his belly. Recognition would push him back to the shadows of Kensington Palace, behind a wall of guards.

He couldn't worry about that now—Eliza was marching along, gripping her cloak around her. The wind was lifting the edges of it, and it looked as if she might take flight. He jogged across the street to catch up to her. "Eliza!"

Her head came up with a start. The rain was coming down now, and he reached his hand for her. "Come!"

She didn't hesitate to slip her slender hand into his, allowing him to pull her along in a mad dash to the carriage. He opened the door, pushed her up inside, then jumped in after her. He felt the carriage rock as his men climbed onto the driver's seat. He opened the vent overhead. "Bedford Square," he barked, then closed the vent.

Eliza's bonnet was dripping. She was breathless, her eyes glittering with delight. She removed the bonnet and shook the water onto the floor. "You are my savior!" she gaily proclaimed. "I would have been soaked by the time I reached Bedford Square." She leaned back, running her hand over the velvet squabs, taking in the velvet wall coverings. "Is this your carriage?"

"No." Sebastian tried to stop looking at her mouth and force his thoughts to the issue at hand. And yet, a part of him refused to stop taking in every little thing about her. The way she crossed her feet at the ankles, one foot bouncing merrily atop the other. How slender and elegant her hands resting in her lap were. "Were you able to discover anything useful?"

She suddenly smiled so sunnily that he felt knocked

back by it. Her eyes sparkled like two stars. "We've worked it all out!"

"We? Who is we?" he asked. "What have you worked out?"

"Caro—that is, Lady Caroline Hawke and I have worked it out. Miss Heath knew nothing, really, other than that your friend asked if her father, the banker, would introduce him to a French banker who is presently in England."

"A French banker?"

She nodded. "Miss Heath said that your friend wanted to make his acquaintance while he was in England. Something about a debt."

This made no sense to Sebastian. Why would Matous wish to speak to a French banker about a debt?

"That seems to explain it, doesn't it?"

Her eyes were still shining at him, distracting him. "Pardon?"

"Well, I think it is obvious, don't you? Your friend owed a debt. He wanted help with it, obviously, for why would he want the English banker to speak to the French banker on his behalf? He must have needed money. The debt must have been…important."

Sebastian mentally shook himself from tracing the lines of her neck with his eyes. "You believe that Mr. Reyno was murdered because he owed someone money?"

"Doesn't that seem plausible to you? It must have been a sizeable debt. And when he failed to repay it, well…unfortunately, there are some very corrupt people in this world."

"Did the lass say his debt was sizeable?"

"No." She frowned thoughtfully. "But it must have

been. Otherwise, would he not have waited until he'd returned to Alucia to borrow money?"

Sebastian didn't think so at all. "Did the woman say anything more?"

"Miss Heath?" She suddenly laughed. "That's when Lord Hawke came into the room and she lost her head for anything else. We could have poured tea on her lap and she wouldn't have noticed. You look bemused. He is very handsome."

Sebastian felt a fragile bit of kinship with Miss Heath. But he was wondering why Matous would want to speak to a French banker about a debt Sebastian was certain he didn't have. The Reyno family had been granted a huge estate and trust in the last decade. They were quite wealthy and he knew very well Matous didn't need money—so who did? Was Matous wanting to speak to the banker on someone's behalf? That would be just like him, seeking to help a friend.

"Beck—we call him Beck—is a coveted matrimonial catch," Eliza said. "Someone like you, really, but on a far smaller scale, naturally, since he might only make his wife baroness and not a queen."

Sebastian was listening with one ear. What could Matous have been doing? Clearly, he needed someone to speak to this banker.

"But he never has shown the slightest interest in marriage," Eliza said as the carriage rolled to a halt. "Oh! We're here! Well, that's certainly quicker than walking, isn't it?" She glanced out the window. So did Sebastian. The rain was a deluge now, but here they were, drawn to a halt at the house with the red door on Bedford Square.

She fell back against the squabs and picked up her bonnet. "Thank you, Sebastian Chartier. I will be forever grateful for your carriage. I would have asked Caro for a carriage to see me home, but Beck hadn't intended to make Miss Heath's acquaintance, and he was still terribly cross that Caro had arranged it. Siblings," she said by way of explanation. "They were having quite a row and I thought it best not to interrupt. So I do owe you a debt."

"I'm the one who owes you a debt, Miss Tricklebank."

"Eliza!" she cheerfully reminded him.

"Eliza," he said, but the name seemed to want to stay in his throat. "Your help has been crucial."

She beamed with pleasure. "I'm so glad I was able to solve the mystery for you." She donned her bonnet as if she'd not only solved his mystery but had tidied up and was ready for supper now.

"I don't think we can say the mystery is solved just yet," he said.

"I suppose you mean the question of who was the actual murderer. But at least you know the reason for it now. That must be some comfort." She scooted across the squab toward the door.

Sebastian wasn't ready for her to leave just yet. "There is a flaw in your reasoning, if I may point it out."

"*Is* there?" She leaned forward, her bright eyes still sparkling, as if she expected to be diverted by whatever he would tell her.

"Matous Reyno was a very wealthy man. I am certain he had no debt."

She leaned back against the squabs. "Oh. Was he?"

"I'll have to ponder what you've told me. Nevertheless, I thank you for your help."

"You're very welcome, Sebastian." She smiled,

reached for the door and pushed it open. The rain was coming down in sheets. "Will you look at that!" she exclaimed. She moved as if she intended to launch herself through the opening.

Sebastian clumsily caught her hand before she could and bent over it, brushing his lips against her knuckles. Her skin felt soft beneath his lips and smelled a little like pastries. Heat began to spread through him, alarming him.

It was absurd—it was hardly a touch at all, but this irreverent woman had somehow wormed her way into his imagination. When he lifted his head, she was beaming at him. "It's been a true pleasure, Your Highness. I wish you the best of luck." And with that, she hopped out of the carriage and ran to the door of her home. Even with the rain he could hear the dogs barking wildly on the other side of it.

She turned around and waved, then disappeared inside, the door closing behind her.

She'd waved as if they were friends, and a strange sense of longing settled uncomfortably over Sebastian. He knocked on the ceiling, sending the carriage on, then fell back against the squabs, feeling a little morose. He was sorry that he wouldn't see the cluttered, warm house again. That he would not be faced with the spoiled little beasts. That he would not have to suffer the disdainful look of an unimpressed cat.

That he had these feelings at all was unsettling. It was absurd that he'd feel anything at all—it was a modest house, with ordinary people inside. But he did feel it. He felt it burning a hole in his chest.

Unfortunately, his longing was only sharpened when he reached Kensington. Servants stepped out of his path, courtiers curtsied and bowed, their smiles too sharp, too knowing. It was the deference that had been paid to him all his life, but he'd never really taken note of it until he'd lost that deference in Bedford Square.

Patro met him in his suite of rooms. His butler readily accepted the wet outer garments without hesitation or question.

Sebastian carried on into the sitting room and glanced around. The furnishings were quite expensive. Velvet upholstery with gilded legs. Massive paintings, marble hearths. Everything was neatly ordered, everything in its place. It was a palace after all.

But this sitting room, which he'd occupied for a fortnight, and would occupy at least a month if not longer, looked as if no one lived here at all. There was not a single personal touch. It needed, he thought, a ball of yarn.

Later, he joined his advisors in the dining room for supper and talk of the trade negotiations, which, in spite of everything else, were proceeding well. Sebastian glanced around at all the men gathered and wondered if he could trust any of them with what he'd learned. He eyed Rostafan surreptitiously but with particular attention, watching him eat heartily and speak louder than anyone else. He seemed unbothered by any care in this world.

But Sebastian needed help to seek the truth, and after dinner, when the other gentlemen retired to a drawing room for tobacco and whisky, he decided to trust Caius Anastasan, and drew his old acquaintance aside.

"Your Highness?" Caius asked expectantly.

"I need your help and your discretion," Sebastian said.

"Of course."

"Not even your wife can know what I ask," Sebastian warned him.

Caius looked surprised, but he didn't hesitate. "You have my word."

Still, Sebastian found it difficult to say what he wanted. It was a veiled accusation and a dire one to make. He looked at Caius's dark brown eyes and said, "I need to know if Rostafan has an unusually large debt."

Caius's brows dipped. "Pardon?"

Sebastian said nothing, allowing his foreign minister to work it out and reveal anything he might know. "What sort of debt?" Caius asked.

"I don't know. But one large enough that he would need the assistance of a banker to see it paid."

Caius pressed his lips together. "May I ask why?"

Sebastian debated how to answer his question. "Something has come to my attention and I don't know what to make of it. At present, I am looking for information. I'm not certain it's even relevant to...anything. I don't know how you will do it, Caius, but I want no one—" he paused and looked Caius directly in the eye "—*no one* to know that I've inquired. Especially not him."

Caius nodded. "I understand, Your Highness."

With nothing left to be said, Sebastian gestured to the door. "Shall we join the others?"

"If I may, sir?"

Sebastian nodded.

"You are acquainted with my wife, Sarafina."

"Of course." He'd known Lady Anastasan for many years. She was petite, her skin as pale white as Caius's was olive. She was always quick with a greeting and a smile. She was well liked, from what Sebastian knew.

"She has made a suggestion that bears your consideration, in my opinion. She suggested that she might serve as your secretary until our return to Alucia. She is quite adept at correspondence and calendars and the like."

In his grief, Sebastian hadn't thought about a replacement. He tried to picture Sarafina reviewing his schedule and responding to correspondence from home and the English government. He'd never had a woman in his employ, but he had to admit the idea intrigued him. If Sarafina was even half as clever as Miss Tricklebank—which seemed impossible—he could indeed use her services. "Send her round on the morrow to speak to me," he said.

Caius nodded, and the two of them joined the other men in the drawing room.

The following morning, Lady Anastasan was shown into Sebastian's sitting room. She'd brought freshly baked *molete*, a sweet pastry from Alucia. "An unexpected treat," Sebastian said, pleased by it.

"The queen once mentioned they are your favorite," she said with a winsome smile.

Yes, Sebastian thought, this might work very well. After some discussion, he offered her the position until they returned home to Helenamar.

The day after that, Caius was back with news: Rostafan had no significant debts. In fact, he'd recently come into quite a lot of money, as much as thirty thousand pounds.

That surprised Sebastian—that was a very large sum for a field marshal to come into. "How?"

"I couldn't ascertain," Caius said. "I should be able to learn it once we've returned home."

Sebastian nodded and thanked Caius, and said nothing more to him or anyone else.

But he couldn't get one thought out of his mind. He was probably sliding down a rabbit hole with his suspicion, chasing after something that wasn't even there. But it occurred to him that if Rostafan was involved, and if Matous had spoken to Mr. Heath on Rostafan's behalf, perhaps the need for the banker was not to borrow money—perhaps the need for a banker was to deposit a large sum of money out of sight.

Why Rostafan would need to do that was the question that plagued Sebastian. Another, more pressing question was why Matous would know of Rostafan's money at all. What could he possibly have had to do with it? And why would Rostafan need the services of a French banker? Why not Alucian?

The questions swirled in Sebastian's head through one long meeting after another in which he had to concentrate to discuss the terms of trading ore. He wished he had Leopold's counsel, but his brother had gone back to Cambridge and his studies. In Leopold's absence, he needed desperately to talk to someone.

Someone he could trust.

He knew precisely whose counsel he wanted—that of a woman whose image had been dancing around his mind's eye for two days now.

CHAPTER THIRTEEN

Alas, a pretty peacock who had hoped for wedding bells to ring across the Continent was not invited to dine with princely company at a ducal table of six-and-thirty at the home of Lord Rutland. Are the sins of the fathers visited upon the children?

Ladies, do have a care when walking the streets of London as a murderer still roams free.

—Honeycutt's Gazette of Fashion and Domesticity for Ladies

ELIZA HAD PICKED up all the yarn that Pris had strewn throughout the ground floor of the house. She'd walked the dogs down to the butcher's shop for a bone and had chatted with Mr. and Mrs. Thompkins about the infamous murder at Kensington Palace—without giving anything away, of course—and listening to all the speculation. Everyone in the butcher shop had an opinion. It hadn't happened at all, claimed one—the Alucians only claimed it had to gain favor with the queen. No, said another, it was a Whig plot to keep England from entering a disastrous trade agreement. Eliza's favorite theory came from Mrs. Thompkins. She claimed it could be none other than a jealous lover. Why else had no one seen men coming or going from his room? Because it was a lover, and she'd been smuggled in somehow.

From there, Eliza came home to help Margaret in the kitchen to store some vegetables and make dough. Afterward, she'd balanced the household accounts, read three legal briefs to her father and helped Poppy hang laundry in the garden. She repaired two clocks and sent them off with Ben to the homes of people who'd asked for her help.

She'd done everything she possibly could to distract herself from her thoughts, but it was no use. She could not stop thinking of that blasted prince, Mr. Chartier, the cart driver. She couldn't stop thinking of how his gaze had darkened, how he'd grabbed her hand before she'd stepped out of the carriage.

Her obsession was ridiculous. She'd gone from wanting to punch him square in the mouth to wanting desperately to kiss him. But it was so foolish! She could never take a prince as a lover, even if he was so inclined—that was another fantasy she'd allowed herself to enjoy—and it was absurd to entertain it.

It didn't help that Caroline and Hollis were almost rabid with their questions about him. Caroline had spotted him outside her house Saturday after the tea. Eliza had told them both that he'd come to call, but clearly, it was shockingly impactive to actually *see* him waiting for Eliza like a suitor than to hear of it.

Eliza had invited Caroline and Hollis to dine tonight because she was still seeking a distraction—something else, *anything* else—to think about.

Unfortunately, none of them could think of anything but the prince.

"You've lost all perspective, the three of you," the

judge said, having listened to them speculate as he ate his meal. "You shouldn't be thinking of foreign princes at all. It's beyond the bounds of lunacy if you ask me."

"I've got it!" Caroline said brightly to Eliza. "You might send the prince a note!"

"What sort of note?" Eliza asked curiously.

"One that tells him how pleased you are to have made his acquaintance, of course. Clearly, you are *quite* pleased." She laughed.

"Eliza should not be sending notes to anyone from Alucia," her father said sternly.

Hollis put a slab of bread on his plate and guided his hand to it. "Why not, Pappa? He must get notes from *everyone*. I know! We could invite him to dine."

"What, *here*?" Eliza exclaimed. "Would you have a prince sit at our scarred table?"

"There is not a thing wrong with our table," her father sniffed. "A few scars indicate a happy household and a life well lived."

"To a certain point," Eliza said. "You've not seen it in years, Pappa. It looks as if we dragged it through the street."

"Then I shall invite him," Hollis declared. "*My* table is not scarred."

"Don't be ridiculous," Eliza said. "Why would he come to your house? He doesn't even know you."

"Well, obviously, I hope to change that. Can you imagine what bits I could publish if I met him?"

"Hollis, don't be ridiculous," Caroline said. "Eliza, don't you *want* to see him again?"

What a foolish question—of course she did. "No woman in her right mind would not want to see a prince again, would she?"

"*You* didn't want to see one again just a few days ago," Hollis reminded her.

"Yes, well, I've changed my mind. I think I would like it very much," she said primly. "Under the right circumstances, of course."

"Of course," her father said firmly.

"But I think he would not want to see me," Eliza continued. "Surely the crown prince of Alucia has much more important things on his mind than some spinster in the middle of London."

"Surely," her father said gruffly. "Such as a trade agreement on which everything rests for Alucia. Surely *that*."

"Don't say *spinster* as if you are nothing," Hollis chastised Eliza as she poured more wine into her glass.

"Why not? I *am* a spinster. I'm not ashamed of it. Disappointed, perhaps, but not ashamed."

"I don't see why we must designate anything about ourselves at all. You're a spinster, I'm a widow, Caro is a debutante. We're all unmarried women. What difference should it make?"

Eliza could see her point, but she shrugged. She was a spinster, and even if her sister wanted to forget it, society would never allow her to, particularly after her spectacular fall from grace. She had discovered Mr. Daughton-Cress's perfidy and lies at a supper party, at the moment when the host had stood to announce his congratulations to Asher on his engagement.

Eliza had been so stunned that she hadn't realized she'd spoken until it was too late. "What?" she'd demanded loudly.

The seventeen heads around that table had all turned toward her.

"No, there must be some mistake," she'd said, while even as she spoke, she knew in her heart there was no mistake. That feeling was confirmed when she looked at Asher. And then she'd very nearly lost her mind.

Who could blame her? She'd done everything she was to do! She'd waited patiently and faithfully. She had given herself to him, she had planned her trousseau, she had foolishly believed every lie he'd told her, and in that moment she'd understood that he'd deceived her terribly, and she'd exploded into grief and anger.

She'd gained her feet. "Asher, is it true? Are you offering her what you have promised to offer *me*?"

Thank God Beck had been there to physically remove her before she'd said any more than she did. Eliza hadn't wanted to go, she'd wanted an explanation from a pale-faced Asher, but Beck wrapped his arms around and lifted her off her feet, carrying her from the room while Eliza shouted at Asher that he was a liar.

Once Beck had removed her, she'd collapsed in his arms. "He promised me!" she sobbed.

"For heaven's sake, Eliza, men freely promise things to have what they want," Beck had said. "Poor girl. I'm so very sorry this has happened, and you won't believe me now, but you're much better off without the bugger."

Eliza had been extremely careful with her affections since then—she'd withheld them completely. But many in society had long memories and could easily recall the scandal.

"You're all very lovely as far as I'm concerned," her father said, and pushed his plate away. "As much as I would love to remain at this scarred table and listen to a lot of wistful thinking about a foreign prince, I am tired and should like to retire. But before I go, I think

I must be the voice of reason here. Eliza, my darling, you suffered a great hurt once. I would not like to see that happen again, and it is my opinion that your gallivanting about with a prince who has no business with you cannot end well. Now, where is Ben?"

"I'll fetch him, Pappa," Hollis said.

Eliza helped her father to his feet, and when Ben came for him, the three women resumed their seats. Eliza sipped her wine as Margaret cleared the plates. Her thoughts kept sliding back to her few days in the company of a powerful man with arresting green eyes… until Hollis ruined it.

"Is there any word, Caro, on whether Katherine Maugham or Elizabeth Keene has gained any interest from the prince?" Hollis asked.

"I beg your pardon—I thought you were determined to put him with me," Eliza said.

Hollis laughed. "It's fun to pretend."

"No, but I *have* heard that Elizabeth Keene has caught the eye of Lord Prudhome." Caroline arched a brow.

"Really?" Hollis asked, perking up. "Everyone knows the Prudhome fortune is entailed for generations."

"Precisely," Caroline said with a wicked little gleam in her eye. "Which is why Lady Elizabeth's dowry looks so appealing to him. He's twenty years older than her if he's a day."

"Where is paper when I need it?" Hollis exclaimed and hopped up to search about the dining room.

"I've got some in the parlor," Eliza offered. She didn't want to hear the news of who would strike a marriage bargain with whom, and left the dining room and went to her desk. She found paper, and decided Hollis probably would be asking for a writing implement next. She picked up a pen and the inkwell, too. But the sudden barking of the dogs gave her heart such a start that she bobbled the well, and it slipped, sloshing ink onto her hand and the desk. "For heaven's sake, those dogs will be the death of me," she muttered as she used her finger to swipe up the spill.

But then a knock at the door gave her heart another start, and Eliza managed to smear the ink onto the palm and back of her hand. She used her apron to wipe it from her hands as she hurried to the door to open it.

Before she opened the door, however, she brushed a loose bit of her hair from her cheek with the back of her hand, then glanced down, realizing it was the hand smeared with ink. "On my *word*," she breathed irritably.

Whoever it was knocked again, and Jack and John threw their wretched little bodies at the door as if they meant to go through it.

"Jack! John! Come away from there!" Hollis shouted, having come into the hall to see what the commotion was about.

The dogs obediently turned and trotted to Hollis. She pointed toward the kitchen. "Off you go," she commanded them.

Eliza opened the door as her sister corralled them.

She heard Hollis's gasp—well, more of a shriek, really—before she herself could even draw a breath. But there he stood, the crown prince of Alucia, one elbow braced against the door frame, a hand on his waist. He was dressed in princely clothes, too, and not those of a cart driver. He was wearing a fine wool greatcoat that gaped open and revealed an elaborately embroidered waistcoat. His silk neckcloth was so perfectly tied she could imagine a small army of valets had constructed it together.

Eliza was struck so dumb by his appearance that she fixated on the neckcloth.

The neckcloth of a future king.

A future king who was standing at her door.

Again.

"Good evening, Miss Tricklebank," he said in his lovely accent. "My apologies for arriving unannounced."

She managed to tear her gaze from his neckcloth. "This is quite a surprise."

He smiled uncertainly. "Not an unpleasant one, I hope. I don't mean to intrude at this late hour, but I was in the vicinity."

Somewhere behind Eliza, she was vaguely aware of high-pitched voices in a distant room. "You were in the vicinity of Bedford Square?"

His wince was almost unnoticeable. "You seem skeptical."

"I am. Bedford Square is nowhere near Kensington Palace, which I am sure you've ascertained by now?"

"That may be true, but my acquaintances are far and wide." He dropped his arm from the door and glanced over his shoulder. Of course there were men standing on the sidewalk beside an ornate carriage. "And then again, perhaps I am near to Bedford Square because I, ah..." He looked back at her and said softly, "because I desired to be."

Well, then. Eliza's heart was going to claw right up her throat and go skipping off down the street. She needed a moment to think, but she could hear Hollis and Caroline fluttering behind her like a flock of sparrows.

The prince's gaze moved down the length of her and he murmured, where only she could hear, "I need some advice."

Advice? He'd come for *advice*? That was not what she'd hoped he meant. She had hoped he meant he'd come to take her to Alucia and marry her there or, at the very least, to whisk her off for a private tour of Kensington Palace. Just because a spinster was approaching her thirtieth year didn't mean she didn't harbor some lovely, romantic fantasies, and his seeking advice was definitely not one of them. "I see. Unfortunately, my father has retired for the evening."

"Your fa—Not from him, Eliza. From *you*."

And just like that, her fantasy came roaring back to life. She blushed. She thought herself so practical, and yet, she didn't know what she was to do in a situation like this. "You want advice from *me*?"

"If you would indulge me."

This man could have the advice of the finest minds in the country, and yet, here he was, seeking her advice. Advice he had not wanted before, she had to admit. She stared at him, trying to sort it out. "Why?"

His gaze moved over her, lingering on her chest. And then her waist. "I believe I can trust your discretion. And I believe you will be diligent in refusing to tell me what you think I might want to hear."

She couldn't help but smile at that. She supposed she ought to tell him that his assumption was wrong, and that she would tell Hollis and Caroline *every* word he said. Or that she wasn't so bold or brazen that she wouldn't couch her words to make them more palatable than her actual thoughts. But then she glanced past him, to the men and the coach on the street.

"They will drive on and come round for me in a half hour if you agree to see me. We'll not call attention to your residence and I won't take much of your time."

Too late for that, she reckoned—everyone on the square had probably noticed his grand carriage by now. Nevertheless, she must be living a dream—Prince Sebastian was actually asking her if she would deign to see him, and the realization made her feel hot and thrilled and maybe a little nauseated. "My sister and my friend have come to dine."

"Just a few moments, please," he said, and he looked as if he feared she would not grant him even that.

How could she deny him? She didn't *want* to deny him. In fact, now that she'd gotten her bearings, she very much wanted him to come in if only to parade him in front of Hollis and Caroline. So she opened the door a little wider. "Welcome."

The prince turned around and nodded at the men. They moved at once, two of them jumping onto the coach as it pulled away from the curb. She stepped inside, pressing herself against the wall so he could pass her. He paused in the middle of the foyer to remove his greatcoat and drape it over his arm. He was wearing Alucian clothing beneath the greatcoat—the long waistcoat, the longer coat. And on his chest, he wore a ribbon badge, and at the center, gold and diamonds in some sort of crest.

She turned, intending to invite him into the parlor, but Hollis and Caroline were there, both of them staring at him in astonishment and, for once, both of them remarkably speechless. Caroline was the first to gather her wits, sinking into a perfect curtsy and tugging at Hollis's gown to do the same.

"Ah…if I may?" Eliza said, stepping around the prince. "May I introduce my sister, Mrs. Hollis Honeycutt," she said. "And my dear friend, Lady Caroline Hawke."

The prince looked at Hollis. "You must be Mrs. Honeycutt of *Honeycutt's Gazette*."

Clearly delighted he would know her gazette, Hollis beamed with pride. "I am indeed, Your Royal Highness."

"Lady Caroline, how do you do," he said inclining his head.

"I am… I am well," she stammered. Neither she nor Hollis could stop staring at the prince with wide, dazed eyes and glossy smiles. Eliza couldn't help but feel a bit smug about it, too—for once, she was the one with the dazzling news and was not living vicariously through their adventures.

The prince clasped his hands at his back and politely waited.

Caroline grabbed Hollis's hand and gave it a squeeze. "I've had the pleasure of meeting Prince Leopold." She was practically levitating.

"Ah, Leo. And where did you meet him?"

"Last summer, at a country house near Chichester."

Eliza hoped to high heaven that Caroline didn't mean to review the brief encounter she'd had with the younger prince in the detail she normally reserved for her and Hollis.

"Leopold is fond of the beautiful English countryside. I think it almost as beautiful as Alucia." Sebastian smiled. Hollis and Caroline twittered like silly girls. Eliza began to fret that they'd make complete cakes of themselves. The prince must have feared it, too, because he turned to look at her. "Miss Tricklebank, if we might have that word?"

Caroline's and Hollis's eyes widened even more.

"Of course," Eliza said smoothly, and motioned toward the parlor. He waited for her to precede him, and she started in that direction. So did her sister and her friend. Eliza stopped, smiled sweetly and said, "If you would be so kind as to wait in the dining room?"

Hollis's mouth fell open.

Caroline put her hand on Hollis's arm, pulling her back. "Of course!" she said, as if that was what she'd intended all along. And even as she pretended to be the courteous, reasonable one, she was craning her neck to see around Eliza to the prince.

Eliza walked into the parlor and the prince followed her. She quietly shut the door behind her, turned around and leaned against it. "I must apologize for—"

"Not at all." He pointed at her cheek. "Have you been painting?"

"Painting?" She suddenly remembered the ink. "Oh! I blame the dogs entirely. Not that they were painting." She gave a nervous little laugh. Of course they hadn't been painting, why would she say that? "Neither was I. No one was painting! I mean that they startled me half out of my wits while I was holding an inkwell."

"I think they startled all of Bedford Square half out of their wits."

She self-consciously rubbed at her cheek.

The prince moved closer, frowning at the ink. He took a handkerchief from an interior pocket. "May I?"

She hesitated, and he stepped closer and dabbed at the ink on her cheek. His gaze roamed her face as he did, leaving a trail of heat in her skin. "There we are. That's most of it."

She was certain her blush was as red as an apple. She touched her cheek where he'd swiped the ink from her skin. She felt a bit dizzy. No, not dizzy, precisely. It was more like she was on fire. Yes, that was it. She was on fire.

But the prince moved away, wandering around the room, looking at things. Her clocks. The painting of a dog she'd done many years ago. The stacks of books and papers.

He turned back to the mantel. "You have a lot of clocks."

"Yes. I repair them."

He looked at her with surprise. "You?"

She gave another nervous little laugh and fidgeted with the hem of her sleeve. She didn't think *clock repair* was the sort of thing one should admit when one wanted to impress a prince. "It's a hobby. People bring me their clocks and I repair them. Or I buy broken ones and repair them." She shrugged. "It keeps me busy."

He looked at the clocks again.

"Do you have a hobby, Your Highness?"

He looked at her sidelong. "I thought we were friends."

She smiled. "Do you have a hobby, Sebastian?"

"Not an exciting one, I'm afraid. Recently, I've undertaken the chronicling of Alucian military history. Would that be considered a hobby?"

"It may only be thought a hobby if no tutor is forcing you to do it." She giggled at her own jest. She had a tendency to laugh at herself when her nerves were jangled.

"But how interesting that must be," she added quickly. Lest he think she was laughing at him. She was not.

He gave her a rueful smile, almost as if someone had dared to laugh at him about this before. "You needn't pretend that you find it anything more than tedious. I am aware it does not evoke the proper image most people seem to have of princes. It is a solitary occupation, but as my life does not lend itself to more public sorts of hobbies, I find it an interesting way to pass the time when necessary."

"Oh, but I don't think it tedious!" she hastened to assure him. "I read history to my father quite a lot. He says a society without history is a like a tree without roots."

"Yes." He nodded, and appeared almost intrigued.

The Lord knew her father offered opinions on so many things she scarcely thought about them at all. She gestured to the couch. "Would you care to sit?"

He indicated she should sit first, and when she'd settled on one end, he sat on the other, pushing the hem of his coat out, then sitting on the edge of the couch, one arm braced against what looked like a very firm and powerful thigh.

Eliza faced the fire and tried not to look at him. She'd gone completely round the bend, apparently, because she couldn't seem to keep from ogling him. "Well, then!" She sat up straighter. "How may I help you?"

"I don't have a question as much as I have a need to discuss. My brother has returned to Cambridge and there is no one else in whom I have complete confidence."

It was a stunning admission, and Eliza was taken aback. "Do you have confidence in me?"

He looked almost disconcerted by her question. "Should I not?"

"Yes! That is, I will tell you true, you have my word. But you scarcely know me—"

"And in the short time that I have, you have been unfailingly and brutally honest with me." He smiled lopsidedly. "I can't say the same for others."

This pleased her enormously, and she straightened in her seat a little more. "What is it you would like to discuss?"

He shifted his gaze to the fire. "It has to do with Matous. I have been mulling over what he might have been after in speaking to Mr. Heath, particularly in light of what Miss Heath has said and the fact that Matous had no significant debt. None that would require a loan of any sort."

"Oh." That was curious—Miss Heath seemed rather sure that it was an issue of a debt.

"Field Marshal Rostafan, however, has come into a sizeable fortune, the origins of which are unclear."

"Oh." That was interesting. "But what has that to do with Mr. Reyno's conversation with Mr. Heath?"

"I don't know, exactly. But I think it is possible that Matous was speaking to Mr. Heath on Rostafan's behalf."

"Is it?" she asked.

"You think it is too far-fetched?" he asked.

"Me?" She realized he was studying her. He looked as if he really wanted to know what she thought. That was certainly a new experience for her. While her father valued her opinion, Mr. Frink and the barristers who came around could hardly concern themselves with what she thought about anything. Wouldn't they be surprised to know that Prince Sebastian wanted to know what she thought? Wouldn't they be surprised to know that he actually valued her opinion? His interest in what she had to say was exhilarating.

"Why do you suppose the young woman characterized the conversation about it as a debt?" he asked.

Eliza thought back to the exact words Miss Heath had said. *My father said there was some discussion of a debt.* But she hadn't said what sort of debt, and Eliza and Caroline had assumed it was a debt of money, as the parties in question were bankers. That made the most sense, but it occurred to her now that it could have been something else. "What if it was not that sort of debt?" she said aloud. "What if the conversation had been about a type of debt, and not necessarily one that involved money?"

"I don't understand," Sebastian said.

"Such as a debt of gratitude. Or a debt of favor owed."

The prince pondered this. He stood and walked to the window, his hands on his waist. He suddenly turned around. "You may very well be right, Eliza."

There it was again, her name said in his rich, deep voice, and she was thrilled all over again. She was easily thrilled in general in his company, she was learning.

"I think I should speak with the banker directly. I'll have him to dine at Kensington."

"What? *No,*" she said instantly, and stood, too.

"I should speak to him directly, and as you have pointed out, I can hardly go to him."

"But neither can you invite him without proper introduction. Can you imagine the speculation? If he knows anything at all, he'd be on guard. No, Sebastian, you need to meet him and speak with him naturally, as you would if you encountered him at an event. At a supper party, for example."

The prince groaned. "Surely by now I've dined at every available house in London."

Not at hers, but again, there was the issue of the terribly scarred table. And the dogs. And various and sundry other things that didn't seem appropriate for a prince. "I could arrange it." The words tumbled out of her mouth and she instantly regretted it, because what on earth was she saying? She had no society, not really, and lived vicariously through her sister and dearest friend. How could she *possibly* arrange a supper that would include a banker she'd never met and a prince she should have *never* met?

Sebastian looked dubious, too.

"I could," she stubbornly insisted, because nothing was worse than being forced to admit in the next breath that she didn't know what she was doing. "Caroline would help me. If Lord Hawke can't be persuaded to host it, she knows everyone in Mayfair. She could easily arrange a supper party and invite dozens if she liked." Yes, that sounded entirely plausible.

He eyed her studiously. "You would do that for me?"

Good Lord, he believed her. Of *course* she would do it for him. She couldn't say why she was so willing to get involved in a matter her father had expressly commanded her to stay away from, other than a need to prove something to herself and—yes, all right—to be in his company. But she was so uncertain as to how she might actually make her boast happen that she had to look away from his intense gaze.

What in blazes was the matter with her? Why was

she saying things she knew she couldn't possibly do? "There must be some occasion that I can find where you and Mr. Heath will both be in attendance."

She could feel his gaze on her and made her situation worse by declaring, "In the meantime, I intend to keep an eye out for the man who delivered the note. I've seen him in the markets from time to time." She should have thought of this before.

"No, it's too dangerous," he said with a firm shake of his head. "I won't allow it."

"I beg your pardon?"

"I know," he said, putting his hand up before she could argue. "You will not accept a command from me, as I am not your prince. But in this I insist. It's wrong enough that I'm searching for answers instead of leaving it to the proper authorities, but to have you search as well is unacceptable. I've no idea who is behind Reyno's death. It could be an entire nation. It could be very dangerous, Eliza."

Nothing set Eliza's teeth on edge more than a man telling her *no*, as if he was her husband or father. "I go to Covent Garden several times a week. You can't stop me from walking through."

"Then I will accompany you."

"You can't! You'd be noticed at once. *Haut monde* gentlemen are not common on Bedford Square. My father is as *haut monde* as they come. And they are certainly not seen in the markets."

"No one knows if I am *haut monde* or not," he said sternly, as if he found the suggestion that he carried himself like a future king to be both insulting and absurd.

"You move with the confidence of a man who will one day be king."

He snorted. "There's a look to it, is that it?"

"There is."

He grunted some remark and walked to the window and looked out, as if pondering this fact.

"What are you doing?" Eliza exclaimed. "Come away from there—everyone on this square is watching this house. They saw your coach, they saw your clothes."

"What must they think, Eliza? That you've received a gentleman caller in the night?" He smiled, apparently pleased with the idea.

"They will think that the caller has come for my father, as they always do. Please step aside so I may close the drapes."

He didn't move.

Eliza pushed her way in front of him, her back against his chest, and yanked the drapes shut. And still he didn't move. She cleared her throat and turned around. He didn't move as much as an inch, so she was still squeezed in between the window and him. So close to him that she could see the folds in the knot of his neckcloth. Or the tiny script on the medal he wore on his chest. She could see the way his beard had begun to show itself again, and how his mouth tipped up in one corner in a grin of amusement, ending in a soft dimple. She could see the low light in his green eyes and could feel that light rushing through her.

He was staring into her eyes, almost as if he was searching for something there. Eliza could feel her nerves crackling like fire on a new log. They stood so *close*. The air around them was charged with the heat between them.

Sebastian lifted his hand and slid two fingers very

carefully beneath her chin, hardly touching her at all, and slowly tipped her face up. Her skin turned to gooseflesh with anticipation. She knew what she *wanted* him to do. She knew what *she* wanted desperately to do. She was bold and she was brazen, but when it came down to the moment, she didn't have the courage to kiss a crown prince. So if he didn't kiss her, if he continued to stand there and look at her like he was that very moment, she would disintegrate. There were no degrees of disintegration for her—it would be complete.

"You've been a tremendous help to me, Eliza."

Oh, but the way he says my name. She swallowed. "I'm happy to be of any assistance."

The tip of his tongue skirted over his bottom lip as he considered her. His fingers traced a feathery line from her chin, down her neck, to her collarbone. "I don't know how to properly thank you." This, he said to her mouth, and the flames of the fire began to lick at her spine, little waves of heat scorching through her.

"There is really no need," she said to his lips.

"There is every need." He lowered his head, his mouth so close to hers. He hesitated, as if he wasn't certain what he meant to do. "Do not search for the delivery man, do you hear me?" he murmured, and touched his soft, rose-petal lips to hers.

Eliza closed her eyes. She thought she might have sighed. It had been so long since she'd been kissed, so long since she'd felt a man's touch. It had been so long since her hopeful life had ended and her life of the invisible spinster had begun.

He deepened the kiss. Still soft, but insistent. Easy, but demanding. She was feeling things cracking open, things she'd not felt properly in a very long time. She was sparkling. Blood and bone were sparkling in her, and the heat was running a course over and over in her, down to her toes and fingers, and up again, to her head and her heart.

He slipped his tongue into her mouth. Eliza moaned softly. She shifted closer, so that her body was fully touching his. His arm went round behind her back and pulled her tighter to him. She could feel the hardness of his body pressed against hers from her knees to her chest. He was a rock, all muscle and sinew, and she angled her head and slid her hands up his firm chest. Was she allowed to do that? She couldn't stop herself from doing it. She was not going to have a virile man, a prince, kiss her and stand like a chaste log, oh no. She was going to squeeze every bit of pleasure out of it. *Gather round, children. I once met a royal prince and I kissed him.*

She put her arms around his neck and tangled her fingers in his hair. She pressed her breasts against his chest, and if she could have, she would have crawled inside his coat. He smelled lovely—sandalwood and rosewood and something else delicate and heady. His body was so firm beneath her touch, and in spite of his clothing, she could feel the hard planes, the breadth of his muscles in his shoulders and arms.

She had sunk into him, had pressed against his chest. *I am burning.* She was a blaze in a winter's hearth, a burning effigy on Guy Fawkes Night. She was a conflagration of hope and lust and tingling so intense that she could hardly think.

And then it was over.

Sebastian lifted his head. His eyes skated over her face and lingered on her mouth as he deliberately ran his thumb across her bottom lip. He kissed her forehead and stepped back. "I should...perhaps I should go."

"Go?" she asked dizzily. She was reeling from that kiss. She didn't move. She *couldn't* move. It was as if her entire body had been paralyzed with desire.

He touched his fingers to her chin. "No sleuthing about Covent Garden. Good night, Eliza."

"Good night, Sebastian," she said with an old, ingrained meekness that normally would have annoyed her, but in the moment it was all she could manage. She hadn't yet gained control of her body.

She watched him walk across the room. She heard him go out the door, his footfall down the steps, to the carriage that had undoubtedly come around. She drew a breath and remained standing in the very spot he'd met her wildest dreams and kissed her.

She heard the dogs barking in the kitchen, Ben or Margaret walking around the sitting room overhead. She heard Hollis's and Caroline's voices drifting out of the dining room.

She didn't move. There she stood, a charred effigy, burned up by a single kiss.

CHAPTER FOURTEEN

A formal supper at the home of Lord Stanley saw an abundance of trains on the evening gowns of English ladies, though not as lavishly embroidered or as long as the Alucian trains. Wide sleeves are a must. Printed silk is vogue, with beading along the bodice in a trend one hopes will continue into the spring Season.

New information suggests that if a lady wishes to enjoy a romp without consequence, trotting a horse briskly the day after the romp should remove said consequence. If the lady does not have access to horseflesh, vigorous jumping up and down immediately after the act may be substituted.

—Honeycutt's Gazette of Fashion and Domesticity for Ladies

SEBASTIAN HAD UNDONE his neckcloth and had handed off his greatcoat by the time he strode into his suite of rooms at Kensington. He had scarcely noticed the footmen who took his hat and gloves, had scarcely looked at the chambermaid who scurried out of his path and out of sight.

He was thinking of a kiss.

He was thinking of a kiss in a way he'd never thought

of a kiss before. Generally, when he kissed a woman, his goal was simple—he wanted to bed her. There had been many infatuations through the years, many tender kisses. But all of them had come from a need that was not rooted in his heart, but in his groin.

Sebastian wasn't so smitten as to think that kissing Eliza had come from the heart, exactly. He couldn't really say where the kiss had come from, other than it had been remarkably…fresh.

He wanted more of the fresh.

His thoughts full of Eliza, he was caught off guard by the presence of Lady Anastasan. She quickly rose from her seat at his desk and sank into a deep curtsy.

Sebastian looked at her. He looked at the desk.

"I've put your weekly schedule on the desk, Your Highness," she said, bowing her head. "Please forgive the intrusion."

She'd been tidying up, too, it would seem. Some documents he'd left in a spread across his desk had been neatly stacked. "Thank you." He didn't know quite what to make of this. He hadn't asked her to tidy up. He hadn't asked her to do anything other than take notes. He walked cautiously into the room, glancing around, looking for other changes. Other people, perhaps?

Lady Anastasan lingered, standing uncertainly next to his desk.

"Is there something you wish to say?"

"No, Your Highness. Rather, I…ah… I wondered how you're getting on."

How he was *getting on*? What an odd question. He couldn't think of a time that Matous had asked him how he was getting on.

"You've been through so much, Your Highness. I thought perhaps that you might need…help."

"I am well." He turned away from the desk. This felt wrong to him. He didn't expect his staff to inquire after his well-being.

"Is there anything I might help with? Anything at all?"

Sebastian glanced curiously over his shoulder at her. "No. Thank you, Sarafina."

She smiled a little thinly and glanced at her feet. He had the impression she had something else to say, but Patro chose that moment to enter the room. *"Bon notte, mae principae,"* he said with a bow. "Shall I send Egius?"

"Bon notte," Sebastian responded to his greeting. "Not yet. I should like to read first."

Patro nodded. His gaze flicked over Lady Anastasan before he went through another door.

Lady Anastasan, however, remained. Sebastian was growing impatient with her. "Is there more, Sarafina?"

"No, Your Highness." She touched an earlobe. "I don't want you to think…that is, I want you to know that I am here because I didn't want to leave your things unattended."

"What things?"

She looked confused by the question. "Your things? Rostafan was in earlier, you see, and he said that the correspondence pouch contained sensitive information—"

"Rostafan?"

Lady Anastasan blinked big brown eyes. "*Je*, Your Highness."

"When was that?"

"Oh, an hour or two at least."

Rostafan had been at the supper at the home of Lord Stanley, as had Sebastian. When they'd left, Rostafan had said he meant to ride along with Mr. Botley-Finch to a gentlemen's club on Bond Street.

So when, exactly, had he come here and left a pouch of sensitive correspondence?

"Is something wrong?" Lady Anastasan asked.

"No. Thank you, madam. You may go."

She seemed reluctant, but curtsied and went out of the room as he'd requested.

Sebastian sat down at his desk and called for his butler.

Patro appeared almost instantaneously. "Sir?"

Sebastian leaned back in his chair, propped his feet on the desk and templed his fingers as he considered his butler. "I've a hypothetical question for you."

Patro clasped his hands behind his back and waited.

"Do you think it is possible to have a private supper in these rooms? Without anyone knowing who dined here in my company?"

Patro looked around him as if to acquaint himself with these rooms. "I should think it theoretically possible."

"Possible, but not probable?"

"*Je*, Your Highness."

"Mmm," Sebastian mused. "Another hypothetical question for you. If a man wanted to dine privately with someone, where might he do so?"

"I would suggest he let a home. Or have someone in his trust do that for him."

That was not a bad idea. "No one would know?"

"I think it could be arranged, sir. Would we expect His Royal Highness Prince Leopold to dine?"

Sebastian shook his head.

Patro nodded. He'd been Sebastian's butler for a very long time and knew Sebastian well.

"I'd need a way to come and go without being seen by either Alucian or Englishman. Except, of course, those who serve."

"I should be delighted to serve, sir," Patro said evenly.

"And I'd need someone to fetch the person. With all due discretion, of course."

"Of course, Your Highness, as you wish."

Was this what he wished? Sebastian didn't know. He had so many feelings that he could scarcely think. Exuberance. Dread. Contentment. Agitation. All of those feelings seemed to apply to him right now in equal measure. This sounded like something Leopold would do, and something Sebastian would caution him against doing.

But damn it, he very much liked Eliza Tricklebank. He liked her forthright manner and the way she kissed him as if she feared he might disappear if she let go. He wanted to see her, to be alone with her without a cat watching or people listening around the doors. Was it possible for him to have this one thing?

"You're certain?" Sebastian asked. "It can be done?"

"I would need assistance," Patro said. "May I suggest Egius? The man would die on a sword before he'd utter a word."

Sebastian smiled. "*Je*, Egius."

"Then I am certain. If you like, I can make some very discreet inquiries about the let of a house."

Patro was a married man with five children at home in Alucia. Sebastian wondered what Patro must think of his prince. He wondered if he understood the invisible bars that surrounded Sebastian in everything he did, and how there were times, like now, that he desperately wanted to break free of those invisible bars.

Whatever Patro thought would be carefully hidden behind his inscrutable expression. "You have my leave to make inquiries," Sebastian said. "Come to me with what you find."

Patro bowed and went out.

Sebastian watched him go, as efficient in his stride as he was in his duties. With a sigh he turned to the pouch of correspondence on his desk. He picked up the pouch and noticed the small leather strap that bound it together was untied. Had Rostafan done that? Or Lady Anastasan? He opened the pouch and withdrew the papers.

There were communiqués from Helenamar. Documents he'd requested having to do with outstanding trade items to be negotiated. A schedule of tides for the next two months so that he could plan the Alucian contingent's departure.

How could he leave England without knowing who had killed Matous?

He put the papers in the pouch and tied the strap. He laid it down on his desk and stared at it. Frankly, he couldn't imagine Rostafan being particularly careful with the thin strap that bound the pouch. If he'd wanted to have a look, he would have ripped the strap in half. But why would Rostafan have even bothered? Whatever was in this pouch would be briefed to him on the morrow.

Then who had opened it? Lady Anastasan? What interest could she have? Would Patro have done it? No.

Patro would sooner die than touch something that belonged to Sebastian without his permission.

Sebastian sat at his desk for a very long time, thinking through who might have looked in the pouch, and what they might have been looking for.

But gradually, his thoughts turned to Eliza Tricklebank with the curious smear of ink on her fair cheek.

CHAPTER FIFTEEN

A birthday soirée to be held in Mayfair, featuring the finest ales from a distinctive brewery, in honor of the birthday of a young woman who will undoubtedly be quite sought after when she makes her debut next spring, assuming she is not soon snatched off the marriage mart by a princely gesture.

It also has been said that a young man only recently come into the title of earl is eager to marry and settle his ancient seat with heirs so that he may quickly flutter back to the pretty bird with the warbling voice on the Strand.

Ladies, a half teaspoon of sugar added to a proper starch mixture will keep your petticoats stiffer for longer. This remedy has not yet been tested on husbands.

—Honeycutt's Gazette of Fashion and Domesticity for Ladies

CAROLINE AND HOLLIS made Eliza review everything that happened between her and the prince twice through. Each time, they fell into cries of utter delight when Eliza recounted the kiss, still breathless with the excitement of it. Where did he put his hands, they asked. Did he apologize for taking such liberty? *How was the kiss?*

Eliza laughed along with them, but there were no words to describe what she'd experienced. They were teasing her, she knew, thinking it all a lark, but it was no lark for her. That kiss had awakened something in her, had aroused her to at least a healthy lust, if not something more.

She couldn't stop thinking about it. She couldn't stop wishing for more of it, for all of him. She couldn't stop wanting all the things that had been denied her when she'd fallen in love with the reprobate Asher Daughton-Cress.

She was not without experience in these things and knew very well what she wanted. Asher had lured her into his bed between his whispered promises that an offer would be made forthwith, the bloody bounder. She should have known—his kisses had been too urgent, too demanding. In hindsight, it was quite clear that he'd been looking for a portal to slake his thirst. He'd used her and left her to bear the mark of a fool.

The kiss from the prince was more reverent than any of Asher's ever had been. She sensed that his thirst was vastly different from Asher's.

And so was hers.

She pondered this the next day as she wandered around the house, humming to herself, trying in vain to make some sense of this sudden new phenomenon in her life.

She had clumsily dropped some books she was carrying in the afternoon, and when Poppy dipped down to help her pick them up, she said, "All right, then, I can't hold my tongue another moment. What has happened?"

"Happened?" Eliza asked, confused as they rose to their feet.

"Aye, happened! You've been wandering about in a fog all bloody day! Something has happened and I'll know what it is. Is it the judge? Is he ill?"

"No." Eliza laughed self-consciously. Poppy had been out last night. She had no idea that Sebastian had come again. "I'm preoccupied, I suppose."

"With what?"

Eliza looked at the door of her sitting room and quickly went to close it so that Ben or Margaret would not hear. "Last night, while you were away, the prince came to call."

Poppy gasped. *"Again?"*

"Again," Eliza spoke low and felt the smile on her lips. Oh, blast it—it was impossible to keep that telling smile from her face.

Poppy frowned. "But why?"

"He wanted to discuss something with me. He said Prince Leopold had returned to Cambridge, and he had no one else with whom he could discuss the matter." Her grin was getting larger.

Poppy's frown went deeper. "All right," she said, folding her arms across her body.

"He did indeed need to discuss something, but..." Good Lord, she was *giggling.* "He kissed me."

Poppy stared at her.

Eliza giggled again. *"Ah!"* she said to the ceiling. "I can't stop smiling and giggling and I—"

Poppy sat so hard in a chair that Eliza thought she'd fallen.

"Poppy! What is the matter?" Eliza exclaimed.

Poppy shook her head. "You will be lost to us."

Eliza laughed. "What are you talking about?"

Poppy lifted her gaze from the floor. "You are the one he will choose, Eliza."

"Oh, *Lord*," Eliza said. "Have you been going round to the palm reader again?"

She meant it as a jest, but Poppy stood up, clearly offended. "I can't speak of this now. I can't." She started for the door.

"Poppy, what in heaven is the matter?" Eliza said after her. "He will not choose *me*. A man like that must make a match with someone of significant standing."

But Poppy wouldn't hear it. She opened the door and went out of the room. Eliza heard her run up the stairs. She sighed and sank down onto the chair Poppy had vacated. The poor dear didn't understand the way these things worked.

But Eliza very firmly understood it, and she harbored no illusions whatsoever.

IF POPPY FEARED losing Eliza to a foreign land, Hollis and Caroline began to fear she might be losing her mind. That she'd made too much of it. That perhaps she had instigated it. *They* did not believe her in any danger of being whisked off to Alucia.

They were at Caroline's that evening, admiring the new gowns Caroline had commissioned. Eliza couldn't help wonder how she might possibly hide them all from Beck, but Caroline seemed unconcerned. Later, they sat down to dine on roast beef and potatoes, strawberries that had been brought up from the southern part of England at a dear price, and wine.

Talk naturally turned to the prince, but Eliza had something else on her mind that evening. "I promised him a supper party or something like it."

"You what?" Hollis said. "Why would you promise such a thing?"

"Because Sebas—" She caught herself. "The prince desires to speak to Mr. Heath. He intended to invite him to Kensington!"

"So?" Caroline said.

"If he was invited to Kensington, the entire government would think it had to do with the trade agreement. I said I thought he should do it in a place so crowded no one would think anything of him exchanging a few words. Do you see? It's not as…official."

"Oh, *Eliza*," Caroline said. She put down her fork. She glanced at the open door of the dining room and abruptly stood. She walked to the door and closed it very quietly, then hurried back to the table. "We can't risk Beck hearing this, can we? Now listen, Eliza," she said, and pushed her plate aside, folded her arms on the table and leaned forward. "Darling, you've met your prince. You've had your kiss! But that must be the end of it, mustn't it?"

"The end of what, exactly?" Eliza asked.

"You're trying, very gamely, to solve a *murder*," Caroline said. "What do you know about murder? You can't possibly carry on with this."

Eliza bristled. "I don't see why not. You seemed quite at ease carrying on with this when we invited Miss Heath for tea. And you, Hollis, started the whole thing by printing the note."

"Well, that was different," Caroline said. "I wanted to get a good look at Miss Heath. And Hollis always prints the gossip."

"And Eliza, you agreed to printing it!" Hollis reminded her. "You *helped* me do it."

"Dearest, what you're doing is madness," Caroline said. "You're cavorting with the *crown prince* of Alucia! It borders on ridiculous."

Eliza gasped. "I am *not* ridiculous, Caro! And I'm not cavorting, for God's sake. You can't disagree that there is something awfully wrong about this. No one seems to care that a man was murdered in his own bed."

"I think we all know what is really happening here," Hollis offered.

"Do we, indeed?" Eliza drawled.

Hollis reached for her hand and squeezed it. "You're falling in love with him."

"Oh, for the love of Pete," Eliza groused. She yanked her hand from Hollis's and fell back in her chair.

"You're charmed by him," Hollis continued. "And it's been very exciting, even from our perspective."

So they'd been discussing her. *Poor, dear Eliza, the spinster who fell in love with a prince.* "It *has* been very exciting. But I'm not a fool. You both know how practical I am."

"Not anymore you're not," Caroline said with a sympathetic wince. "Don't you understand? We don't want to see your hurt again, that's all."

"I won't be *hurt*," Eliza said petulantly. She loved them dearly, but Caroline and Hollis seemed to doubt her emotional capacity. That was what an outburst at a supper party did for you—no one would ever again believe that you could bear up to disappointment. "The two of you have been eager for every detail of my encounters with him, and suddenly you're concerned for me?"

"It's not that," Hollis said. "It's been quite diverting. But he's kissed you, and it seems more intense now. I would not want to see you hurt, and if you allow yourself to get entangled, you *will* be hurt. He'll go back to Alucia with a marriage agreement and a fiancée who brings a very large dowry and influence in the English government. And besides, if you keep chasing ideas about a murderer, you may be physically harmed, as well."

"You think I believe in fairy tales," Eliza accused them. "You think I'm unsophisticated in the ways of the world, as proven by my horrible mistake with Asher."

"That is not true," Caroline said. "I would say this to Hollis just as readily."

Eliza didn't believe that, and didn't know if this conversation made her angry or sorrowful. Life wasn't the same for her as it was for them. She didn't meet gentlemen every day like Caroline. She hadn't been happily married as Hollis had once been. She knew she wasn't as fashionable as the two of them, that she was not invited to soirées around town. But she was *not* naive. Not anymore.

She slowly sat up, looked at Caroline and said, "I need a supper party or something like it. I'm asking you as my friend to help me."

Caroline's eyes widened. "I can't possibly have one here. Beck would never allow it, not for something like this."

"Then surely you know someone who will."

"Eliza! One cannot simply conjure up a party—"

The door suddenly swung open with a bang and Beck strode into the room, drawing up when he saw them all at the table. "Lord. Are you all here *again*? Is there no food in your house, Eliza? Or yours, Hollis?"

"Your food is better," Hollis said, and popped a strawberry into her mouth.

Beck rolled his eyes and sauntered forward. He held a stack of correspondence in his hand and tossed an envelope onto the table. It slid across the polished surface to Caroline.

"What is this?" she asked, picking it up.

"It would appear to be an invitation."

She opened the envelope and withdrew thick vellum and unfolded it, her eyes scanning the page. "Juliana Whitbread is having a grand party in honor of her birthday," she announced.

"Now that will be quite the affair," Beck said as he looked at the rest of the post. "I should think all the important people will be invited to attend." He glanced up at them. "Not any of you, naturally. People of significance. Not those who conjure up my imaginary attachment to a miss who is blind as a bat and print the damn thing."

"Ah," Hollis said. "It would seem you *do* read the gazette. You're peeved."

"*Peeved*, Mrs. Honeycutt, does not begin to describe what I thought of your made-up gossip. I hold absolutely no esteem for Miss Lucille Heath."

"Are you certain?" Eliza asked sweetly.

"Why are you two always here?" Beck demanded.

"Who will attend this party?" Hollis asked curiously, accustomed as she was to completely ignoring Beck.

"You wouldn't know them," Beck said.

"You might be surprised," Hollis chirped and ate another strawberry.

"Well, *I* know them," Caroline said. "Who is coming?"

"Everyone," Beck said. "The princes you're all so agog about."

Eliza, Caroline and Hollis exchanged a look.

"Mr. Heath?" Eliza asked.

"Who in bloody hell is Mr. Heath?"

"The banker!" Caroline exclaimed. "Whose daughter you've been rumored to be considering for matrimony." She giggled.

Beck glared at Hollis again. "Probably. Half of Parliament will be there. It's to be quite the affair, an autumn carnival designed to entice the Earl of Leicester to offer for the young beauty, Miss Whitbread. Her father is an ambitious man."

"Not the prince of Alucia?" Hollis asked.

Beck snorted. "Undoubtedly, his august person has been invited to spur the earl. But there is no question an alliance with Leicester is what is desired. Everyone knows it."

"I know Juliana very well," Caroline remarked.

"Bully for you," Beck drawled.

"The invitation is addressed to us both, Beck."

He looked through more of the correspondence. "I don't intend to waste a day petting monkeys and watching a spoiled daughter swan about."

"Why not?" Eliza asked. "Are you in love with her?"

Hollis giggled.

Beck groaned. He looked around at the three of them. "What have I ever done to deserve this? What? You may send my regrets, Caro. I'm not going."

"I never doubted that for a moment."

"Hollis, God help you if you eat all the strawberries," Beck warned. "They were not purchased for you."

"All right," she said cheerfully as he turned and

walked out of the room. When he'd gone, she ate another strawberry.

"Well, Eliza, I think we have your event," Caroline said, waving the invitation at her.

"But I'm not invited," Eliza pointed out. Not that she needed to be there for the prince to make Mr. Heath's acquaintance, but still, she felt she ought to be there.

And she desperately wanted to be there to see him again.

"No, but *I'm* invited, and as Beck is not planning to attend, I will bring my very dear friend. Juliana won't mind in the least."

Eliza felt a sudden surge of elation that was not warranted by an invitation to accompany Caroline to the party of someone she didn't know. "Are you not concerned for my tender feelings now?"

"But of course," Caroline said. "But this will be a party like none other and I'd hate that you miss it. And who knows? Maybe you'll meet a *true* suitor." She winked at Eliza.

"I meant only to warn you," Hollis said with a sniff. "You'll do as you please, no one knows that better than me. But you're my sister and it's my duty and I care about you."

Eliza softened a little. She would do the same if Hollis was going around kissing foreign princes, she supposed. "I love you for it, Hollis, but you're right, I will do as I please."

Hollis sighed. "I know, darling. Go, then. I'll stay at home with Pappa."

"But what will she wear?" Caroline asked.

"What will she wear indeed," Hollis said. "You leave that to me, Caro."

"It's to be a carnival followed by a ball that evening," Caroline warned her. "See that she is dressed accordingly."

"As accordingly as I can make her," Hollis said, studying Eliza.

"Do you both realize I am sitting here with you and can hear every word you say?" Eliza demanded.

"A low décolletage, of course," Hollis said. "We'd not want the prince to be disappointed."

Caroline giggled.

"And sleeves, of course. Oh! And a proper train. Do you have any dresses with trains, Eliza?"

Eliza gave her a pointed look. "You know how many dresses I have, Hollis. And you know that not one has a train."

"You'll have one when we're done with you." She leaned over and took another strawberry.

"The party is in a few days," Caroline said. "You haven't much time."

"For the love of—Am I so hopeless?" Eliza demanded.

"Yes," Caroline and Hollis said in unison. With a wink, Hollis held out the plate of strawberries.

The three of them ate all what was left except one, which they graciously left for Beck.

CHAPTER SIXTEEN

The latest fashions were on full display at Worthington Hall, the site of the birthday carnival honoring Miss Juliana Whitbread. Ladies in attendance were attired in dresses that were worn off the shoulder and with trains. The English trains were not as long or as elaborately embroidered as the Alucian ones, but the Alucian sleeves paled in comparison to the embellished sleeves of the English dresses.

Miss Juliana was the object of many male eyes, resplendent in sky blue with white trim, pearls as pale as her skin. At dusk, an elaborate garden maze hid any number of sins, including those of a lady of Mayfair whose child has scarcely been weaned from his wet nurse, and a gentleman old enough to be her father. Who is, in fact, a dear friend of the family and apparently even more indulgent of her than her father.

—Honeycutt's Gazette of Fashion and Domesticity for Ladies

THIS BALL, THIS birthday for a girl who was not even out, was not an event Sebastian wished to attend. But Caius had impressed upon him that Mr. Whitbread, a former Member of Parliament, was a voice of influence when it came to trade. He had lobbied successfully for tariffs on cotton and the Alucians wanted to see them lifted. Furthermore, Whitbread wanted the Alucian princes at his daughter's birthday as leverage toward a match with another English lord. If Sebastian could make an appearance, Caius explained, Mr. Whitbread would be more inclined to advise the lifting of the tariffs.

Sebastian, always dutiful, dressed in princely clothing and went. But not without Leopold—he'd summoned his brother to Kensington.

Leopold was happy to have been summoned. "Of course I want to attend. Every woman with five thousand a year and a pleasing face will be in attendance," he'd joked as he'd straightened his neckcloth.

The contingent of Alucians numbered fourteen. They arrived after the carnival and in time for the ball, but the carnival was still set up on the grounds and some of the afternoon revellers were still going in and out of the tents, still engaged in the games, still putting children on the backs of ponies. By the look of things, plenty of porter ale had been served throughout the day—people were laughing and singing as the day faded away and servants went about, lighting torches on the grounds.

Sebastian and Leopold rode in a chaise with Caius and his wife. As they rolled up to the doors of the mansion, Caius cleared his throat. "Your Highness, if I may?"

Sebastian nodded.

"Two familiar young ladies in contention for your hand will be in attendance tonight, and one more, whose family, I am delighted to say, has found their way to supporting your terms for the trade agreement."

Sebastian suppressed a groan. "Who?"

"Lady Katherine Maugham, Lady Elizabeth Keene, and Lady Mary Brazelton."

The names were familiar, all of them having appeared on a list before they'd ever departed Alucia. "How will I know them?"

"I will see to it," Caius said. "You have made the acquaintance of Lady Katherine and Lady Elizabeth. I believe you have only briefly made the acquaintance of Lady Mary."

He couldn't conjure any face but Eliza's.

Sitting next to her husband, Lady Anastasan gave the slightest hint of a smirk before turning her attention to the window.

"I don't want a production of it, Caius. No lines of ladies, no formal introductions."

Caius nodded. "I understand. But if I may be so bold—"

"You may not," Sebastian said, not wishing to be reminded of his lack of enthusiasm for this very important task.

"You may," Leopold said, and frowned darkly when Sebastian shot him a look.

"If I may be so bold, Your Highness, we've only a fortnight, perhaps three weeks left in England, and you have not as yet settled on a match. We need time to negotiate the terms."

Sebastian glared at him. "Do you think I don't know what must be done? Do you think I don't understand the importance of this choice?"

Caius kept his expression even. "I am responsible for reporting to the king. I am doing my best to meet all of our objectives."

"Leave him be, Bas," Leopold said. "It's no one's fault but yours."

"How happy I am that my future wife is the subject of so much scrutiny from men who will not bed her," Sebastian snapped. And then, "My apologies, Lady Anastasan."

She smiled thinly and dropped her gaze.

Sebastian sighed. "All right, I will do what I must, Caius. This is as important to me as it is to you. But I will not have you orchestrate it."

"*Je*, Your Highness," Caius said quietly, and exchanged a look with Leopold.

The coach rolled to a halt and a moment later, a footman opened the door. Sebastian was the first to alight, followed by Leopold. They stood impatiently while Caius helped his wife from the coach and footman after footman rushed out to greet them and see them in.

The moment they walked into the entrance hall, Sebastian felt the weight of his title. He often felt it when entering a room—it was a millstone, the heavy weight of expectation and of all eyes on him. It never got easier. People who were introduced to him turned quite serious, sometimes utterly tongue-tied. He never felt entirely human in these circumstances but a thing of wonder to be openly studied.

Perhaps that was the reason he'd made so little effort to find a wife. Perhaps it was because no one had yet looked at him like he was a *person*.

With the notable exception, of course, of Miss Tricklebank. And her maid who was not a maid.

"Your Royal Highness." An Englishman bowed low before him.

"Mr. Samuel Charles Whitbread," Caius murmured behind him.

"Mr. Whitbread," Sebastian said. "How good of you to include us in your daughter's birthday celebration."

"We are most honored by your presence and that of Prince Leopold. Please." He indicated the princes should walk with him. They moved through the hall. Sebastian nodded at every greeting and smiled at the curtsies from women who tried to catch his eye.

They had hardly made it into the ballroom when Sebastian was cornered by a pair of gentlemen from Parliament. He nodded along as they proclaimed themselves happy to support and ratify a trade agreement with Alucia. One of them was speaking at length about a trade issue the English were experiencing with the Americans when Sebastian heard a laugh that shot through him. It lifted his heart. *She was here?* Could he be so fortunate? In the last few days, he'd tried to think of reasons to call, but he'd been involved in long meetings with the English, sometimes well into the night.

He abruptly turned, studying the crowd around him. He couldn't see her, but he was certain that was her laugh he'd heard, that glorious, irreverent laugh.

Or maybe it was mad, wishful thinking. When he didn't see her, he turned back to the two men.

As one of the men resumed his tale, Sebastian heard the laugh again. "I beg your pardon," he said politely, and turned around once more. There were so many people crowded into the hall it seemed impossible that he could hear a single laugh, and yet, he was certain he had. He bent his head, looking around a group of women who were looking directly at him, all of them with hopeful smiles on their faces.

He saw her.

It was just a glimpse, but he knew it was her, and his heart skipped several beats with excitement and anticipation. He'd not expected this lovely surprise. Suddenly, the night didn't seem so interminable after all.

He shifted a little to see better. She was standing in the corner conversing with a gentleman, a glass of wine in her hand carelessly bobbing about as she spoke. She was highly animated, laughing so roundly at something that she swayed backward a little. The gown she was wearing was gold, matching the strands of gold in her hair, and it looked, from where he was standing, as if a headdress was floating above her like a little cloud.

He couldn't see her as well as he would have liked, because unlike every other woman, she was not looking at him directly or surreptitiously stealing a glimpse.

"Your Royal Highness."

Sebastian remembered himself and turned back to the two gentlemen. Caius had joined them with a young woman on his arm. Sebastian recognized her. He'd met her before at some supper or another.

"May I introduce Lady Mary Brazelton?"

Ah yes, Lady Mary, the daughter of Richard Brazelton, the Earl of Branleigh, the lass with a wandering eye that tended to look away from the other. "Of course. How do you do, Lady Mary?"

She shyly extended her hand. Sebastian reluctantly took it and bowed over it. She sank into a cursty. "A pleasure, sir." Her voice was shaking. He lifted her up. She let go his hand and gave him a tremulous smile. "Have you, ah…have you seen the gardens, Your Highness?"

Deo, is this how they coached them? He could imagine the lesson. *Invite the prince to walk the garden. Take care to demonstrate your knowledge of horticulture as it will add to your list of accomplishments.* "I have not. Would you care to show them to me?"

"I would be delighted."

Sebastian offered his arm, and Lady Mary put her hand on it. She was still trembling and he wondered why she found him so intimidating. He'd hardly said a word.

He escorted her out past many curious onlookers. He could almost hear the whispers behind them, could hear the guessing begin. But just as they stepped out onto the terrace, Sebastian heard Eliza's laugh drifting up behind him, and then promptly slide down his spine. It was amazing that with all those people talking and watching, he could hear her laugh and hers alone.

So let them all guess what was truly in his heart at this moment. It was not Lady Mary.

In the garden, Lady Mary shivered so uncontrollably that he could scarcely bear it. He turned her about and returned her to the house. "Perhaps another time in the garden, Lady Mary. It seems the cool night air doesn't agree with you."

She couldn't meet his eye. "You are too kind." She spoke so softly he had to lean in to hear her. The little mouse, uncertain as to how she'd performed, scurried across the hall to a gentleman who he assumed was her father. Sebastian could well imagine she would be forced to give an accounting of every word uttered between them and how she'd comported herself.

As for him, he would tell Caius to mark her name from any list. He could not abide the thought of a woman trembling every time he came near.

He scarcely had time to adjust the sashes he wore and

look around for Eliza when he was accosted by more people. Surprisingly, Mrs. Forsythe, his lively lover, was among them, sidling up to him with a cool smile.

"Your Highness." She sank low and rose again. "How well you look, if I may say." She smiled in that sultry way she had, and under any other circumstance, he would have been delighted to entertain that smile. But he'd been informed about the gloves and trusted her even less than he had before.

"Thank you."

Botley-Finch had reported that the English had determined Mrs. Forsythe was in no way involved in anything to do with Matous's death, but rather had embarked on a bit of spying at the behest of Lord Montpassen, who was firmly against the trade agreement. The plan, Botley-Finch explained, was for Mrs. Forsythe to leave a glove indicating she was with the prince behind closed doors, and a gentleman in the room next to the one they'd arranged would listen for any word on his position about the trade agreement, Wesloria, or any other state secret he might share in the throes of passion.

Sebastian had told the attaché that it was a ridiculous plan. "I am not in the habit of speaking about trade in the bedchamber," he'd drawled.

"No, Your Highness. No one has accused Montpassen of possessing any intelligent qualities other than a penchant for gathering wealth."

Mrs. Forsythe's smile deepened, and she managed to touch her finger to Sebastian's. "Have you seen the maze, sir? It is truly a feat of design."

"I have seen it. Did you find your missing glove, Mrs. Forsythe?"

Her smile faltered and a bit of color rose in her

cheeks. But the woman was practiced and she smiled quickly. "Indeed, I did. Thank you."

"I beg your pardon, Mrs. Forsythe, but your presence is needed across the room."

It was Caius, come to Sebastian's rescue. Mrs. Forsythe tried to catch Sebastian's eye, but he looked away. He had nothing to say to her. They had used each other for the purposes they'd desired and there was no need to pretend it was more.

"Good evening," she said uncertainly.

Caius directed Sebastian to more people, and reminded him of having met others. From the corner of his eye Sebastian saw his brother laughing in a circle of women, enjoying the evening, unconcerned with protocol or meeting the right people, or assessing women for their suitability in a royal role or as a wife for the rest of his bloody life.

One of the Alucian guards put a glass of wine in Sebastian's hand. It was safe to drink, then. Sebastian drank it to dull the tedium of having to discuss intricacies of trade with various Englishmen who came forward, to make empty, polite conversation with women he would never see again. An elderly gentleman had managed to get an audience with him, and talked in great detail about iron ore.

Sebastian's mind wandered to a soirée he'd held at the palace once when he was a very young man. His friends had come, including some of the daughters of courtiers he'd grown up with in the palace. His friends were rambunctious young lads with more lust in their heads than brains. They'd donned ladies' dresses and had danced waltzes with each other, performing for the young ladies who had laughed until tears rolled down their cheeks.

That was the charm and silliness of his youth. He'd had true friends then. He'd trusted the people around him then. That was before rumors of rebellion circulated like air. *Where was Eliza?*

"You see, then, Your Highness, how my ideas for improving the smelting of the iron ore would be of benefit to you and your country."

"Yes," he lied.

He wondered idly if he might have a soirée like that again. Perhaps gather some of his old friends when he returned to Helenamar. He hadn't seen some of them in many years. He could hope that some had not succumbed to the dreaded deference that had infected Caius.

"The extraction of the metallurgy is infinitely—"

"I beg your pardon, Lord Dalton."

Caius again, saving Sebastian from the conclusion of Lord Dalton's sentence.

"I must have the prince," Caius added apologetically.

"Oh. Yes, of course," Lord Dalton said, then looked at Sebastian. "We might continue this conversation later, if it pleases Your Highness."

It does not. "Absolutely." Sebastian gave him a ghost of a smile and turned toward his foreign minister.

His wife was with him, and she gave him a cheerful smile. "Do you mean to dance, Your Highness? Shall I have a covert look at some dance cards for you?"

The musicians were warming up. It sounded like a waltz.

"*Je*, Sarafina, darling, an excellent idea. Fetch Lady—"

"No," Sebastian said. He looked around the room,

searching the crowd, desperate to find her and not seeing her. Just when he began to believe she wasn't in the ballroom, he spotted her with another woman. "There," he said, nodding in her direction. "The woman in gold."

Caius squinted, finally spotting her. "I beg your pardon, Your Highness, I am not familiar."

Exactly. "You don't need to be, Caius. I am familiar." He stepped away before Caius could dispatch his wife to find him a more suitable partner.

As Sebastian moved across the room, everyone parted like the Red Sea, bowing and curtsying.

Eliza was speaking with quite a lot of verve. She hadn't noticed his approach, not until he was upon her. And really, the woman she was talking to was the one to notice him, her mouth dropping open as she fell into a curtsy.

Eliza was smiling with laughter when she turned, and she stilled a moment, obviously surprised to see him. A light sparked in her eyes and she sank into a very deep and very crooked curtsy. "Your Royal Highness!" she said, her voice full of delight.

He didn't respond right away—he couldn't. He was dumbfounded by the sight of her. He was used to Eliza in her plain clothes, her hair dropping tendrils around her face. She was to him a beautiful woman, but the woman who stood before him looked like a princess. She looked as if this ball should have been held for her.

The bodice of the gown she wore, gold silk with pearls, was fitted tightly to her body. Her headdress was made of the same diaphanous material that covered the skirt, threaded with silver to catch the light and sparkle. The curls of her hair bounced at her temple with her laugh. She was elegant, and she was beautiful, and her expression was filled with joy. Had he not known her, he would have mistaken her for someone of great importance. Why weren't the men in this room surrounding her? Why hadn't every eligible bachelor found his way to her side? What in bloody hell was the matter with Englishmen?

Her friend, still in a curtsy, stared at Sebastian in disbelief. "I think you can rise up," Eliza said to her friend.

"Forgive me," Sebastian said quickly to that woman, awkwardly reaching out to help the woman as she came up. *Get hold of yourself, man.* "Miss Tricklebank, good evening." He bowed.

"Good evening," she said with a playful wink. "Oh! I beg your pardon. May I introduce Mrs. Keller?"

Mrs. Keller was so stunned she didn't move at all, but just kept her gaze fixed on him. Sebastian gave her a nod of his head. He wished Mrs. Keller would disappear. He wished everyone in this room would disappear. He noticed Eliza's dance card dangling from her wrist. She was twisting a little in time to the music, turning this way then that way. He felt clumsy and unpracticed in the art of flirting. "Would you do me the honor of accompanying me in this dance, Miss Tricklebank?"

She smiled. She slowly leaned to her right to see around him. Then leaned forward and whispered, "Are you certain?"

He leaned forward and whispered, *"Quite."*

"Then I'd be delighted," she said, holding out her hand with a sunny smile that made his blood rush. Something had ruptured in Sebastian—a tear in his tightly woven fabric.

He presented his arm. "If you will excuse us, Mrs.

Keller?" she asked, and with her head held high, allowed him to escort her to the dance floor.

Once there, Sebastian bowed. She bobbed into a scarcely passable curtsy and slipped her hand into his, then placed the other one on his shoulder. "You can't say I haven't warned you before," she said before the music began. "You can't blame me if your toes are broken."

He put his hand on her back. "Ah yes, dancing is not your talent." He smiled fondly at her.

One dark gold brow arched above the other. "So you *do* remember."

He began to move them along. "Some things I remember very well." His gaze fell to her mouth. "Some things I will never forget."

Her lips parted slightly with her breath.

He twirled them to the right.

"My sister informs me I am passable at the waltz. The Alucian dances, however, would require a lifetime of instruction."

He wished he could give her that lifetime of instruction. "You dance very well, Eliza."

She smiled with gratitude. "It's a pity you can't report as much to my former dance teacher. Alas, he has passed, no doubt slain by his own expectations."

Sebastian laughed and twirled her again. All he wanted to do was kiss her. To look into her eyes. To feel her body against his. "Has anyone told you how stunning you are tonight?" he blurted.

Her eyes sparkled with delight and surprise. "Why, *thank* you, Mr. Chartier. As it happens, Mr. Robinson has said so. He's an old friend of my father's, and his sight nearly as bad as my father's. All right, I'm desperate to know," she said, leaning slightly forward as they moved around the room. "Have you seen him?"

"Mr. Robinson?"

"No!" She glanced quickly right and left, then mouthed the words *Mr. Heath*.

He'd forgotten about the banker. He'd forgotten everything but how beautiful Eliza looked. "I don't…no. Is he here?"

"He is, indeed. It's the perfect opportunity! I'll point him out, if you like." She looked around them, as if searching for the man.

Sebastian looked at her. "Eliza, you have…"

She returned her gaze to him.

Sebastian swallowed. He twirled her again. His tongue felt a little thick in his mouth. *"Belius,"* he croaked.

"Oh dear." She smiled. "I have that?"

Why was he so graceless? It was as if years of training in decorum had deserted him. "What I'm trying to say, and very badly at that, is that you are beautiful. It's the nearest translation." But *belius* meant more than that. It was transcendent of beauty. It didn't mean physical perfection; it referred more to the soul.

"Oh." Her blush returned. "You are plying me with compliments, Mr. Chartier. I don't know what to make of it."

He didn't know what to make of it, either. But he was enchanted.

"If I may say so, *Your Highness*, you look quite dashing yourself this evening, what with all your sashes and medals." She looked at the pin that he wore at the center of his neckcloth. It was made of obsidian, a precious gem that was mined in Alucia. "What is it for?"

"It is a medal of valor."

"Really! Have you been valiant?"

"I have endeavoured on occasion. This one came after the four-year war with Wesloria."

She blinked. "You fought in a war?"

"Military duty is mandatory for royal sons." War was devastating, but he could honestly say those years had been some of the best of his life. He'd discovered his true mettle. He'd discovered what sort of man he was when the trappings of his royal blood were stripped away.

"You continue to surprise me," she said brightly. Her smile had changed. It was full of regard for him. He could feel that regard in his bones and it had the effect of making him feel invincible. "And to think I thought you a boor."

He laughed and twirled her around again. He hadn't enjoyed a dance like this in years. But as all bright spots of joy in his life, this one, too, had to come to an end.

The music drew to a close. He had to work to release her hand. He wished he could keep holding it and walk straight out the door with her. Just keep walking, away from the throne. Away from Matous. Away from London and Helenamar—just the two of them into the world.

"Would it be unseemly of me to dance with you again?" he muttered as they joined the others leaving the dance floor. "I was thinking perhaps an Alucian set."

"Not if you value your feet. The waltz was *quite* diverting. I shall be the talk of the ladies' retiring room."

"And the gazette, I should think."

"Without question. I'll pen the on dit myself." She smiled up at him and bowed her head. "He's just behind you, you know. Portly fellow. A gray moustache so heavy that one shudders to think what might lurk there."

"Pardon?"

"Mr. Heath," she whispered. "Have you forgotten that you wanted an opportunity to speak to him?"

"Yes," he admitted. He'd forgotten everything about himself that didn't have to do with her. "Thank you for the reminder." He bowed. She smiled pertly and walked away with a bounce in her step.

When he could see her no more, he turned around, intending to meet this Mr. Heath. But when he did, he saw that the other guests were still here, many of them watching him. How many of them had just seen him reluctantly let go of Eliza? How many of them had deduced his true feelings?

He spotted Caius moving toward him through the throng. He saw the smiles of many women hoping they might be his next dance partner. He saw the portly gentleman with the unsettling moustache moving away from him, strolling toward the door. Sebastian abruptly followed, nodding politely at those who caught his eye, artfully stepping out of the way of anyone who looked like they meant to intercept him.

Mr. Heath was headed for a sideboard and two large bowls of punch. As the gentleman helped himself, Sebastian stepped up beside him. Immediately, a footman materialized from thin air. "Your Royal Highness, may I?" he asked, gesturing to the punch.

The footman's question startled the banker, and he jerked his gaze to Sebastian. "How do you do," Sebastian said.

"Ah. Your Royal Highness, good evening," the banker said. He inclined his head and looked as if he meant to move on. Sebastian didn't have to look back to know Caius was bearing down on him.

"You look familiar," Sebastian said, and turned to nod to the footman who was so desperate to serve him punch.

"Pardon?" The banker looked startled. "I beg your pardon, but I don't think that is possible. We've not been introduced."

"No," Sebastian agreed as he accepted the punch from the footman. "But you were acquainted with my secretary, were you not?"

The ruddy color began to drain from Mr. Heath's full cheeks.

"I recall seeing the two of you speaking at the masquerade ball," Sebastian said casually. He sipped from his glass. "Excellent punch, wouldn't you agree?" His guards were probably apoplectic, watching him drink from an untested glass.

"I…ah…yes, indeed it is."

Mr. Heath looked very uncomfortable. From the corner of his eye, Sebastian could see Caius drawing closer. "If I may—Mr. Heath, isn't it? If I may, Mr. Heath, what did Mr. Reyno want with you?"

Mr. Heath blanched. "I beg your pardon, Your Highness, but I've spoken at length to the authorities—"

"But you've not spoken to me." Sebastian shook his head at Caius. Caius hesitated—for a moment.

"Would you be so kind as to step out into the hall with me? I won't take much of your time." He smiled.

"I don't—I'm sure there is nothing I can tell you."

"Perhaps you will tell me all the same," Sebastian said, and smiled coolly. He could see the calculation in Heath's eyes, the internal debate over what to do. So he put his hand on the man's elbow and helped him make the decision, nudging him toward the door and the hall before Caius could reach them.

"I would be grateful if you would tell me what it was Mr. Reyno spoke to you about?" Sebastian asked when they stepped into the hall.

"I spoke to him only briefly." Mr. Heath sounded a bit frantic. "I greeted him. We talked of the weather."

Sebastian glanced over his shoulder. "You spoke to him three times if you spoke to him once, and while I know that Mr. Reyno liked a discussion of weather as well as anyone, I cannot imagine he'd have three different conversations about it."

The ends of Mr. Heath's moustache trembled. "I want no trouble," he said in a low voice. "I didn't know Mr. Reyno before that evening and I wished him no harm, you must believe me."

"Then please do tell me what you spoke about. I have no desire other than to find who did this."

Mr. Heath glanced down the long hall. With his chin, he indicated Sebastian should follow him. They moved quickly down the hall, reaching a corner, and then stepping into another, darkened corridor. Once there, Mr. Heath looked back, then said quickly, "Your secretary inquired if I had been contacted by the French banker, Adolphe d'Eichtal. It had to do with a debt, he said. Someone wanted to repay a rather large debt and would transfer the money to the French bank."

"Through the Bank of England?"

"That was what I understood."

That made no sense. Why would Matous want to do that? "Did it have to do with our negotiations?" But Sebastian realized the moment he asked the question that it couldn't be. Matous was his secretary and would never discuss the trade negotiations with anyone.

"Unfortunately, I don't know what it had to do with or who had the money," Heath said.

"Do you know d'Eichtal, then?"

"We've met, yes, in the course of various country-state business dealings. But I know nothing of this. As I explained to Mr. Reyno, I had not spoken to Monsieur d'Eichtal, and it would be highly unusual for him to contact me directly about a transfer of monies. There are bankers and clerks to handle the transactions. Not the bank governors."

Sebastian put his glass aside on a console and settled his hands on his hips. "You had more than one conversation with him."

"He asked the question in different ways, Your Highness. In the end, I told him that if there was a large amount of money to be moved from one bank to the next, it could certainly be achieved, but that I had no knowledge of it."

"Why were you reluctant to tell me this?" he asked curiously. "Why pretend it had something to do with the weather?"

Mr. Heath looked down.

Sebastian stepped closer. "What did you tell your government?"

"The same. We spoke of the weather in London."

"Why dissemble, Mr. Heath?" Sebastian pressed him.

"I suppose because none of it sounded above board," he said. "Frankly, it sounded quite wrong to me, and apparently, my instincts were right."

But the question remained *who* would transfer a large

amount of money through England to France? Why would Matous, of all people, know of it? "Did he mention on whose behalf he was speaking? Or..." He had to make himself ask the next question. "Was he speaking for himself?"

Mr. Heath shook his head. "On my word, I don't know. He never gave me a name or indicated it had to do with him. But I feel certain he was not inquiring for an English subject. I am certain he was inquiring for an Alucian."

"What makes you think so?"

Heath looked off for a moment. "I can't rightly say, but that was my impression. It had to do with an Alucian. Perhaps because he seemed so...unsettled."

Unsettled.

"I've told you all I know," Mr. Heath said. "I've not spoken to another Alucian since that night."

Sebastian said nothing. He was still trying to absorb this news.

"If I may have your leave—"

"Of course," Sebastian said. "Thank you, Mr. Heath. You've been too kind to entertain my curiosity." He moved to one side so Mr. Heath could pass. The man escaped quickly, striding down the hall, away from Sebastian.

Sebastian held back a moment, his hand braced against the wall, thinking. Rostafan had come into a great deal of money. Had he brought it to England, and if he had, why would he? Why not the Alucian bank? And did Matous know of it?

"Everyone is looking for you. You've got your guards in quite a frenzied search."

Sebastian looked around to his brother. Leopold had a glass of wine in his hand. He grinned. "Come on, then, old man, there is dancing and drink to be had." He threw his arm around Sebastian's shoulders, pulling him along.

Sebastian allowed it—his thoughts were too far away, too muddied, and he couldn't think of this now.

In the ballroom, more women were presented. More walks were taken around the gardens. Sebastian danced more and made more empty chatter about the beauty of Alucia and the wish for warmer days. Over and over again.

And so on.

And so on.

CHAPTER SEVENTEEN

There is no better time for dancing than the celebration of a young woman's birthday. A pair of princes were among those to take to the dance floor, partnering with all the young ladies rumored to be potential queens. But who was the beauty in gold, with the pearls strung across the bodice of her gown? One prince seemed particularly entranced.

Ladies, if you desire another child, add saffron liberally to your cooking.

—Honeycutt's Gazette of Fashion and Domesticity for Ladies

ELIZA HAD DONE it again, had drunk too much of the rum punch. Well, who could blame her for it? It was her season for revelry, for she was never invited to such events. She never looked this stunning, either, even if the corset she wore in order to fit into Caroline's altered dress had stopped all blood flow to her head and her limbs.

Whether it was her lack of breath or the delicious rum punch, Eliza had been wandering around the ballroom radiating a warm glow. She was not an honoree of this party, but she might as well have been. After dancing with Sebastian she was floating on air, smiling at passers-by, sometimes stopping to laugh at a conversation she was not part of. When Caroline introduced her to Miss Whitbread, Eliza gave her a buzzy little smile and effusive well wishes for her birthday.

Oh, but Miss Whitbread was a lovely young thing, with a gown of white and lavender, and a train that seemed to float behind her when she moved. She looked to be having a grand time of it, judging by her happy smile and shining eyes. As well she should be—she was a beautiful woman, much younger than Eliza, with an entire life of privilege and comfort stretching before her.

The tightness in Eliza's chest had nothing to do with envy, but the blasted corset. Why would she be envious? Her life was perfectly satisfactory, and she'd learned a long time ago that wishing for a different circumstance was pointless.

But then she saw Mr. Asher Daughton-Cress. He was *here*, in the flesh, the first she'd seen him in ten years. He was a little gray at the temples, but was as trim and fit as he'd ever been. And standing beside him, his beautiful wife, who was, by all outward appearances, about to give birth. How many children was that? Four?

All right, maybe she did feel a stab or two of envy. How lovely it must be to know that your lot was a good marriage, with all the luxuries that afforded, including healthy, happy children. How awful to have been lied to about something as fundamental to life as that.

Eliza turned and went the other way so that she'd not encounter the happy couple and thereby remind them all what had happened all those years ago.

She refused to dwell on it. The hurt had long subsided, and besides, she was having a wonderful time of it this evening. She didn't want to think about him or what he'd done. Or the fact that he'd never offered an apology. She wanted to have fun. There was nothing to be done for her lot in life, so Eliza had another glass of rum punch and celebrated Miss Whitbread's birthday.

She danced with gentlemen she didn't know and flirted coyly, studiously avoided any sight of Asher, and generally felt as if she had conquered the evening… until she realized the commotion on the far end of the dance floor was due to the performance of a quadrille by the crown prince of Alucia.

He was dancing with Lady Katherine Maugham. The peacock. The one Caroline was certain would win the prince's hand. Eliza could imagine how *thrilled* the peacock must have been with that invitation to dance.

That was enough to tip the balance of her good humor into the category of despairing. Not only did she have Asher and his wife and happy life to contend with, she had to watch Sebastian court the woman he would marry.

It was the latter that sobered her the most. She couldn't seem to tear her gaze away from Sebastian. She kept stealing glances in his direction, struggling to see him through all the shoulders of gentlemen and the gowns of ladies whom Sebastian danced with.

Her sparkle faded. She glumly realized, there was a veritable parade of women before him. But every now and again she thought—or imagined—that Sebastian tried to catch her eye. And she thought—or imagined—that he smiled faintly when he did.

And every now and again she felt it necessary to help herself to another cup of punch.

Of course she understood, without the slightest equivocation, that it was important he pay heed to these women. He would be a king! He had to marry and provide heirs to his country's throne. He would choose from these women with the proper training and pedigrees and social connections to be considered a potential future queen.

Would the peacock find marriage to him pleasurable? Would her house be very grand? Eliza supposed it would, as she guessed that the Alucian royal family lived in a palace much like Buckingham. Would the peacock wear a crown? Was a crown something that was worn every day, a day crown as it were, with more elaborately jeweled crowns for formal occasions? Eliza would save these questions for Hollis, who would surely know.

Would the peacock see her husband every day? Take tea with him? Sit quietly with her clocks—or needlework, she supposed, as she was the only one she knew to be intrigued by the working of clocks—while her husband read important papers and remarked on this or that? Would they together ride out for a hunt, or play croquet, or be invited to parties and suppers of the Members of Parliament?

Sebastian was now dancing a reel with a woman with glistening blond hair.

Well, Eliza had danced with him first, so there was that.

Frankly, his request to dance with her had surprised her. She couldn't believe he'd sought her out at all, not with all the courting he clearly had to do. She'd felt like a queen in a beautiful dress in that moment. She'd felt utterly regal as he escorted her onto the dance floor. She'd felt all eyes on her and, honestly, Eliza hadn't hated it.

She *very* much hoped Asher and his wife had seen her.

Eliza smirked and turned back to the sideboard for more rum punch. A woman was there before her, daintily ladling punch into a glass.

"It's rum punch," Eliza announced.

The woman flashed a smile.

"We were served rum punch at the Royal Masquerade Ball," Eliza added, apropos of nothing.

The woman looked up and around, as if she thought Eliza was addressing someone else. When she saw no one, she looked uneasily at Eliza.

"I was there," Eliza said proudly. "It was quite a spectacular ball, really. You've not seen such beautiful masks, I assure you. And they served the best rum punch. I've heard it said it was the *queen's* rum punch—"

"Eliza! I've been looking for you all night!"

Eliza glanced over her shoulder at Caroline. "You *have*?" Generally, Caroline used these evenings to accept the attentions of all the gentlemen she would never consider for a husband.

Caroline smiled at a point past Eliza and said, "I beg your pardon, madam, but may I borrow Miss Tricklebank away?"

"By all means," the woman said, and with her punch, hurried off.

Caroline pulled Eliza away from the punch.

"How rude, Caro. She might have wanted to hear more about the masquerade ball."

"She didn't, trust me."

"And I didn't fill my glass."

"You don't need to fill your glass, Eliza. Your cheeks are as red as apples. And besides, I need you. Prince Leopold is in the gaming room," she said gravely.

Eliza stared at her, waiting for further explanation. Caroline arched a brow as if Eliza should understand.

"Is that *bad*?" Eliza asked carefully.

"Well, he's not here dancing, is he? And he's yet to

acknowledge me, and I stood directly behind him for almost a quarter of an hour!"

"No," Eliza said with mock concern.

Caroline frowned with exasperation. "Do you think you're the only one with prince problems?"

"I don't have a *prince* problem."

"I don't know why he pretends he's not acquainted with me!"

"Is it possible he simply doesn't recall?"

Caroline sighed. "Really, Eliza?" She fluttered the fingers of both hands in the direction of her face. "You think he may not recall?" She clucked her tongue. "I want to know what he's about. You need to join a table."

"Join a table?"

"In the gaming room!"

"Me?"

"For me, Eliza! Does he mean to stay all night in the gaming room?"

"I don't know, Caro! How could I possible know?"

"That's why you must join a table! Go round to the gaming room and—why are you laughing?"

"I can't join a table! I'm a wretched gambler, and I haven't a purse."

"You don't need a purse," Caroline said, and turned her around, giving her a push toward the door. "I'd be most obliged if you'd go and play a hand or two and tell me what he's about."

Eliza tried to step away before Caroline shoved her out the door, but she caught sight of Asher moving in her direction. He hadn't seen her, but a few more steps, and they'd be nose to nose. Eliza did not want that. She couldn't possibly greet him as if he was some old acquaintance. She whirled around. "All right," she said.

"But I have no purse, and if lose a hand and am challenged for it, you will have to stand in for me at the duel."

"Don't lose," Caroline said. "Oh dear," she muttered, looking past Eliza. "It's Mr. Daughton-Cress."

"Yes, I've seen him. Find another way from this room before I do something I'll regret and I'll go and spy on your prince."

"It's not *spying*, exactly," Caroline muttered, and looped her arm through Eliza's. "It's gathering information." She pulled her toward another exit.

The gaming room was just across the corridor. Inside, the room was almost as big as the ballroom, with enormous mirrors on the wall that reflected the light of the four chandeliers. That made it so bright that one could believe it was a sunny spring day.

There were several cloth-covered tables set up, and all of them were full with men and women engaged in games of chance. Eliza couldn't spot an empty seat—she couldn't join a game even if she desired.

She did not so desire. She desired only to remove any chance of meeting Asher.

However, she did spot Prince Leopold straightaway as she was quite familiar with him after he'd stood so slack-jawed in her parlor. He was seated at a table with two gentlemen and a pretty Alucian woman.

A *very* pretty Alucian woman.

Well, that wasn't good—Eliza could tell by the way the woman smiled and glanced at the prince there was a flirtation between them. She didn't think she'd have the nerve to tell Caroline.

"I beg your pardon, madam."

The beautifully accented feminine voice was directly behind Eliza, and she turned to see an Alucian woman with big brown eyes smiling warmly at her. *"Bon notte."*

"Ah...good evening."

The woman cocked her head to one side. "Have we been introduced, madam? You are familiar to me."

"No. At least, not that I recall. I'm Eliza Tricklebank."

"Ah." The woman smiled again. "No, I think we have not met. I'm Lady Anastasan."

She said her name as if Eliza should know who she was, but Eliza didn't know. So she smiled and said again, "Good evening."

Lady Anastasan suddenly grinned. "*I* know where I've seen you! You danced with His Royal Highness, Prince Sebastian! The very first dance, wasn't it?"

Lady Anastasan was smiling, but there was something in her eyes that didn't seem quite as friendly as the rest of her face. "Ah...yes. Yes, that was me," Eliza said. "He was very kind to invite me."

"Indeed! *Everyone* wants to dance with the prince. How did you make his acquaintance?"

She wondered if perhaps Lady Anastasan was in love with Sebastian. Before Eliza could think of how to explain her acquaintance, Lady Anastasan pressed the tips of her fingers to her forehead. "How tactless of me. I meant only that there are so *many* ladies wanting to make his acquaintance."

"I first made his acquaintance at the masquerade ball at Kensington Palace."

"Oh, wonderful! I thought it very clever to have a masquerade, didn't you? But the masks were uncomfortably warm after a time."

"*Weren't* they," Eliza agreed.

"I suppose Lady Marlborough invited you to make

his acquaintance?" the woman asked with a thin smile. "Quite a line *that* was. So many of your fellow English ladies desire to meet the prince, don't they?"

She seemed pleasant enough, but Eliza didn't care for Lady Anastasan. There was a faint, yet discernible hint of disparagement there. "Well, as you know, we haven't any bachelor princes of our own."

Lady Anastasan laughed. "No, you don't, do you? It was a pleasure to make your acquaintance, Miss Tricklebank. Do enjoy your evening."

"Thank you."

Lady Anastasan walked away. Eliza watched her, curious. No, she didn't care for her at all. But she did admire the train on her gown. It was intricately embroidered, and Eliza imagined it had taken a dozen seamstresses and a full month to create it. She was so entranced with the train that she watched Lady Anastasan walk all the way across the room, and past a table where an Alucian gentleman with a barrel chest and a deep bark for a laugh was playing cards with two Englishmen. Lady Anastasan touched the big man very quickly and lightly on his back as she circled around the table, and when she'd passed, she glanced over her shoulder, smiled and, Eliza was fairly certain, winked. She then carried on to the far end of the room and joined a table of ladies.

Eliza assumed the gentleman was her husband. There was something about the look between the two of them that seemed very familiar.

She shifted her attention to Prince Leopold. He was leaning across the gaming table, his eyes locked on the Alucian woman. Poor Caroline. She decided to leave the gaming room, but when she reached the door, there was quite a crush. She stood aside as people streamed in, then stood aside again as some gentlemen were eager to go out before her. When she finally managed to step into the wide hall, she was blocked by a group of Alucians. She stepped around them, but as she tried to pass, she saw Asher and his wife, her hand protectively resting on her belly. They were standing not three feet away.

Eliza turned about and went in the opposite direction. There had been times she'd imagined an encounter like this, and had imagined she'd be perfectly at ease. He meant nothing to her anymore. But when she saw him, she didn't trust herself to be particularly civil. He had scored her with his betrayal, and she did not care to speak to him at all.

She passed another clump of Alucians, and as she skirted around them, she felt a hand on her arm.

She jerked around, startled. "Miss Tricklebank, how do you find the ball?"

Sebastian. She smiled with relief. "It's wonderful! And how do *you* find it, Mr. Chartier?"

"Tedious," he said. He looked at the door to the gaming room. "Did you try your luck?"

"No. I thought I might, but then I realized I had no pockets to carry all my winnings."

He smiled. "That is indeed a dilemma."

The gentleman behind Sebastian had noticed her and was studying her curiously. "I should like to suggest pockets as the next innovation in ladies' fashions. By the bye, Your Highness, did you have an opportunity to—"

"I did."

One of the gentlemen behind him stepped forward, his gaze on Eliza for a moment. "Your Highness, Lady Amelia Darnley is waiting."

Something flickered in Sebastian's eyes. He said

nothing but smiled almost sadly at Eliza. "Good night, Miss Tricklebank."

"Good night."

She carried on into the ballroom. Her heart was racing and lurching and racing again in ways she had never quite experienced. This wasn't fair—she wanted a word with whoever was in the heavens above doling out fairness and miracles. She wanted to be the only one for Sebastian. And she wanted to be nowhere near Asher when Sebastian realized it.

In the ballroom, she had another glass of the punch—she didn't care if her cheeks looked like apples. She danced another set with a gentleman who had thick lips and a limp that surprisingly did not hinder his dancing in the slightest.

But as the hours ticked by, and the women piled up in front of Sebastian, Eliza grew weary. She wanted to go home. She was tired of playing at princess. It had been quite diverting, but the reality of her true situation kept crawling into her thoughts with every sighting of Asher or Sebastian.

Worse, it occurred to her that tonight was probably the last she'd ever see Sebastian. She'd pointed out Mr. Heath—what other reason would they possibly have to communicate? She would have to subsist on the memory of their dance and those few moments she'd felt like a queen.

She sought out Caroline, hoping she'd be ready to go. Unfortunately, Caroline was in the middle of being doted on by two men.

So Eliza slipped out onto the terrace. The cool night air was a welcome respite from the sweltering heat of the ballroom.

"Miss Tricklebank?"

Eliza started. An Alucian gentleman had stepped out onto the terrace. He had dark brown hair and darker eyes. "How do you know—"

"Madam, I've a message for you."

His accent was much stronger than Sebastian's, and for a moment, she thought she might have misunderstood him. "A message? What sort of message?" She tried to see behind the man, but he was rather broad in the chest and blocked her view of the door.

He stepped closer. Eliza stepped backward. "His Royal Highness has asked me to tell you to expect to hear word from him soon."

"Word?" Eliza stared at him. Was this man to be believed? Was this some sort of trick? "But why is—"

"He asked me to tell you only that," the man said, and with a sharp bow, he turned and stepped back inside.

Eliza slowly turned her gaze up to the moon. It all seemed very odd, but Eliza didn't care—it dawned on her that tonight would *not* be the last she saw of him. The understanding filled her with light and hope.

She suddenly smiled. Maybe she wasn't finished pretending at princess after all.

CHAPTER EIGHTEEN

The mystery of who will win the contest for princely affections has only grown in the last week. The wall-eyed daughter of a prominent coal baron has risen in interest. Could she be the perfect trading partner? Could a gentleman with royal manners overlook a shifting eye?

Ladies, you must try Damiana Wafers for lethargy. Two wafers a day will give you the stamina of a woodcutter. However, the manufacturer does not recommend any actual woodcutting.

—Honeycutt's Gazette of Fashion and Domesticity for Ladies

SEBASTIAN WAS SURPRISINGLY, uncharacteristically tense.

Patro had done the impossible: he'd found a small but richly appointed townhouse off an alley in the Mayfair district. All necessary precautions had been taken, and Sebastian had arrived in English clothing and in a plain carriage. A cook had been hired and told the meal was for a Member of Parliament. A fire was blazing in the hearth, and there were at least four guards present in the house but thankfully out of sight. Sebastian was alone in the small salon.

He was alone and waiting. Anxious. Uneasy with the fear she might not come.

He'd sent the message to Eliza at half past six. It was now nearly eight o'clock. He'd relentlessly paced in front of the hearth, convincing himself he'd done the wrong thing. Why would she come? The invitation (or perhaps she would see it as a summons) went beyond the pale of decency, really, and if anyone had suggested he would do the thing he was doing now even a month ago, he would have been indignant. But he couldn't stay away from her, and it wasn't possible to proceed in a normal fashion. He'd left the trade talks early, angered by the high tariffs suggested for ore, which would leave Alucian iron ore languishing in the market. And because he couldn't seem to concentrate his thoughts properly.

Eliza could well think his note too brazen, too outlandish, too crass. She could send back a response that was—

He heard the sound of a carriage on the cobbled stones of the street below and went to the window to have a look. The nondescript carriage that had delivered him here rolled to a halt. He watched a driver leap off the driver's seat and open the carriage door.

She had come.

Sebastian stepped back and released the breath he hadn't realized he was holding. *What am I doing here, like this? Who have I become?*

It was the same question Leopold had asked him when he'd overheard Patro speaking to Sebastian about the hire of this house. *What are you doing, Bas?*

Unfortunately, Sebastian couldn't find words to explain it satisfactorily. His brother didn't have the same view of life—Leopold could do as he pleased, bed women as he liked. But Sebastian's position was different. He had to be careful. He couldn't risk paternity. He couldn't risk scandal. He was always on guard.

But it wasn't as if he was without feminine companionship—accommodations were made for princes and future kings. He'd had a mistress for many years, a young widow, wealthy in her own right. The affair had ended when she'd become too needy, wanting more from him than he could or wanted to give.

It was a relationship held at arm's length. He had to remain reasonably chaste, had to keep his eye on the future and the family lineage. He had to carry the mantle of responsibility and leadership, whereas Leopold was free to live his life as he pleased…within the bounds of reason.

"What of Matous?" Leopold had asked that same afternoon. "What about your burning desire to see his killer brought to justice?"

"Do you think I have any less desire? I told you, I am looking into Rostafan's finances." Two days ago, he'd sent a letter to Alucia with instructions for his father.

Still, Leopold had stared at him, his gaze sharp and assessing. "For God's sake, Bas, have a bloody care. What if she gets with child?"

"I haven't—I *wouldn't*," Sebastian had blustered, but even as the words had tumbled from his mouth, he knew them to be a lie. He would. In a heartbeat, he would.

All right, so he was a cad, a disgrace to his title and to the king. To his parents. To himself. But he would take her in his arms if she were willing, and he'd not think twice.

"You haven't much time," Leopold had pleaded with him. "The talks have stalled, we are no closer to Matous's killer, and everyone wants to know who will receive an offer of marriage."

"I haven't time for one private supper?" Sebastian had snapped. "I am well aware of what has not yet been accomplished. Have I worked any less diligently?"

"You haven't time for carrying on. You need to make a match, Bas. You need to redouble your efforts to finish what you came here determined to do."

Sebastian had said nothing. What could he possibly have said? Leopold was right.

"Who is it, then?" Leopold had asked.

"Who will I dine—"

"No," Leopold had said, shaking his head. "Who might be a queen of Alucia? Surely you have some idea."

Leopold's dogged determination had annoyed Sebastian. He had suddenly become the responsible one after all his years of freedom. Sebastian had been so annoyed that he'd walked out of the room, unwilling to discuss a marriage he did not particularly want when he was planning a private evening he very much did want.

Was he not allowed this one moment in his life? Was it necessary to be the crown prince every single moment of every day? Was he ever allowed to just be a man who was enthralled with a pretty woman?

Sebastian couldn't think of his argument with Leopold just now. He ran his hands over his head and smoothed back his hair. He couldn't believe he was as anxious as this, like a lad scarcely out of short pants. But he desperately wanted Eliza to esteem him.

He heard voices in the foyer, and a moment later, Patro opened the door to the salon, stepped inside and bowed. "Your Royal Highness, Miss Eliza Tricklebank."

Eliza walked in behind Patro with a smile of delight and looked all around her before settling her gaze on Sebastian. He broke into a surprising and cheek-stretching grin.

"Your Royal Highness!" she said, as if she'd just encountered a friend on the street. She sank into her crooked curtsy and bounced up. "I think my curtsy is improving, don't you?"

He did not, but nevertheless, this was the thing he admired about Eliza—she said whatever came to mind without a care if it was proper to say in front of him or not.

"Eliza," he said, and took both her hands in his. "Thank you for coming."

"Well, I *had* to. Such a mysterious message you sent me!" She pulled her hands free of his to remove her cloak. Patro was instantly on hand to take it.

"Some wine, Patro," Sebastian said in Alucian. Patro quietly went out with her cloak.

Eliza was looking at the velvet drapes, the tall windows, the painted ceiling. "Where are we?"

Sebastian looked around, too. The salon was small, but the furnishings expensive with a lot of gold and porcelain and he didn't know what all. His vision glossed over everything in the room except Eliza. "I couldn't say, in truth. I've borrowed it for the occasion."

"You've *borrowed* it?"

Did she disapprove? "I...ah... I thought perhaps we could not be sufficiently at our leisure at Kensington."

A broad smile shaped her lips. "Are we at our leisure?"

He swallowed. His tongue felt so thick suddenly.

Her smile faded a little and she peered closely at him. "What is the matter?"

"Pardon?"

"You look as if you've swallowed something and it won't go down."

"I do?"

"Yes, Mr. Chartier, you do."

He rubbed his forehead. "I think I would be more at ease if you called me Sebastian."

She smiled. "You're quite right. It wouldn't do to go back on our friendship at this late date. Very well, then, Sebastian. I am at my leisure." She bowed.

If only he could be at his leisure. He felt so bloody awkward and anxious.

Patro returned with a silver tray and put two goblets of wine on a small table between chairs arranged before the hearth. Sebastian gestured to the chairs as his butler soundlessly disappeared.

Eliza sat carefully, arranging her blue cotton and muslin gown. It was rather plain, really, and in spite of being bowled over by her at the Whitbread affair, Sebastian thought this gown suited her. It was just plain enough that one's attention was drawn to the lovely gray of her eyes and the golden brown of her hair. She had appealing features, a beauty that settled quietly in his chest. Her face was indelibly printed in his heart.

"Please," he said, gesturing to the wine.

"I am fairly certain one waits until the prince has picked up his glass."

"Ah." He was truly out of his element. Things around him were done so automatically and without question that he barely noticed the intricate details anymore. He picked up a glass. "Let's pretend I'm not a prince this evening." He tapped his glass to hers.

"I don't think I can possibly forget it, but I'll certainly

try." She smiled and sipped her wine. The moment she did, her eyes lit. "Oh, my! It's *very* good. Is it French?"

"Alucian."

She gasped. "*Alucian!* My sister will be green with envy." She sipped again and closed her eyes for a moment. "Delicious." She smiled with delight. "The messenger said you had something you wished to discuss. I'm on tenterhooks. I couldn't guess!"

"Couldn't you?"

"I assume it has to do with Mr. Heath?"

No, it had nothing to do with Heath. But he said, "Yes." Mr. Heath had been the ploy to bring her here—he couldn't very well ask her to come just so that he could kiss her again. "Did you enjoy the ball?" he asked, subtly changing the subject.

"Oh, I did, very much! Not as much as the birthday girl, I'd wager, but quite nearly. I danced so much that I am certain my dancing has miraculously improved. You'd be impressed."

He was plainly, achingly, impressed.

"Did you see the monkeys and the jugglers before the ball? Fascinating!"

He shook his head.

"Oh, a pity!" She put down her glass. "Have you been to a carnival?"

He nodded. "Carnivals and a circus, all brought to court."

"Really?" She sat up straighter. "What's it like, the circus?"

"Displays of horsemanship and amazing acrobatic feats."

"I will add that to my list of things I must see one day. Did you notice the moon tonight?"

"The moon?"

"It's as big as a sun. It's so close it feels as if you could reach up and touch it. My mother used to sing a little ditty to us about a man who lived on the moon. What was it? *The man in the moon came down too soon and asked his way to Norwich.*" She laughed. "Why ever would he want to go to Norwich?"

"Ours was a bit different." Sebastian eased back into his chair. "I'm not certain of the translation, but it went something like *See the man in the moon, and how his bundle weighs him down. His sticks...*" He paused, thinking through the translation. "I assume that means there are sticks in his bundle. *His sticks the truth reveal, it never profits man to steal.*"

"I think I prefer the English nursery rhyme."

He smiled. "So do I."

She picked up her wine glass and drank, watching him. Sebastian felt unsteady and unduly aware of himself and his every movement. People were always so eager to talk to him that he never really had to do much of it. There was so much he wanted to know about her, so many things he didn't know if he could inquire after. Or even how.

Eliza put down her glass again. "You seem ill at ease, Sebastian."

"I'm not," he said quickly. "Not at all."

Her eyes narrowed. "Why did you ask me to come here?"

"To…to see you. To speak to you."

"About the banker?"

The banker! Had he made such a complete mess of this? "No, Eliza. About you. I want to speak to you about…you."

She blinked. "You want to *speak* to me?" And then

she burst into laughter, falling back against the chair in a fit of giggles.

"What?" he demanded, trying to understand what he'd said that was so amusing.

"For a moment I thought you meant to offer for my *hand*!" she cried with delight. "You're so very serious, and when a gentleman says..." She waved a hand. "You must ignore me." She giggled again.

His heart climbed to his throat. He'd been so blinded by his infatuation that he hadn't really thought how this could seem to her. "Oh God. Eliza, I—"

"Good heavens, I can be such a silly goose," she said, still giggling. She sat up and carefully wiped a finger beneath each eye. She straightened herself and put her hands in her lap. "All right, there we are. I am composed and I do beg your pardon." Her brows dipped and she leaned toward him. "But it does bring to mind the question of who *will* you offer for?"

He was knocked off balance by *that* question and didn't know what to say. No one beside his brother would dare to ask him so bluntly.

No one but Eliza Tricklebank.

She must have seen his consternation because she waved a hand. "Don't trouble yourself, really. I should never have asked. But of course it's the question on everyone's mind in London. *I* don't wonder," she said confidently. "It would do me no good at all to wonder. Would you like to know what I *do* wonder?"

"I would."

"I wonder why you've not been married already."

He was taken aback again, made speechless by another question few would dare to put to him. "It's...

complicated," he said. He didn't want to talk about marriage. He wanted to talk about her.

"Oh, I'm certain it's all *terribly* complicated. And yet, I would think the entire kingdom of Alucia would be preoccupied with that very question. Much like everyone here is preoccupied with the queen's many pregnancies. She's with child again, my father has told me."

"Is she?" His head was spinning around the many things she was saying.

"Did you not notice when you met her? I think it will be soon."

"I..." He had to think back to the evening at Windsor. What he remembered about Queen Victoria was how small she was. No bigger than a child herself. "I didn't notice," he admitted. "The English skirts are very full."

"Oh, *aren't* they?" She sighed. "So much trouble, these full skirts. I prefer the Alucian way of dressing. Such lovely trains."

The door opened and Patro slipped inside. "Shall I serve, Your Highness?" he asked in Alucian.

Sebastian nodded.

Immediately, the door was pushed open and Egius entered with a tray, followed by one of the guards with another tray carrying the dishes of food. Patro took each dish and expertly spooned food onto the plates. Lamb with carrots and leeks. Freshly baked bread. When Patro had filled the plates, he stood back.

Sebastian glanced at Eliza. "Shall we?"

"I am astonished! I hadn't expected this."

Once again he felt uncertain. Should he have told her he meant to dine? Would she not have expected it, given the late hour? "I hope...do you mind?"

"Of course not! I'm ravenous," she said, and stood

up and walked to the table before he could escort her. With a nod of his chin, Sebastian sent Patro and Egius on their way.

He managed to help Eliza into a seat before she sat on her own. He took his seat, refilled their glasses with wine and lifted his glass. "To our friendship."

She lifted her glass and smiled brightly. "To our friendship," she echoed, touching her glass to his.

"It's good, isn't it?" Sebastian asked as they began to eat.

"It's *divine*," she agreed, forking more. "I have long thought that no cook can compare to our Margaret, but I might have been mistaken. And by the bye, Sebastian, you didn't answer my question, if I may be so bold as to say so. You haven't said why you are not yet married with a dozen little prince heirs. Isn't that what future kings do?"

The way she flowed from one topic to the next fascinated him. But her question unnerved him. She was right—that was precisely what princes did. "It doesn't sound very appealing when you put it like that."

"Really? I would *adore* having a dozen little princes running around."

"I might ask the same of you," he said. "Why haven't you married? I would think that you would be in great demand, and I don't understand why you have kept yourself from it."

She looked surprised. "I haven't *kept* myself from it. I will tell you, but I inquired of you first." She smiled pertly.

"You did," he conceded. He sat back. He sighed, thinking through the years, of the reasons he'd…avoided?…his duty. "The truth is that if ever I met a woman who engaged me, she was not suitable to marry a crown prince in either her standing or connections. And the women who were suitable did not engage me."

"Well, that sounds perfectly wretched."

Was she teasing him? Making light of his situation? "It's really beyond my control." He stabbed a bite of the lamb. "So much of my life is beyond my control, really. So many decisions must be made based on the needs of the country and not the man."

"I believe a person should be allowed to marry on the basis of compatibility and affection and nothing more," she said firmly.

It was as if she was reading his thoughts. "They should, I agree."

She held his gaze for a long moment. Sebastian could feel something highly charged slip between them like a whisper before she dropped her gaze to her plate. "The rules for marrying a prince," she murmured. "There ought to be a book to instruct all the ladies who wish to be a princess." When she looked up again, she was smiling once more.

How he wished he could wake to that smile every day. How he wished he could marry for compatibility and affection and nothing more. "You've not yet answered my question," he said gently.

"Ah yes, the perennial question on the minds of strangers everywhere. Why in *heaven* has Miss Tricklebank not done her duty and married?" She sipped her wine as she considered him. "You could very well be scandalized."

"Scandalize me, then," he challenged her. "Tell me everything. Is the truth so awful?"

She laughed. "It's not particularly pleasant from my viewpoint. *Lord*, I can't believe I mean to tell you!" She fanned her face with her hand. "Hollis is forever telling me I say things I ought not to say outside of our parlor, but what have I to lose by being truthful? My situation can't possibly be made worse by it. All right, Sebastian, brace yourself. We are alike in ways you don't even realize. We are both hemmed in by expectations and rules. As for me, there *was* a gentleman once upon a time."

"A gentleman seems to me a good start."

"He *appeared* to be one," she corrected.

"That's tantalizing. Go on," he urged her.

"My father is a justice, as you know. The gentleman's father was likewise a justice. We had met on several occasions, and after some of those meetings, he expressed his desire to marry."

Sebastian felt a swell of resentment against this gentleman. "And you said no?"

A laugh burst from her. "How I wish I had said no. The truth is that I was quite naive. He didn't actually *make* an offer of marriage, you see, but promised he would. I assured him that when the time came, he could count on my enthusiastic and favorable reply."

"Ah." Sebastian put down his fork. He had no right to ask, but something in him needed to know. "Did you love him?" He closed his hand into a fist and laid it against the table. "My apologies. How rude of me." How odd that he was apologizing to her for a second time.

"It's a fair question. Yes, I loved him. Quite a lot, actually. I thought I'd have a dozen little princes around me in short order." She smiled ruefully.

This story was making him feel strangely ill. Was it indignation that nauseated him? Or was it envy? "Why didn't you marry him, then?"

"Well, that's the interesting thing. He never asked. He made a lot of promises, and he assured me it was only a matter of time. He took full advantage of my esteem for him," she said with a flutter of lashes, "but can you imagine? When the time came, he offered for someone else."

Sebastian stared at her.

The color in her cheeks had gone deeper, and Eliza smiled with a twinge of bitterness. "She had twenty thousand pounds a year. I had a blind father and a smaller dowry. A respectable one, mind you, but nothing like that. I suppose she solved a few financial problems for him."

He couldn't fathom it.

"He played me for a fool. He never meant to offer. He was lying to me all along, meant only to seduce me, and I will not lie—he was very successful. And it turned out that I was one of the very few in London not to know about the other engagement." She laughed again, this time to the ceiling. "The truth was made known to me at a supper party, when the host stood to toast the newly engaged couple. And I..." She sighed and looked at him. "Suffice it to say I did not react well at all."

"Deo," he said. *God.* "Eliza, I am so terribly—"

"Please," she said. "It was at least ten years ago. I feel nothing for it." She drank more wine.

How could a man treat any woman so ill? But especially Eliza? He understood the base instinct—she was lovely. But to be so cruel? So lacking in morals? It was unfathomable. He dropped his gaze to his plate. "There was never another opportunity for you?"

"Not really. Mr. Norris was quite keen, but he was in search of a housekeeper and not a wife. I don't know how it's done in Alucia, but in London, when a woman has been deemed..." she paused and tapped her finger on her lips, as if searching for the right word "*...notorious.* Yes, notorious. When she is deemed such, her prospects dim. And as she grows older, like me, she grows more undesirable to wed. The invitations cease to come. She is labeled a spinster, and when she walks down the street, no one notices her. She becomes invisible. She helps her father with the law and they pay her no mind. She's a ghost at his side." Her smile was tinged with sadness. "Isn't it ironic? I feel as if the rules that surround me must be as strong as the rules that surround you. The only difference is that you are highly visible and desired."

Sebastian was dismayed for her. Youth and vitality and wealth were the measures of a good match in Alucia. But Eliza was such a vibrant, beautiful woman. There was truly no one like her and he would expect healthy men to be calling on her every day, vying for her attention.

He was certainly vying for it.

"Look, I've made you forlorn! You mustn't be, not on my behalf!" she said cheerfully. "Life has a way of putting you where you should be. My father needs me. I help him with his work and as it happens, I know quite a lot about the law. And clocks."

She smiled, but Sebastian leaned forward and covered her hand with his. "Are you content with it, Eliza? Isn't there more that you want?"

She seemed bemused by his question. "I don't...no. No, I don't want more. What is the point of wanting more? My circumstances will not change. I will not suddenly become a mother to a dozen little princes. All I want now is for my father to be comfortable." She looked off for a moment. "And perhaps see a bit of the world. At least go beyond London."

Sebastian leaned back, his hand sliding from hers. He wanted more for her. He wanted everything for her. She should have everything.

"Are you properly scandalized?" she asked.

"Not in the least," he said quietly. "And you're not a ghost to me. I see you very clearly."

She smiled happily. "Good! I rather like our friendship." She resumed eating.

He'd lost his appetite. He was still pondering what she'd said about their situations being similar. How the circumstances of his birth and her affair had rendered them both completely helpless when it came to choosing a life mate. Oh, but he knew there were men across the globe who would envy his position. Who would welcome the flotilla of beauties who sailed through his world trying to catch his eye on any given day. But Sebastian had grown weary of it. There had been so many of them through the years that they all seemed the same to him now.

What he wanted was what Eliza wanted—the peace and comfort of a life mate. A happy home. A dozen little princes.

"Are you going to tell me about your conversation with Mr. Heath?"

That again. He picked up his fork and willed away the image of Matous that suddenly popped into his head. "It was not particularly helpful. He said only that my secretary had wondered if he'd been contacted by a French banker. That he understood someone with a large sum of money wished to use the English bank to transfer the sum to the French bank."

"Why?" Eliza asked.

"I don't know. I don't know why anyone from Alucia would bring a large sum to England only to transfer it to France."

"Could it have been winnings from a bit of gambling? I understand that great sums can be won."

"It could have been, I suppose, but why transfer the sum to a French bank? Why not to the Bank of Alucia?"

"Because he didn't want anyone in Alucia to know," she suggested. She put aside her fork and settled back against the chair, her arms folded across her as she thought it through. "And naturally, access to a French bank would be a bit easier than access to the Bank of England if one was in Alucia. But who would he be hiding it from?"

Sebastian shrugged. "The government, perhaps, to avoid taxation."

"Or family. Perhaps he didn't want to share his winnings. Perhaps he had sworn off gambling and didn't want to disappoint them. But why would your secretary know of it? Why would he ask?"

"That's the rub," Sebastian agreed.

"I can think of one possibility."

"What?"

She stood up, which struck Sebastian as odd—no one ever rose from a table before him or the king or queen. But Eliza had already gone to the hearth and held out her hands to the heat, blissfully unaware of such archaic rules. "If the money was destined for something nefarious, it might be detected if it was in an Alucian bank."

That was true. The Bank of Alucia was governed by the crown.

"What if the money was destined for some place like Wesloria? What if the reason the money was in England at all was so that it might travel from England to France to Wesloria, so that no one in Alucia would be the wiser?"

That made sense to him on some level.

Eliza began to sway from side to side, apparently warming to her idea. "If that were the case, one would think that your secretary knew something of it. One would think he was the one who sent my father the note, which obviously, he couldn't have done. It means someone else knew of it, too. The thing, I should think, is to find the man who delivered the note. Someone gave it to him. That someone would know."

It was so wildly improbable that it actually made sense to Sebastian. "You're very clever, Eliza, do you know that?"

She laughed. "You flatter me."

"It's not flattery." He stood up from the table and walked to the hearth to stand beside her. He wanted to say something, but whatever it was, it swelled in the back of his throat, a lump of unformed words, mangled by feelings that were overwhelming.

He touched his fingers to her hand, then laced his fingers through hers as they stood side by side staring into the fire. "Eliza… I want you to know…" He paused and swallowed. "I want you to know that I wish…"

Words were wretched. They sounded cheap. They did not adequately describe what he wished, and he swallowed down the bitter aftertaste. "I wish things were different for us."

She squeezed his fingers. "Don't you dare say it, Sebastian Chartier. Don't you *dare*. Do you think I expected anything from you at all? I'm not a debutante without any notion of how the world spins around me. I don't wish a single thing had been different." She turned to him, her face even lovelier in the golden light of the fire. "I met a prince. A *real* prince. And now he is my friend. So no, I don't wish for a single thing to have been different. Except the death of your friend, naturally."

The swell in his throat began to choke him. "I *do* wish it was different," he said earnestly. "*Deo*, how I do." He touched his knuckles to her cheek. Her skin was warmed by the heat from the fire, and her shining gray eyes were anchored in his. Sebastian slid his hand to the hollow of her throat, spreading his fingers against the column of her neck, and down, to her décolletage.

Eliza did not move. She did not object. "How would it be different?"

"I would take you in my arms," he said softly. "I would behave in all the ways a prince ought not to behave."

"How?"

She was so close now that he could feel her breath on his chin as he rested his palm against her heart.

"In a way that would scandalize tender young hearts," he muttered. He could feel her heartbeat thrumming with determination against his hand, beating as strong as his. He slid his hand lower still, to the swell of her breast, and Eliza drew a shallow breath. Color shaded her cheeks.

She shifted closer to him. "I don't have a tender young heart."

Sebastian's blood began to roil. He bent his head and touched his lips to hers, and the moment he did, his heart leapt nearly out of his chest. He drew her lip between his teeth and probed deeply, his tongue swirling around hers while he filled his hand with her breast.

Eliza's soft sound of pleasure was the thing that sent him barrelling past all common sense. He caught her with an arm around her waist and hauled her into his body, pressing his hardness against her so that she would feel what she did to him, would know how much he wanted her, how his body was simmering, building to the boil of raw need. He slipped his hand into her bodice.

"The door," she whispered.

He was slipping into a fog and couldn't hear her. "Mmm?"

"The door."

It took a great deal of effort for Sebastian to reel himself back from the sea he was about to dive into. He glanced over her shoulder to the door and reluctantly let go of her. He strode forward, grabbing a chair on his way and dragging it behind him. He wedged it beneath the doorknob like a rotten bounder.

Eliza was standing where he'd left her, one hand on her throat, the other on her hip. She smiled and slowly arched a brow, as if questioning why he dallied.

Sebastian fairly leapt back across the room to her, grabbed her up and lifted her off her feet, eliciting a squeal of delight from her as he whirled her around and onto a settee. "You have captured me completely, Eliza," he said, and then abandoned all thought.

This, he thought desperately to himself, was a moment like no other, like none would ever be, and he would never forget it. He kissed her with all the passion and emotion that sort of feeling aroused in a man.

CHAPTER NINETEEN

A long-married lady known for her lace caps has recently supplied her daughters with a remedy for love. Hold rainwater in a crystal vase for three days, then boil with apple and rosemary. Pour the water into ale and serve to the object of affection. Love will be returned tenfold. Careful you do not serve the ale to someone whose affection you do not want, for you will not be able to end it. Our lady with the lace caps avows she knows this to be true.

—Honeycutt's Gazette of Fashion and Domesticity for Ladies

IT SEEMED ALMOST preternatural to Eliza how her body could feel the fall before her mind could even grasp it. It was the same sensation as when she was a child, the same sink of the gut she would experience before falling from a tree or tumbling off a horse. Her body sought to protect itself from harm and twisted or moved however it needed to while her mind struggled to catch up.

That was exactly what happened to her when Sebastian touched her—she fell at a perilous pace with no hope of breaking the fall, and really, when she thought about it afterward, no part of her desired to break the fall—her heart slammed the door on that notion.

The moment Sebastian's mouth touched hers, Eliza was done. The only desire she had was to keep falling. She'd meant what she said—she didn't want a single thing to be different. *Children, gather round. I kissed a prince, I made him a friend, and before he set sail for his kingdom, I bedded him. Pin that to your pretty little bonnets.*

His hands were on her body, on her breasts, squeezing her hips. They were frantic, as if they'd caged raging desires for years. He held her tightly, bending her body into his, his fingers sinking into the curls of her hair as he kissed her with the same, desperate need that was eddying in her. Another breath, and she was on her back on the settee, Sebastian's hands beneath the hem of her gown, shoving the fabric up, then his hand sliding up her leg, to the top of her stocking and her bare thigh, to the space between her legs.

Eliza dug her fingers into his shoulders and gasped into his mouth when he touched her there. She was damp in anticipation of his touch, and as his fingers danced in the furrow of her sex, shivers of delight and desire began to radiate through her body.

Her skirt and petticoat was bunched between them. She held him in her arms, her fingers clawing down his back as he stroked her with his hand. If she hadn't been incinerated by the burn in her veins, Eliza might have laughed at their inglorious and frantic arrangement. But she'd turned to ash, and there was nothing she could think of, nothing she wanted more than this man. It was so urgent between them, so much overwrought attraction and desire boiling between them that it couldn't come fast enough.

Sebastian was braced above her, his gaze taking her

in. His green eyes had gone dark, like the shades of a forest. He was breathing hard as if he was sprinting toward the finish line. He quickly shed his coat, his waistcoat and neckcloth.

Eliza watched him with fascination. His body, apparent to her beneath a silk shirt, was hard and the contours sculpted to the most alluring figure she could hope for. As his gaze slid down her body, she hoped he found her just as appealing. His eyes fixed on the low cut of her gown. His arousal was evident, and he made a soft moan of pleasure before he lowered himself to her bosom. He slid his hand into her dress and freed a breast, then took it into his mouth.

The sensation was divine; Eliza's head fell back and she closed her eyes, floating along on a river of desire he'd created for her, digging her fingers into his shoulders as he teased her with his lips and his tongue. "You're *ruining* me," she said, breathless with pleasure.

"You've already ruined me." His hand found her leg again, and he moved his hand up, pushing her gown and petticoat out of the way.

"Are we mad?" Eliza asked breathlessly as she slid her hands beneath his shirt to explore his body.

"*Je*, utterly so." He abruptly gathered her in his arms and stood up from the settee as if she weighed nothing, and twirled around, coming down onto one knee and putting her on her back before the hearth. He settled in between her legs.

Her intense lust for Sebastian would be her downfall. She was so eager to feel him inside her that she hooked her leg behind his back and raked her fingers down his chest. She arched her back into him, opening her mouth beneath his, her tongue twirling around his. She pressed against him and boldly moved her hand to the front of his trousers and slid her palm down his erection.

Sebastian lifted his head as if he intended to speak. His eyes had gone dark with the longing that was annihilating her, and there seemed to her no time for words. This was too urgent, too imperative. She cupped him, rubbed her hand against him.

"Eliza," he said hoarsely.

To hear this man whisper her name with such raw desire was astonishing in its capacity to arouse and incite. The dam of yearning burst within her, and it was unlike any corporeal thing she'd ever experienced. It was hedonistic, without the slightest apprehension, nothing but need for his flesh in hers. She began to fumble with the buttons of his trousers in a dire need to free him as he removed his shirt.

When he pulled the shirt over his head, Eliza was momentarily paralyzed. He was truly magnificent, all curved muscle on bone. She kissed his chest, her tongue on his nipples, her hands moving on his body, trying to touch every part of him.

Sebastian shifted his weight between her legs. He paused, his gaze devouring her as he guided himself into her body, sliding in with excruciating care, pushing into the very core of her.

Eliza was filled with his flesh and a pleasure so immense that she surrendered instantly. She was speechless, all thought departed and nothing remaining but raw desire. She pushed against him and said, "More."

Sebastian understood her. He began to move in her, his desperation as hard as hers. Eliza let go to ride the wave that started in her ankles and rose up, filling every vein, wrapping around every fibre. It was wild and lawless, hard and frenzied. They moved together and against each other, her clinging to his hips as if she could pull him closer and deeper, him with his arm around her waist to anchor her as he drove into her while his eyes darkened even more.

"More," she said again. She had no idea what she meant by that, other than she wanted every bit of him, every inch of him, galvanized by the undisguised need they both apparently shared. She could feel the earthquake building, could feel her body beginning to detonate. He kissed her, his tongue swirling in her mouth, his hands stroking her along with his body.

This would end in a blaze of fireworks. All the charges were flaring, the skies opening, and there would be nothing left of her.

Sebastian grabbed her hand, held it to his chest, and lifted his hips, thrusting deeper. Eliza cried out with ecstasy, her body convulsing as she shattered around him. Sebastian thrust faster, then abruptly pulled himself free of her body with a gasp as his release racked his body. He dropped his forehead to her shoulder, panting.

Neither of them could speak for a long moment. Eliza could scarcely breathe. When she could at last draw a breath, she brushed the lock of dark hair that had fallen over his brow, then pressed her palms to his cheeks and lifted his head.

He returned her gaze with glassy-eyed contentment and smiled. "I didn't know such pleasure was possible," she said, and caressed his face with her palm before she kissed his mouth.

He dipped his head and nibbled at her collarbone. "Where did you come from, Eliza Tricklebank? What heavenly being put you in my path?" He lifted his head and kissed her, his mouth lingering on hers, so gentle now. So tender. He slowly pulled away from her and rolled onto his side beside her, his arm draped across her middle.

Not only did Eliza feel sated, she felt free. Free of the burden she'd carried for years, free of the past that had defined her. She felt affection and a different sort of desire now—to be cocooned in his arms, safe from the world, happy and moved and complete.

She felt all those things, but she also felt a bit of sorrow. It lurked on the edges of her happiness and contentment, seeping into the cracks.

Sebastian came up on his elbow, traced a finger over her lips, then lowered his head to kiss her forehead. "I've the house let for a week."

She was surprised by this news and turned to look up at him. He looked so hopeful, as if he wanted her to approve. "You want me to return?"

His brow furrowed. "*Je*, of course. Surely you didn't think I…that this was—"

"No," she said quickly, although she wasn't entirely certain what he would say. She thought this was a tryst, a clandestine sexual encounter. She didn't expect it to be more. "But surely you have many invitations and meetings you must attend?"

He frowned and closed his eyes a moment, pressing the bridge of his nose with his fingers. "I'll find a way, Eliza—I *will* find a way."

It moved her that he wanted to find a way. And she'd be delighted if he did. But there was a part of her that wanted to ask him toward what end. She felt strangely unsteady. The complete surrender she'd experienced only moments ago had begun to dissipate as the reality of how difficult it would be to say goodbye to him began to creep in. To try and reconcile that against the spectacular physical release she'd just experienced made her feel unmoored.

He traced a line across her neck with a tress of hair that had fallen from its tie. "Are you all right?"

"Yes!" she said, forcing gaiety into her voice and her smile. Oh, but she knew how to do that, didn't she? She was as practiced as anyone at the art of pretending to be perfectly fine, and she could do it for the prince.

He helped her up and they dressed. They sat at the table, bantering back and forth like lovers. She supposed they were lovers now. But Eliza was increasingly cognizant that this had been a profound night for her, one that had transcended all other nights. She'd experienced an extraordinary culmination of desire, and behind it, the hard beginning of despair.

Eliza generally considered herself to be a confident woman. She'd learned to be one after Asher's betrayal. She reasoned that if she could survive his betrayal, she could survive anything. But when she looked at the man across from her, so eager to please her, so handsome and enticing, she couldn't help but wonder if she might have made a grave mistake.

CHAPTER TWENTY

It has been reported, by those with a Keene eye, that the favored daughter of a certain magnate is currently considered to be the favorite to earn a princely offer of marriage. Perhaps this explains the sudden commission of a new style of gowns with very long trains from a French modiste.

—Honeycutt's Gazette of Fashion and Domesticity for Ladies

SEBASTIAN KISSED ELIZA once as she put on her cloak and prepared to leave. And because he couldn't bear it, he drew her back and kissed her again before removing the chair and opening the door.

Patro was waiting just outside. He'd probably heard everything. He'd probably made note of the way Eliza's curls had come undone and that Sebastian's waistcoat had gone missing.

Sebastian followed behind Eliza and Patro to the door with the sullenness of a child about to be left behind by his parents. Eliza was nattering on, her voice high and breathless. Sebastian realized that while he was accustomed to having an audience for everything he did, she was not. How foolish he'd been, how unseemly it had been to take her on the floor. But the moment had got the best of him, and it had all seemed so urgent and compelling and he hadn't thought clearly. He'd been beyond even an ability to think. He'd been overwhelmed by his desires.

The Alucian crown prince was mortal after all.

He watched one of his men hand Eliza into the carriage, and watched it pull away.

"Your Highness," Patro said behind him. "Please do come away from the door, lest you risk being seen."

Sebastian reluctantly stepped back and allowed Patro to shut the door.

He couldn't think of much else but Eliza, and when the carriage came back around for him, he brooded all the way back to Kensington Palace.

The way the evening had played out had not been his intention, had *never* been his intention. He'd wanted only to spend time with her and her alone. He'd never intended to seduce her with all the finesse of a lad in a barn on a bed of hay.

That he could feel so passionately about this woman surprised him and intrigued him. There had been times that he'd wondered if he had anything in the way of passion left in him at all. He'd been so intent on his duty for so long, so determined to drag Alucia into the modern world, that heart fires rarely flared in him.

His heart flamed for Eliza Tricklebank.

She deserved a proper bed, with down pillows and silk bed coverings. But how could he possibly even think of it? Did he think he would carry on with her for another week or two? And then what, simply leave her behind as if it had never happened?

And what of his business here? There were still a few small but critical items outstanding in the trade negotiations, and he could not return to Alucia empty-handed—the prime minister would see to it that he was removed from any discussions about war or trade if he did. He would be made into a useless figurehead.

And there was also the matter of choosing a potential bride, a thought that made him queasy. And what of Matous? Was it possible his death had been part of a Weslorian plot, as Eliza had suggested? Didn't that deserve every ounce of his attention?

What he was doing was illogical, but it was as if his heart was moving independently of his head.

He was still trying to work out his own feelings about it when he walked into his apartment suite at Kensington. He instantly drew up when he saw Lady Anastasan sitting near the hearth.

She rose instantly. "Your Highness." She gave him a ghost of a smile, but it was, Sebastian thought, a bit of a smirk.

Sebastian looked around him. Was there anyone else making themselves comfortable in his rooms? This was the second time he'd caught her lingering when no one was around, and it left him feeling uncomfortably exposed. Did the whole bloody contingent of Alucians know what he was doing?

Deo, how he resented the prying eyes everywhere around him. He was a man, for God's sake, and a man was allowed to have an affair of the heart. It was *natural*. What was unnatural was the requirement that he somehow choose a woman whose name he would have to commit to memory, a woman he scarcely knew. What was unnatural was walking into the sanctity of his rooms and finding this woman here.

"Who has given you permission to be here?" he asked sharply.

"I beg your pardon, Your Highness. I stayed to keep an eye on things while you were away. Patro is not here, and neither is Egius."

"*What* things?"

She clasped her hands together at her waist as if she were frightened. "I…ah… I saw Mr. Rostafan coming from this room earlier. I knew you and the others had gone out for the evening, and I thought things shouldn't be left unattended."

"And so you thought you'd do the attending, madam? Do you distrust Mr. Rostafan? Do you think it is your place to question his business?"

Lady Anastasan didn't answer. She clenched her hands tighter.

Well, he distrusted Rostafan. What the bloody hell was he doing in these rooms again? Sebastian looked at his desk, wondering what the man could be looking for.

He looked at Lady Anastasan again. "This may surprise you, Sarafina, but I have guards to keep an eye on things. I don't require my foreign minister's wife to stand lookout."

"I do beg your pardon, Your Highness," she said, clearly chastised. "I suppose I feel protective."

Yes, well, he felt restless and he didn't feel like soothing her ruffled feathers or explaining to her that her position here was temporary. A mere favor. And he most decidedly did not feel like reminding her that she was not, in fact, his mother—Queen Daria was alive and well in Alucia. "Where is Caius?"

"Abed, Your Highness. He wasn't feeling well."

Sebastian turned away from her. "Thank you, Sarafina. You may go to him."

He heard the rustle of her skirts as she moved across

the room. He heard the slide of the door as she opened it and the quiet close behind her. Even still, he glanced over his shoulder to assure himself she'd gone.

He stalked into the adjoining dressing room and began to undress. He tossed his coat onto a chair. Egius had his waistcoat, so Sebastian pulled his shirttails free of his trousers.

He was pulling his neckcloth free of his collar when he heard someone in the sitting room. Assuming it was Patro or Egius returned from Mayfair, he strolled into the sitting room but was brought to a halt by the sight of Rostafan.

His field marshal looked startled. He quickly bowed. "Your Highness. I didn't realize you'd returned."

"Obviously not. What are you doing in my sitting room, uninvited?"

"I beg your pardon, sir. I was searching for Lady Anastasan. I was told she might be here."

"What business would you have with the foreign minister's wife, Rostafan?"

Rostafan's expression changed. He looked almost insulted. "I have no *business* with her, Your Highness. I meant only to inquire after the whereabouts of the foreign minister. I need to speak to him."

Sebastian didn't believe this man. He moved closer to the giant of a man. "Why didn't you send a servant to inquire? Are you in the habit of entering rooms when no one is about?"

"Not at all, Your Highness," Rostafan said calmly. "The door was ajar."

That was not true—the door had been very much closed. He knew, because he'd looked at it after Lady Anastasan had left. What the devil was Rostafan after?

"I have offended you, sir," Rostafan said with a bow of his head.

"*Je*, you have indeed," Sebastian said.

Rostafan clasped his hands behind his back. "With your approval, I will take my leave."

"Go," Sebastian bit out.

Rostafan wheeled about and strode for the door, closing it behind him. The door stayed closed and did not suddenly come ajar.

Sebastian turned his attention to his desk. He walked across the room and found a sealed pouch from Alucia on top of the desk. He opened it and sorted through the contents. There was correspondence for Anastasan. A letter from his father asking when he would complete his work, and informing him that they'd captured rebels in the north. Sebastian's letter to his father had not had time to reach him, so there was no news about the finances of Rostafan. There were some papers from the minister of finance, information Sebastian and his negotiators needed to discuss a tariff that seemed designed to discourage trade.

There was nothing else in the pouch. Nothing to tell Sebastian why Rostafan was skulking about. He wondered what Eliza would say of it.

Sebastian sat at his desk to mull it over, but his thoughts were interrupted by the arrival of Patro and Egius. He put the correspondence in the pouch and sealed it while suspicions began to stack in his thoughts.

He woke up the next morning with a sense of unease rooted firmly in his chest, wedged in beside his feelings for Eliza. He'd dreamed of her, had relived the experience before the fire in that house in such detail that he'd felt bothered and unsatisfied when he awoke.

He was at his desk when Patro announced Foreign Minister Anastasan and his wife.

"Bon den," Caius said, bowing. Lady Anastasan curtsied but kept her gaze on the floor. She seemed nervous, and Sebastian guessed she had not told her husband of his dismissal of her last night.

"What is it?" Sebastian asked.

"I should like to speak to you regarding Lady Elizabeth Keene and Lady Katherine Maugham," Caius said.

Sebastian steeled himself. "What of them?"

"I would suggest that we issue dinner invitations to the ladies and their families. A small affair, perhaps no more than twenty-four?"

An image of Eliza's smiling face slashed across Sebastian's thoughts.

"I should think their families would be delighted," Lady Anastasan said.

Caius shot his wife a dark look full of warning. This was not her affair. She was a secretary, not Sebastian's advisor. "That is for the prince to decide."

"Of course," Lady Anastasan said. "Perhaps His Highness has someone else he'd like to invite? Perhaps one of the ladies he danced with at the Whitbread ball?"

What a curious and dangerous thing to do. What was wrong with the woman?

Her husband's expression turned very dark. "Madam, I forgot some papers. They are on my desk. If you would be so kind as to fetch them."

Lady Anastasan bit her lip but nodded and went out.

"My apologies—" Caius began.

"Not necessary," Sebastian said. "But I've decided I don't have need of a private secretary now that we are nearing the end of our stay here. You and I seem to manage fairly well."

Caius blanched. He opened his mouth, thought better of what he would have said, and then closed his mouth as he bowed his head. "As you wish, Your Highness."

"I wish." Frankly, Sebastian could go the rest of his days without seeing Lady Anastasan. How odd it was to have no opinion of someone, and then to have one develop so quickly and strongly. There was something about her that didn't set well with him. He didn't like the way she lingered, the way she looked him directly in the eye, as if they shared a secret.

"This supper," Sebastian said. "Tell me again—Elizabeth Keene, is she blonde? Brunette?"

"Blonde," Caius said. "Her father is a leading industrialist involved in ironworks and a distant cousin of the queen. Lady Katherine Maugham is the daughter of a prominent member of the House of Lords. On her mother's side, there are ties to Prince Albert's family in Saxe-Coburg and Gotha. Both would be excellent options."

Excellent options for the state, but not for him. Sebastian could scarcely remember either of them. Did it matter? He would come to know whomever he married well enough, he supposed. He would sire the children, and then he would return to his work. "Both families, then. No more than twenty-four. No dancing, if you please." He didn't think he could stomach another ball.

"Will Friday suit?"

That gave him only three days at the house in Mayfair. Three days with Eliza. Three precious days. *"Je,"* he said quietly.

He felt a roil of guilt. What would come was inevitable. He should tell Eliza himself that an announcement would come soon. She knew it would come, she was no fool. But he wanted to be the one to tell her. He wanted her to know how much it pained him.

Even that made him wince—as if his regret was any consolation.

It was no consolation at all. It was gut-wrenching to be called a future king and be so bound by duty. He should be the one man in all the world who could have what he wanted. And yet he was the one man in all the world who could not.

CHAPTER TWENTY-ONE

Ladies, if you install a water pump in your kitchen, do have a care. Recently, a new pump brought such joy to this wife that she pumped until the apparatus flew off and flooded her floor, causing her to fall and break her arm. Some manufacturers suggest that a water pump might be better suited for a garden rather than the house.

News from the Thames is that the Alucian ships are being provisioned for the journey home and will carry away the prince seen often about town.

—Honeycutt's Gazette of Fashion and Domesticity for Ladies

ELIZA WENT TO the market for Poppy and Margaret in a restless bid for something to do, to have something to think about other than Sebastian and this unlikely rabbit hole she'd tumbled down. She slung her cotton bag over her shoulder and wandered through the stalls, idly viewing various wares. She'd promised a new skein of yarn for her father, eggs for Margaret, and three yards of gray muslin for Poppy, if she happened on it.

She had the yarn and muslin. On her way to the booth where the old woman sold eggs, she stopped to admire the flowers that had been cut just this morning and brought to Covent Garden. She was perusing them, wondering if she ought to buy a few for the dining table when someone walked by and caught her eye. He was a very short man, and at first, she hardly spared him a glance, but in the next breath, she realized who he was. The man striding briskly along with a slight limp and his arms swinging was the man who had brought her the post that fateful day.

"Hey!" Eliza shouted. "You there, sir!" She went after him, hopping over and around a pair of chickens that were pecking along the path, past a barking dog, and through two fruit stands. *"Wait!"*

The man glanced curiously over his shoulder, but when he saw her, he started to run.

So did Eliza. She wasn't as quick as she used to be, but she could still keep pace. She picked up her skirts and ran past people who had stopped walking, so startled were they to see a woman chasing a man through the market stalls.

She chased the man into an alley that had no way out. Eliza stopped to catch her breath, her hand pressed to her heart. "There is no need to *run*," she complained. "My lungs are near to exploding!"

"Don't hurt me," the man pleaded with his hands clasped together at his chest, his back to the brick wall.

"*Hurt* you? Do I look as if I could hurt you?"

"I don't know! Perhaps you've got men."

Her laugh turned into a wheeze. "I have no men, sir—look around you! I had some yarn and some cloth, but your reluctance to speak to me caused me to drop my bag. What will I tell my father, I ask you? He was expecting new yarn."

"Please," the man pleaded.

"Do you remember me?"

He nodded warily.

"Splendid. Then perhaps instead of pleading for your life, you'll answer a simple question," she said, coming closer. "I really must know who gave you the note intended for my father."

The man, who was a good head shorter than she, took a pair of steps backward. "What note?"

"The note that was stuck among the letters you handed me that day."

"I don't know about no note, mu'um. I was given five pence to deliver the post, and that I did. I didn't look at it."

"Who gave you five pence? What did he look like?"

"Wasn't a he."

"What do you mean, it wasn't a he?"

"'Twas a she."

"A *she*?"

"Aye, mu'um. Pretty lass, she was."

Well, this was an interesting turn. What woman would be delivering a note like that? "What did she look like?"

"Hair like yours, a bit darker, I suppose. Brown eyes. Small. A far sight smaller than you. But bigger here," he said, gesturing with both hands to his chest. "*Quite* a lot bigger, and spilling out of—"

"All right," she said with a withering look. "Does she live nearby?"

"How'd I know that? Don't know her a'tall. Never seen her before that morning. She don't live round here, I think. Had an odd way of speaking, she did."

What did *that* mean? "Do you mean a lisp?"

"Like she'd come from somewhere other than London."

"An accent?"

He looked at her blankly.

"Did she sound as if she was from the north?" Eliza tried.

"Didn't sound like any Englishman I ever heard."

Was it possible the woman had been an Alucian? Eliza stepped closer. The man's hands came up again as if in prayer. "For heaven's sake, put your hands down. I won't touch you. What did she say?"

"Said she'd give me five pence to take round the post to the judge on Bedford Square. I know who that is, everyone knows Justice Tricklebank on Bedford Square. He's got no eyes."

"He has eyes," Eliza said. "He's blind. It's different. Go on, what then?"

"Well…nothing. I said all right. She give the five pence, and I took the post from her and went round and handed it to you."

How odd. What was she doing with her father's post? "Where did she go?"

He shrugged again. "Disappeared into the market. Just wandered away."

Eliza tried to think who it might possibly have been. A *woman*?

"Will you let me go now?" the man asked.

She studied him, looking for any sign of prevarication or artifice. She saw nothing but a poor man who had earned a bit of extra money and seemed unusually afraid of women. "Yes," she said. "But you ought not to be taking a five pence from every stranger you meet."

"No, mu'um." He was already skirting around her as if he didn't trust her to let him pass. When he had managed to get past her, he took off running again as if the hounds of hell were chasing him.

"I said I'd never hurt you!" Eliza called after him. "How could I possibly *hurt* you?" She sighed and walked out of the narrow alleyway, retracing her steps back to the flower stall, where she found her dropped cloth bag. Trampled, of course.

When she'd purchased the eggs, she started home, still surprised and flummoxed with the idea that a *woman* had given that man the note to deliver.

It was late afternoon and dark clouds were rolling in. There was a chill to the air and a sense of melancholy settled on her. It would be winter soon. She didn't mind winter so much, but it meant that Sebastian would be gone sooner rather than later. She would guess that the Alucians would want to depart before the prevailing winds turned icy cold. Not that she knew a blessed thing about sailing, but the idea seemed plausible to her.

Sebastian had been much on her mind these last few days. The memory of that night—the sounds, the scents, the *feelings*, all of it—had been her constant companion. She had no regrets—it had been magical, really, and something she had never dreamed could happen to her. She'd hardly given a thought to her personal chastity—at least she could live a long life remembering that man's touch.

But a small doubt kept pushing to the forefront. She craved to feel it all again, to look into his green eyes… but she also knew she'd be mad to think of meeting him again, alone. Every time she was with him, she only felt closer to him. Her imagination raced further and further ahead. It would race right off a bridge and into the Thames if she wasn't careful.

He *would* be gone soon, there was no way around that. He was an Alucian prince and he would return to Helenamar with a suitable English bride. He'd have beautiful and hopefully exceedingly healthy children when he assumed his throne, and she…

Well, she would have memories. That was it.

This interlude in an otherwise humdrum life would come to an end and she would at least have the memory of it.

It hardly seemed fair. It was so unfair, in fact, a part of her thought she ought not to make it grossly unfair by refusing to see what was plainly in front of her.

Eliza was so lost in thought that at first she didn't notice the postman until she all but tripped over his satchel. But there stood Mr. French on Mrs. Spragg's stoop, the two of them deep in conversation. A few steps below him on the sidewalk was his satchel with all the post, lying carelessly open.

Eliza waved and looked down at the satchel. The mouth of it was unusually large, presumably so Mr. French could easily search the contents. Anyone walking down the street could dip down and take a letter or two without Mr. French's notice.

She glanced up. Mr. French was leaning against the little stone wall that surrounded Mrs. Spragg's landing, one leg crossed casually over the other, his back to the sidewalk. Eliza could take the whole bloody bag and carry on and he'd never know it. She could certainly rummage around it for a minute or two until she found a few pieces of correspondence addressed to her father.

She leaned over—there was a thick stack of letters and correspondence, bound by a leather tie, the top letter addressed to her father. She suddenly realized how the culprit had done it—Eliza's father received all manner of correspondence at home, whereas most of the residents on this square received perhaps a letter or two on any given day. It would be very easy to find the post destined for number 34.

Eliza waited patiently until Mr. French finally came down the stairs favoring his left leg.

"Miss Tricklebank, what a delight! Shall I hand you the post, then?"

"If you would, please. I thought I'd save you the walk."

"That's very kind of you. I should like to get home to Mrs. French before it's too late." He picked up the bag and set the strap on his shoulder. "I suppose I dally too long on some days. Mrs. French likes me home."

"Of course she does. But you're so very reliable that she must miss you terribly every day."

"I take a bit of pride in that, I do. Can't say that for all the postmen. But me? I deliver every day without fail."

"I know that you do! That's why I was so very surprised when another man delivered our post one day."

"What?" his brows rose, then knit into a frown. "When?"

"Oh, a fortnight or so ago," she said airily.

His frown deepened. "I beg your pardon, Miss Tricklebank, but I don't see how that might have happened. I walk the same route every day. You could set a clock by me, you could."

"Which is why I thought it odd."

He shook his head and gave her a kind, indulgent smile. "I think you must be mistaken, Miss Tricklebank."

As if she were a doddering old woman confused about her whereabouts. She wasn't confused about a thing. "Perhaps you're right." She smiled sweetly. She knew very well that a woman had taken the post addressed to 34 Bedford Square from his bag, had put the note in it, then paid a stranger from the market to deliver it.

"Very well, Miss Tricklebank, if I may leave the justice's post to you, I shall carry on this way and finish my work for the day."

"You may. And good day to you, Mr. French."

He touched two fingers to his cap and started down the walk with his limp and his satchel.

Eliza walked on, pulling her cloak even more tightly around her.

As she neared number 34, she saw a coach was parked at the far corner. It was big, shiny and black, fully enclosed. It looked like the coaches that carried the queen out of Buckingham from time to time. Was it *him*? Her heart began to race. Surely he hadn't come like this, in broad daylight, with a coach as big as a shed.

Oh, Lord, *surely* he was not inside with her father.

Eliza hurried home.

There were three men standing about the coach, all of them in greatcoats, which made it impossible to see if they wore Alucian clothing beneath them, but she didn't really need to see. She knew who they were.

She darted up the steps of the house, tripping over the top step in her haste, then shouting at Jack and John to move away from the door. She squeezed in through a crack so they'd not escape.

"Eliza!" Poppy hurried down the hall to her, eyes wide as moons. "You won't believe it!"

"Oh, but I think I will." She thrust her things at Poppy. "Where is he?"

"In the parlor. The judge is coming down for tea at any minute."

As if on cue, the judge called downstairs, "Eliza, is that you come in?"

"Yes, Pappa!" she called.

"Who has come?" he called.

"Ah… I'll see," she said, and exchanged a frantic look with Poppy. She tried to remove her cloak as she hurried into the parlor, Jack and John racing ahead of her.

Sebastian was standing at the mantel, either admiring her clocks or Pris, who was perched atop one of them. He turned when she banged in the door, and Eliza had only a moment to collect herself. He was so striking, so virile, and the way he smiled at her made her feel warm and a bit wobbly.

With a quick look over her shoulder, she whispered loudly, "What are you doing here?"

Jack and John, their tales wagging, were sniffing around Sebastian.

"I must speak with you," he said, moving forward through the dogs as if he didn't realize they were there.

"My father is expecting me for tea," she said.

"Then I should like to make his acquaintance, if I may."

"Eliza?" her father called.

She was panicked—how would she explain the Alucian prince to her father? "Lord help you, I think you've lost your mind," she said softly.

"I can't disagree." He suddenly strode across the room and grabbed her up and kissed her hard on the mouth, then let go and stepped back just as her father entered the room, his hand on the strings tacked to the wall to guide him.

Eliza turned toward her father, her eyesight slightly blurred from being thoroughly dazzled. “Pappa!” she said, far too brightly. She went to him, took his hand and helped him to his chair.

“Where have you been?” he asked as he seated himself.

“The market. I brought the yarn like you wanted.”

He turned his head toward the room as if he had sight and was looking for something. “What color?”

“Blue—”

“What is the matter?” he asked.

“Pardon?”

“You’re too anxious, darling.” He stilled a moment, as if listening. She tried to calm her breathing and looked nervously at Sebastian. He looked as if he wanted to speak.

“Who is here?”

“Um...”

Sebastian opened his mouth as if to speak.

“You are right,” she said quickly before he could utter a word. “Someone has come. Poppy, will you bring wine or tea or...better yet, whisky.”

“Yes,” Poppy said from her place at the door.

“Who in the blazes is here?” her father demanded.

“I will tell you, Pappa.” She put his knitting on his lap and guided his hands to the needles. Pris leapt onto his chair and stretched along the back of it.

“We’ve a caller,” Eliza continued. “Well, *I* have a caller. But he would like to make your acquaintance.”

“*He?* Have you been keeping a secret from me, darling? You don’t mean to leave me, do you?”

"What? No! Of course not, Pappa. I should tell you that he's rather a notable caller."

Her father's brows dipped. "How notable?"

"He's a prince," she said quietly.

Her father fixed his glassy gaze into space. "That is indeed a notable caller. Why is he calling?"

"To have a word with me, actually. We're friends—"

"Friends," he scoffed.

Sebastian stepped forward, but Eliza shook her head. "We are, Pappa. I've helped him in a personal matter."

Her father snorted. "You will forgive me, Eliza, my dearest, for you are a very capable woman. But I cannot begin to imagine how you might have *helped* this man. Particularly after I expressly asked you to stay clear of any matter having to do with him."

"You did, Pappa," she said, wincing. "But I didn't. And now we are friends and I—"

"Am I to meet the gentleman?" her father demanded.

Eliza didn't hear what more her father said, because there was suddenly a raised voice coming from the entry. Bloody hell, it was Hollis. Eliza bolted for the door to head her off, because her sister was perfectly capable of making a tense situation even worse. Unfortunately, Hollis was already at the door of the salon. She came to a halt just over the threshold and stared at them all in confusion.

"Hollis, dearest, come in!" Eliza said gaily, opting to pretend it was perfectly natural for Sebastian to be standing in the parlor. "One more for whisky, Poppy!"

Hollis stared at Sebastian. "Eliza! What is—"

"I was just about to make introductions," Eliza interjected.

"I think you should," Sebastian said. He bowed to Hollis. "Mrs. Honeycutt."

"Your Highness," she said coolly, but curtsied elegantly.

"Pappa, please allow me to introduce His Royal Highness, Prince Sebastian." Was that how it was done? Eliza really had no idea. She looked at Sebastian for help, but his expression, so earnest only moments before, was politely shuttered. "My father, Justice William Tricklebank."

Sebastian reached down for her father's hand. "A great pleasure, Your Honor."

"The pleasure *should* be mine," her father said, and slowly withdrew his hand. "But until I know what business you could possibly have with my daughter, I will reserve it."

Hollis clamped her hand over her mouth in mortification. Eliza was not terribly surprised. Sebastian took her father's tone in stride.

"I appreciate a man who comes straight to the point," Sebastian said. "Miss Tricklebank spoke true—she has been a great help to me and dispenses excellent advice. I arrived tonight hoping to seek more of it."

"She is invaluable in her advice," her father agreed. "But I would hope that in the course of seeking her advice you have not extended assurances or promises you do not intend to keep, sir."

"Pappa!" Hollis and Eliza exclaimed in unison.

"You have my word as a prince and a gentleman," Sebastian said solemnly.

Eliza's face was flaming. She wanted to point out to her father that she was a grown woman and not an innocent maid. Before she could make her point, Poppy returned to the room with the rickety rolling cart they used when they had several guests, the small whisky tots rattling against each other. She bumped into a stack of books on the floor and knocked them over, then backed up and went around them, rolling the cart to a halt before her father.

"Ah, here is the whisky," Eliza said. "I think we could all use a bit. Please do sit, Your Highness."

"Are we not on more familiar terms, Eliza? You must call me Sebastian."

"Oh *no*," Hollis said faintly. "Oh dear."

"Right you are," Eliza said with a dark look for him. It wouldn't take her sister or her father much effort to understand what had happened between her and Sebastian. "Will you please sit, Sebastian?"

"I shudder to think how the two of you have come to a first-name basis in such a short time of acquaintance, but for now, I should like to know what advice you've sought from my daughter," her father said, as if he'd read Eliza's thoughts. She tried to put a tot of whisky in his hand. He waved her off.

"She's been indispensable to me in discovering what happened to my personal secretary," Sebastian said, and accepted a tot of whisky from Poppy, who almost bobbled it right into his lap, she was so struck by him. "As you might imagine, after a tragic loss such as we experienced, everyone is suspect. But I have come to trust Eliza's point of view."

"No doubt she has come to trust yours, as well," her father said curtly.

"Pappa!"

Hollis, who would not miss an opportunity to find

something to print, asked quickly, "Have you discovered who was behind it?"

Sebastian shook his head.

Eliza wanted to tell Sebastian what she'd learned today, but she'd not do so in front of her family. She'd always been proud that her family was free with their opinions—it had made for some healthy and honest debates over the years. But today, she preferred not to hear any of their opinions on any subject.

"You may trust her opinion, sir," her father continued, "but I assure you, Eliza knows nothing of murder and should not be involved. I resent that you might have put my daughter in danger."

"Of course he hasn't!" Eliza exclaimed. Her father was speaking as if she were a child.

"Eliza is very clever, Pappa," Hollis said. "Far cleverer than any of the sheltered young debutantes His Highness may have met here—"

"Hollis!" Eliza said sharply. "All right, that's enough, both of you," she said, holding up both hands. "Pappa. Hollis. I do appreciate your care and concern for me and my reputation…such that it is," she said with a shrug. "But I'm not a fool, and the prince has been a perfect gentleman. We are *friends*. I am not in danger. In *any* way," she said, with a pointed look for Hollis.

Hollis frowned into her tot of whisky. "We care about you, Eliza."

They cared about the poor Eliza who had once been the biggest fool in all of London, and they did not want to see a repeat of that terrible time. "I know you do, and I love you desperately because of it. I made a wretched mistake ten years ago, but I am a very different person than I was then. You know that I am."

Hollis's lashes fluttered as she looked down. "Don't say more, Eliza," she softly warned her.

"I've nothing to hide," Eliza said.

"I have found her honesty to be refreshing," Sebastian said. "In my daily dealings, there are many people I meet who are not entirely truthful with me because of misguided notions about what a prince should or should not know. They tend to keep things from me, or present them in a pleasing way. Eliza has been quite blunt in her assessments of both me and my situation. She speaks the truth, no matter what."

"She does indeed speak the truth, and I, too, rely on her advice. But she is my daughter and I would not see her harmed," the judge said firmly.

"I am not *harmed*," Eliza said.

"Be that as it may, you are in no position to advise a prince," her father insisted. "If that is the sort of advice he seeks, then perhaps he will agree to dine with us this evening and see what other wisdom can be gleaned from all the Tricklebanks of Bedford Square. We are all of us dreadfully honest and free with our opinions, no matter how wrongheaded we might be."

"A very kind offer," Sebastian said. "Unfortunately, I am expected elsewhere." He looked at Eliza. "I had hoped for a word with your daughter, if we could be spared a moment?"

Eliza looked at her family. Pappa's eyes were fixed in her general direction, and the rest of them were all looking at her—Hollis, Poppy, the dogs…even Pris. "I can be spared," she answered for them all. "Please excuse us."

Her father said nothing. His hands rested on his lap and he turned his head.

"It has been my pleasure to make your acquaintance, Your Honor," Sebastian said gracefully. "Mrs. Honeycutt," he said, bowing. "Poppy."

Poppy smiled sheepishly at him. At least her opinion had changed for the better.

Eliza walked to the door of the parlor and opened it. The prince would not go through before she did, so she shot a look at her family before passing through. She walked across the hall to the small sitting room she sometimes used to work on her clocks. There were several of them around in various stages of disrepair. Sebastian followed her inside, pulling the door closed behind him. For a fleeting moment, she thought her father was right—she had no business advising a prince. But she had to share with him what she'd just discovered. "Sebastian! I have news," she said, grabbing his arms. "I found the man who delivered the post to me!"

Something flickered in Sebastian's eyes. Something hard. "I told you not to look. Where did you find him?"

"At Covent Garden. You won't believe it! He said the person who asked him to take the post for five pence was a *woman*."

"A woman?" He looked stunned. "What woman?"

"He claimed not to know her, but he said she was small, with hair darker than mine, and had brown eyes."

"That could be any woman in England," he said.

"He also said her…ah…bosom was large. And that she spoke with an accent. Not an English accent, but a foreign one."

Sebastian's face began to darken with a frown. "Did he recognize the accent?"

"No—but she must have been an Alucian, don't you think?"

He considered that and shook his head. "It's not possible."

"Of course it is!"

He rubbed the back of his neck, thinking. "There are no more than five women in our party. Could she have been French?"

"Why would a Frenchwoman want to deliver the note? Unless she was somehow tied to the French banker? But it could have been an Alucian woman who is not in your party. Someone who was here already, or arrived after you. A rebel who knew you'd come to England."

He didn't reject the idea. He turned away from her, thinking. "And I suppose it could have been one in my party."

He stared at the floor for a long moment.

"What did you want to tell me?" Eliza asked.

Sebastian suddenly turned around. "What is the time?"

An ironic question, given the number of clocks stacked around the room. Eliza picked up a pocket watch she'd recently repaired and glanced at the face. "A quarter to six." She handed the pocket watch to him. "For you."

He looked down at the small pocket watch she held in her hand.

"I bought it from an old man who was selling it for parts. It was so lovely I wanted to repair it. And I have." She traced her finger over the engraving on the back of the watch. *Amor loyal*, a Latin inscription that meant *Love is loyal.* She had assumed that the watch had been a gift and had wondered, as she'd bent over the small timepiece when she'd worked on it, who had made it for whom. It was such a lovely sentiment and it seemed…it seemed fitting somehow to give it to Sebastian. "I want you to have it. A token of our friendship." She lifted his hand and put the watch in his palm, folding his fingers over it. "Something to remember me by."

Sebastian slowly lifted his gaze from the watch. His beautiful green eyes looked suddenly dull. "I will cherish it," he said softly and slid the watch into his pocket. He took both hands in hers. "I must leave you now."

"So soon?"

"I am expected at Kensington. I should have been there by now."

"Oh." She tried to smile at him, but for some reason, the smile would not come. *I must leave you now.* It sounded so final. That was what she wanted, wasn't it? To end before the inevitable crash?

"I am dining with the usual array of dignitaries."

She nodded.

He glanced down at her hands, brought one to his lips, then the other. "As well as the families of two young women."

There it was. Eliza's heart began to sink. And curiously, her knees began to quake. She felt as if she was skirting around the possibility of a faint.

"Decisions must be made," he muttered hopelessly. "When I came to England, it was with two objectives in mind. One was to strike the trade agreement we are very near to finishing. It is the first of its kind for Alucia and will bring my country into the age of industrialization."

Eliza nodded.

"The agreement was my idea, but an unpopular one. There are those who advise my father that all our efforts should be pointed toward Wesloria. But I see our future as something brighter than war."

"Oh, I hope that is true."

"It is imperative that I conclude a negotiation that results in an advantageous trade agreement for Alucia, or I will be pushed aside by our parliament. In order to be given the opportunity, I had to make a trade of sorts, Eliza. There is the pressing issue of succession and the agreement I struck with my father and our parliament was to make an advantageous marriage with an Englishwoman who could bring some assurances with her. Do you understand? I mean that am to marry someone who will keep England on our side if war should occur with Wesloria. Do you see? Decisions *must* be made."

Eliza could feel herself nodding. She wanted to sit down. To put her head between her knees. Of course decisions must be made. How odd he should say it that way—as if the decisions would not be made by him.

"But you must know, you *must* know, that I never in my wildest imaginings thought—"

"You mustn't fret about me," she said, interrupting him. She pulled her hands free of his. "Just tell me who, Sebastian. I would like to know."

He grimaced slightly. "Lady Elizabeth Keene," he muttered. "And Lady Katherine Maugham."

The peacock. He was going to offer for the peacock. Eliza didn't know if she should be surprised or if she should go on and vomit on his shoes as she felt on the verge of doing. But she politely swallowed down that swell of nausea.

"Are you acquainted?" he asked.

Of course she wasn't acquainted. She was no one.

She shook her head and tried to breathe properly. "I know of them, but I am not acquainted."

Sebastian's gaze moved over her face. He gathered her in his arms and held her. "I would give the sun and the moon to say something else to you now," he said into her hair. "You can't know how ardently I wish I could. If I could have been anyone else. *Anyone* else."

But he wasn't anyone else, and neither was she, and this had been the inevitable conclusion all along. There had never been even the slightest whiff of another possibility. "You should go," she said into his shoulder, then slowly pushed him back. She made herself look up at him. She made herself smile. She would not, *would not*, let him see that she was crumbling. He owed her nothing. "You don't want to keep them waiting."

Sebastian's face wore his internal conflict. "Perhaps I shouldn't have come, but I wanted you to know," he said. "I needed to tell you myself, Eliza. I couldn't bear for you to hear it from anyone else."

"I understand." She was still smiling.

"Eliza." His voice was full of anguish, but he didn't say anything more. There was nothing left for either of them to say, really. And he was a true gentleman—he wouldn't give her false hope.

She felt tears building behind her eyes and willed them away. She would not cry. She'd known from the beginning that it would end this way and she had no one but herself to blame for the pain it was causing her. "You should go," she said again.

He kissed her cheek, then went out of the room and to the front door. Eliza followed him.

People had gathered around the coach. All of Bedford Square would know that a prince had come. She watched him vault into the coach, watched as it pulled away for what was surely the last time. When she could see it no longer, she backed up, intending to shut the door, and bumped into Hollis.

"Good Lord, Hollis, you frightened me."

"Eliza..." Hollis said sadly. "Darling, please don't fall in love with him."

"I haven't," Eliza insisted. "I *won't*. I'm very clear-headed." Honestly, she didn't know what she felt. Was it love? Was it infatuation? Was it sadness so deep that she could feel it all the way to her toes? She couldn't possibly identify the pernicious mix of feelings in her.

Hollis did not look like she believed her—and she looked incredibly sad.

"Don't look at me like that," Eliza said, trying to pass her sister. "I know what I'm doing."

"Do you?" Hollis asked. "Do you *really*, Eliza? Do you at least have a plan?"

Eliza laughed. "Are you asking if I have a princess plan? A plan in which I somehow seduce a crown prince to love me and marry me and make *me*, a judge's poor daughter, his future queen?" She laughed bitterly. "No, Hollis, I don't have a princess plan. This might hurt in the end, but I don't care. At least I've had a bit of life these last few weeks. At least I was kissed by a prince and loved by a prince and I won't apologize for it or regret it. I would do it all again." She pushed past her sister and went into the parlor.

She *would* do it all again. In a heartbeat.

"Pappa, shall I read to you?" she asked cheerfully.

"Has the prince gone?"

"He has. He is dining with his marital prospects this evening."

She ignored Hollis's gasp of surprise and picked up the book *Catherine* by W. M. Thackeray. A book about a woman who had murdered her husband. It suited her mood, as she would very much like to murder something just now.

She read as Hollis picked up her embroidery. Her father, still agitated, finally felt around for his knitting. The dogs slept, and the cat tried to catch the string of wool from her father's needles. Poppy collected the whisky no one had drunk.

Eliza read, her mind telling her what to say. Her heart…well, her heart wasn't listening.

Her heart was busy shoring up for the storm that would soon hit it.

CHAPTER TWENTY-TWO

A Keene observation has been made as to the withering prospect of marriage between an English lord and a debutante whose father has recently recorded some significant debts. Now she must hope that a more royal interest will bloom for the sake of the family.

Brown cloth soaked in vinegar and pressed against the temples is sure to alleviate the worst of headaches.

It is rumored that fine Alucian lace will soon be abundantly available to all of London's best modistes by summer.

—Honeycutt's Gazette of Fashion and Domesticity for Ladies

IT HAD BEEN harder for Sebastian to leave Eliza this evening than any other time before. But what had he expected? He knew what was in his heart, and every time he was in her presence, his heart played a little longer with fire. It was the look in her eyes that caused the painful swell of guilt. He realized he was burning her heart as well as his.

He wanted to put his fist through a wall. Strike a blow to something. He was better than this—he was not the sort of man to toy with the affections of a woman, particularly Eliza's, and yet, he was doing exactly that because he was not able to deny himself the pleasure of her.

That didn't excuse him in the least. All his life, he had known his path. There was no question of it, no possibility it could be altered. And now he couldn't bear the thought of chatting up two women who held no interest for him whatsoever.

It was nauseating.

His feelings did not matter—that was the naked truth of his position. His feelings had been consumed by the state of Alucia. He would make a match with an English woman who could bring some influence in the English Parliament with her, just as he'd explained to Eliza. He would, presumably, produce heirs, and that would seal them forever and that would be that.

His only solace was that there would be times in the quiet of the evening, when he was alone in his library recording Alucian history, that he would remember and imagine what might have been if he'd been any other man.

He was late. The guests had already been shown to the privy room. He was hurried up the stairs to the rooms he used, and Egius worked quickly to drape him in the sashes and medals that marked his royal blood.

A half hour later, he walked into the receiving room and the curtsying and bowing began.

Lady Elizabeth Keene and her family were the first to reach him. "Your Royal Highness," her father, Richard Keene, Lord Vasser, said, bowing low. "We should like to invite you to our country home for a weekend of hunting. The game there is unsurpassed anywhere in England. I've built the home in the style of a French chateau and I think you would be quite at home."

Sebastian wondered why he thought the style of a French chateau would make him feel quite at home.

Vasser had angled himself in front of his daughter so that Sebastian could hardly see her at all. Vasser seemed to have forgotten that if Sebastian offered marriage, he would offer it to his daughter, and not to him and his French chateau.

Caius, however, always steady, understood the rules and said, "Lady Elizabeth, we are pleased to have you dine with us this evening."

Her father had no choice but to step out of the way. His daughter flushed and curtsied. "How pleased I am to attend." She lifted her gaze and smiled sweetly at Sebastian. How old was she? Seventeen? Eighteen? She seemed terribly young. A child, almost. But he asked if she had seen the view of the gardens from here and invited her to see it with him now. They strolled across the red carpet and stood at the window beneath the painted cupola of the privy room. He inquired about her family. She reported she had a younger brother and a sister, the latter reportedly very good at the piano.

"And you? What would your family say of your talents?" *What is your talent?* He'd asked that of Eliza in the passageway.

"I enjoy singing," she said, and a faint blush touched her cheeks.

She probably feared he'd ask her to sing for him here and now. She could rest assured nothing would bore him more. "I'd be delighted to hear you sing one day," he said blandly.

She beamed. "How do you find England?"

Why was that the question on the tip of every English subject's lips? What did it matter? "I like it very well."

"Is Alucia like England?"

"In some ways." The poor girl had no idea how to converse. She was grasping for anything to say, as nervous as a mouse cornered by a cat. She was too young, he decided. He did not want to marry a child.

"Your Highness." Caius's voice was soft but insistent, and Sebastian was grateful for it. "If I may draw you away."

Sebastian bowed to Lady Elizabeth. "Will you excuse me?"

She glanced nervously across the room, probably to her father. But she executed a perfect curtsy. Sebastian thought of Eliza and her crooked curtsies, more of a hop up and down than a show of deference. He was smiling to himself as he walked away.

"Lady Katherine is by the hearth," Caius said in a low voice. "Her father is one of the most influential gentlemen in the Lords."

"Do we care more for iron ore or parliamentary concessions?" Sebastian asked in Alucian.

"Both are excellent prospects," Caius responded in Alucian as they reached the Maughams.

"Good evening," Sebastian said, bowing before Lady Katherine.

"Your Royal Highness," Lady Katherine said. Her father stayed well behind her. Smart man. Let his beautiful daughter be the shiny lure that drew the fish. Lady Katherine was beautiful, indeed, and there was a little spark in her eye that, in any other privy room, in any other time of his life, would have made him curious.

As it was, he only compared it to Eliza's eyes and found Lady Katherine's lacking.

He quickly discovered that Lady Katherine had taken her quest to become a queen more seriously than Lady Elizabeth. She had studied Alucia. "I understand Alucia has some of the largest lavender fields in Europe," she said as they strolled around the room, looking at portraits.

"True."

"And your seas are particularly good for fishing."

"I wouldn't hesitate to say they are almost as good as the seas around England."

Lady Katherine smiled, clearly proud of herself. "You must miss your home."

How odd, that a few short weeks ago, he would have agreed that he was desperate to go home. But tonight, he could hardly bear to think of going. There was too much hanging over his head—it wasn't just Matous, although that continued to plague him. But his grief and anger over Matous's death had been eclipsed by his longing for Eliza. He wasn't ready to leave that vibrant woman behind.

He wasn't thinking clearly. He was in over his head.

Here was a beautiful woman standing before him. A young woman with her best childbearing years ahead of her. Her father was influential in the Lords and sympathetic to the Alucian position. There was much to be gained from such a union. But as he smiled at her and listened to her talk about her family's seat in Norfolk, all he could see was Eliza with her plain gown, her ink-stained apron, and the wisps of hair around her face. He could only think of the clocks and the dogs and the judgmental cat. And the strings tacked around that small house to guide her blind father. And the boots and bags and hats in the narrow entrance.

When supper was announced, Sebastian was seated at the center of the table, an English minister on his right. On the other side was Lord Prescott from the House of Lords, who had some sort of relationship with Prince Albert. He was supposed to befriend the man. But Sebastian's thoughts wandered as they often did during these formal meals, and tonight they wandered to the Alucian women here tonight, all of them engaged in conversations.

Were any of them particularly small?

Any of them particularly voluptuous?

Would any of them betray their country and their king?

He decided somewhere between the last course and the dessert ices that he needed to see the man who had accepted five pence for delivering the post.

A man's laugh boomed from one end of the table, and he turned his head. Rostafan slapped his hand hard enough against the table to rattle the dishes as he guffawed at something. He leaned to his left and said something to an Alucian woman beside him. Sebastian knew the woman—she was the wife of one of the field marshal's lieutenants. Was it her? No—she was taller than most, if he recalled. And flat chested. But she smiled up at Rostafan with such delight he couldn't help but wonder.

Sebastian listened attentively to the English minister of finance as he described some of the work they'd done for the trade agreement. He thought that he should have sent for Leopold and had him here to help him decide which woman would be the future queen of Alucia. Sebastian felt almost outside himself, as if he was hovering above the table, observing them all with detachment. Observing his life as it was now—women who might have already betrayed him, women who might someday betray him, and all the men who controlled them.

The feeling only worsened as the supper wore on. He was conversing, he was smiling, but he felt nothing. He was void of emotion. The two young women and their families, whose connections were the best England could offer, kept casting anxious smiles in his direction. Lady Elizabeth's father, probably feeling a bit behind in the race, stood up and offered a toast to the prosperity and good health of the crown prince and the kingdom of Alucia.

Sebastian wondered what Eliza would make of this scene. He could imagine her laughing and talking and blissfully ignoring the politics of it all.

After dinner, the ladies repaired to another room, and the men were served brandy and cigars. Sebastian stood up from the table and went to look out the window at the darkened gardens. In the reflection of the window, he could see Rostafan laughing uproariously as an Englishman stood by him. The Alucian field marshal, always jovial. What made him so jovial?

"Your Highness."

It was Caius again, bowing before him. Always deferential. Always careful and cautious around his old schoolmate.

"It is time to rejoin the ladies. We've set the room for cards."

"And I'm to play with each of them, is that it?"

"It would be advantageous to advancing the issue of a union, yes."

Another trade deal, that was all his marriage was to his foreign minister. But it was Sebastian's life. He looked at Caius's carefully composed face. "Who do you think killed Matous?"

Caius blanched. "Pardon?" he glanced toward the guests, probably fearful someone had heard Sebastian's ill-timed question.

"I would like to know what you think," Sebastian said. "We've not discussed it since the day after it happened and I want to know if you have any theories."

"I would respectfully reserve judgment until Mr. Botley-Finch has given us the final results of the investigation."

Sebastian stepped closer and spoke in Alucian. "Caius, I am asking you—do you have any theories?"

Caius lifted his chin. "A dispute, sir. I think Matous must have been involved in some bad business."

"What sort of bad business? Rebellion?"

"Rebellion!" Caius sputtered. "Not Matous. He was loyal to you and the king. He was loyal to his core."

"Is everyone in our party?" Sebastian asked, and his gaze drifted toward Rostafan.

Caius looked shocked by his question. "*Je*, I believe so."

"What sort of dispute would have caused someone to take Matous's life?" Sebastian asked curiously.

"Gambling. A woman, perhaps. One never knows what goes on after our work is done."

Sebastian considered this. That was true in theory, but Sebastian did know what went on with Matous. He was with him for most of every day. He'd heard the bits and pieces of his personal life. He knew how he loved his wife, Maribel. The sorrow they'd both felt when his wife had lost a child she was carrying. His concern for his mother's increasingly fragile state.

"Shall we adjourn?" Caius asked, clearly eager to be done with any speculation.

Sebastian pulled the watch Eliza had given him from his pocket and glanced at the time. He ran his thumb over the Latin inscription. *Love is loyal. "Je."*

For the rest of the evening, Sebastian forced himself to smile and banter, recalling to mind the lessons of one of his many tutors, Master Thaddeus. It was Master Thaddeus's job to teach Sebastian how to be a king one day and for weeks had drilled into him the decorum, the manners, the rules of etiquette, the many expectations of polite society.

Master Thaddeus would be proud.

And so the evening went, Sebastian's body going through the motions at Kensington Palace while his thoughts swirled vaguely around Matous and, more acutely, around 34 Bedford Square.

CHAPTER TWENTY-THREE

A certain eligible young lady with the countenance of a peacock was spotted shopping for a trousseau on Bond Street Wednesday past, leading some to speculate that a royal engagement will soon be announced.

An unfortunate fainting event at church services in Belgravia last week has led us to once again urge ladies not to lace their corsets too tightly. We would not bind wild animals as tightly as some of us bind our waists. Remember, good health is essential to a successful marriage, and that includes the ability to breathe.

—Honeycutt's Gazette of Fashion and Domesticity for Ladies

IT WAS A quiet early Saturday afternoon when Caroline arrived, breathless with excitement. When she had kissed the judge and fallen onto the settee as if in a faint, she said, "Elizabeth Keene is *distraught* and her father *furious*! It appears Katherine Maugham has won."

Eliza didn't need to ask what Katherine Maugham had won. Her heart began its frighteningly rapid descent to her toes. "He will choose the peacock?"

"I heard her family brought in a tutor to teach her everything there is to know about Alucia. They say by the time she had occasion to meet the prince again, she knew more than he!"

"That sounds a bit far-fetched," the judge said.

"And Elizabeth Keene thought all she had to do was appear pleasing to win his hand."

"That's arrogance for you," Hollis said. "Although I dare say she would be generally correct. Men are such simple creatures."

"Present company excluded, I should hope," the judge said.

"Oh dear, Eliza, are you all right?" Caroline asked.

"What?" The blood had drained from her face and she felt a desperate need to pant, but other than that, she was quite all right. "I'm perfectly fine!" She bent over the clock she was repairing. The balance wheel had somehow come out of balance. How was that possible? The one thing the balance wheel had to do was keep the balance, and it had, ticking along as it ought for decades, until suddenly, just like that, it became unbalanced.

A bit like her life of late.

"I'm shocked, really," Hollis said. "I would have thought Elizabeth Keene. I understand she is not as free with her opinions as Lady Katherine."

"What's wrong with offering opinions?" Eliza asked, looking up from her clock.

"Eliza, darling, don't you know anything, really?" Caroline asked. "Gentlemen don't care for women to have opinions. We are to be demure and do as we are told. We are to be a helpmate, not a thinker. Once Lady Katherine is married and wearing a crown, she may present all the opinions she likes."

"Balderdash," the judge said from his chair. His fingers were flying through the yarn, his strip of knitting growing longer by the day. "Women are entitled to their opinions as equally as men."

"Goodness, Your Honor!" Caroline laughed. "You know very well that's not true. Women are entitled to opinions, but they are not entitled to *offer* them, and it would serve Lady Katherine well if she did not offer hers until the deed is done."

Hollis laughed.

Eliza couldn't laugh. She picked up her cloth bag she'd tossed onto the back of a chair yesterday. "I'm to the market," she announced cheerfully.

"What? Why?" Hollis asked. "Caro is here!"

"Yes, I see her plainly, stretched across the settee as if she's had a fainting spell. She won't mind in the least, will you, darling?"

Caroline wiggled her feet, crossed at the ankles at one end. "Not at all. I don't intend to go anywhere. In fact, I may rest. I'm awfully knackered—I was out until four o'clock this morning at Lucille Heath's."

"Well, you're fast friends now, aren't you?" Hollis asked. She was painting a watercolor of the basket full of the judge's yarn.

"What do you need from the market stalls, Eliza?" the judge asked.

She should have thought of that before she jauntily slung her bag over her shoulder. What she needed from the market stalls was to be away from her sister and her dearest friend. She couldn't hear another word of Katherine Maugham.

"I'll go along if you like," Poppy suddenly chirped from the small stepladder on which she was standing. She had been determined all week to dust the books, and had kicked up enough dust they'd all walked around sneezing for two days. "The milkmaid didn't come round again today, and Margaret needs it."

"You don't want to carry milk all the way back to the square, Poppy," Hollis said. "It's too far. Really, we ought to have a milk cow, Pappa."

"And do what with it, my love? Shall it share the parlor with us?"

"Come on, then, Poppy, unless you want to stay for the debate on whether or not the Tricklebanks of Bedford Square should have a milk cow. If you like, I can tell you how the debate will end on our way to the market," Eliza said.

"I'll just fetch my cloak and money from Margaret."

"How long will you be, Eliza?" her father asked. "I had in mind to go round to Mr. Fletcher's for supper."

"Please do, Pappa," Eliza said. "I'll be all right. Poppy and I will share a meal." She walked across the room and bent down to kiss her father's crown. She touched Caroline's forehead on her way by the settee, and Hollis's arm on her way to the door. "A bit more blue there," she said, pointing to Hollis's water coloring.

"Don't wake me when you return," Caroline muttered, closing her eyes.

POPPY AND ELIZA stopped at the butcher shop to say hello to Mr. and Mrs. Thompkins on their way to the market. "Good afternoon, Mr. Thompkins," Eliza said cheerfully. "Will you have any lamb this week?"

"Thursday, lass. I'll send a lad round with a special cut for the justice. Any royal balls this week? Any fancy dancing?"

A woman at the counter looked curiously at Eliza. "Not this week, I'm afraid," Eliza said.

"I reckon the royal balls will be over for everyone, then, eh? The *Times* said he's made his choice. They say we'll witness a big wedding at Westminster in the spring."

"A foreign prince, marrying here?" Mrs. Thompkins said. "It should be in Alucia, shouldn't it? Mustn't they knight her or some such?"

"They don't knight ladies, Ellie," Mr. Thompkins informed his wife. "I reckon he's already a knight. What is he, Miss Tricklebank? Is he a knight, you reckon?"

"I wouldn't… I have no idea."

"I should like to see the gown she wears that day," Mrs. Thompkins said. "She'll be pretty as Queen Victoria on the day she wed."

Eliza smiled thinly. She was feeling a little dizzy—the butcher shop was too close. "Come, Poppy. We should carry on." They bade goodbye to the butcher and his wife, and she and Poppy stepped out onto the street.

The dizziness did not dissipate. It was as if there was a force swirling around her head, sucking out all coherent thought. She hadn't yet imagined Lady Katherine in a wedding gown, *thank you, Mrs. Thompkins*, and now that she had, she wanted to sit down until the dizziness passed.

"Are you all right?" Poppy asked.

"Perfectly fine," Eliza chirped for the second time that day. But she wasn't fine. She felt adrift—so adrift that she didn't notice the man who stepped into her path until she very nearly collided with him. "Miss Tricklebank?"

Eliza and Poppy gasped at the same moment. The man had an accent, but he was dressed like an Englishman.

"Who are you?" Poppy demanded.

"I beg your pardon. I called for you at Bedford Square with a message, but the man who answered the door said you'd gone to the market."

Eliza linked her arm through Poppy's and eyed him suspiciously. "You were calling on me? Whatever for?"

The man looked flummoxed. "Your…ah…your friend sent me?"

"Is that a question?" Poppy demanded. "What friend, then? Friends don't send messengers, do they, sir? Friends come round on their own."

The man cleared his throat, looked directly in Eliza's eye and said, "Your *friend*, madam. He asked that you come to Mayfair. I am to see you there."

Eliza took a step backward. "I'm not going anywhere with you! I've never laid eyes on you in my life!"

The man looked bewildered.

"You heard her," Poppy said fiercely.

He suddenly seemed to remember something. He dug in his pocket, then held out his hand, his palm up. He was holding the pocket watch she'd given Sebastian. "He said to show you this. He said you'd understand."

She took the pocket watch from his hand.

Sebastian wanted her to come. But what was she to understand? Everyone in London believed his offer for Katherine Maugham was imminent if not already made. "Who are you?"

"A guard in His Majesty's service."

Poppy looked at Eliza, one brow high above the other. "That's right fancy, isn't it?"

"But my so-called *friend* has come to Bedford Square

on his own before, or sent a note. Why doesn't he come now?" Eliza asked.

"Everything is different now, madam. I only know what I'm to do."

Yes, things certainly were different now. There was a season to everything, and her season with Sebastian had come to an end. What good would it do her to go now? It would only make her heart ache more.

Poppy made the decision for her. "Go," she said, sliding the cloth bag from Eliza's shoulders. "The judge will be out this evening. I'll tell him you've called on a friend for tea. It's the truth."

"Poppy!"

"Eliza," she said sternly. She glanced at the man, then shifted so that she was standing before Eliza, blocking his view. "You're the *one*, dearest," she whispered. "But if you don't go now, you may miss the chance."

Eliza blinked. She held Poppy's gaze for a long moment.

"Miss?" the guard said.

Eliza stepped around Poppy. "How do I know you don't intend to kidnap me?"

His eyes rounded with surprise. "I beg your pardon?"

"He doesn't mean to kidnap you," Poppy said. "Look at him! He's got the face of an angel."

The young man blushed. "Bring this one, then," he said, gesturing at Poppy. "Two against one, as it were." He pointed to a hired carriage. "If you please, madam." She looked at the pocket watch she was still holding and closed her fingers around it. She wanted to see him. Dear God, how she wanted to see him, no matter how heartbreaking it would be in the end. She looked at Poppy, who gave her a fierce nod.

All right, she would go. She would see Sebastian one last time, in her plain day dress and old but very warm cloak. "All right," she said, so softly that she hardly heard herself. She stepped off the curb and followed the man to the waiting carriage. He put her on the back seat, climbed to the driver's seat and told the man to drive on. Poppy waved cheerily from the sidewalk.

Eliza watched London roll past on the way to Mayfair. The carriage turned down the same little cobblestoned street and came to a halt in front of the same house she'd been to before. A door opened before she could even alight. The same man who had attended her before was waiting, his gaze fixed at some point over her head.

Eliza jogged up the steps.

"Good afternoon, madam. If you will follow me," he said, and walked briskly down the same hall to the same door of the same salon and opened it.

Eliza hesitated one last moment to quickly question her good sense, and then stepped inside.

Sebastian was still in his greatcoat, as if he'd just arrived. A swell of pride and enchantment rose through her. She imagined this man could inspire armies to march and great swathes of women to swoon, and Eliza was suddenly very envious of Katherine Maugham. So envious that she also felt impotent rage, her feelings tumbling and tossing about in complete anarchy.

Sebastian's smile was a bit hopeful and fearful at the same time. "You came," he said, as if surprised by it. "I didn't think you would."

"I shouldn't have."

He pressed his lips together. He nodded, as if reluctantly agreeing. "But you did, and thank God for it." He moved warily across the room toward her, almost as if he expected her to bolt. When he reached her, he lifted his hand and carefully brushed his knuckles against her cheek, then touched two fingers beneath her chin. "It astonishes me how you seem more beautiful every time I lay eyes on you."

Eliza choked on the compliment and glanced down at her spinster attire. "You should save your flattery for your future wife." She glanced up and instantly took pity on him—his hope was so evident, and in spite of the anarchy of murderous, sorrowful lust in her breast, she pressed her palm against his cheek. "Sebastian, you can't send for me again, because I am powerless to resist the call. But by all accounts you've come to a decision, and you must honor—"

"I haven't," he quickly interjected. "Don't believe what you hear, Eliza, unless you hear it from my own lips. Speculation is often presented as fact."

Her hand fell away. "Everyone has said it."

"I give you my word, I've made no decision. I've said not a word to either woman."

This was news she needed to absorb. So many questions were swirling in her now—what did it mean that he hadn't yet made a decision? What in blazes was he waiting for? She abruptly turned and walked away from him, removing her gloves, holding them tight in her hand and knowing she needed to probe his statement for her own sake, as it was filling her with useless, injurious hope. Did he intend to offer for Lady Katherine or not? She needed him to tell her now who he would marry, who he would learn to love, and she didn't care to be standing so close when he did.

"I don't believe you. Surely you've decided by now

who you will choose. You said decisions had to be made, and you gave every indication it had to be soon. An offer will require negotiation—"

"On my word, Eliza, no decision has been made, not by me or anyone. I've obviously hit a bit of a stumbling block."

A stumbling block. She glanced at him over her shoulder. "The trade agreement?"

"The trade..." He laughed a little, shook his head and smiled fondly at her, as if he found her ignorance charming. "Not that." He shoved a hand through his perfectly coiffed hair, making it look windblown. "I find this difficult to say, as I actually fear the consequence of it," he said with a strangled little laugh.

She imagined all sorts of horrible things. "The consequence of what?"

He looked fixedly at her. "Do you really not grasp what I mean? Do you not see that I've fallen in love with someone who makes any other offer impossible?"

Eliza's breath left her.

He pushed his hand through his hair again. "Forgive me, I am wretched at this. I've never in my life..." He shook his head pressed his lips together, his brow furrowed.

The anarchy of her emotions grew to full revolt. She was so flabbergasted she couldn't speak.

"I am... God help me, I am at sea. I have come to love you ardently, Eliza, and yet I find myself in this damnable predicament of being an heir to a throne." He laughed bitterly. "That must sound as deranged as I feel."

She could not seem to catch her breath. She couldn't believe what was happening, not in her wildest fantasy. He was telling her that he loved her, and her heart was nearly bursting with joy, but at the same time, her head felt as if it were in some sort of vise. How could he tell her this when nothing would come of it? How could she accept it when she would read of his nuptials? It was wrong to fill her with this dead hope. "Sebastian! What in heaven are you saying?"

He suddenly moved across the room to her. "For the love of Christ, Eliza, don't dissuade me, please. I know how it must seem to you, I do. I am a prince, I should do as I please, but it's not possible, not in this. The king, my father, depends on me. My *country* depends on me. It was never my choice, I have always known it—but I never expected to fall in love."

He was truly distressed. The pain of this admission was clearly evident around his eyes and in the set of his mouth.

"You think less of me, and I don't blame you. But I had to tell you."

She wanted desperately to help him. She wanted desperately to help herself. "It's infatuation—"

"No. *Deo, no,* Eliza. Can you not see with your own eyes? Can you not look at me now and see it?"

He cupped her face in his hands, forcing her to look at him. She could see what he said was true. It both frightened her and enthralled her. "How can you do this to me?" she asked weakly. She wasn't Caroline, who could marry at any time if she desired, but who preferred to tease and pretend she had the affection of a prince. She wasn't Hollis, either, who had experienced the love of her life, if even for a short time. Eliza was a woman who lived on her own private island in a bustling city, who could only dream of a moment like this. And that she could have it, but from someone who was as far removed from her as any man could possibly be, wounded her soul.

She knew she was headed for an ugly and painful fall.

He splayed his hand across her cheek. “I love you, Eliza Tricklebank. Do you hear me?”

She set her gaze on his mouth.

“Don’t say anything,” he said gruffly. “Just allow it to be for now. Can you do that?”

Conscious thought had deserted her, leaving nothing but the riot of her emotions.

“I am desperate for the few moments of happiness we have together. It’s unfair of me to ask—”

“It is,” she said curtly. “It’s horribly unfair.”

Sebastian stilled. He slowly removed his hand, nodding. “Of course it is,” he said. “I beg your forgiveness.” He stepped away from her, wandering to the hearth.

The poor man looked so lost.

Her heart ached for him. Eliza needed these moments of happiness, too, and she understood him completely. Even in her sorrow she could feel the connection between them, the pull of his heart to hers. It seemed cruel that everything she had ever wanted was standing right before her, wanting her as much as she wanted him. Just as it must seem cruel to him to feel those things as the divide between them widened with every passing day.

He lowered his head, his hands clasped tightly at his back.

“Sebastian.”

He didn’t turn.

“My power to resist my own feelings has gone missing.”

That brought his head up. He turned partially toward her with an expression of unspeakable sorrow.

Eliza lost the last rags of her reason. She couldn’t

bear it and suddenly ran to him. "If you kiss me, I will encourage it. I will fully encourage it all." She threw her arms around his neck and pulled his head down so that he would kiss her and she could encourage it all.

Sebastian crushed her to him and returned her kiss hard and deep, the feelings he'd been trying to express suddenly roaring to life in physical touch. She understood him completely. She knew what she was doing, even in the dense fog of sexual arousal. She understood that this was the only time in her life that she would be so completely desired. Or that she would desire someone so completely in return.

Sebastian whirled her about and pushed her up against the wall, his body covering hers, his mouth, warm and wet on hers. The sensation electrified her, rattling every bone, every fibre in her. She pressed against him, trying to blend into him, but the cloaks they wore were an impediment. Sebastian seemed to realize it, too. He lifted his head and looked at the door. He took her hand in his. "Come," he said. He went to the door, opened it slightly and said something in Alucian, then closed the door.

"What are you doing?"

"Give it a moment." He gave her a quick kiss, then opened the door and pulled her out into the hall.

Eliza knew where they were going, and she didn't care that she'd already made this mistake once. She cared only about this moment and etching it into her heart.

CHAPTER TWENTY-FOUR

A formal supper by invitation of the queen in honor of the soon-departing Alucian crown prince has been cancelled due to a brief illness in the queen. Or perhaps it was cancelled due to foul weather, as has been said among certain members of the House of Lords, particularly from one who had hoped to have his daughter affianced by now.

The foul weather did not keep one bird who has hatched six little hatchlings in eight years from hopping across Marylebone Road to call on an old friend who was once her Latin tutor. She did not hop out again until the following morning, leaving one to assume that Latin is a difficult subject.

—Honeycutt's Gazette of Fashion and Domesticity for Ladies

IT WAS AMAZING to Sebastian how quickly a man could lose his mind to devotion and love and all manner of things he had not felt until his thirty-second year. But here he was, racing down a hall like a stable lad clinging to the landowner's daughter. Up a flight of service stairs and down another, narrower hall. Bedrooms, he assumed. He moved all the way to the end of the hall, passing the closed door, not knowing what he might disturb. But when they came to the last door in the hall, it was thankfully standing open. He saw only a bed, drew Eliza inside and shut the door behind him.

It was a master bedroom, judging by the size of it. It was at the corner of the house, with windows on two walls. He let go of Eliza's hand and went to a door on the only wall with no windows. He opened it, saw a dressing room. He latched it shut.

Eliza was standing in the middle of the room, looking around at it, frowning at the canopied bed. "Who lives here?"

He didn't know, he didn't care. The evidence of anything that happened in this room would be erased by Patro before the day was done. What Sebastian cared about was that they were alone. There was no servant standing outside the door. There was no one lingering in the hall waiting for him to finish.

And there was a proper bed.

His pulse began to ratchet. He felt almost as if he'd been waiting for this moment all his life. He shrugged out of his greatcoat and let it lay where it fell. He moved to Eliza, unfastened the clasp of her cloak, removed it from her shoulders and tossed it onto a chair. He took the gloves she held tightly in her hand and tossed them aside, too. And then he took her into his arms.

Her body curved into his and she clung to him, her fingers digging into his arms and shoulders. Sebastian pulled the pins from her hair and watched golden brown curls tumble down her back and around her shoulders. She was so beautiful, the perfection of the fantasy that he carried in his mind.

She sighed and pressed her mouth to his, her tongue

meeting his. Sebastian's need was rapidly building, brick upon brick, towering over him.

He caressed her side, his hand sliding up to the plumpness of her breast. He began to unfasten the buttons of her gown, and pushing it from her shoulders, watched it slide down her body to reveal her undergarments.

He turned her around, began to unlace her corset, pulling all the ties free until the corset gaped open. Eliza removed it and tossed it aside. She was standing in a chemise so light that he could almost see her through the fabric.

The drum was beating louder in his veins. He removed his coat and waistcoat, pulled his shirt over his head, then took her into his arms again. He kissed her as he picked her up by her waist and twirled her around, settling her against the foot of the bed. He dipped to the hollow of her throat and felt the flutter of her pulse beneath his lips. Her heart was beating rapidly, and he could feel the staccato of it in his blood.

He sought the bottom of her chemise and slid it up. His hands were on bare skin now, and white-hot rivers of anticipation shimmered in waves down his spine. He pushed the chemise over her head, then pushed her back onto the bed and removed her pantalets.

She was gloriously bare before him and Sebastian thought there was nothing more beautiful to him in nature than a woman's body. He quickly disrobed, so that he was bare before her, too, his erection thick and pulsing with anticipation.

She drew a deep breath as he came over her. He cupped her face, pressed his forehead to hers. "I do love you, Eliza," he said earnestly. "I've never uttered those words to a woman before."

She pushed a lock of his hair from his forehead, encircled him with her arms. "I want to remember every second," she said, and pulled him down to kiss her.

Sebastian began to explore her body, his hands and mouth on her breasts, on her smooth, warm skin. He reached for the soft flesh of her inner thigh and into the folds of her sex.

She groaned softly and reached for him, wrapping her fingers around him.

The dam burst in Sebastian. He couldn't contain his lust or his regard for her. He swirled his fingers around the core of her pleasure, and when she began to gasp, her breathing coming quick, he anchored his arm around her and thrust into her, filling her up.

The physical experience was like no other—he was riding a crest of intense pleasure, but with an undercurrent of despair knowing it might be the last time he touched her.

He willed that from his mind. He couldn't think of it now—he wanted every moment, every stroke to count. He wanted to lift them to heights neither of them would ever experience again. He wanted this to be the instant when all things would be illuminated and understood. He wanted it to be magic.

Eliza latched onto his arms, arching her back and whimpering as he moved in her, riding along toward her completion until he could scarcely contain his own. He rolled with her, putting her on top of his body so he could see her. Eliza began to ride him, her fingers digging into his chest.

She gazed down at him with her gray eyes, and her

hair spilling everywhere in long, glorious curls. "I curse the day I met you," she breathed.

"So do I," he agreed.

Her body clenched around his. "You've been my undoing, Sebastian. But oh, what a glorious undoing it has been," she said, and closed her eyes.

Sebastian came up on an elbow, thrust his hand into hair at the back of her head and stopped them from moving. "All my life, I've believed that joy like this was not possible for me. If nothing else, Eliza, if nothing else, you have showed me what love is. Do you understand what a gift that is? I would never have known love had it not been for you."

Eliza smiled. She framed his face with her hands and leaned down to kiss him tenderly. "Neither of us will ever be the same, then, will we?"

Oh, Eliza. He could not possibly express how profoundly he had been changed.

He began to move in her again, slower, and with deliberation, wanting it to last as long as he could possibly could manage it.

She continued to kiss him, her body moving in rhythm with his. The build was excruciating and wonderful, but when he could contain it no more, he embraced her and rolled onto their sides.

Eliza was gasping with exertion, her chest still rising with each furious breath, and when she came, she cried out at the sensation of it.

It was the end for Sebastian. He jerked free of her and spilled onto her thigh.

"Oh dear God," Eliza said breathlessly. "Oh my stars." She kissed him on the mouth, lingering there, then sighed happily and fell onto her back, her arm flopping to one side.

Sebastian kissed her cheek, her forehead, and then tenderly kissed her mouth before gathering her in his arms and holding her to him. He had never felt so utterly connected to another human being. He could feel her heart beating against his chest, and it was almost as if she was a part of him. Love and good fortune and all that was right with the world was shimmering above them, blanketing them.

Several moments passed before Sebastian put his palm to her cheek and kissed her again, this time with reverence. He reached for the coverlet and pulled it down, and the two of them crawled into the bed and lay in each other's arms, their gazes on the boughs of the tree dancing on the other side of the windowpanes.

"It's still day," Eliza said. "I feel like I've been away for a week."

"I wish we'd been away for a week," Sebastian murmured.

"Do you suppose marriage is like this?" she asked.

"I don't know." He hoped that he could find this in his life, this feeling of peace and contentment. He ran his fingers through a long tress of her hair. "Certainly not with anyone but you."

She turned her head, resting it on his chest. "If I were married to you, I would insist we begin and end every day just like this."

He chuckled and traced a line up and down her arm. "I would happily oblige. But is that all, madam? Or is there more you would demand of me?"

"Yes. Horsehair crinolines for my dresses. It's quite

expensive according to my sister, and only the fanciest of ladies can wear them."

"Then you would have an entire herd of horsehair crinolines. What else?"

She looked at him. "That you tell me you love me every day, without fail." She put her hand against his cheek.

Sebastian pressed his cheek against her palm and closed his eyes. "That would be the easiest thing in all the world to do." He kissed her palm and allowed himself to imagine it, but hard reality began to ram the door of consciousness, demanding to be let in.

He turned his gaze to the canopy overhead.

"What would you demand in marriage to me?" she asked.

"That you be by my side through good times and bad. That you would be forever honest with me as you are now."

"That, too, would be the easiest thing in all the world to do, for I don't know how to be any other way." She giggled and rolled onto her back beside him. "I hope you have that, Sebastian. I truly do."

He closed his eyes against the pain that wish caused him. How could she be so generous with a wish like that?

Eliza suddenly sat up, clutching a bed sheet to her, revealing her smooth back to him. He ran his finger down the knobs of her spine.

"I hope you find who killed your friend, too," she said, swinging her legs off the side of the bed. "Did the information about the woman help?"

She stood up, began to root around for her clothes as he watched.

She was eager to be away, he guessed. Her reality must be knocking as adamantly as his. "No. The English government wants to wash their hands of it."

"Why?"

"They want to finish the trade agreement. This is an Alucian problem as they see it. They are probably right."

She had found a stocking and sat on the bed to pull it on. "But what about the man who delivered the post? Doesn't what he said help?"

Sebastian shook his head. "There could be any number of Alucian women in London now."

"Still, you should speak to him."

"How shall I speak to him, *mung lief*, my love?"

She glanced over her shoulder at him."I will take you to him, that's how."

He began to shake his head, but Eliza leaned across the bed wearing only one stocking and pressed her hand to his chest. "What have you to lose, Sebastian? If the government won't help you, this may be your only hope."

She had a point. The clock was ticking, his time here running out. He sat up, too. "Do you know where he is?"

"Well, no. But I think he is in Covent Garden most days looking for work. It's Saturday—I'm certain we can find him. But you can't go as a prince. You'll have to be a cart driver again."

"I was not a *cart driver*—"

"Oh, but you were, Your Highness." She grinned, kissed him on the tip of his nose and hopped off the bed and began to dress.

Sebastian watched her, memorizing the details of her body so that he'd not forget. He would take these images to Alucia with him—the freckle on her right hip.

Her breasts, one slightly smaller than the other. The way her waist flared into her hips, and her ankles, as slender as his wrists. These were the images he would cling to.

She glanced up and pushed the hair from her face. "Are you coming?"

How he hated to leave the warmth of this bed. The scent of their lovemaking. The feel of her skin against his. How he hated everything that was to come. *"Je,"* he said softly, and slung his legs over the side to stand.

When they'd dressed—Sebastian without his waistcoat or neckcloth, and Eliza with her hair bound in a loose knot at her nape—he went out of the room to find Patro. He explained what he needed from his butler, and as usual, Patro and Egius efficiently fulfilled his request without as much as the lift of a brow. When Sebastian returned to the bedroom, he was wearing someone else's coat. He had no idea whose and didn't care. "Shall we?" he asked, and held out his hand to Eliza.

"There is something missing," she said, eyeing him critically. She reached into her reticule and withdrew the pocket watch she'd given him. She dangled it before him like a pendulum and then slipped it into his coat pocket. She patted the pocket and smiled up at him. "Now you look like a proper cart driver."

He laughed, put his arm around her shoulders and kissed her temple. God, how he loved her.

THEY WERE DEPOSITED on an inconspicuous corner from an inconspicuous carriage. Sebastian's guards had come, dressed in Alucian-style clothing, as Egius complained he couldn't outfit the entire Alucian party in drab English clothing. Sebastian instructed the guards to keep a stealth distance from him so that no one would suspect. One of the guards attempted to persuade him that this was a bad idea, but Sebastian refused to hear his case.

Eliza pulled her bonnet down low so that one would have to dip to see her face, and the two of them began to wander through the stalls like an old married couple, stopping to look at delicacies and goods for sale, commenting on the things they saw as if they had nothing at all to concern them but their supper.

Sebastian had never strolled through a market without a horde of onlookers following him.

They stopped at a flower stall, and Eliza bent to smell the roses that had been gathered into bunches and tied with twine. "They're lovely," she said. "Do you have flowers stalls like this? I can't imagine there are any in the world as lovely."

"I'm...not sure," he said.

"Then I am very sad for you. I think there is nothing better than a leisurely stroll through the markets on Saturdays. Oh, look!" She grabbed his hand and tugged him toward a shopfront. It was filled with clocks. "I've bought a few clocks here." She stepped through the low door and down a pair of steps. Sebastian followed her. The shop was close and crowded with clocks of all sizes. Large cabinet clocks. Delicate porcelain clocks. Wall clocks, some of them gaudy, some of them gold. He wished he could give her all these clocks if that was what made her happy. But he didn't even have a purse.

From there, they went to the food stalls and sampled chocolate and bites of pastries. "Oh dear," Eliza said, and her eyes fluttered shut when she bit into a lemon tart. "It's heavenly!"

She offered the rest to him. She was right—it was heavenly.

In spite of the circumstances, the day was one of the best of Sebastian's life. He strolled along, unremarked by anyone, unrecognizable and anonymous to the world. He was moving through a dream where responsibilities did not weigh him down, and people did not vie for his attention. For the space of an afternoon, he was allowed to merely exist in the company of a beautiful woman whom he loved.

They came to the end of the stalls. A public house was on the corner, and judging from the cacophony of voices filtering out the windows and door, it was crowded.

"Let's have an ale," Eliza suggested.

Sebastian had not been in a public house since he'd attended university here. He looked warily at the door.

Eliza tugged on his hand. "You can't come to England and not have a pint, sir." She dipped into the pub. Sebastian helplessly followed her.

He watched Eliza walk straight up to the bar and shout, "Two pints!"

Moments later, a man slapped down two tanks of foamy dark ale, sloshing the contents on the highly polished wood surface. Eliza handed him a few coins, then turned back to Sebastian and handed him one of the ales. He sipped. She laughed and wiped the foam from his upper lip.

"It's quite good."

"When I was a girl, my father would bring me to this very public house, and we'd sit with his friends. Believe me when I tell you I've heard every tale a man could possibly tell in this public house." She laughed, then looked over her pint at him. "What did you do for amusement as a boy?"

"Amusement? I didn't frequent public houses, unfortunately. I learned French and English and decorum. I studied economic theories and battle histories." He shrugged.

"Surely you had some diversion. Didn't you?"

"I liked to read," he admitted. "And ride. I had a pair of horses." It struck him that he had little to say about his childhood. He'd rarely seen his parents, and though Leopold had been his constant companion, there hadn't been any other children to speak of. Most of his time had been spent in training and classrooms.

"That seems—"

Eliza lost her train of thought, as did Sebastian, because just a few feet away, a man stood up and took a healthy swing at another man and sent him tumbling onto his arse.

"Oh, he got a good piece of him, didn't he?" Eliza exclaimed excitedly.

The man got up from the floor and leapt across the table for the offender, knocking tankards left and right and spilling ale onto the floor. People around them scrambled out of the way.

Sebastian stepped in front of Eliza, putting himself between her and the fighting. "We should step out."

"Why? Don't you want to see who wins?" She tried to push him aside.

"I think for—"

Eliza suddenly gasped and gripped his arm. "It's him!" She put down her tankard and began to dart around the people who were crowding together to watch the fight.

"Wait—Eliza!" Sebastian went after her, but by the time he was able to shove his way out of the public house, Eliza was already running down the street. Sebastian went after her, perturbed that she would run off like that, and intended to tell her so, but when he caught up to her, Eliza had managed to intercept a short, stout man wearing a stained cap.

"There you are!" she said to the man brightly, as if she'd just found her lost companion.

The man seemed alarmed. He turned to flee but ran straight into Sebastian.

"Why are you always running away from me?" Eliza demanded. "I don't want to take offense, sir, but how can I not? I'm not going to hurt you—I mean only to ask you a question."

"You've already asked your questions," he complained.

"But I have another one."

Sebastian set the man back. He was at least a foot taller than this one and warned him, "Don't run, do you understand? If you do, I'll catch you and pummel you."

Eliza's eyes widened, and then she laughed as if he'd made a jest. "No, he won't," she assured the fellow, whose eyes had gone round as gold crowns. "Now, see here—I must know who gave you five pence."

The man went from looking frightened to exasperated. "I *told* you. There's no more to say than what I've already said, aye? A man's got to make a living, that's all."

"Perhaps I could entice you to say more," Sebastian said. "Perhaps I could entice you to have a look at a few faces and see if any of them jog your memory."

"No," the man said, shaking his head. "I don't want trouble."

"I'll give you twenty pounds," Sebastian offered.

"*Twenty* pounds!" Eliza gasped, her hand clamped to her heart. "That's far too much!"

The amount sounded reasonable to Sebastian in exchange for something of this magnitude. "Too much?" he repeated uncertainly.

"I'll take ten," the man offered.

Eliza gestured to the man as proof that she was right.

"Very well," Sebastian said uncertainly. "Ten pounds."

"Where am I to see these faces?" the man asked, his apprehension completely erased with the promise of ten pounds.

His question, however, presented something of a tricky wicket. Sebastian needed him to come to Kensington Palace and look at the Alucian women in his party. How he might do that without drawing unwanted scrutiny was the quandary.

"To Kensington Palace," Eliza answered.

The man's eyes rounded even more.

"Not *inside* the palace," Eliza said, reading his mind. "Do you think the whole world has gone mad?"

"I've a better idea," Sebastian said.

Eliza and the man looked expectantly at him.

"I will take the ladies to Bond Street on the morrow for hats. A souvenir of London, as it were."

The man looked from Eliza to Sebastian. "Bond Street? I've been chased off Bond Street, I have."

"Fancy that," Eliza drawled.

Sebastian had to think how to accomplish this amidst a full schedule and without raising suspicion. "When the ladies arrive, five of them in all if I am not mistaken, you can view them from the window of a coach and determine if any of them are familiar."

"A coach," the man said dubiously. "*What* coach?"

"What coach," Eliza repeated with impatience. "Any coach will do for you, sir."

"One of my men will accompany you."

"He means me," Eliza said quickly. "I will accompany you and watch out the window with you." She looked at Sebastian and shrugged. "I've seen several of the ladies. I can help."

"What of my ten pounds?" the man asked.

"You'll have it when you've done as the gentleman has asked," Eliza said pertly.

"And how am I to *find* this coach?" the man asked, as if he thought he'd stumbled on a difficult question they couldn't answer.

Eliza sighed. "I should think that if the gentleman is inclined to pay you as much as ten pounds, he will see that you find the coach."

The man studied them with suspicion, and at last nodded his agreement. "All right."

Still, Eliza didn't seem to trust him. "What is your name?"

"Paul Oates," he said, and yanked on his soiled waistcoat as he lifted his chin.

"Very well, Mr. Oates. You should know that my father is a judge on the Queen's Bench. If you renege on this deal, I will personally see to it that you are hauled before him and made to account." She smiled sunnily.

"No need to threaten," Mr. Oates sniffed. "I could do with the ten pounds, that I could."

The deal struck, they worked out the details of when

Eliza would meet him here on the morrow and proceed to a coach.

"Am I free to go?" Mr. Oates asked.

Eliza looked at Sebastian. He hated to let the man go, for like Eliza, he didn't trust him. But he could hardly hold him against his will. He nodded.

Mr. Oates scurried away like a rat.

Sebastian and Eliza watched him go. "He won't appear on the morrow, will he?" Sebastian asked.

"He will," Eliza said confidently. "Ten pounds is a king's ransom to him." She turned her smile to him. "*Twenty* pounds, Sebastian! Are you mad?"

"I think we've established that I am," he agreed.

He was mad, all right. Mad about Eliza. Madly, madly in love with Eliza.

CHAPTER TWENTY-FIVE

Alucian fashion is not superior to English fashion in all ways, as some Frenchmen have suggested. England has the finest milliners in all the world, a fact recognized by Prince Sebastian himself, who was seen purchasing fine English bonnets from a Bond Street modiste for the ladies in his entourage.

For English ladies, commissions may be placed for spring bonnets at the end of next month. Satin, silk, straw, and chip-plate bonnets with ribbons and flowers are expected to be in high demand.

—Honeycutt's Gazette of Fashion and Domesticity for Ladies

PAUL OATES WAS a hungry man. He had negotiated, in exchange for his participation, some bread, cheese and dried meat. He'd arrived at the appointed place, at the agreed time, but would not step foot inside until he'd had a tankard of ale and food brought to him.

He exclaimed over the fancy coach that was really rather plain, then ate like an animal as he and Eliza waited on Bond Street.

"Who's the bloke, then, this gentleman?" he asked with a greasy smirk through a mouthful of food.

"I should think it plainly obvious that he is my friend."

"A *friend*." Mr. Oates snorted his opinion of that. He pointed a gray finger at her. "You think yourself high and mighty, like him," he said, fluttering his fingers toward the ceiling of the coach. "But you're not like him, miss, not at all. *Kensington Palace?* Think I don't know who lives there?" He shook his head and shoved a hunk of dried beef the size of Eliza's fist into his mouth.

She had to look away. And frankly, she would be astonished beyond comprehension if Mr. Oates knew who lived at Kensington Palace.

"The *queen*, that's who," he said through his dried meat, as if answering her unspoken question. "The bloke's her brother."

This man was an idiot, and she sincerely hoped she hadn't placed all of Sebastian's hopes in him. "How did you arrive at that conclusion, Mr. Oates?"

He shrugged and took another enormous, smacky bite of the bread. "Makes sense, it does. I've seen the likeness of Prince Albert, and the bloke's not him. He's her brother. Looks just like her."

"Well, you're a clever one, aren't you? He is indeed the queen's brother." She doubted she was in any danger of Mr. Oates ever discovering that the queen lived at Buckingham Palace, not Kensington, and that she had no siblings.

He tapped his temple with the same gray finger. "Knew it," he said proudly.

Eliza resisted rolling her eyes. She had only to endure an hour or so with him and then hopefully never meet the fool again. Although she probably would see him again, wandering about the markets looking for work.

Nevertheless, the plan, as they'd determined yesterday, was really very simple. Sebastian would bring round the Alucian ladies in his party to Bond Street, and as they strolled down the sidewalk to the door of Mrs. Cubison's shop, Mr. Oates would look to see if he recognized any of them. Sebastian would arrive last, and before he stepped inside to Mrs. Cubison's shop to arrange payment for the selected bonnets, he would step up to the coach that contained Eliza and Mr. Oates, and hear Mr. Oates's answer. The coach would then return Eliza and Mr. Oates to Covent Garden, where one of Sebastian's men would present the ten pounds, and Eliza…well, she would wait at home.

Sebastian had promised her he would come to her. *"Wait for me, Eliza. I will come, I swear it, on my oath."*

Mr. Oates had finished gorging on his food and had settled back, spreading his grubby hands over the leather squabs. "I been in better coaches than this. If he's the queen's brother, why he ain't got better than this?"

"Not half an hour ago, you were rather impressed, as I recall," Eliza pointed out.

"Aye, but this ain't as fancy as those I seen carrying the queen."

"Of course not, Mr. Oates. She is the queen, and the gentleman is merely her brother."

He nodded as if that was a correct assumption.

He closed his eyes. Not a minute later, he was snoring. Eliza balled herself into a corner on the bench opposite him and prayed the Alucian ladies would arrive soon.

They did not arrive soon, but a full hour after they'd been expected. She heard them before she saw them. She sat up, kicked Mr. Oates with her boot, and surged toward the window. A coach was disgorging them onto the sidewalk, and they were gathered around, shaking out their skirts and adjusting their bonnets. "Come quick!" Eliza hissed at Mr. Oates.

He crowded in beside her at the window, filling her nose with the scent of unwashed clothes. "Can't see them."

"What do you mean you can't see them?" she asked frantically.

"Their bonnets," he said.

"Oh, *Lord*." They were coming closer, but Mr. Oates continued to shake his head. "Can't see a one of 'em."

Eliza made a quick decision. She opened the coach door and pushed him out, then leapt out behind him. She linked her arm through his filthy clothing and yanked him toward a shop window.

"What's this?" he asked, peering into the window.

"Pretend you're looking at the apothecary's shop window, Mr. Oates, then turn your head as if you are speaking to me and *look at the ladies*!"

"Oh." He turned his head. He leaned around her as the ladies reached Mrs. Cubison's door. "Not her," he said. "No. No. No—aye, that's the one. That's her, all right."

Eliza glanced to her left. "Which one?"

"The one in the yellow and blue gown and the blue cloak."

Eliza noticed her right away—her gown was beautiful. The woman was a few inches shorter than anyone else, and Eliza realized with a start that she'd met this woman. She was the Alucian woman she'd spoken to in the gaming room at Juliana Whitbread's party. *What was her name?* Anastasan! Lady Anastasan!

"Are you certain?"

"I know who give me five pence, miss."

The ladies gathered at the door and window of Mrs. Cubison's, peering inside and waiting for a footman to open the door for them.

"She's a bonny thing, she is. Small and dainty. And quite a big—"

"Yes, I see it," Eliza snapped before he mentioned her bosom again. For one who was so petite, Lady Anastasan did indeed have a rather large bosom.

The footman opened the door to the shop and the ladies filed inside, laughing and chattering, Lady Anastasan in the middle of them.

When they'd gone, Eliza hurried Mr. Oates back to the coach.

Another quarter of an hour passed before a sleek carriage arrived. Two men came down from driver's bench and moved to the sidewalk. The door swung open, and Sebastian stepped out. He strolled to Eliza's coach, spoke to the driver and then stood back.

Eliza opened the door with a smile so broad it made her cheeks ache.

Sebastian's smile was nearly as broad.

"I was right," Mr. Oates proclaimed, pushing in next to Eliza. "She's got a big chest," he said, and held up his cupped hands to his own chest to demonstrate.

"It's Lady Anastasan," Eliza said.

Sebastian physically reacted as if she'd struck him. "Pardon?"

"She's wearing a blue and gold gown. Mr. Oates said she is the one who paid him five pence to deliver the post to our house."

Mr. Oates nodded.

"You're absolutely certain?" Sebastian asked him.

"Won't forget the looks of her," Mr. Oates confirmed with a leering grin.

"How do you know her name?" Sebastian asked, directing his attention to Eliza.

"I made her acquaintance at the birthday ball," Eliza said. "She was there with her husband."

"You met Lord Anastasan?"

She nodded.

He seemed confused by this. "A slender man, his complexion olive?"

"What? No. A very large man, really."

Sebastian looked even more confused. "Are you certain?"

Eliza thought back to that night. "He was at a gaming table. She walked past him and touched his back, then as she passed, she looked back and smiled."

"I don't understand," Sebastian said. "What made you think he was her husband?"

What *had* made her think it was so intimate? "There was something about the look between them, I suppose."

Sebastian's color had changed. His face was dark, his eyes even darker. "Describe him, please," he asked briskly.

"He was quite a large man. A very large chest."

"Like his wife." Mr. Oates snickered.

"He sports a beard. Oh, and his laugh was quite loud. In fact, that's why I noticed it at all—his laughter drew my attention to him."

Sebastian's eyes looked almost black to her. "Are you very certain, Eliza?"

His voice was so full of deadly calm that it sent shivers down her spine. "I am."

Sebastian's expression was suddenly so cold that Eliza recoiled. "Is everything all right?"

"It will be. Thank you, Mr. Oates. Thank you, Eliza. You've been a great help." He shut the door without looking at Eliza, banged on the side of the coach, and just like that, Eliza and Mr. Oates were ferried away.

She was stunned. She didn't know what had just happened. Mr. Oates, on the other hand, felt he'd done his job very well, and when they reached Covent Garden, he accepted his ten pounds from the driver and smiled at Eliza through a few missing teeth. "No one will believe I met the queen's brother," he boasted.

"No, they certainly won't," she agreed. She shut the coach door and sank back against the squabs and let the driver take her home.

In the hours that followed, she felt very much at odds. Disquieted. Alarmed, even. Something had changed and she didn't know what, and she didn't like it. Sebastian had seemed both shocked and furious, and something between them, that spark, that glow, had shifted when he'd heard the name Anastasan.

Eliza remained at home, alternately pacing the parlor, or trying to busy herself with the household accounts, or tidying up her father's books, or playing with the dogs. One long minute after another, waiting for Sebastian to come. Nothing helped ease her nerves, however, and by the end of the day she was undone by what had happened. Tripped up by it. Consumed by it.

The next day, she had a firm talk with herself and issued a stern reminder that life was always destined to go on. So she dressed and went to the market as she did two or three times a week. She wandered the stalls, bought some flowers and bread. And then she bought some expensive Belgian chocolates, because she deserved them after the trial she'd just been through. When she returned home, Poppy was sweeping the entry.

"Blustery day!" Eliza said, feigning cheer as she removed her bonnet. "Has anyone come?"

"Not today," Poppy said as she swept around Eliza. "That milkmaid's gone missing again. The lass doesn't come regular as she ought." She paused and opened the door to have a look around the square. "Quiet as Sunday morning out there," she said, and shut the door and resumed her sweeping.

The next day passed in the same way, with no word. As did the day after that. On the fourth day, Eliza could bear it no more and walked Jack and John round to Hollis's house.

Her manservant, Donovan, answered the door. He had shed his coat and had rolled up his shirtsleeves to reveal thick forearms. He had a towel draped over one shoulder and held a feather duster in his hand. "Good morning, Donovan," she said, eyeing the duster. "Are you the chambermaid today?"

"Mrs. Honeycutt does not employ a chambermaid, Miss Tricklebank. She does, however, employ a housekeeper, but Mrs. Edison had taken ill."

"I am very sorry to hear it. Is my sister at home?"

"Aye, she is. Working away at the gazette." He opened the door wider. "Come in."

He led her down the hall to Hollis's former sitting room, which she had transformed into an office. Gazettes were stacked on a dining table set in the middle of the room, where they put the gazette together. Today, Hollis was busy pouring over the gazette layout.

"Your sister," Donovan said. "And her dogs."

"Wonderful!" Hollis said without looking up from her layout.

Jack and John trotted over to examine Hollis before curling up beneath the table.

"I'm almost done," Hollis said. "Have you seen the new style of pantalets?" she asked with breathless excitement. "Shorter and more open than before. They tie with a lovely ribbon." She held up a flyer from a well-known manufacturer of ladies' undergarments. "I'm going round to have a look tomorrow. Would you like to come?"

"Perhaps," Eliza said.

"What are you doing here?" Hollis asked as she bent over the gazette again. "I wasn't expecting you until the morrow. Where's Pappa?"

"At court." Eliza fell into a chair.

Hollis looked up. She frowned. "What is it? You look very glum."

"I've not heard from Sebastian in three days."

"What? The cheek of the man!" Hollis laughed. "Don't be cross, darling. He must have a dozen things to attend to if he has one."

"Something is wrong," Eliza insisted.

Hollis stopped working on her gazette. "Why do you say that?"

Eliza didn't want to tell her sister about their foray into Covent Garden, or the one with Mr. Oates. Not yet. "It's a feeling."

Hollis stared at her. Then slowly sank back into her seat. "Oh dear. You've gone and done it, haven't you?"

"Done what?"

"Fallen in love."

Eliza blushed. "*No*, Hollis—"

"Don't you dare lie to me, Mary Eliza Tricklebank. I know you better than anyone. Lie to Caro or Pappa, but not to *me*."

Eliza sighed. "Fine. Perhaps I have."

Hollis gasped. "Oh, Eliza!"

"I know, I know, I shouldn't have, but we were so compatible in all ways. Like you and Donovan."

"What? Donovan and I are not compatible in all ways—" She suddenly gasped. "Certainly not in *all* ways," she said. "Are *you* compatible with the prince in *all* ways?"

Eliza didn't answer that, and Hollis clamped a hand over her mouth, presumably to keep from squealing. When she'd composed herself, she lowered her hand and said, "*Eliza!* What else have you not told me?"

Eliza sank lower in her chair, her legs sprawled before her. "So much, Hollis." And so she told her. She told her sister about the meetings at the house in Mayfair, about her assistance in helping him find the woman who had paid to have the note delivered. She told Hollis about their conversations, and how similar they were, both of them cornered by society's expectations and duty. How he'd confessed he loved her but was bound by duty, and Eliza, not knowing if she loved him or not, had not returned the sentiment.

Hollis listened, her eyes glistening. "Oh dear, darling," she said softly, and came around to where Eliza was haphazardly slung across the chair, perched on the arm of it, and put her arms around her. "I feared this might happen."

"I'm glad that it happened! As painful as it is, I haven't a single regret."

Hollis didn't say anything to that. She stood up.

"Caro might know a way to get word to him, do you suppose?"

"What if she did? What word would I send?"

"That you love him, silly. At least let him know before he leaves England. Poor man, to utter those words and not hear them in return. I told Caro I'd come round today. Shall we go?"

Eliza shrugged. She didn't care what they did, as long as she didn't have to return to her house to wait for a call that was not going to come.

They gathered the dogs, called to Donovan for a cloak for Hollis, then went out, their arms linked, Eliza leaning against her sister as they walked.

Caroline was at home, of course—it was too early for her to be making a round of calls, and she was rarely dressed before the early afternoon. In fact they found her in her sitting room in a dressing gown, her hair unbound. She was on the floor and all around her were fashion plates.

"These are the latest from France," she said with delight. "Lady Halsem has just returned from Paris with them and has lent them to me. Will you look at this yellow dress?" she asked, holding one of the plates up. "Jack! Keep your snout from my plates!" she exclaimed, shooing away one dog.

Hollis fell to her knees to have a look at the plates.

Eliza sat on an ottoman and stared glumly at the fashion plates.

"What brings you two and the beasts today?" Caroline asked as she held up one plate and then another one beside it, to compare.

"Eliza has been at mischief behind our backs, and I

would never be able to tell you everything, so I brought her along to tell you herself."

"Really?" Caroline sounded delighted. "Tell me *everything.*"

Hollis did, in fact, do most of the talking, but when she got to the part where the prince had declared his regard for Eliza, Caroline screamed and fell onto her back and the fashion plates, pushing away two very excited dogs. "You've *slayed* me, Eliza! How have you kept this from us? How have you—"

"What is the screaming about?" Beck demanded from the door of the sitting room. He was dressed to go out, his hat in hand. The dogs raced across the room to examine his boots.

Caroline sat up. "Where are you going?"

"To meet Lord Ailesbury at White's and hear the latest about the talk going round town."

"What talk?"

"What talk, indeed. You haven't heard?"

"I've heard nothing!" Caroline said. "I was with Lady Halsem all day yesterday, and she's only just arrived from France."

"And neither does your little gossip know?" he asked, and smiled smugly at Hollis.

"No, I don't," Hollis said.

Beck laughed. "I thought you three would be the first to know about the plot to kidnap one of your precious princes and hold him hostage."

Eliza's mouth gaped, but no sound came. She couldn't make a sound—she had no breath.

"What?" Caroline demanded.

"There is no call to shout."

"What are you talking about, Beck?" Hollis demanded.

"I'm rather shocked your ladies' gazette doesn't know of it," he said, grinning. "What's wrong, Hollis, are you behind the latest news?"

"Beckett!" Caroline exclaimed.

He was clearly diverted by their pique. "That's all I know, really. It seems that in the course of investigating the murder, they uncovered a plot to kidnap the crown prince when he sails to Alucia. He was to be held for ransom by the Weslorians. Apparently, his secretary got wind of it and was murdered for it. Or so the talk goes."

Hollis and Caroline turned to Eliza, both of them agape.

"He's surrounded like an infant in swaddling now. They are wrapping up trade negotiations and intend to sail by the end of the week."

"W-who are the traitors?" Eliza asked.

"How would I know, Eliza? They are Alucians. That's their business, and the sooner they are gone, the better for all of us. There is no call for that dirtiness in jolly old England." He pulled on the ends of his waistcoat. "Don't eat all the food," he said, and quit the room.

Caroline and Hollis looked helplessly at Eliza.

"I think I feel a bit sick," Eliza whispered.

"You must get a message to him," Hollis said. "How can she do that, Caro?"

"I wouldn't possibly know! My talents only extend so far."

"But you must know of *someone*," Hollis insisted.

She and Caroline argued whether she did or did not know someone else, but Eliza heard none of it. Her heart had burst into pieces and fallen into a dark hole of despair. There was no way to get a message to him, not now, not after a plot against him had been exposed. He'd said he would come to her. But he wouldn't come now—they wouldn't let him out of their sight. When a man had attempted to assassinate the queen three years ago, they kept her surrounded as tight as a corset afterward.

She closed her eyes and covered her face with her hands. She thought of the house at Mayfair. Was it possible one of the men was there? Could she perhaps send him a message through one of them? She abruptly stood up, and when she did, Jack and John did, too, trampling over Caroline's fashion plates. "The house in Mayfair!" she cried. "I have to go."

"Wait! What are you talking about?" Hollis said, and came to her feet.

"We met at a small house in Mayfair. Twice. Where is my cloak? Caro, ring for Garrett, please."

"Good *Lord*, Eliza, what if someone had seen you?" Caroline exclaimed.

"It doesn't matter. I have to go there."

"You're not going alone," Caroline said, and came to her feet, the fashion plates clutched to her chest.

"I have to go *now*, Caro. I can't wait for you to dress!"

"I won't be long!" Caroline said, hurrying from the room. "Hollis, hurry down and tell Garrett to bring round a cab!" she cried as she disappeared into another room.

A moment later, they heard her shouting for her maid.

A half hour later, Caroline, Hollis, Eliza and the two dogs were squeezed into a cab that smelled of decay, and were hurtling across Mayfair.

Eliza found the house easily enough, as she'd always had a strong sense of direction. But the house looked completely different. There was no light coming through the windows. The drapes were drawn, and it looked as if the house had been closed for the winter.

"Oh no," she murmured. *"No."* They climbed out and went to the door. Eliza knocked. Hollis cupped her hands around her eyes and tried to peer in a window. Eliza knocked again, only this time, with her fist. "Surely one of you is still in there!" she shouted. "You can't all have disappeared!"

"Eliza," Caroline said gently. "There is no one here."

They pulled a reluctant Eliza away and got back in the cab and started for Caroline's. Eliza couldn't hold it back any longer—she cried the tears of grief that she'd held at bay these last few days.

She had known this would happen. She'd tried to prepare herself, but one could never prepare for this sort of heartache. Just like that, he was gone from her life. The last image she had was of him standing on the sidewalk outside Mrs. Cubison's, staring at the ground, his expression dark and brooding.

Hollis and Caroline folded over Eliza, desperately trying to comfort her. But there was no comfort for Eliza, not today, at least. She was despondent. She had no idea the devastation would run so deep. It left her utterly breathless.

CHAPTER TWENTY-SIX

All of London is paying close watch to the tide schedules that will be the first to predict when the prince and Alucian contingent will set sail. Will he embark on his journey home with a princess? A certain peacock is more attentive to the possibility than anyone else. Word is that all betrothal negotiations have ceased due to the tragic circumstances of an Alucian's death, but that they are set to resume shortly and an announcement may be expected at any time and will be received with much notoriety and fanfare.

Ladies, if you are planning to set sail soon, don't be without Mrs. Billard's belladonna potion for nausea, perfect for rough seas.

—Honeycutt's Gazette of Fashion and Domesticity for Ladies

THERE WAS AN image Sebastian would never forget, and that was the look that came over Caius's face when his tearful wife had admitted, after pointed questioning, to conspiring with Rostafan to kidnap Sebastian while at sea. And that when Matous suspected something was afoot, she had risen in the middle of the night, unbeknownst to her sleeping husband—who had assured the investigators that he and his wife had long been in bed—and had murdered Matous.

Sebastian had been shocked when she'd admitted she'd done it. "You drew the knife across his throat?"

"He was sleeping," she said through her tears.

"Did Rostafan direct you to do so?"

She shook her head. "I told him afterward. He was quite cross with me."

Sebastian's shock had been nothing compared to that of her husband. Caius looked like a man who had been shot through the heart. He sat immobile for several moments before he leapt from his seat and slapped his wife so hard across her face that she was knocked from her chair.

Leopold had grabbed Caius before he could kill her. "She'll hang for it," he'd said. "You can do no worse to her, and besides, we need you now more than ever."

It was a lot for any of them to absorb. When confronted with the news that a man had pointed her out as having paid him to deliver a message implicating Rostafan, Sarafina had collapsed under the weight of her guilt. She'd admitted everything. To her adulterous affair with Rostafan. To Rostafan's plans to kidnap Sebastian as they sailed home, part of a conspiracy funded by the Weslorians to draw Alucia into conflict. To the money the field marshal intended to funnel to Wesloria to aid in a rebellion. She admitted that she'd become frightened, and had attempted to shift the blame to Rostafan for Matous's death out of fear of being caught and accused of murder. She didn't know Justice Tricklebank but knew from an Alucian barrister, who had shared ale with Tricklebank and some other justices, that he was blind and his court was hearing the criminal cases.

She didn't know if her plan would work, but she knew if confided in an Alucian, it would come round to Rostafan. It had been easy to pick out the blind justice and follow him home one afternoon.

Hers had been a bungled, desperate attempt to hide a heinous crime, and would likely cost her life.

Rostafan had fled when news of Lady Anastasan's detention became known. He was caught trying to board a ship bound for the Continent. Mr. Botley-Finch had assured Sebastian he would be held until the Alucian contingent set sail.

As for the Alucians in England, Lady Anastasan pointed to three who knew of the plot to kidnap him. Two of them were in his guard and had been paid to seize him once the ship left English shores.

All of them were being held now, accused of high treason.

How Caius managed to keep his head through these stunning revelations, Sebastian didn't know. As for Sebastian, out of an abundance of caution, he'd agreed that he had to return to Helenamar at once.

The trade agreement was very nearly complete. There was one last issue between the two countries, one that would require a legal ruling. And of course, there was the issue of his engagement.

Caius, who had somehow managed to compose himself in a way Sebastian thought was Herculean, had suggested they proceed post-haste to an agreement with Lady Katherine Maugham and leave England as soon as possible. There was too much at risk now, too many unanswered questions, he said. "Lady Katherine is eager for the match and her father is frankly desperate to have a foothold in Alucia for trade," Caius said in making his case.

Sebastian decided he was not as strong as Caius. With all the turmoil around him, Sebastian could not bring himself to give consent to proceed.

He couldn't stop thinking of Eliza, and hadn't stopped, even in the darkest of hours. But in the aftermath of the trauma they'd just endured, he was even more keenly aware of how important it was to keep those close whom he loved, and those he trusted even closer. He was painfully aware that Caius and Sarafina's marriage had been arranged as was custom for the privileged class in Alucia. All those years spent in bed with a woman, and Caius had never really known her.

"I'll think about it," Sebastian said.

Caius nodded. He turned to leave, but Sebastian said, "Caius."

When his foreign minister turned back, Sebastian saw a glimpse of his old schoolmate—just a flash of that lad before Caius's expression shuttered. "Perhaps we best leave the negotiations to the finance minister."

"To Lord Benedick? But he knows nothing of it."

"It's a betrothal agreement—he is perfectly capable."

Caius looked shocked.

"You've suffered quite a shock, my friend," Sebastian reminded him.

Caius's face turned dark. "Have you lost trust in me, sir? Do you suspect me?"

"No," Sebastian said honestly. "I admit there are times I've wondered what changed between us after Oxford. If you grew distant because of something I couldn't see. But I have always trusted you."

"You wondered what changed?" Caius gave a sorrowful laugh. "You became the crown prince. You became *my* prince, one I was sworn to protect and defend. We had gone past boyish games."

His answer surprised Sebastian. "Did that put an end to our friendship? I have missed it."

Caius studied him in a way he had not looked at Sebastian in a very long time. "I love my country, Bas," he said quietly. It was the first time he'd called Sebastian by his nickname since they were lads. "I have worked very hard to afford you the respect you are due. That my wife has betrayed Alucia, and you, and the king—that she has betrayed *me*..." He paused, and swallowed hard. "I am determined to do everything in my power to set it to rights. I should rather work to finish our business here than dwell on what she has done. I beg your leave to do just that."

Sebastian suppressed a sigh of weariness, of the weight that every personal relationship he had must bear because of who he was. "If that is what you need to do," he said.

Caius bowed, turned sharply and strode from the room. But he paused at the door and glanced back. "I meant no harm," he said stiffly. "On my word, I meant no harm."

Sebastian nodded. He understood Caius to mean he'd meant no harm in putting him at arm's length all those years ago. But it didn't make it any easier to accept.

Caius disappeared into the hall.

Sebastian did trust him, but his gut told him the two boyhood friends would always be a memory. After what Sarafina had done, he doubted if Caius would ever let down his guard. He wondered idly for a moment what he would do in a similar situation to Caius's…but then remembered he had his own gut-wrenching situation.

He sat down and picked up his pen to write the letter to Eliza he'd been trying to write all day. To explain to her what had happened. To tell her how sorry he was. But every time he put his pen to paper, his words sounded either hollow or deranged.

Leopold appeared the next morning, obviously sent in by the Alucian officials who remained, all of them wanting to leave straightaway. "What is the matter with you?" he asked without preamble.

"I beg your pardon?"

"We've come down to the last stipulation of a trade agreement that will revolutionize Alucia. All you must do is choose a bride, Bas."

"I know what I must do," he said.

Leopold sat across the desk from him, leaning forward. "Then why haven't you? I've seen these women. They are appealing in their looks and their nature—"

"I don't love them," Sebastian snapped.

Leopold's mouth gaped. "I would laugh if that weren't so absurd. You're not supposed to love either of them, not now. Not yet. That will come with time—"

"You took your lessons well, Leo, as did I," Sebastian said. He stood up and began moving restlessly about the room. "Do your duty and all will be yours. But in this, they were wrong. I love someone else. Someone entirely unsuitable according to the dictates I've been given. And I cannot form the words to extend an offer of marriage merely for political expediency when I love someone else."

Leopold's brows rose to his hairline. "Is she a chambermaid?"

It wasn't unheard of. Sebastian shook his head. "Miss Eliza Tricklebank."

Leopold stared at him in confusion for a moment. "The woman who ordered you from her house? The judge's daughter?"

Sebastian sighed and rubbed his eyes with his hands. "*Je.* Her."

Leopold stared at him for a very long time. But his expression changed to a smile.

"Don't laugh," Sebastian warned him. "It pains me enough as it is."

"Why her?" Leopold asked. "There are two women *groomed* for someone like you, who would be pleasing companions and versed in the ways of a queen—"

"Because she has *not* been groomed for me," Sebastian said bitterly. "Because she shows me the least bit of deference of anyone! Because she is honest, and she speaks her mind, and she sees me as an *equal*, Leo, and not her lord and not her purse. I am not her path to riches and privilege. I'd wager those things haven't entered her mind. She speaks to me of things no one ever speaks to me. She is a passionate lover, she is full of laughter, she is…" He put his hands on his waist and bit his tongue.

She was everything, that was what. Everything he'd ever wanted, even if he hadn't known it. Everything he could not have. Or couldn't he? It suddenly occurred to him that he hadn't been able to write that letter because something else was teasing his thoughts. He suddenly knew what he needed to do. "I need to determine a way I can offer for her," he said quietly.

His brother was very still for several moments. He stood from his chair. "Don't be ridiculous. She has neither connection nor pedigree. Can you imagine the hue and cry if you returned with an offer for a judge's daughter, someone who brings nothing to our table?"

"She can bring an heir," Sebastian said. "Isn't that the most important thing?"

"You're not thinking clearly," Leopold said. "You've been through quite a lot, Bas. Losing Matous, discovering the plot against you. But you can't marry this woman. There is no way for you to address the things she is lacking."

Sebastian waved him off. "She lacks nothing but a name," he muttered. The moment those words left his mouth, an absurd idea clicked in his head. She needed a name. She needed a proper name. One that suggested influence. How to do that? "She must have a name," he said to Leopold. "A title."

Leopold stared at him. "How in hell can you manage that?"

"I don't know," Sebastian said. "But I will think of something."

Leopold sighed. "There is no time left, Bas. You sail at week's end."

"That gives me a few days, does it not?"

Leopold sighed and shook his head. "You are headed for disaster. Everything you have worked so hard to achieve will be lost because you've lost your mind."

Sebastian didn't argue with him. He knew how ridiculous he sounded. But it was all that he had, a last grasp at happiness, and damn it if he wasn't going to take it.

He began to think how, but every idea ended at a dead end.

Sebastian's bad humor followed him through the night and into the next morning. He thought only of Eliza, his gut twisted with the agony of knowing she'd wonder what had happened to him, why he'd never come. She'd surely heard the news by now, and maybe she understood. But it wasn't enough.

He could get a letter to her, that wasn't the issue. What was at issue was his paralysis in writing it. His inability to speak his heart in a way that would soothe her. *I love you, thank you for that.* He sounded like a grandfather on his deathbed. *I love you, I can't live without you, and yet I must.* That sounded like a weak man with no autonomy. *I love you, but you can bring nothing to Alucia.* That was the honest truth, but it was harsh.

His misery pressed against the feelings of love that still stirred in him and left him bleary-eyed. *How to give her a name?*

The idea came to him in the middle of a fitful sleep.

He summoned Leopold and Caius the next morning. "I have an idea that will finish the trade agreement and the betrothal at the same time."

"What?" Leopold asked.

"I will make Miss Eliza Tricklebank part of the final trade agreement."

Leopold and Anastasan exchanged a look. "Are you honestly suggesting that you *trade* England for a woman?" Leopold shook his head. "Bloody hell, Bas."

"At least hear what I have to say," Sebastian urged him. "There is one last item that is set to go before an English court, is there not? It must be determined if a tariff on Alucian iron ore can be reduced. Do you see?"

"No," Leopold said flatly.

"If I may, Your Highness," Caius said, and to Leopold, he explained, "One of the Members of Parliament has suggested that a proposed tariff in the agreement is prohibitive in its nature. Others think it is not prohibitive but generates much needed revenue. It must be looked at by a judge before Parliament will consider it. It is scheduled to go before a judge on the morrow."

Caius understood him, and that gave Sebastian a wild surge of hope.

"What of it?" Leopold asked. "What has that to do with Miss Tricklebank?"

"I will ask that it go before her father, Justice Tricklebank. If he rules favorably—and we have every reason to believe any judge would, as the proposed tariff is quite prohibitive—I would insist that for his participation in this important trade agreement, he be given an appropriate title. A reward, so to speak."

Leopold looked at Caius. "That is madness."

Sebastian was determined. It was his only hope, no matter how far-fetched it sounded, even to his own ears. "If he is given a title, his daughter, is by rights, Lady Eliza Trickebank. She is the daughter of a Queen's Bench justice, Lord Tricklebank."

"What does this solve?" Leopold angrily demanded. "Her connections, her ability to provide some gain is still absent! And who, precisely, would convince the queen to elevate this judge to baron? How in God's name does any of this serve you?"

"Mr. Braeburn of Norfolk is very keen to import the ore," Caius calmly explained. "He is very keen to see the tariff reduced. It happens his maternal grandmother hails from Saxe-Coburg and Gotha, the birthplace of Prince Albert. Prince Albert and Mr. Braeburn are favorably acquainted, according to Mr. Botley-Finch."

"So favorably acquainted that he would make Tricklebank a baron?" Sebastian asked.

"Does it matter?" Leopold scoffed. "Everyone knows

the queen and her husband have very little sway with Parliament."

"In some things, that is true," Caius agreed. "But it is also true that most men seek to please the queen in ways that do not interfere with the designs of men."

Meaning, Sebastian understood, that they would grant her this leave to name a judge baron as long as the agreement was signed with the reduced tariffs. It was nothing to them if Tricklebank was made a baron. Their profit was what mattered.

"How can this be achieved?" Sebastian asked Caius.

"Given what happened here at Kensington, the English would like to see us depart, and sooner rather than later. There is a certain amount of exposure as long as you are here on their soil, Your Highness—frankly, they fear being pulled into war or another altercation with the Weslorians. They likely will make these concessions that have nothing to do with them as long as the agreement is signed. I need your leave to arrange a few things."

Leopold groaned.

Caius ignored him. "I can arrange this. I am confident I can do this."

"Bas, please, this is foolishness," Leopold begged him. "This stunt could destroy everything you have worked to achieve here. You are to arrange a betrothal to a woman with *influence.* A match that can be manipulated if necessary. Make your offer for one of the women who have been vetted and be done with it. Our father will never agree to this match."

Sebastian looked at Caius. Caius's expression was fierce. He needed to do this. For his prince. Perhaps for his old friend. Whatever his reasons, for the first time in days, a small sliver of hope snaked into Sebastian's heart. "I have negotiated an advantageous trade agreement, one that will benefit Alucia for generations to come. As for my marriage? I will take my chances. Go," he said to Caius.

Caius left the room.

Leopold looked at him in disbelief. "God help you if it falls apart, Bas. God help you."

"*Je*, God help me," Sebastian agreed.

He waited until Leopold had left the room, then removed the watch from his pocket and rubbed his thumb over the engraving. He wasn't very confident that Caius could actually make this happen for him. Men who had responsibilities to their constituencies would not agree to such foolery, and this was a very thin reason to give a man a title. And yet, he hoped harder than he'd ever hoped for anything in his life.

He looked down at the letter he'd been trying to write and stared at the words he'd written. Like the other letters he'd attempted before this, he wadded it up and carried it across the room to the fire and tossed it in, watching the edges blacken and curl until the whole thing was ash.

He couldn't bring himself to write words that would break his heart, or hers. And he couldn't bring himself to leave her behind. He was clinging to a very small hope that Caius could accomplish the impossible.

The door opened behind him. He turned; Patro bowed. "Your Highness. I am informed that a coach will arrive in an hour. You are to dine with members of the Conservative Party at the home of Sir Robert Peel. Shall I send in Egius?"

"Je," Sebastian said, and steeled himself for another

luncheon of trying to look detached and unconcerned when his heart and head were raging with want.

He needed Eliza to bear with him. He absently moved his thumb over the engraving of the watch and looked down at the Latin script. He suddenly did have something to say to her. He returned to his desk, picked up his pen and dashed off his note. Before he could change his mind, he called for Patro.

"Deliver this to 34 Bedford Square," he said, and went into his dressing room to prepare for the luncheon.

CHAPTER TWENTY-SEVEN

Ships flying the Alucian flags are being provisioned for the journey home. Many predict the ships will set sail at midnight on the fourteenth of this month. Aboard the ship will be two cloth merchants destined for the Helenamar markets. Silk cloth from Alucia should be available next autumn.

No one can ascertain if a bridal suite has been set aside on any of the ships, but clouds of hope still abound in salons across Mayfair. In a few salons, it is heard that there is relief that their daughter will not be involved in a murderous scandal before she's said her marital vows. A very *few salons.*

—Honeycutt's Gazette of Fashion and Domesticity for Ladies

ELIZA WAS WEARY unto death of people asking her if she was all right. "I'm fine," she'd say, sometimes as much as three times a day.

Her family meant well, she knew that they did. Poppy and Margaret meant well with their sad eyes and whispers behind Eliza's back. The butcher meant well, too, particularly as Mr. and Mrs. Thompkins had no notion of what had happened to Eliza in the last few weeks. She told them she was fatigued.

She tried to keep her thoughts occupied by working on her clocks. She sometimes took as many as two apart a day, then put them back together.

Sometimes when she worked, her father nattered on about his day at work. One day, he said, he had as many as four cases come before him on the Bench. The next day, only one. Wasn't it interesting, he said, how the wheels of justice spun some days like a rogue cart with no driver, and some days, not at all?

He was most perplexed about the day only one case came before him. "It had to do with the Alucian trade agreement, which I understand has been completed save a few nicks here and there."

Eliza had a clock wheel in her hands, and was rubbing it with oil. She didn't really care about that agreement. All she cared about was that no one had come to this house, not even a messenger. She supposed Sebastian was entirely occupied with the revelation of rebellion and finishing the trade agreement. He was probably seeing to it that all his things were packed and readied to go. Maybe he was entertaining the two young women who wanted to be his bride.

Hollis dined with Eliza and her father one night and reported that the London papers were full of scandalous bits of gossip about the Alucian plot of murder and betrothal intrigue. She seemed rather envious of the gossip but claimed to be offended on Eliza's behalf.

"The announcement of any engagement has been put on hold, naturally, for it wouldn't do to uncover a scheme to *murder* the prince, then announce his engagement."

"Murder!" Eliza exclaimed.

"Well, not murder but kidnapping, which one could reasonably assume would lead to murder."

"I don't think you should assume anything, darling," their father said.

"The *Times* alluded to many adulterous affairs among all the Alucians. I even heard," Hollis said, leaning forward, "that some think it was the *prince* who was having an affair with the lady, and when his secretary discovered it, he had him murdered so that it would not be discovered." Her eyes widened.

"That makes no sense," Poppy said from her place at the table. "Why would he murder the secretary? Could he not have merely threatened him with his job instead?"

"This is precisely the problem with untoward speculation," their father said. "It is presented as fact. None of us truly know what happened, and *none* of us should be spreading gossip."

Hollis looked guiltily at her plate.

But later, when their father had retired for the evening, Hollis told Eliza that she'd heard that the engagement would be the last thing to be announced before the prince's departure at the end of the week.

"Oh?" Eliza tried to keep her voice light and carefree. "Has a date of departure been set?"

"According to the *Times*, the Alucians will depart at midnight Wednesday, weather permitting."

So that was it. She had only a few days left to hope of any word from a butterfly trapped in a royal cocoon, kept away from any and all who might do him harm.

Oh, Eliza, what have you done to yourself?

"Eliza?" Hollis said.

"I'm fine," Eliza said quickly, and yanked so hard at the door of a cuckoo clock that she broke it off.

"Leave the clock—"

"No," Eliza said, and slapped away Hollis's hand. She had to keep her hands busy. She had to keep her mind fixed on little problems that had clear solutions with not the slightest ambiguity.

That night, Eliza read to her father from some mindless, wretchedly tiresome legal tomes having to do with government tariffs.

"I should think the question obviously answered," her father said when Eliza had finished reading. "The tariff is, by its nature, prohibitive. Would you not agree, darling?"

She had no idea what he meant, for her thoughts had been elsewhere while her mind had read the words. "Oh, I… I wasn't really listening," she admitted.

As the days marched toward Wednesday, Eliza grew more despondent. One day, she was in her room, lying face down on her bed, her head hanging off the side, tracing a circle over and over again on the carpet with her finger. She felt ill. Her feelings for Sebastian had coagulated and hardened in a lump in her belly, constantly there, constantly aching. She wished he would set sail as soon as possible so that she could suffer in peace.

She heard voices at the door, her father and his friend, Mr. Fletcher. She heard Jack and John barking as if an army had invaded their cozy house. "Eliza!" her father called. "Are you home, darling?"

She sighed, pushed herself up. She paused in front of the mirror and noticed how unkempt she looked. She ought to do something about that. Perhaps she would on the morrow.

"Here I am, Pappa," she said as she walked into the parlor. She greeted him with a kiss to his cheek. "Margaret has made a stew this evening. Would you like some wine before we dine?"

"Oh, I think I'll have a whisky this evening, my love. And how are you this fine day?"

"Very well." She walked to the sideboard, passing by her desk. When she did, she noticed the post that was stacked there. She'd not attended to it in days, really, too despondent to care. But tonight, she happened to notice the corner of a light blue envelope sticking out from the pile. She paused to pull that one from the stack of official correspondence and saw that it was addressed to her.

"I've had a very interesting day, all in all. The infamous trade deal returned to me."

"Did it?" she asked absently, and turned the letter over. It was sealed with wax, but the markings weren't familiar to her. She broke the seal.

"Tariffs can be a tricky thing, I suppose, but as I explained to the barrister, this was rather straightforward. Of course the tariff was prohibitive. All tariffs are prohibitive by nature, but the question is *how* prohibitive."

She unfolded the letter. *Amor loyal—S.*

The blood immediately drained from her face.

"What do you think?" her father asked.

"What? Oh. Yes, of course," she said. "Whisky, you said?"

"Please, darling. I wasn't expecting the case, as the preliminary inquiry was brought a few days ago, and Mr. Frink had advised it be sent to another justice who was more familiar."

Eliza quickly poured the whisky and put it in her father's hand, then took her note and sat in the chair beside him, her fingers tracing over the lines of the ink. *Love is loyal.* He'd sent her a note after all, and in her general malaise, she'd failed to notice it. But when had it come? And what did the note mean? Was it his goodbye?

Ben entered the room with fuel for the hearth.

"Ben, did the post come today?" she asked.

He looked at the desk. "No post today, miss. That's been sitting there, what, two, three days now?" He went down on one knee and began to place logs on the fire.

She'd been wandering around like the dead, apparently.

Poppy suddenly swept into the room carrying a stack of books that she placed next to another stack on the shelves. "You're late tonight, Your Honor!" she said brightly. She picked up a shawl and went to the judge to drape it around his shoulders while the cat tried to catch the tail of it.

"I had a pint with the lads," her father said jovially. "We had quite a bit of excitement today."

"Did you?" Poppy asked, and bent down to pick up the cat.

Amor loyal. Was he asking her to remain loyal? Well, she'd need more information than this. She looked again at the letter, at the words he'd written, so neat. So blessedly regal.

As her father explained to Poppy and Ben his views on tariffs or God knew what, Eliza felt slightly panicked. As if she was supposed to know something. To understand this note. To *do* something. Was she to have done something?

So when a knock came at the door, she leapt up as quickly as the dogs did. "I'll see who has come," she said before Ben or Poppy could say it. But the moment she stepped out of the parlor, Hollis's voice rang out. "It's me, darlings!"

Eliza walked into the hall, still clutching the letter.

Hollis took off her coat and bonnet and hung them on the pegs. "Why are you looking at me like that?"

"I was hoping you were someone else."

"I beg your pardon! Then you'll be pleased to know someone else has come."

"Who?"

"I don't know. Mr. Frink is outside with another gentleman."

Hollis glanced at herself in the entry mirror, then jumped when another knock came to the door. Jack and John nearly bowled her over. "For God's sake, those dogs!" she cried.

"Jack! John!" Eliza commanded.

The two terriers raced toward her and veered off, following her pointing into the parlor.

Hollis opened the door. "Oh! Good evening again, Mr. Frink."

"Mrs. Honeycutt."

Behind Mr. Frink, Eliza could see two gentlemen. Englishmen. They quickly doffed their caps.

"I beg your pardon for the intrusion, but is the judge at home?"

"Didn't you bring him?" Hollis asked.

"Not tonight," Mr. Frink said. "I was detained with some pressing business."

"He's here," Eliza said, and gestured Mr. Frink in. The two men entered behind him, nodding politely.

In the parlor, the dogs began to bark again.

"You better come with me before they attack," Hollis said. She indicated the men should follow her and stepped into the parlor. "Down, Jack, for heaven's sake! Pappa, you have callers. Mr. Frink has come!"

One of the gentlemen had left the door open, so Eliza went to close it before joining the others. But at the door, she noticed several men gathered on the sidewalk. She pulled the door open wider. And her heart, which had hung so low that it had dragged the floor these last few days, sprang into her throat. Sebastian was standing on the walk in the middle of those men.

He was dressed in full princely regalia—a sash across his chest, pinned with a crest of some sort. A slew of medals arrayed on his breast. He wore a top hat and a greatcoat and looked as if he was on his way to a ball. Or an opera. His dress confused her—what was he doing here, dressed like that?

She blinked, half-expecting him to disappear. But he didn't. He stood there, looking up at her with a peculiar mix of anguish and joy.

Eliza did not understand what was happening, but the butterflies were swirling madly in her belly. "I don't… has something happened?"

He stepped forward, out of the group of his men. "You received my note?"

She was still holding it, she realized. The paper was growing damp with her grip. "Not a few minutes ago."

He took another step forward. "Is there some place we might speak?"

Eliza glanced down the street. Lights were illuminating windows. Most people were home for the evening and she was certain many of them had been drawn to their windows by all the commotion of carriages and men. It was the curse of living on a square. "My father has callers."

"I know." He took another step forward.

He must have seen them come in. "We could speak

in the square," she said, indicating the patch of green behind him.

"Wherever you like." He held out his hand to her.

She was very aware that she looked as if she'd been drowning in self-pity for days. Because she had. She tucked a bit of hair behind her ear and came down the steps. She did not take his hand or put her hand on his arm—it was more than she could bear to touch him, so she folded her arms across her body.

Sebastian accepted that and clasped his hands behind his back. He wordlessly escorted her through that throng of men—all of them eyeing her very curiously—and across the street to the green. When they reached the square, he slowly turned to face her. Her rubbed his nape with his hand, drew a breath and said, "Eliza, I… I have something I must say."

All her nerves, all her worry, all her grief, collapsed in on itself, and she couldn't bear to hear it. "For heaven's sake, don't make this any harder than it is, Sebastian, please. I understand. You needn't have come all this way to explain."

Except that he did need to explain. But she didn't think she'd survive it.

"You—"

"Of *course* I do," she said with a dismissive wave of her hand. She was shaking, she realized. His nearness, her feelings for him, had all got the better of her. "You didn't honestly believe I was foolish enough to harbor any illusions, did you?"

He didn't respond.

"I only wanted the chance to say goodbye, Sebastian. That's all. Just to say goodbye, and thank you, although that must sound very odd. But you can't possibly know what your friendship means to me. *Meant* to me. And I wanted to tell you…well, I hadn't intended it like this, I thought at least I'd be properly dressed, but I wanted to tell you before you set sail that I…" She gasped in the breath she'd not been able to take. "I love you, too." She gasped for another breath after admitting it. *"Loved,"* she whispered sadly.

Sebastian stared at her, looking a wee bit stunned. "You wanted to tell me goodbye?"

That was what he'd heard? "That, and the other part. Most sincerely, the other part."

His brows dipped. "The part about loving me?"

"Yes, that part! Oh, I am making a mess of it. I had intended to say it in a more poignant way, obviously, and a more poignant place would have been better," she said, glancing around the square. "But I wasn't expecting you." She laughed a little hysterically. "I've thought all these long days that you'd leave without seeing me, and I was devastated, really, and I hadn't seen the note, and I don't even know when it arrived because I've been terribly out of sorts, but I didn't see it until tonight, and when I did, I was very touched, but I wasn't quite certain what you meant. What did you mean, Sebastian? That I'm to remain loyal to you? Or that you would remain loyal to me? Or was it simply a lovely sentiment to say fare-thee-well? I wasn't certain at all, and I've had no time to think it through, really. Or prepare for this moment." She gestured to her hair.

"You look beautiful."

"I look like I've been sweeping chimneys!"

He chuckled. It almost erupted out of him, as if he'd been trying to hold it in. But once it was out, he laughed.

He laughed so that he bent over with it. Some of the men came around the carriage to see if anything was amiss.

"Why are you laughing?" she demanded. "This is not at all how I would have had our last moment happen, but it's here and I've done the best I know to do!"

"Dearest Eliza," he said, and wiped a tear of laughter from beneath his eye. "You cannot possibly imagine how you've tormented me these many days."

"How *I've* tormented *you*?" She sobered. "You said you'd come."

"I know," he said, sobering, too. "It proved impossible with the things that unfolded after our meeting on Bond Street."

"I suspected as much." She touched his hand, laced her fingers with his. "So this is where it ends, then," she said morosely.

"That is my fervent hope," he agreed.

"Oh," she said, feeling a little stung. "That is...you hope it will end?"

"Eliza." He put his hand to her neck. "Did you really think I could leave England without you?"

"Pardon?"

"There are men in your house at this very moment, explaining to your father that he is to be made a baron. So that you will be made a lady."

She didn't understand him. "I don't want to be a lady—"

"But do you want to be a princess? And one day be a queen? No, don't answer me. Listen to me first, please."

She couldn't have answered even if she'd wanted—he'd knocked the breath clean from her lungs.

"I came here tonight to ask if would you do me the

great honor of becoming my wife, but I can't ask you that without explaining to you that it won't be easy."

"What?" The world felt as if it was tilting into a dream. It had to be a dream, because it made no sense. Was he mad? Had he been mad all along? Had she embarked on a lark with a madman—

"What I mean is that you must understand there is constant scrutiny. Your every move will be studied, your every word examined. Every manner reviewed in the papers, in the salons. It's not an easy life, the one I offer."

"What life? I think… I mean, some of what you have said—"

"Of course there is privilege and crowns and horsehair crinolines if your heart desires it. And I vow to you now I would protect you with all that I have. But it's not fair—I must make you understand the truth before you answer. I must tell you that in addition to all that, I live a quiet life with books and horses, and it's not terribly exciting."

He spoke almost apologetically, and quite earnestly.

"I need you to know all of this before I tell you that I have fallen so hard in love with you, Eliza. *Deeply* in love. I am forbidden by our laws from marrying a commoner, but I may marry the daughter of a baron. So I… I made it part of the final trade agreement negotiation."

Eliza was stunned. She wasn't entirely sure what was happening. "You *what*?"

"My terms were simple—I must have you. We arranged to bring a legal question to your father—"

She gasped—her father's nattering suddenly rushed back to her. "If the tariff was set for purposes of revenue or to prohibit trade!" she exclaimed. "And it was a very simple answer!"

"*Je.* It was a simple answer. We made the case that the judge had cleared the last hurdle for the agreement and should be made a baron in appreciation for his service, and we reserved a few things to offer in exchange for it, and...and it doesn't matter how it happened, or why, but there are men in your parlor explaining to your father now that he has been granted a title by decree of the queen, and I love you, Eliza. I *love* you. And I won't leave this island without your favorable reply."

It really was a dream. A true and proper dream, and she didn't want to wake from it, ever. Eliza couldn't believe this was happening to *her*, the spinster of Bedford Square. The scandalized daughter of a justice on the Queen's Bench. All she'd wanted to do was meet a prince so she could say that she had, to add a little color to an otherwise drab existence, and the prince was standing before her, asking her to marry him and telling her how ardently he loved her. "Good Lord!" she said, and pressed her fingertips to her cheeks. "Am I dreaming?"

"Not unless I'm dreaming, too."

"But I haven't the slightest notion how to be a princess!"

He pulled her closer. "You *are* a princess, Eliza. I will help you. There are scores of people to help you. So now I beg of you to release me from the claws of dread and answer me—will you marry me?"

"Sebastian! You are utterly mad! But of *course* I will marry you! I hardly care what anyone says of me, only you. Oh my heavens! *Yes*, Sebastian. A thousand times, *yes*."

CHAPTER TWENTY-EIGHT

All of England is desperate for a glimpse of what Lady Eliza Tricklebank will wear on the occasion of her marriage. London's finest dressmaker predicts it will be white and trimmed in Alucian lace.

Nuptials are expected for a Keene young woman whose dowry was enhanced by the trade agreement with Alucia. Unfortunately, a certain peacock will enter another Season without prospect. Unless one would consider the elderly bachelor acquaintance of her mother who pursues her, but we understand the peacock does not consider him at all.

Ladies, if you are planning your own bridal trousseau, none should be without at least one black silk petticoat and eight pairs of gloves, of which three pairs should be kid leather. A pair of sturdy walking boots is also considered a must.

—Honeycutt's Gazette of Fashion and Domesticity for Ladies

SAYING GOODBYE WAS the hardest part. So difficult that there were moments Eliza wished she'd never met Sebastian.

Her father's fear of losing her was not as acute as she'd imagined it. It turned out that he was far more concerned with her happiness. "My darling, I will miss you terribly, you know that I will. But my greatest joy as a father is sending my daughters to their personal happiness. Now listen to me, Eliza. You will have very good times and you will have difficult times, but if you safeguard the joy of your love, you will survive it and be richer for it."

Poppy was the least affected of them all. "I knew it all along," she'd said, reminding Eliza that she'd said as much to her weeks ago. "I knew from the start he'd choose you. Don't fret about the judge. I'll read to him."

"You!" Hollis had complained. "*I* will read to him."

"You will not," Poppy said. "You have enough to do with your gazette. Who will help you now?"

Hollis suddenly remembered her gazette, which had experienced amazing growth in the last weeks, thanks to the hints she printed about the prince's search for a wife. She was currently seeking to employ someone to help her. "You'll have to help me with that, too, Poppy," Hollis warned her. "And Caroline, although she insists she is far too busy with the many invitations she now receives because she is friends with the future Queen of Alucia."

Eliza said goodbye to Ben and Margaret, and Mr. and Mrs. Thompkins, and as she was walking out the door, to Jack and John and Pris, none of whom seemed particularly moved that she was leaving.

It was a beautiful spring day that she and Hollis, Caroline and Beck—who had insisted it wouldn't do to send three unmarried women into the world without proper escort, and determined the guards Sebastian had sent to escort them insufficient—set sail for Alucia.

They arrived on the shores of the Alucian capital,

Helenamar, a city framed by white sandy beaches and blue-green mountains that rose up from the sea. The biggest coach any of them had ever seen was on hand to ferry them to the palace.

They drove through a bustling port, up cobblestoned streets lined with glistening limestone buildings, and over lanes shaded by leafy green trees.

"It looks almost mythical," Caroline said, her voice full of awe.

"It looks like spring anywhere on the Continent," Beck said, trying very hard to sound unimpressed. But his gaze was glued to the window, too.

The drive to the palace was long and lined with elm trees. Sheep and horses and cows grazed in fields of green and gold. When the coach rounded a corner, Hollis gasped. She grabbed Eliza's hand and yanked her to the window. *"Look."*

The palace was as long as a town, built of pink and gold sandstone. The gates were formidable iron features with swirling gold crowns and emblems embedded in them. From a distance, they could see the massive sculptures of leaping horses in the fountain at the main entrance.

Eliza could not believe what she was seeing. How had she stumbled into this? What celestial miracle had been visited upon her?

The coach rolled around the paved circular drive that was as wide and as long as a boulevard, and came to a halt. Beck was the first one to alight, handing out the ladies one at a time.

Large doors swung open, and through them, Eliza could see a glittering entrance, the sparkling chandeliers blazing. A dozen footmen ran out and lined the stairs to the entrance.

"Is this where you will live?" Caroline whispered.

"I certainly hope so," Eliza said. She grabbed first Caroline's hand, and then Hollis's, and together, they started their ascent up those stairs and toward her future, Beck walking behind them.

When they entered the soaring foyer, Eliza felt a little dizzy. It was too grand. The white-and-black marble floors. The gold-and-crystal chandelier overhead. The tall portraits of people dressed in crowns and jewels. And there, at the top of the formal staircase stood Sebastian. He was dressed in a military uniform, a sword at his hip.

"God help me, I think I'm going to vomit," Eliza said.

"That would certainly make an indelible impression," Beck drawled.

"Don't you dare, Eliza," Caroline said. "Don't you *dare*. He will never forget this moment, so take a deep breath and look like a princess."

She didn't know if that was quite possible. But she took several deep breaths as Sebastian started down the long flight of stairs toward them. Behind him, people were arriving on the landing, lining up along the balustrade and looking down to observe her.

Thankfully, Caroline remembered what they were to do, and yanked Eliza into a curtsy as she hissed at Hollis to do the same. "I dearly hope they have an etiquette coach," she whispered. "You're going to need one."

But Eliza forgot what Caroline had tried to teach her about court life and rose up, slipping her hands from theirs. She had been thoroughly beguiled by this man and had missed him for three long months. She'd forgotten how very handsome he was, and when he smiled at her, she felt it in her heart. So they would forgive her if she couldn't help herself and suddenly ran forward, throwing her arms around him and kissing him fully on the lips. Sebastian wrapped his arms around her and squeezed her tightly to him. He had missed her, too.

Eliza heard the murmurs above her, the whispers of Caroline and Hollis and Beck as they complained about her behavior, but she didn't care. All she saw was Sebastian.

"Good morning, Mr. Chartier," she said.

He grinned. He wrapped his arms around her, kissed her again and said, "Welcome home, Princess Eliza."

Home. What a beautiful word that was, filled with all the love and joy she would need to sustain her in the years to come. She was home, and this man loved her, and she loved him, and if she let go of him, she would probably fall flat on her back and laugh hysterically at her incredible dumb luck.

* * * * *

New York Times bestselling author

JULIA LONDON

returns to her unforgettable Scottish series with The Highland Grooms.

Join these sinfully seductive Scottish heroes and sensual yet headstrong heroines as they surrender their hearts to love in the lush green Scottish Highlands.

"London delivers a fresh take with an old-fashioned yarn full of danger and romance that makes the happy ending feel genuinely hard-won between two characters perfectly suited for each other."
—*Entertainment Weekly on Devil in Tartan*

Order your copies today!

HQNBooks.com

PHJULHG18